Henry Taylor

Autobiography of Henry Taylor - 1800 - 1875

Vol I: 1800 - 1844

Henry Taylor

Autobiography of Henry Taylor - 1800 - 1875
Vol I: 1800 - 1844

ISBN/EAN: 9783337031237

Printed in Europe, USA, Canada, Australia, Japan

Cover: Foto ©Andreas Hilbeck / pixelio.de

More available books at **www.hansebooks.com**

AUTOBIOGRAPHY

OF

HENRY TAYLOR

1800—1875

'Small sands the mountain, moments make the year,
And trifles life.' (YOUNG)

IN TWO VOLUMES

VOL. I.

1800——1844

LONDON

LONGMANS, GREEN AND CO.

1885

INTRODUCTION.

THIS WORK was begun in 1865, continued as leisure served till 1877, and then privately printed for communication to a few friends. Any readers who may reach the last pages will find that it was intended only for posthumous publication; and till the end of 1884 no other was contemplated. I mention this because, had it been otherwise, it might have been somewhat differently written. But publication in the 85th year of a man's life comes rather near to posthumous publication; and, after a little revision, I have not found much difficulty in consenting to its present appearance.

BOURNEMOUTH: *March*, **1885.**

CONTENTS

OF

THE FIRST VOLUME.

CHAPTER VII.

CHAPTER VIII.

CHAPTER IX.

CHAPTER X.

CHAPTER XI.

CHAPTER XII.

CHAPTER XIII.

CHAPTER XIV.

CHAPTER XV.

CHAPTER XVI.

CHAPTER XVII.

CHAPTER XVIII.

CHAPTER XIX.

CHAPTER XX.

CHAPTER XXI.

CHAPTER XXII.

APPENDIX.

AUTOBIOGRAPHY

OF

HENRY TAYLOR.

CHAPTER I.

BIRTH AND PARENTAGE.

WHEN a man's life is written it is expected that something should be said of his birth and parentage, however little there may be to say in which any one but himself and his family can take an interest.

I was born at Bishop-Middleham, in the county of Durham, on October 18, 1800. It would have been pleasant to me to have been high-born. Pleasantness to the imagination, however, seems to be in these days (perhaps in other days too) almost the only advantage of high-birth taken in itself and by itself. For if by any accident it is stripped of the wealth and the rich or powerful connections with which it is commonly attended, it seems to do nothing for a man's worldly advancement, and often indeed to be lost sight of.

It would have been pleasant to me also to have

inherited a pleasant sounding name. To have a pleasant sound connected with one's life at every step of it, is surely no contemptible addition to the pleasantness of life ; and though changing an ugly sounding name for a pleasant sounding name is not to be approved, because fanciful changes of name, becoming frequent, might occasion public inconveniences, yet, if there were no such reason against it, I do not think it would be to be despised merely because the motive of it is connected with the fancy and the imagination and the love of pleasing sounds. It is now readily excused in the case of a man who changes his name for an estate, and it is then said that he had 'good reasons for it' ; meaning, apparently, that if he changes his name from mercenary motives there is no fault to be found with him, whereas if he makes the change from motives connected with the imagination, he is more or less despicable.

My father, George Taylor (born June 6, 1772), was the son of George Taylor (born 1732), who inherited from his father, William Taylor (my great-grandfather), the estate of Swinhoe-Broomford, in the parish of Bamborough, in Northumberland. It was entailed, but when my grandfather's eldest son attained his majority, the entail was broken. I am the sole surviving heir in the male line of my great-grandfather, and a plan of the estate is all of it that has come into my possession. From the plan I learn that it consisted of 717 acres ; and I infer that the status of my great-grandfather was that of an inconsiderable squire. From some Latin and other books in my library in which he had written his name, I infer that he was a not uneducated squire.[1] The only other thing I know of him is, that one day when following the hounds close at the heels of the husband of a lady who was said to be the most beautiful person in the county, the said husband's horse fell, and my great-grandfather unhappily riding over him and killing him, was in due season married to his widow.

Of my forefathers, before the times of my great-grandfather, I know little or nothing; how long they had been proprietors of Swinhoe-Broomford or whence they came. I have heard that they came from the other side of the border, under some persecution in the time of John Knox, connected in some way with a marriage of one of them with a daughter of a Sir Andrew Hume of the Merse, the Chief of a Border Clan. But these are merely confused recollections of what was told me when I was hardly old enough to receive distinct impressions. Mixed blood makes, in my opinion, the best breed; and I should not be sorry to surmise that some proportion of mine may be Scotch; but I think my family did not care much whence they came or from whom. Except once or twice, very early in my childhood, I do not remember to have heard it spoken of.

---

[1] In a copy of Florus, which must have belonged to a son, to the name 'Wm. Taylor' is added 'Vir—1744.' Whether he meant that he was more of a man than his neighbours, or only that he had attained the age of manhood in the year 1744, I am unable to say.

My grandfather, George Taylor, married (May 5, 1761) Hannah, the daughter of Thomas Forster of Lucker. All that I know about them is what I find in a letter of February, 1807, to Sir Walter Scott from Robert Surtees, the antiquary and historian of Durham, who, in giving an account of a search after Jacobite ballads, writes : ' Much of the above, such as it is, I owe to a very intelligent neighbour, now a temporary resident in this county, who has a hereditary right to be a retailer of Jacobite poetry, for his maternal grandfather, Thomas Forster, Esq., of Lucker, a near relative of General Forster, was condemned in 1715, and escaped out of Newgate by an exchange of clothes with his wife, and afterwards recovered his estates ; [1] and Mr. Taylor's paternal ancestor was begot between the double walls of Chillingham Castle, where his father was secreted in the Duke of Monmouth's rebellion. Mr. Taylor remembers that his own father, whose estate was at Swinhoe, in Northumberland, used to maintain an old man in the capacity of writing-master to the children, who had been engaged in 1745, and was supposed to have been a person of some rank and property. He used on particular occasions, when tipsy, to sing a Latin Jacobite song, which I am sorry Taylor does not remember a word of.' General Forster took refuge in Italy, whence he sent to his

[1] Sir G. Grey tells me this is a mistake, and that it was General Forster himself and not his brother who escaped by the exchange of clothes.

mother a present of a fan, which has come down to me with a memorandum of its history attached to it.

With the estate of Swinhoe-Broomford, my grandfather inherited a disputed title to an estate of greater value called Limeage, in Kent, and the lawsuit thereto appertaining, the expenses of which brought incumbrances upon Swinhoe-Broomford, and these incumbrances increased until the sale of the estate after it had come into my father's possession on the death of his eldest brother. The sale, which produced 23,400*l.*, did little more than pay off the incumbrances.[1]

Thus my grandfather, who died before I was born, had been latterly in embarrassed circumstances, and had left Swinhoe to live by himself in a lodging in the village of Rothbury; and from the silence maintained about him and his separation from his family, I imagine that there must have been something amiss in his habits of life. His children, three sons and two daughters, went to live with his younger brother John, who had no children of his own, and was supposed to be rather rich, having married a lady of good fortune, a daughter (if I recollect right) of a Sir George Wheler.

---

[1] My father, writing to me on July 30, 1826, to announce the completion of the sale, added, 'Thank God!—The estate and the family have been encumbered for a century—to my knowledge for 40 years—once more, thank God!' A Mr. Tewart was the purchaser. I have heard that a certain Mr. Henry Taylor has occupied it since. If so, he was not related to us.

This John, my great-uncle, had a house in Durham. I recollect him well ; for his latter years were passed in my father's house, as my father's early years had been in his. He was the leanest man I ever saw, small in the bone and rather tall, the spare shanks ending in gouty ankles, with a refined, blood-less, meagre countenance, in which self-sufficiency was in some degree tempered by self-respect. He was vain and supercilious, but there was an ease and repose in his deportment which gave him an air of distinction rather than pretension. I suppose he must have had some claims to be considered literary, for there was in my father's library, and there ought to be in mine (though I cannot find it), a quarto volume of poetry, by a Mr. Percival, dedicated to him ; and those of my books in which his name is written are rather beyond the range of ordinary reading. The manners which prevailed when his were formed, had made ceremony a second nature to him, and he treated us children with the same formal politeness as our elders ; and his compliments gained in length and slowness from a distressing impediment in his speech. He was a man of some acuteness and ability (which were of no use to him) ; he was brought up to no profession, made no money, and allowed almost everything he had to melt away from him. Being childless himself, he gave his nephews to understand that there would be a good provision for them all at his death, and when it took place the provision proved very scanty indeed.

In the meantime the three boys were sent to a grammar school at Witton-le-Wear, whence the two elder went to Trinity College, Cambridge. My father, the youngest, had had bad health, through which the sight of one eye was lost and that of the other impaired, and he was kept at home with his uncle, who could not be brought to any decision as to what was to be done with him.

At about twenty-three years of age, however, circumstances led him to take a decision for himself. He fell in love with Eleanor Ashworth, the daughter of an ironmonger in Durham. I do not know whether provincial tradesmen were more frequently well educated in those days than in these, or whether this ironmonger was exceptional. I have no reason to think that his birth was above his station, not having heard anything about it; but I believe he was a man of some education ; for I recollect to have seen when a boy a literary correspondence extending over many years between him and an eminent man of that time, Dunning (afterwards Lord Ashburton); and his house was the resort of such scholars and men of literary tastes as a cathedral town may be supposed to bring together.

The little I know of my mother (who died whilst I was an infant) is derived from some letters of hers which have come into my hands, for after her death my father could seldom bear to mention her name. I have been told by others that she was not pretty, but that in her looks as well as in her ways she was attractive ; and amongst the letters there are three which relate to rejected suits, and one which shows that my father's was not successful at first. The earliest of these is dated February 4, 1786, when she must have been a very young girl. It is addressed to a brother in India.[1] Some extracts from it will exhibit the manner of a courtship and declaration by surprise in the eighteenth century :—

'This gentleman dined at Mr. Landell's[2] about three months ago, which was the first of my seeing him ; and he afterwards, at his own request, rode out once or twice with my uncle L. I saw very little more of him at Newcastle, but very unexpectedly received a visit from him at Durham soon after my return. I had fixed the day following to meet my friends, the Miss Johnsons, at Blue House ;[3] I mentioned my intention to Mr. H., when he immediately proposed accompanying me, as it would make but a few miles difference in his ride to Newcastle. This I consented to very readily, and without the remotest suspicion that he meant to show me any particular attention. How I could possibly be so blind is, to be sure, totally unaccountable, unless he administered some stupifying potion to lull my senses asleep,

---

[1] A Captain Ashworth, who seems to have been a man of some note ; for the Indian army was then in a high state of discontent, and it was said of Captain Ashworth, that he ' had but to lift a finger and he could have set the Ganges in a flame.' I believe he was afterwards chosen as a delegate from the army to represent their grievances at home. He is spoken of in a letter of May, 1796, as 'General' Ashworth.

[2] Her mother's brother.

[3] A seaside hotel.

which indeed was very likely to operate in his favour.
However, if this was the case, he had not the power
of perpetuating its effect ; for I was presently roused
by his telling me upon the road that it was quite
immaterial his returning to Newcastle, that he thought
Blue House a very pleasant place, and could spend a
few days there very comfortably. To this proposal
I made some very awkward reply, not knowing how
to prevent him putting his plans in execution, and
being too anxious to extricate myself from such a
disagreeable situation to hit upon the right method
of doing it. So we arrived at the end of our journey
without coming to any explanation. He, however,
to my great relief, left us that night, but returned
again the evening following in the midst of a storm
of wind and rain that Don Quixote himself would
have shuddered to encounter. To these exploits he
added various others of the like nature and tendency
too tedious to mention ; but to crown all, I heard very
soon after that he had (with the utmost prudence I
must allow) made open declaration and application to
Mr. Landell to act as proxy for him and woo his
niece, having had proof which no man could miscon-
strue, that he himself would never have an opportunity ; more than this, he had asked and obtained
the full consent of all his kindred, and I daresay the
remotest branches of the family held themselves in
readiness to pay their compliments to their *cousin
elect* before I had the slightest intimation of what was
going forward, an affair of which I sincerely wish

they had suffered me for ever to remain in the darkest
ignorance ; for from the first proposal of the connection I have never been able to think of it without
utter repugnance and a degree of horror which can
only be imagined by those who have experienced a
similar situation, and who, from the dread of bitter
misery, have been reduced to the sad obligation of
rejecting the advice and solicitation of their best and
most esteemed friends. I must talk seriously and
rationally to you now ; I have been in a wonderful
merry mood when I wrote the above, or I never
could have treated a matter so lightly which has been
the cause of so much heaviness to me ; for in truth
no neglected maiden ever sighed so deeply for an
admirer as I have sighed for neglect from mine. . . . .
Many will tell me that perfection is not to be found
in mortals, and that I must take the bad with the
good, and such-like pretty stories ; but though I am
neither fool enough nor wise enough to expect an
Addison or a Johnson, much less a Locke or a
Newton, yet if I do make an engagement of such
importance, I expect a man that has sense enough to
discern right from wrong, who will not contradict
me when I am in the right and caress me when I
am in the wrong, and with whom I can spend a
winter evening by my fireside without gaping till I
am in danger of getting a lock'd jaw. I have said
more of this affair than I at first intended ; but I
wished to vindicate to you, and to all those who
kindly interest themselves in my welfare, my refusal

of an offer which certainly had many advantages, and particularly lucrative ones. My uncle has behaved to me in the handsomest manner, which I shall ever hold in grateful remembrance ; and it is needless to tell you that my dear mother at least equalled him in affectionate compliance with my wishes. Only my brother,'—not the Indian brother—'has urged it with a degree of earnestness very distressing indeed to me, who have always locked up to him as the most able director of all my actions : but he has at last desisted from persuading me to a step the very idea of which is repugnant to every feeling of my heart.'

The next of the three letters has no date of the year, but from the changed handwriting and the less redundant diction, I have no doubt it belonged to a more mature period of girlhood. It is a common-place specimen of civil and considerate rejection :—

'Dear Sir,—I received yours of the 18th only yesterday, which gave me pain in proportion to the regret I must ever feel in disappointing the wishes of any one whom I believe to have a regard for me. Many reasons, which I think it both useless and improper to communicate, determine me to request that you will think no more on the subject of your letter. The union you solicit never can take place ; but I sincerely wish you a much greater degree of happiness than it could possibly have afforded. I remain, &c., &c.' ·

But this not having been enough, and some answer having been returned to it which seems to

have given her offence, there follows a rejoinder
which is more peremptory, and, indeed, somewhat
severe :—

'Dear Sir,—I must once more give you my most
serious assurance that the reasons which dictated my
answer to your letter of the 18th are equally solid
and unanswerable. It seems to me next to impossible that I should ever change my sentiments ; therefore you may judge how far it is worth your while
to give yourself any farther trouble about it. Pecuniary considerations, you may rely upon it, have no
influence in my present determination. Your prospects of preferment appear to me extremely promis-
ing ; but were you Bishop of Durham, my resolution
would remain the same. However, you will remember that I never told you I had made any vow
against matrimony ; for, in fact, I should be heartily
ashamed of doing anything so absurd. I trust I
shall, on every important occasion, be enabled to
pursue the best direction my judgment shall afford
and make no vows or protestations about the matter.
Forgive me if I tell you, *your* vows are made with a
degree of rashness that might justify a distrust of
their performance. Is it either prudent or rational
to venture to involve yourself in a connection for life
with a woman whose character and dispositions you
can only be acquainted with from hearsay ? You
have had the good luck to escape for once ; but let
me warn you against such desperate proceedings in
future ; for, believe me, no woman worth a farthing

will set any value on an opinion that rests on such very slender foundations. I am, &c., &c.'

Some time in or before 1794 my father's courtship had begun; but with doubtful prospects. She had suffered from a disappointment of the particulars of which I know nothing.[1] She had returned my father's affection in a measure, but not in full; she at first avowedly preferred the happiness and wishes of her mother and her brother, Captain Ashworth, to his; and if her brother had been prepared to give up his Indian career, she would have elected to make a home for him rather than to marry. But her brother was vacillating, and seemed likely to decide upon returning to India, and she wrote to explain her sentiments to him :—

'To be once more left without a single friend on whom we had any claim for aid or protection—the wretchedness in which the accident of a moment had so lately overwhelmed me fresh in my recollection— my mother's very slow if not precarious recovery— together with many other circumstances of inferior distress, threw a deeper shade of despondency over my mind than I think I ever before experienced. Mr. T.'s situation, and the probable consequences of his regard for me (the strength of which I have no more doubt of than I have of mine for him), were no small aggravation of my anxiety. But great as my affection for him is, it is not yet equal to that I feel

---

[1] I have said I *know* nothing. I believe her attachment had been to an author, then of some celebrity and not yet altogether forgotten.

for you and my mother; and therefore, much as I would encounter for him myself, I cannot purchase his happiness at the expense of yours. Your offer of pecuniary assistance I was not unprepared for, my dearest John. I know there is nothing kind and affectionate that you would not do for me; and if you could afford it I would accept it as thankfully as I would the power of contributing to your comfort in a similar way; but if our scheme cannot be prudently accomplished without that, I will never proceed one step farther in it.'

On September 30, 1794, however, she writes to my father in terms of encouragement, though still inconclusively; for, after expressing ardent feelings of friendship, she proceeds that she will not presume to say how far her sentiments may hereafter change, or how far her future conduct may be in opposition to what she now thinks and feels :—

'I have seen ingratitude, perfidy, and inconsistency carried to an extent that had never before entered my imagination; and though the wounds this discovery made can never be healed and are ready to fly open on all occasions, yet such was my confidence in the honour and integrity of those who inflicted them, that I have disputed my own ever since the failure of theirs. That you will form future attachments equally strong with that which engrosses you now, believe me, it is irrational to doubt; possibly still stronger, for you have time enough to look about you for an entire and unbroken heart, which, whatever your prejudices may be, you certainly ought to prize more than one which has been torn into ten thousand pieces.'

She probably came to a decision in the following year ; and my father, having then to look about for the means of marrying and maintaining a family, put himself in pupilage for a year to one of the foremost farmers of those days, and then took a farm at Bishop-Middleham (a few miles from Durham), whence, on April 23, 1797, my mother writes to a sister-in-law to announce her arrival, after having been married that morning. There are two letters from the same place,—'the sweetest place under the sun, or above it either,'—in the latter of which, dated October 18, 1797, she writes to her brother,—' Since the 23rd April, there has been a charm spread over the whole of my existence which I might in vain attempt to describe.'

But before I pass to her married life, I will transcribe a letter in a lighter vein, which, though not dated, must belong to the period of her girlhood.

' You play the termagant so prettily, that I verily believe you have had a lesson from Nature ; and if all *her* scholars were not adepts, I should give her great credit for your proficiency. But all the actors of the *old school* were equally correct and particularly remarkable for that inimitable chastity of expression of which you have given so finished a specimen. And so you would have me live and die at Newcastle ! leave my country and my friends to—sit, as Miss

Wilson says, "playing at being agreeable" with half
a dozen "Virgin Automatons" who hail the hour of
enlargement as if it were the period of human misery
and the dawn of future bliss. The variety and animation of a convent, I daresay, are nothing compared
to this. But I will not be so ill-bred as to say I like
Durham better than Newcastle while you are in it ;
though, upon my honour and truth, I should if you
were here. The perpetual hurly-burly of the place
distracts me, and the incessant visit*ors* and visit*ings*
disturb my peace of mind. To be obliged to be
always witty, amiable, and good-humoured, when,
perhaps, I would often choose to be sulky, peevish,
and disagreeable; to smile, admire, and look gay,
when, perhaps, I had rather cry, sleep, or sit looking
at the figures in the fire; to have one's thoughts and
countenance for ever in full dress, powdered and
perfumed, ready for the necessities of the moment,—
are duties that I was never born to perform. You
know I can be extremely agreeable *with you* for an
hour, and patient enough with other people for a
little time. But is there any such thing as eternal
happiness? Seriously now, my dear girl, what do
you think of *everlasting* happiness? I can conceive
happiness to be exquisite and perfect beyond all
expression—everything in kind and degree,—but in
duration,—alas! not unlimited. We can so much
more easily comprehend the existence of everlasting
pain than of everlasting pleasure! and for this sad
reason—that all pleasure that we know of inevitably

becomes pain, but pain never becomes pleasure. Not that I have expressed myself very philosophically, but never mind that . . . . One firm article of my belief is, that the great Author of all good never created pain, and that it is some unaccountable necessity of Nature that will be explained to us hereafter. What a strange letter this is ! I am half inclined to burn it. If I send it, you must remember that I never mean to be gay on serious subjects, and that if I express myself at all equivocally, it is without the consent either of my judgment or feelings.'

During the short term of their married life my father and mother seem to have been seldom separated; but once, in 1798, my father rode up to London, and some letters which then passed between them still exist. They are expressive of devoted attachment on the part of both, and portions of them are curious as exemplifying the enthusiasm on one side and the hostility on others which was then felt for Godwin, author of ' Political Justice,' ' Caleb Williams,' &c., and his wife Mary (born Wollstonecraft), authoress of 'The Rights of Women ' and ' Letters from Norway,' who had then lately died, after giving birth to another Mary (afterwards married to Percy Bysshe Shelley). My mother writes (May 27, 1798) :—

' I am mistaking B. more and more every day. I spoke of him yesterday as the disciple of Godwin; and to my utter astonishment Godwin seems to be the object of his thorough contempt. Miss A. is mild

and tender in comparison. Yesterday afternoon I
was observing to him that I had never heard him
speak of Godwin and Mary, and asked what he
thought of their last publications. He said he had
never read them, but understood that the memoir
was a pitiful piece of biography. Peggy and I were
speechless,—both, I believe, from unutterable vexa-
tion. However we soon recovered, and attacked B.
less temperately, perhaps, than became the sober voice
of candid criticism. But, upon my word, Moyse's
criticism on Hartley was little less provoking. He
gave us several little paltry hearsay anecdotes of G.,
such as his calling his wife " the other party," his
observation on her declaring in his arms that she was
in heaven, &c., which certainly, abstracted from the
overpowering evidence of all his writings, and above
all of the simple narrative of his own feelings and
conduct towards Mary, must excite the idea of that
priggishness, coldness and pedantry which B. conceives to be the leading features of his character.
But that man who can call the lover, husband, and
biographer of Mary a cold-hearted pedant, must be
himself an impenetrable stone. And B. has read the
memoirs without retracting,—without indeed ever
mentioning the subject to Peggy or me,—and as I
saw he could read it without feeling a momentary
inspiration of the candour and feeling it exhibits, I
have done with him. He is indulging himself in
visions of fame and celebrity which will never be
realised. He says he had rather be eminently bad

than not eminent at all. I did not hear him say it, but Peggy did. What a monstrous offspring of vanity such an idea is! What other embryoes of deformity he may be hatching besides, God only knows.'

And in a subsequent letter (June 1, 1798) she recurs to the subject.

' So you really have seen Godwin and had little Mary in your arms! the only offspring of a union that will certainly be matchless in the present generation. Poor Godwin! what a melancholy tinge must all its infant sportiveness assume in his eyes! Fenwick has been reading Mary's letters to Imlay, and he says if he had 150 wives and were in love with 150 more, he must still be in love with *her*. . . . If you do not remember every word you hear Godwin utter, woe be to you !'

I believe my father's ride of between two and three hundred miles to London was chiefly with a view to make Godwin's acquaintance. He was then supposed by a large party in the country to be a political philosopher who had achieved imperishable renown. His two large volumes sleep on my shelves, and written in the fly-leaf in the hand of one of my uncles is, ' Hoc nescire nefas.' If so, the last two have been nefarious generations. This fast fading of literary celebrities would be melancholy, were it not that transitory admirations give birth to permanent results and he who strongly affects his own generation must, through it, affect those that follow, though his work and his name be forgotten.

Of my mother nothing remains to be said, for I was cut off from the knowledge of her by her early death. And as there is but one more of her letters left, so much of it as is characteristic shall take its place here. It is addressed to the lady who twenty years later became my father's second wife :—

' My dear Miss Mills,— . . . . It is scarcely possible that you could ever come inconveniently to us, even though we knew nothing of your intention, and you might perhaps often come much more conveniently to yourself without the delay of writing. As I now sit by my own fireside from one century to another [the letter is dated in the first month of the new century, January 10, 1800], I am more desirous than ever to render it as acceptable as possible to those I love, that I may not degenerate into a mere cricket and fatigue George's delicate ear with my monotonous notes. I wish you had seen Mrs. Turner. I have seldom seen a mind so masculine joined to manners so pleasing, I will not say feminine ; for her manners, like her opinions, are exclusively her own, and would disdain to fashion themselves in the same mould that has served the purpose of thousands before her. Yet she is free from all whimsical singularity ; and when she does differ from the rest of her species, it almost uniformly seems to proceed from that most interesting of all sources, originality of thought. She is also completely free from parade or ostentation of any kind, and never seems to think herself at all above the level of human nature. Yet I do not think she has the best opinion of human nature ; but her minute acquaintance with it seems to have rendered her invulnerable to surprise, and the strangest vagary that could enter into the mind of man would be to her very much a thing of course. Why this character, with all its excellences and superiority, has excited in me admiration rather than affection, I do not yet venture to determine ; because I am afraid the cause rested solely in me, and I feel rather inclined to sneak off from the investigation of it. Certain it is that if in one hour I was led to respect the moderation which taught her to censure without acrimony, in the next I was chilled by the coolness which allowed her to praise without enthusiasm. But I have not time to add more.

' Very affectionately yours,

'E. TAYLOR.'

The sentence she added last is an echo, which no one can mistake, of the Johnsonian cadence ; and I believe she had seen Dr. Johnson in her childhood. He had drunk tea (some two dozen cups) with her mother ; on which great occasion her aunt had incurred everlasting ignominy by leaving the doctor and going to a dance.

CHAPTER II.

BOYHOOD.

ANNO DOM. 1800-21.   ANNO ÆT. 1-21.

As I have said, it was whilst I was an infant in arms that my mother died. My father, who had by that time removed to St. Helens Auckland, in the same county, where he had taken another farm, pursued his farming operations on a large scale and with more or less activity for about 18 years (*i.e.* so long as times were prosperous), dividing his time between business and literature.

I have said little of my father hitherto, and it is time that I should give some account of him. If I have any difficulty in doing so, it is the reverse of that which I have met with in the case of my mother. Her I never knew. Of him my knowledge is so inward and accustomed as hardly to lend itself to an objective view; for of course it crept upon me insensibly, growing with my growth, and the image of him was never at any one moment presented to me in its totality as something fresh and new : and there is the farther difficulty, that were I to describe him in general terms I should seem to be simply reproducing the model virtuous man of a fiction, who is proverbially uninteresting : I should describe him as good, just, generous, true, affectionate, pure-hearted : and when I attempt to individualise, I find nothing to say except that he was habitually, though not invariably, grave and reserved ; that his abilities, though not pre-eminent in any single kind, were remarkable for the many kinds in which they excelled, and, taken along with his unceasing industry, if he had had as much love of distinction as of knowledge, would probably have made him eminent in his day and generation.

But he had no love of distinction; rather, I think, a preference for obscurity and retirement ; and this prevailed so far as to withdraw him from society as well as from publicity ; and as, for the last thirty years of his life, his wife was the only inmate of his house, and he had no daughter and only one surviving son, he lived too exclusively with his books, and his relations with his fellow-creatures were more limited than is desirable for any man. I may add that he did not read mankind with either the same interest or the same discernment with which he read books. He was open-handed and unsuspicious, and had there not been a more penetrating judgment within reach to restrain him, he would probably have lent and lost and given away everything that belonged to him. He had a lively appreciation of wit, without having any of his own ; and though somewhat taciturn and not brilliant in conversation, he was able and effective when he did take a part in it, and he left lasting impressions even on some whose acquaintance with him was but casual and short. Southey, in a letter to Miss Bowles, January 4, 1826, says in answer to an enquiry of hers, ' The article on Pope in the " Quarterly Review" was written by the father of my fellow-traveller, Henry Taylor, a most remarkable person for strength of character as well as for intellectual powers—the sort of man with whom Cato might shake hands, for he has the better part of an antique Roman about him.' And amongst my letters to my father in 1833 I find one describing the impression he had made many years before, after, as far as I am aware, only a short acquaintance :—

' I met with your old friend, Sir John Sebright, the other day. I did not quite know him by sight, though I soon made a guess after we had been talking for a while, and I led him on by degrees to farming and farmers, and in half an hour's time he began to suspect me, and when the éclaircissement took place I assure you that I never saw an old gentleman burst into a finer fit of enthusiasm. He started from his seat and said that if I was your son, then I was the son of the man in the world for whom he had the greatest respect and admiration, and after (as the Americans say) " a pretty-considerable-damned-long " exposition of your very great merits, he said he had been talking of you and praising you for twenty years, and he hoped that on your account I would allow him the liberty of asking me to put him down

in the list of my friends. He concluded with an invitation to his place in Hertfordshire, which I told him
I should be delighted to accept when leisure served,
and a request that when I wrote to you I would convey to you the expression of his respect and regard
in the strongest language that I could find. He
seems to have about the same impression of the
depth of your learning and the extent of your information that the student had of that of Dr. Faustus,
when he came to learn from him—

> What was and is in heaven and earth
> From chaos and creation's birth ;—

and I daresay he is persuaded that I have learned
nothing less from you, and that I am to turn out a
very agreeable and instructive acquaintance accordingly. When he finds the buckets coming up empty,
I shall have great difficulty in explaining how it
comes that my father's son is not acquainted with
everything that was and is.'

In my father's youth I believe his animal spirits
ran high, and it may have been easy for him to make
friends ; but there must have been something very
congenial to him in Sir J. Sebright, to have brought
out on short notice the powers of pleasing thus indicated. For after my mother's death a deep and somewhat severe melancholy took possession of him, and
I do not think that he was ever again happy till his
second marriage, when he was nearly forty-seven
years of age.

It was under this cloud that my boyhood was passed. Domestic affections had been and were all in all to him. He had strong opinions in favour of home education, and he educated his three boys himself. With my brothers his task was easy, for they had extraordinary gifts and powers. But with me it was otherwise. My mind was slow and languid, and the faculty of acquisition was sadly defective. Perhaps, too, my father made a mistake in attempting to combine the reading he desired for himself with tuition of me. He could do so well enough with my eldest brother, amongst whose boyish MSS. (he died at 20 years of age, in the same week with my other brother) I find versified translations from Lucan, Statius, and Silius Italicus, indicating that the beaten track of tuition had been left far behind : but the path into which my stumbling steps were turned was perhaps the most arduous that could have been found for a lazy boy of twelve or thirteen.   I have a painful recollection of my struggles as I passed through the History, the Annals, the ' De Moribus Germanorum,' and the ' Vita Agricolæ ' of Tacitus, at about that age; understanding as much as I was compelled to understand and no more.   Whether it was that my father was led by my difficulties to form a low estimate of my abilities, or that he found (as he well might) the task of teaching me intolerable, he did not attempt to teach me Greek ; and as I had taken a fancy to the sea (without knowing anything about it), he fell in with my wishes so far as to let me take a year of it on trial ; after which, if I were minded to pursue it, I might.

Accordingly, I was entered in April, 1814, being then 13½ years of age, as a midshipman on board the *Elephant* (74), Captain Austin (possibly the same officer who is now (1865) Admiral of the Fleet, and if so, I should like to see him again, for I admired him in 1814). My father, on returning to the Inn at Portsmouth after having left me on board the *Elephant*, took up a pocket edition of the ' Sylvæ ' of Statius which he had brought with him, and very strangely came upon this passage :—

> Grande tuo rarumque damus, Neptune, profundo
> Depositum.   Juvenis dubiæ committitur alno
> Metius, atque animæ partem super æquora nostræ
> Majorem transferre parat.   Proferte benigna
> Sidera, et antennæ gemino considite cornu,
> Œbalii fratres : vobis pontusque, polusque
> Luceat : Iliacæ longe nimbosa sororis
> Astra fugate, precor, totoque excludite cœlo.[1]
>
> *Lib.* 3, 2, 5.

He noted the date and the circumstances in the margin of the volume, and added ' Sortes Virgilianæ ! ' The *Elephant* was paid off in a fortnight, and I was transferred to a troopship, in which I made a voyage

---

[1] Neptune, to thee and to thy depths we give
A precious trust, the life wherein we live.
Metius, our boy, embarks, and, dubious, we
Send of our soul the better half to sea.
Œbalian brothers, on each yard-arm sit ;
By beams of yours let sea and sky be lit ;
And from Heaven's whole circumference chase afar
Your cloudy Trojan sister's stormy star.

to Quebec, and then to a frigate. I applied to be allowed to join an expedition against Long Island, to which some of my messmates were drafted off; but my Captain had probably reasons of his own for refusing the application. He had, or ought to have had, moneys in his hands placed there by my father for my use, which, it afterwards appeared, were not easily producible. Whatever was the motive, he chose to take me home with him; and of my service in the navy, which lasted less than a year, I remember but little.

If I had been a lazy boy at home, I was not less so at sea. Turning out for the second or third night watch was a trouble to my flesh. I never once went up the rigging—a fact which speaks as ill for the discipline of the ship as for my spirit of enterprise. I recollect mentioning it one evening when I was on a visit to Lockhart at Chiefswood, in the presence of a brown, brawny giant of a sea-captain (Ferguson by name). He lifted up and leant back his neck and head to their utmost stretch as he sat, raising his hands high in the air, which then descended upon his knees with a loud reper-cussion. Lockhart observed, 'That clearly means, "smite my timbers."'

The truth is that my health had always been of the languid kind; my life at home had been somewhat gloomy and dreary, but never rough; the messmates with whom I was now thrown seemed to me a set of abominable blackguards and bullies (one of them, who was about to join another ship, took the opportunity of stealing my dirk, my books, and some of my linen, which I afterwards recovered) ; the food was nothing but hard biscuits, sometimes maggoty, and salt beef or salt pork ; four hours of the night as well as of the day were to be spent on the quarter-deck in all weathers ; and before the year of trial was out, I was so ill that I was unable to walk. Luckily, at this time, my ship arrived in English waters ; and as the war had then come to an end, I had no difficulty (or ought to have had none, for my indebted Captain threw some needless ones in my way) in obtaining my discharge from the navy. It is dated December 5, 1814, and gives me a good character.

I returned home and remained there for about two years ; but I do not remember that my father resumed in any methodical way the task of teaching me, though no doubt he guided and supervised my studies ; and thus I regard myself as, after my thirteenth year, in a great measure self-educated ; with the advantage, however, of a good library, and a house in which literature and knowledge were considered, along with the domestic virtues and affections, all that it was worth while to live for.

It was a house in which the face of a stranger was rarely seen and diversions were almost unknown. The clergyman of the parish was the only neighbour who had any pretensions to be an educated man ; and his pretensions must have been of a humble order, for I remember that, though he himself came to the front door when he had any business with my father, his wife and daughters came to the back door. Such was the position which was sometimes held by a parson in the North of England fifty or sixty years ago.[1]

The house, too, was a silent house. So that, except the dog, who was my chief companion, and the pony, with whom also I was in familiar relations, reading was the only resource for me. There were a very few novels,—' Sir Charles Grandison ' and ' Clarissa Harlowe,' ' Cecilia ' and ' Evelina,' the ' Old Manor House,' and ' Caroline de Lichfield,' a French novel by Mme. de Montolieu,—all of which I read again and again ;—also translations of German dramas,—the ' Robbers,' ' Don Carlos,' ' Count Koenigsmark,' ' Benyowski,' ' The Stranger,' and others,—which charmed me as much ;—and poetry— Southey's, Coleridge's, Scott's, Campbell's, J. Montgomery's, and at last Byron's,—very dear to me all of it. I read Euclid, too, with some interest ; and tried Bridge's ' Conic Sections,' but I could make nothing of that ; and Smith's ' Wealth of Nations,' and Paley's ' Theology,' ' Evidences of Christianity,' and ' Moral Philosophy,' and Cavallo's ' Elements of Natural Philosophy,' Darwin's ' Zoönomia,' and in metaphysics the works of Locke and Hartley. What other books I read at that time I know not. I should think not very many. I was still lazy, and I lounged

____

[1] Written in 1865.

a good deal of my time away in the houses of the farm servants and in the stables ; and, indeed, my favourite place for reading was nestling amongst the hay in the hay-loft.

An intelligent boy, however, will not be the worse for some intercourse with the peasants of the north of England. Their language has (or had then) much of the force and significance which is found in that of the Scotch peasantry as given in Sir W. Scott's novels. 'Is that ye ?' I recollect one man saying, and the other answering, ' Ay, a' that's left o' me. I'm just an auld " has been." ' Such forms of speech were probably traditional or current, and not the invention of those from whom I heard them ; but they belong to a superior race. 'I've forgotten mair na' he ever knew ' is another that I recollect, as the form in which one of my father's farm-servants asserted his superiority to another. 'He has not only mair lair ' (lore, learning) 'than another man, but he has a gift wi't,' was the same man's panegyric of my father. 'What ! are ye there, Molly ?' I heard a man say once to a very old woman whom he had probably not met for a long time, and she answered—' Aye, I think God Almighty's forgotten me.' They were a people whom it was not unprofit-able to mix with and talk to ; though it was from idleness, and not for profit, that I did it.

Once a year a breeze and a sunbeam penetrated into these recesses. My father had had a friend (a relation, I believe, though a distant one) of the name of Davison, much older than himself, an accomplished man who had travelled in the East, had been British Consul at Nice, had come home, married, and died, leaving a widow with the remains of great beauty, and four daughters, one of whom was brilliantly pretty, and all of whom were attractive (in one way or another and more or less), from simplicity and gracefulness of manner, brightness, singleness and saliency of character, softness, and an uncultivated refinement. I can barely recollect the father. Probably I should not have recollected him at all but for his pigtail—one of the last survivors, I suppose, of the latest generation of pigtails. Once a year the widow and the four fresh, pleasant, and graceful daughters came to spend a few midsummer weeks at the Hall at St. Helen's Auckland, or ' The Nunnery,' as it was sometimes called ; for the last occupants had been an abbess and a sisterhood of nuns, driven from France by the revolution. It was a large, old, rambling house, formerly a seat of the Eden family, of which one range was Elizabethan, or perhaps of earlier date, low, with diamond-pane windows ; and at the end of this had been erected a less antique block of building, probably not 100 years old, from which proceeded on one side a still more recent offset. The house had clumps of large timber trees on both sides of it, and pastures divided by a sunk fence in front to give the effect of a park.

The house and its trees made the only picturesque feature in the tract in which it stood, which was flat and uninteresting. I see it now in all its blankness, as I used to see it when it occasionally became my duty to accompany my meagre and solemn grand-uncle in his slow rides. It was a dull situation and a dull life, and I was constitutionally deficient in animal spirits. But the annual visit of the four fresh girls came through the clouds like the chariot of Aurora. I was never *caressed* but by them.

By this time—1815 or 1816—the prosperous times for farming had come to an end, and my father gave it up ; and finding himself no richer than when he began, it became necessary that he should look about for some means of providing for his sons.

His farming avocations had made him ac-quainted with a much more ardent agriculturist than himself, who was also a politician in office, Mr. Arbuthnot, best known as the friend of the Duke of Wellington, and at this time Secretary to the Treasury in Lord Liverpool's Government. My father's inter-course with him was almost entirely by correspon-dence, though he once paid us a visit at St. Helen's Hall, where strangers were so rarely seen and cour-tiers never but this once. He seemed, however, to have a regard for my father, and when a provision was wanted for my brother George and myself, now seventeen and sixteen years of age, he gave us clerk-ships, the one in the Audit Office and the other in a Department then called the Storekeeper-General's, three or four years afterwards reduced and consoli-dated with the Commissariat branch of the Treasury and with the Ordnance Department. This took George and myself to London ; and William, being intended for a doctor, was there already, attending the hospitals. We all lived together for a short time in lodgings in Carey Street, Lincoln's Inn Fields ; and there we all together caught typhus fever, of which William and George died within a fortnight. I had it but slightly.

My father bore the blow as he might. From that time forth his right hand shook, and for many years he was unable to write without using a mechanical contrivance for steadying it. He was devotedly attached to us all three ; but his literary and intellectual pride had been in my brothers.

The elder of them had just completed his twentieth year ; the other was in his nineteenth. Both had written much poetry in the various manners in which boys write before their own is finally formed.

It was precisely in the twenty years covered by their lives that poetry in England was changing its mood. My father's (he wrote not a little, and there is some extant of his eldest brother's also) was of the kind cultivated in the eighteenth century,— ethical and didactic. That of his sons was imaginative and romantic, and I shall have occasion to quote some of it hereafter. What I will quote here is in another kind,—an epitaph on Cobbett, the notorious writer of the seditious and libellous newspaper called ‘ The Register,' who had lately suffered, both from a horsewhip in the hands of a Mr. Newman and from a criminal prosecution. It is a parody of Gray's 'Elegy ':—

> Here rests his body in the lap of Earth,
>   A man to Mr. Newman not unknown;
> The Attorney-General frowned upon his birth,
>   And Debt and Newgate marked him for their own.
>
> His 'Register' it was the vogue to buy,
>   And men thus recompensed him for the lash ;
> He gave to facts, 'twas all he had, the lie,
>   He gained from fools, 'twas all he wanted, cash.

George seems to have had a turn for mathematics and mechanics as well as for poetry. I recollect the roars of laughter in which some one indulged on inspecting an abortive attempt of his, when a very young boy, to produce the notes of the gamut from an Æolian harp, by keys and stops and two pairs of forge bellows borrowed from the village blacksmith, and wooden conduits or pipes to convey the air ; and in 1816 I find his father reproving him for 'applying his mathematics to such nonsense as a machine for shuffling cards.' Both brothers were addicted to music ; and the elder in a letter to the younger (November, 1816), speaking of a meeting with his Newfoundland dog after a long separation, says : 'Fag and I had a most joyful meeting ; if the genius that invented the tune of " Caller Herring " from the women crying them, had been present, what a fine, wild, jovial air he might have composed ! '

After the death of my brothers I lived alone in

lodgings in London (where I had scarcely a friend or acquaintance) till 1820, when I was sent to the head-quarters of the Windward and Leeward Island Command at Barbadoes ; and after a few months of service there, the absorption of the Department to which I belonged being accomplished, I lost my employment and went home.

CHAPTER III.

Anno Dom. 1821–23. Anno Æt. 21–23.

SHORTLY before I had gone abroad, my father, then 46 years old, had married (November 14, 1818) a lady of about the same age, to whom he had long been attached, and had removed from St. Helen's Auckland to a small house near the east coast, about half way between Newcastle and Sunderland; whence again, in about a year, he removed to Witton-le-Wear, the village where he had been at school; and there he remained till his death, thirty-two years afterwards.

It has been my fortune throughout life to be connected, by relationship, marriage, and friendship, with remarkable women. I suppose my stepmother had faults like other people, but I never could find out what they were. She was gentle and affectionate, and yet firm and strong; deeply religious and wholly unworldly; she was—

> true as Truth's simplicity,
> And simple as the infancy of Truth—

she had read well, though not widely ; and she was wise,—perhaps all the wiser for not having addicted herself to thinking thoughts, or thinking for thinking's sake or for the sense of intellectual power,—a practice by which intellectual ambition is apt to—

<blockquote>

o'erleap itself
And fall o' the other.

</blockquote>

Unperplexed by aims or efforts of this kind, but regarding with a singular intellectual acuteness what life and observation presented, she had a direct and undisturbed insight into human nature and a just and penetrating judgment. And to her other gifts there was added what, when I first came to live with her, made her society especially pleasant to me,—a lively wit and a keen sense of the ridiculous. Something lively was much wanted at Witton Hall. The stranger within the gates was as seldom seen there as he had been at St. Helen's Auckland. The companionship of my stepmother was to some extent a substitute for society ; but it could not altogether dispel the gloom. And, indeed, though intellectually bright, she was not of a very cheerful or hopeful temperament. Her views of life were rather melancholy ; and but that she regarded this life as of small account, she would not have been happy in it. I hardly think she *was* happy ; serene rather, and resigned. My father's religious opinions,[1] though not

---

[1] In humility and reverence he was never wanting, and the spirit in which he held his opinions may be seen in a letter to one of my brothers dated June 15, 1814 :—

sectarian, were peculiar, and fell short of what satisfied her. Devoted as he was to her, she made little
impression upon him in this point; and her imper-

'I wrote to you last in the midst of the business of Darlington
Fair and every minute expecting the mail, so you needed not reproach
me with my brief epistle.   Was that a place to

> reason high
> Of Providence, foreknowledge, will and fate,
> Of happiness and final misery?

These are subjects that require all the leisure and consideration we
can ever command; and when these are given, more yet would be
required: for perhaps on none of these questions can we ever decide with
certainty; and it would seem that the decisions, however important
they may appear to us, have not been thought so by the Author of
Revelation, or the Scriptures would have left no doubt on the subject;
"si cette vérité étoit nécessaire comme le soleil est à la terre, elle
seroit brillante comme lui." The Scriptures have left no doubt that
there will be a future life,—that the character of that, as happy or
miserable, will depend on the moral worth of the character formed
here, and they have laid down plain rules for the formation of that
character. The Scriptures, we should observe, speak always in popular
language, as of the stedfast earth and of the course of the sun and
sea. They in no way pretend to inform on natural truths, or to give
precision of language for the investigation of metaphysical subjects;
hence a frequent laxity of expression which renders one author in
Scripture apparently contradictory of another on subjects where they
did not, it seems, think it important to be precise. The duration of
the punishment of the wicked is expressed in all passages in a way
that leaves no doubt of its being of very long duration; and when the
most learned men doubt on the signification of the words used to
express that signification, we may safely interpret them in that sense
which to the best of our judgment is most accordant with what Nature
evinces and the Scriptures declare to be the character of the Deity,
and by no means allow dubious phrases to impeach the general tenour
of the whole. Now in my mind benevolence and mercy are the
characters so strongly impressed by Nature in the Scriptures, that I
am inclined to believe any errors in my construction of particular
passages rather than admit a doctrine subversive, as it might seem, of
these attributes. These are my general sentiments on the subject,
but I by no means wish them to preclude particular investigations on
your part. I did myself at one time enter pretty fully into such

turbable temper and religious acquiescence, which gave her a sort of even contentment under all other circumstances of life, did not save her from anxiety as to this. It was not, therefore, any buoyancy or sprightliness of animal spirits in her, but rather wit and the easy and lively action of a strong intellect, at once acute, direct and simple, together with ardent affections, never expressed but never to be doubted, which gave some warmth and animation even to Witton Hall.

Nevertheless, my health, not at any time vigorous or comfortable, suffered from the want of active employment and the monotony of life. I read with some diligence but with little appetite. I desired to

investigations, and I did not find that etymological reasoning brought any more uniform results from different passages than popular readings, except, I think, in the various cases of αἰών and its derivatives, translated "eternity and eternal," "for ever and ever," &c. Now the Greek word was by no means ever certainly used for our metaphysical use of "eternal;" it is more properly "time" or "life," as has often been observed. Homer uses it for a man's life, and at Iliad 4478 for a short life; so that αἰών so frequently rendered "eternity" does not necessarily include a long time even. I do not pretend to be competent to enter into all the niceties which this subject involves, but I mention t..is one as most frequently occurring to show the uncertainty and in my mind the impropriety of dogmatical inferences on such subjects, especially when those inferences would tend to subvert our ideas of the divine justice or benevolence deducible from far more certain sources. We cannot arrive at mathematical demonstration on these subjects, and must therefore acquiesce in difficulties to be solved only by adhering to the greater probabilities; and even if investigation were to convince you that eternal punishments were reserved (in the metaphysical sense of the expression) for the wicked, according to the Scriptures, it would resolve itself into the question of the origin of evil, which, however it puzzles us to render compatible with the omnipotence of the Deity, cannot annihilate the evidence for *immeasurable* benevolence and *immeasurable* power.'

be well informed, and whether at Witton or elsewhere I was in the habit of setting myself tasks. At an earlier period I had made translations of the ' De Moribus Germanorum ' of Tacitus, and of some cantos of the ' Orlando Furioso ' (versified in *Ottava Rima*), and I had now taught myself a little (a very little) Greek as well as Italian, and had read the whole of Ariosto, much, if not the whole, of Alfieri, and more or less of the other best known Italian poets, the ' Discorsi ' and ' Principe ' of Machiavelli, Hume's, Smollett's, Clarendon's, Burnet's, and Gibbon's histories, Sale's ' Koran,' more or less of Mosheim and of Milner's ' Church History,' and a good many lighter books in poetry and in prose.

Indeed, the solitude of my life had thrown me much upon books. In a letter of my stepmother's (October 19, 1818) written to me before her marriage (for we corresponded for a year or two before that event), she writes :—

' I believe you are quite right in saying that nothing is so favourable to study as the lonely hours you have to spend. . . . I believe there is nothing so advantageous to the formation of character as alternate solitude and society, and variety of society. We feed in society and digest in solitude. Never to be alone is a dreadful bar to reflection and that sort of investigation that makes us adopt the good for our own and cast the evil from us. A society of friends only is far too flattering ; a society of the domestic circle only is too little varied,—our ideas stagnate, our opinions want toleration and liberality ; and in the domestic life we are, generally speaking, too much intruded on to find opportunity for solitude. I have ever found it so ; I never yet have been able to read, write, or reflect but with a divided attention ; and frequently the pains of disturbance, the efforts to repel it, seize upon that little portion of attention I might make my own, and so I lose all.'

At Witton neither she nor I had much of interruption to repel. I read, therefore, some hours every day ; but except the popular novels and poetry of the time—Scott's, Byron's, Moore's, Campbell's—all that I read I read slowly, languidly, and with effort. Two daily walks of an hour each were performed—also as a task. I recollect that I used to have a sort of spring of joy for a moment when I looked at my watch and found it to be an hour or so later than I had supposed it to be—so heavily did time go with me. But when evening came I had some compensation for the tedium of the day. With me, as with many nervous young persons, evening brought, not exactly high spirits, but an excitement which was better. So after my father and stepmother had gone to bed at ten o'clock, I sat up late, sometimes in meditation, sometimes writing verses, sometimes simply abandoning myself to the pleasure of existence. Though I drank nothing but tea, there was a sort of inebriety in the nocturnal state which was no doubt exhausting, and charged the days that followed with the nervous expenditure of the nights. But I was utterly ignorant in the management of my health ; and even if I had known how much it was suffering, perhaps I should not have spared it, for I had no pleasures but these.

It was now, in 1821–2–3, that I began to write verses in more or less abundance. I have not published any of them,—I think I have not preserved any,—not because I thought them all bad of their kind, but because they were in a tone and style borrowed from the popular poets of the day—then the objects of my ardent admiration—and not the style which I found for myself at a more mature age, partly derived from better models, partly, I think, original. I wrote a poem of five or six hundred lines called ' The Cave of Ceada,' on the story of Aristomenes as told by Pausanias ; a longer poem called ' The Flight of Rhadamistus,' on the story of that personage as told by Tacitus ; and a tragedy called ' King Don Philip the Second,' of course on the too often dramatised story of Don Carlos. Some of my poetry of this period was written under not unfavourable conditions.

For dull, almost to disease, as my daily life was at Witton-le-Wear, there were three weeks of it on which I have always looked back as supremely delightful. In the summer of 1822 my father and stepmother went on a tour to see the Scotch lakes ; for my father, notwithstanding his imperfect sight, had the most ardent admiration of picturesque beauty in nature that I have ever met with in any man, and my stepmother, in her degree, loved it also. They were absent for about three weeks. Now, to me, in those days, and indeed in later days also, there was something exciting in the sense of solitude—an absolute inspiration in an empty house. Generally, as I have said, my inebrieties were nocturnal only, and the day paid the penalty of the night's excess. But for these never-to-be-forgotten three weeks, all penalties were postponed, if not remitted ; the lark took up the song from the nightingale, and my delights were prolonged, without distinction of night or day, and with the intermission of but three or four hours of sleep begun after three in the morning.

It was midsummer weather. The house was dark and gloomy, an old square ivy-covered border tower with walls so thick that light and sunshine had their own difficulties. I remember that a sprig of ivy had worked its way inwards and was sprouting in a corner of the drawing-room ; and writing in after years, when my father and stepmother had been from home, and had gone back to 'what they call their nest,' I said it reminded me of Wordsworth's—

> forsaken bird's nest filled with snow
> Left in a bush of leafless eglantine.

But the situation was picturesque, near the top of a steep hill which rose for about half a mile from the valley of the Wear. The river was crossed by a bridge nearly opposite ; its farther bank was steep and thickly wooded towards the west ; towards the east, where the bank was low, there was a wood or grove, through which a burn, called the Lynn, went its way to join the river ; and farther eastward, at the summit of a green slope, stood an uninhabited castle, partly ancient, partly modern.　My habitual walk was down the hill, across the bridge, through the grove, crossing the Lynn by an old plank bridge, and up to the castle, where I paced backwards and forwards on the top of a sunk fence that imitated a moat.　During these three wonderful weeks I took this walk in the middle of the summer's nights, and then mounted by a narrow little staircase from my bedroom at the top of the tower to the flat leads which roofed it, and there walked backwards and forwards till the sun rose.　All the day round I saw no one but the servants, except that I sometimes looked through a telescope (part of my naval outfit in 1814) from these leads at the goings on of a farmstead on a road which skirted our grounds at the farther end. Through this telescope I saw once a young daughter of the farmer rush into the arms of her brother, on his arrival after an absence, radiant with joy.　I think this was the only phenomenon of human emotion which I had witnessed for three years, except one.　That was when my stepmother, who was not in the habit of betraying her emotions as long as she could stand upon her feet, fell upon the floor on the receipt of a letter which told that a niece of hers (the daughter of a clergyman and grand-daughter of an archbishop) had eloped with a married man.

These three weeks were, as I have said, a favourable time for writing verses ; and the best of my juvenile poems, 'The Cave of Ceada,' was written then.   The best was not bad—of its kind—nor without a certain sort of fervour and beauty ; but it was merely built upon Byron.[1]   So far as temperament went, there was nothing wanting.   It is this temperamental element which makes a poetical poet ; it is this, combined with more than ordinary intelligence and thoughtfulness and an easy command of language and of salient and obvious melodies, which makes a popular poet ; it is this, combined with intellectual and rhythmic gifts of the highest order and with wisdom, which makes a great poet.

Throughout youth and middle life, till health failed, and even after that, I had almost habitual accesses of this temperamental kind ; but I was never more of a poet, as far as *this* goes, than when I wrote bad or indifferent poetry ; and I never felt the charm of poetry more deeply than when the poetry

---

[1] I find there is still one little Byronian poem in existence :—

The tide rolls back, the black rocks rear
  Their rugged heads above the deep ;
Thus dark when Hope hath ebbed appear
  The dreams that Wisdom wakes to weep ;
Dark tombstones o'er a darker grave
  Of buried joys, where by the bier
Is ceaseless sung by wind and wave
  The dirge we all are doomed to hear.

which charmed me was (though better executed) not of a higher order than that which I wrote myself.

> Oh many are the poets that are sown
> By Nature ; men endowed with highest gifts,
> The vision and the faculty divine,
> Yet wanting the accomplishment of verse.

If many are these (of which I do not feel any positive assurance), certainly, in our days, many more are they who are poets by nature and temperament, and possessed also of the accomplishment of verse, but wanting in the highest gifts, 'the vision and the faculty divine.' They are true poets so far forth ; and some of them have their just and appropriate reward in popularity.

It was in the earliest of my years at Witton, 1822, that I first saw myself in print. In those days the ' Edinburgh ' and · Quarterly ' Reviews stood supreme as the literary and political organs, each of its own party in the State. They were great powers, not yet hustled by the swarm of other journals which in no long time after came trooping up to take their part in the leading of the Bear. I think the ' Westminster Review ' was the only other quarterly journal in existence ; and whatever it may have been in point of ability, it could pretend to no rivalry with the other two in the 'pride of place.' Of the two editors, Jeffrey and Gifford, Jeffrey, with the aid of Sydney Smith and Brougham, had achieved the higher reputation for brilliancy and wit ; but Gifford's talents were not perhaps inferior to his ; nor his wit inferior either, though he was a graver man, and was now getting old and weak in health. Both were kind men in life ; both were merciless and remorse-less as writers. Southey said to me of Gifford, that all his gall was in his inkstand. The same might have been said of Jeffrey. But they had had to fight their way in life in their youth ; and they, like many others then and since—myself for a time—adopted the evil habit of regarding literary life as a fair fight, of which the honour and glory belonged to him who could use weapons of offence with most skill and effect. Under cover of this view they 'corrupted their compassions,' and they hardened their hearts to acts of literary cruelty and wrong, dealing death-strokes at the feelings and hopes and fortunes of this or that literary aspirant, perhaps with one or another plea or pretext of a public or a party purpose to be answered, but in reality with little other object than that of raising their own credit as journalists by the force and brilliancy of their writings.

There was no malice in all this, any more than there is malice in the soldier of fortune or the mercenary who hacks and hews and slays his fellow-creatures in his pursuit of glory and reward. But there was an utter indifference to human suffering : and it is seldom that human suffering takes a form more acute than in a youthful aspirant to literary celebrity who finds himself suddenly exposed to indignity and shame and made the laughter of mankind. Mankind are always ready to applaud that which makes them laugh, whatsoever victim writhes ; but none was more ready to join in the applause than I was in my two-and-twentieth year. The view which I adopted afterwards (but not immediately nor very soon afterwards) was that no unkind word should be spoken of book or man unless there was something more to be alleged for it than the expurgation of literature by criticism ; inasmuch as, generally speaking, neglect will do all that is necessary in that way.

In 1816, my brothers, in that year aged respectively seventeen and eighteen, had sent Gifford an article on Coleridge (perhaps a joint production) ; and although the article was not accepted, on the ground that another contributor had written one on the same subject, he had given them encouragement ; and in a letter to the younger of them, dated December 4, 1817, he writes : 'How was it that I never heard from you after I enclosed the MS. of Coleridge? I augured well of the mind that produced that little article. It is surely capable of greater things ; but I lost sight of you all at once.' It was probably this correspondence of my brothers with Gifford that suggested to me to make an attempt in the same direction ; and, early in 1822, I sent him a short article upon Moore's 'Irish Melodies.' I heard nothing of it for several months, and I was infinitely surprised and delighted when, in October of that year, I received a letter and a remittance in acknowledgment of my article, which was to appear in the number then to be published. On referring to the article, I find it to be a light and lively piece of criticism on the approved model of sarcastic flippancy; not indeed altogether suppressing the genuine admiration which I felt at that time for Moore, but nevertheless taking such opportunities as arose of mocking at him.

In the blind solitude of Witton Hall this appearance in the 'Quarterly Review' seemed like an opening into the outer world and its sunshine. And, indeed, I think it did lead the way to the outer world; for my father and stepmother, who had seen that I was suffering in health and spirits from an unoccupied and objectless life, were now encouraged to think that if I were to go forth I might find an occupation and career in literature. My stepmother, for these years that I had been at home, had been watching me fondly and wisely, and she understood me well. She had justly considered me as in some points of character unsettled and crude; perhaps even more so than most youths may be expected to be between nineteen and twenty-two. My enthusiastic admiration of Byron was morally stultifying; I do not say debasing, because it was matter of imagination, and did not, in any positive and affirmative sense, work itself into my practical life. What it did was to supplant or stunt other and ·elevating admirations. But great is the loss in youth which is thereby suffered :

We live by admiration, hope, and love.[1]

By love and hope throughout life and in all its seasons ; by admiration eminently in youth, and more or less, but perhaps with a diminishing predominance, afterwards. My stepmother perceived, as she was sure to do, my follies and crudities— looked through and through them. Her temper was imperturbable. She did not remonstrate, admonish, warn, advise, or discuss, with any special reference to myself and my follies. The influence she exercised was that which was necessarily to operate from living with a keen and strong understanding, governed by a pure and strenuous moral mind, as free as any human being's can be from vanity or littleness or self-love. When called upon to speak on subjects involving moral sentiments, she spoke the truth, regardless whether agreeable or disagreeable. But she took no personal aim—none, that is, at me ; for persons were no doubt, as they must be with all practical minds, the groundwork of her moral insights. The persons who presented themselves in her secluded way of life were not many ; but many are not required for a true knowledge of human nature ; and for the purposes of such knowledge there may be more easily too many than too few ; for in this as in other ways 'the hand of little employment hath the daintier sense.'

[1] Wordsworth.

Under this regimen I had so far gained in strength, that within a year after this *début* of mine in the 'Quarterly Review' she had come to the conclusion that I might be safely sent to London to seek my fortunes as an adventurer in literature ; and my father adopted her view.

She had had a powerful coadjutrix. For in these years were the beginnings of an influence founded partly on personal admiration—at least aided by it— which lasted in direct action through the greater part of life, and in its ultimate results, if not defeated by the adverse elements and powers, ought to reach beyond this horizon. My stepmother had a dear friend and cousin, at that time about forty years of age, by name Isabella Fenwick.   Her face might have been called handsome, but that it was too noble and distinguished to be disposed of by that appellative. Her manners, her voice, and everything about her, harmonised with her face, and her whole effect was simple and great, and at the same time distinctly individual. My father says of her in one of his letters : 'All the noblenesses are so obvious, and yet there is so much single-heartedness withal, that one is sure all that is on the surface is also worked into the substance of the character.'

I was then, and have been always, peculiarly amenable to manners and looks. Miss Fenwick was too far removed from me by age, and too far above me in nature and character, for me to be in love with her. My admiration was wholly unamorous, but it was very ardent. She was largely and deeply religious ; gladly and affectionately submissive to the authority of the Church ; but, by a law of her nature, free,—a child of God in the bondage of love and in the ' glorious liberty ' which consists with it. Her intellect was more imaginative, various, and capacious than her cousin's ; her judgment less sure-footed ; her impulses more vehement ; her nature more perturbed. She had the same sense of the ridiculous ; and when they were together, my father (who, rigorous and austere as he was in his morality, had a profound charity and consideration for all men that were not obnoxious to moral censure) used to be somewhat shocked at the treatment which weakness and folly met with at their hands. He could bear ridicule only when it was directed at himself ; and he *looked* so grave and severe that his wife and his son were the only persons who were ever likely to laugh at *him*. But though our ridicule of himself was rather pleasant to him, he could not be persuaded that ridicule of strangers and of the absent was consistent with benevolence towards them ; and perhaps there was in Miss Fenwick at that time, besides what was harmless and stingless, some want of toleration for what, after all, in a just estimate, is tolerable enough,—prudential virtue and worldly respectability. Her theory was that the great sinners are, through remorse and repentance, more in the way to salvation than the indifferently well-conducted people. I recollect once, when the talk was of sermons, she

said the only use of them was to make *respectable*
people uncomfortable. There would be something
to be said for her preference of great sinners to
respectable sinners, if great sinners did commonly
repent; but as the facts are, I am afraid the world
cannot afford that moderately good conduct from
mixed or secondary motives should be despised.
Nevertheless, with all her vehemence of contempt for
what was contemptible and her undue disrespect for
what was merely creditable, she had a most generous
and charitable heart; and out of an income which
did not much exceed 1,000*l.*, she spent (at least in the
portion of her life when the disposal of her income
was within my knowledge) several hundreds a year
in bounties and charities. 'A more generous and a
tenderer heart I never knew,' says Mrs. H. N. Coleridge [1] in a letter to Aubrey de Vere ; and so say I.
Nor was it by money merely or by money most
that her sympathy with misfortune made itself felt.
Her spirits were easily depressed, and by such depression some persons are disabled for consolatory
offices. It was not so with Miss Fenwick. She said
of herself that she was at home in the house of
mourning ; and no words could express her more
truly.

There is a good deal of her mind in my writings.
I wish there were more ; and I wish that she had left
her thoughts behind her in writings of her own. I
think that during some portion of her life she had

[1] Life and Letters of Mrs. H. N. Coleridge, vol. ii. p. 63.

been accustomed to commune with herself in her chamber and write the results. But the diffidence of a constitutional melancholy stopped them there. They were never seen by any one, and were not allowed to survive her. Once when I was writing an article for the 'Quarterly Review,' I told her that it would contain some things which she had dropped in conversation and I had picked up. She replied :—

' You must be most ingenious in making out any-thing from my conversation that could be useful in an article in the "Quarterly." It must be good policy in me to speak to you in half sentences.'—It was very much her way to let a sentence die off when it had gone far enough to show whither it was leading.— ' I do sometimes regret I did not earlier in life get into the habit of committing my thoughts to paper. But to communicate my thoughts then to some living ear seemed all in all to me ; and when from experience I found there were few who would be in-terested in listening to me and I turned to my pen, I found my taste had become too much cultivated for my power of expression, and I could not frame a sentence that did not disgust me. Else, having read a great deal and thought and felt a good deal, I might have written what might have interested others and improved myself. But most of my think-ing has perished within me.'

The change which came over me by admiration in the case of Miss Fenwick, was corroborated by another admiration. In the autumn of 1823 I went to the Lake country and paid a visit to Southey. He was then about 50 years of age. He was the first of our great men with whom I had come face to face. Afterwards I became acquainted with most of his eminent contemporaries and of my own,—with Wordsworth, Coleridge, Scott, Moore, Campbell, Tennyson, and Browning among poets ; amongst historians with Hallam, Macaulay, Froude, Carlyle, and Lecky ; amongst statesmen with all I think that were conspicuous except Canning, Brougham, and Disraeli ; and I have found none who combined with intellectual pre-eminence so much of what was personally attractive. I have given some account of his personal bearing and his ways in conversation in a notice of him printed by his son at p. 4, vol. vi., of his ‘ Life and Correspondence.’ Of the impression he made upon me in my first youth, I made mention in some stanzas written in 1829, which being printed in the notes to ‘ Philip Van Artevelde,’ need not be reprinted here. The beginning of the poem is lost ; but there are stanzas relating to the changes I underwent at Witton, and Miss Fenwick’s part in producing them, and they are these :—

> Three years and five—three passed in scenes remote
>   Where seldom stranger foot was known to stray,
> And every eve the thrush’s dropping note
>   Sang a soft requiem to a studious day ;
>   Glenlynn, did ever evening pass away
> That I came not through all the changeful year ?
>   Like constancy I came in thy green May.

And when thy boughs were fallen into the sere,
The yellow leaf, decay would only more endear.

Three studious years—but not from books alone
  The harvest of those years was gathered in ;
For living minds were there to which my own
  Did in its aspirations then begin,
  As was its right by birth, to be akin ;
The just, the generous, the unworldly wise
  (Sole agonist infallible to win),
The steady and the strong, I learnt to prize,
And would have been the like if wishes might suffice.

And with the wish some weakness past away,
  And vanities withal that spread their lure
For an unsettled nature in that day
  Of danger when the soul is immature
  And yet the wit is forward : these their cure
Found in communion with the minds I name ;
  And there was one beside of heart as pure
The force of whose commanding spirit came
In aid of their old drifts,—new, sudden, yet the same.

In all things noble, even in her faults,
  For power and dignity went thro' them all,
That rare humility which most exalts
  Was hers—the fear the highest have to fall
  Below their own conceptions : I recall
That first impression and the change it wrought
  Upon me, and find something to appal
And something to rejoice the heart,—the thought
How much it did effect, how far, far more it ought.

Superior to the world she stood apart
  By nature, not from pride ; although of earth
The earthy had no portion in her heart ;
  All vanities to which the world gives birth
  Were aliens there ; she used them for her mirth

> If sprung from folly, and if baser born,
>   Asserted the supremacy of worth
> With a strong passion and a perfect scorn
> Which made all human vice seem wretched and forlorn.

This was no idealisation. These were the facts of the case.

CHAPTER IV.

ON the 18th of October I completed my twenty-third year, and before that day I left home, contentedly but with not much of the animation of hope, to seek my fortunes. My stepmother wrote to me on the 15th :—

'After all the chatterings, the jestings, the preachings, and the varieties of conversations that we have held for two years past, you may expect some continuations of each variety now and then per post when you are settled in London ; and I shall hope for reply occasionally also, in some of the crammed sheets that you have to write with all your adventures. . . . You will imagine with how much additional interest Old Jackey [this was the postman] will be watched for on the winter evenings here now. I sometimes fear these evenings will want subject of interesting employment for your father, unless he can suit himself in some kind of authorship. Dr. Holland suggests a subject [the Thirty Years' War] in a letter I here enclose. You will perhaps anticipate your father's reply; but in case you are not quite certain of it, I will tell you what he says to Mr. Turner, granting that it is of an interesting nature—" but having been executed by such a mind as Schiller's, a good translation of his work would be a more valuable addition to English literature than any original work on the same subject by one man in a million, in which distinguished minority I have no pretensions to stand." What is the work in which your father will feel that he must excel ? How frequently do we complain of the intolerable vanity of authors ! How few authors we should have if it was not for vanity ; and though it is a very disgusting quality, even when it is founded, as it *sometimes* is, upon valuable stuff, we are glad to have it spoiling the flavour in some degree, rather than not have the good stuff at all.'

What she here says of my father was not only true in 1823, but remained true for the ensuing twenty-eight years of his life. During those years he wrote a few articles in the ' Quarterly Review ' (about ten, I think), and except a memoir of his friend Mr. Surtees, author of the ' History of Durham,' that was all. In his love of knowledge he had transformed the means into the end ; the uses of knowledge passed out of sight, whilst his unsunned hoards increased from year to year like a miser's money in the days in which a miser's way of hoarding was by heaping up gold in a cellar.[1] I remember

---

[1] So far as the Latin and Greek portion is concerned the hoard exists to this day, but as in a cellar still. For forty years he kept a

quoting to him with the impertinence which always pleased him when it came from me, the words which Miss Edgeworth puts in the mouth of a bookworm to a friend visiting him in his study : ' Here I am reading and reading from morning to night all the year round, and *nobody's the wiser.*'

On the 22nd of October I had arrived in London, and on the 23rd I saw Gifford, and 'found him propped in his chair, with a little thickened milk and a bunch of grapes before him, and all the appearance of a far-gone invalid.'   He had in his hands, and gave me in proof for revision, another article which I had written in the same style as the former, clever and malapert. This was directed against a man conspicuous in Parliament even then, and shortly to be much more so, with whose friendship I was honoured in later years.   I have never told him that I was his anonymous assailant in my youth, though of course he would care no more than if he were reminded of a derisive cheer in the House of Commons of forty years ago ; and had he known it at the time, knowing also how important it was to the young tumbler that his somersaults should attract notice, he would not

Latin and Greek commonplace book,—an 'Index Idoneorum' as he entitled it,—ranging the passages he extracted under the various heads of subject to which they related.   After his death, Dr. Whewell, then Master of Trinity, contemplated the publication of it by means of a fund at Cambridge disposable for the publication of valuable but unmarketable MSS.   On inquiry, however, he found the fund was anticipated for some years then to come.   [1880.   I have presented it now to the Library of Durham University.]

have grudged any little specks of mud that might light upon him.[1]

A great encouragement no doubt it was to me—this second appearance in print immediately on my arrival in London ; and it may possibly have contri-buted more or less towards a greater success which was to come in less than three months. In the meantime I had undertaken to edit the ' London Magazine,' then, if I recollect right, lately set on foot, for which I had written two articles on ' Recent Poetical Plagiarisms and Imitations.' I have looked over them now and am amazed at the display of reading and erudition which I know that I never possessed—Greek, Latin, French, Italian, Spanish, and German. With one or two of these languages I had a fair familiarity ; as to some others, what I may have read I could only have spelt out with a dictionary ; and yet I assumed to appear perfectly at my ease in them—translated Spanish and German ballads, and quoted from Lucan, Claudian, Lucius Varus, Silius Italicus, Statius, Aulus Gellius, Lucretius, Valerius Flaccus, Justin, Tibullus,—scarcely one of which authors I had ever read, and quoted for the most part aptly enough. I have no recollection of the manner in which I managed to put these wares in my window ; but I have little doubt that as regards the Greek and Latin authors I must have had by me

---

[1] *Note, August* 15, 1876. Lord Russell tells me the article had been very useful to him by showing him that it was not to poetry but to politics that he was to devote himself.

my father's marked copies with his marginal notes. But my journalising projects and operations were soon to cease.

Of two or three literary men to whom I had brought introductions, one was Dr. Holland (afterwards Sir Henry). He held an eminent position in his profession and in the literary world, and was in friendly relations with the leading men of all political parties. I had breakfasted with him once or twice after my arrival in London in October, and on the 10th of January he informed me, to my infinite surprise, that he had been in communication with the Under Secretary of State for the Colonial Department, and that, ' if my engagements would allow of it,' it was proposed that I should be appointed to a clerkship in that office with a salary of 350*l.* at once, which it was expected would shortly be increased to 600*l.* —the increase did in fact take place within twelve months—and which would ultimately rise to 900*l.*[1] It was abundantly plain to me that ' my engagements would allow of it.' I could not imagine how it had happened that Dr. Holland, who had not seen me, I think, above two or three times, had been induced to make me his nominee, when asked to recommend a fit person for the office in question. Some relatives of his were old friends of my father's, and on their

---

[1] In point of fact, the prospects thrown open to me did not stop even here ; for, in the course of years, the office of Under Secretary of State, with 2,000*l.* a year, was offered to me, though for reasons which will be stated in their place I did not accept it.

account he may have been glad to be of use to me ; but I daresay his main object was to recommend the man whom he thought most likely to be useful ; for no doubt the facts of the case were represented to him, and they were facts which called loudly for fit men.

The business of the Colonial Office was growing every year more important—in reference to the question of negro emancipation I may say more momentous ; and it was in utter confusion. Several old clerks who took but little interest in it were therefore to be provided for elsewhere, and several new ones to be brought in, who were to be chosen with a view to obtain more effective service. Dr. Holland had but scanty means of estimating my abilities by personal intercourse, for I do not think that in my youth they came to the surface in society ; but there were my two articles in the ' Quarterly Review ' to speak for me ; and when it appeared to be desirable that Lord Bathurst, then Secretary of State for the Colonies, should be furnished with testimony to my abilities, I was enabled to produce a letter from Gifford, opportunely received ten days before, commending my last article, and adding, ' I shall always be happy to hear from you. I know not what leisure you may have, and therefore I do not press you ; but to me your communications, however brief, will always be acceptable.'

In communicating to my father, on the 22nd of January, my instalment in the Colonial Office, I concluded my letter by saying, ‘That this affair will delight you is one of my greatest pleasures in thinking of it.’ And this, I think, was true. As well as I recollect, I was at that time less solicitous personally about this sort of success than was reasonable or even justifiable. I used to think that tea and bread and butter (to me, as I have said, so inebriating) were all that was necessary to my happiness; not knowing that life in its further progress would bring with it other wants. At the same time I have no doubt that I rejoiced and was elated.

The manner in which the news was received at Witton may be gathered from a letter of my step-mother’s :—

‘Your father met your last letter as he was walking down to Auckland with letters that he had written to each of your aunts. His first feeling was to run back with the letter for my sake; but then to add a postscript to the said letters in his pocket and to save the post for your aunts was more important, for he could communicate the good prospects to me at any rate by dinner-time; so accordingly he came panting in to a late dinner, and Margaret, weary with keeping the meat hot, had it popped down on the table by the time he got off his hat, &c. “Take away the dinner, Margaret! bring the candles, and don’t come in till you are called.” “What can have happened!” said I. “Good news, excellent news!” “From Harry?” “Yes, from Harry.” “Make haste.” So then he read away—wonders and marvels indeed, my dear Harry, and the greatest feeling of pleasure to me is, that you are likely to be rewarded for all your patient perseverance in endeavouring to become independent. You give me credit for imagining a scheme that is likely to become productive of so much good ; now, I have no more credit in that than any one who has to dispose of a book, or a broom, or a pen, or any other article, and who finds out that a book must be exposed to sale in a market where readers resort, or a broom where there are housemaids, the pen where there are writers, and so on ; and it was easy to see that one stored as you were *must* be useful to many, and could not be used unless known ; but that you have been so soon discovered and wanted is certainly a piece of good luck beyond our most sanguine expectations. I do not at all regret your not having gone sooner to town. All the time at home was preparatory, and I do think not more at all than what has been advantageous. Two years ago the value of a good income was in great part unknown to you, and consequently you are now better prepared, not only for spending it right, but for the patient performance of wearisome offices which will continue it to you. The life of authorship was a resource when nothing more steady could be had ; and for all its uncertainties and its laboriousness and its vexations, it had in it something very flattering to a mind formed like yours ; and if you succeed in this desirable clerkship, which we trust is pretty certain, you will · have to forego much of that fame you anticipated as an author ; for your mind will have to be given to dry work and to be kept *present* to your employment, or there will be neglects ; and, after all, it seems where talent is not required you cannot have the fame attending talent, but only the fame of being an attentive useful clerk, and your reward is money. I feel sorry for you on this point, for I think it will be mortifying to your favourite source of ambition ; but you must just drive your ambition into another channel ; and secretaryship leads to honours too, and a line of life that may be very agreeable to you ; for general talents are useful in every line and lead to fame ; and there may be leisure moments for your more favourite studies.'

The business to which the appointment introduced me proved to be neither irksome nor ill-suited to me. I plunged into it at once, and by a letter which, though not dated, must have been written in March, 1824, it appears that I was working in Downing Street night after night till one or two in the morning, in the preparation of a paper which was immediately printed at the Foreign Office private press and laid before the Cabinet ; and in furnishing materials for a speech to be spoken by Mr. Canning on the subject of the measures then in agitation for meliorating the condition of the slaves.   My ' remarks nearly in full,' I wrote to my father, ' were sent to Canning ; cram, cram, cram, and on Tuesday night *evolabat oratio.'*

The paper for the Cabinet seems to have been

elaborate and voluminous. ' A clerk was sent to see the types broken up and receive the printer's declaration that he had delivered all the impressions taken off and kept no copy. The impressions delivered I was directed to keep under lock and key and give to no one.'

I do not find any copy amongst the official papers of mine, printed and MS., in my own possession, and I do not know how my task was executed. Lord Bathurst, it appears, was delighted with my work ; but it must have been very imperfect from want of practice and experience ; and the faults which I should imagine to have been most conspicuous, would be arrogance and impertinence. They were faults which tainted my official style, not only in the beggar-on-horseback beginnings, but I am afraid for several years afterwards. There is an indication of this in the letter in which I speak to my stepmother of what I am about :—

' At this time I have scarcely a word or thought for you but such as are born and die in Downing Street ; but I shall be glad to send my thoughts to Witton if they will go there (and there they will go if anywhere) by way of a diversion from foolish governors, furious houses of assembly, methodists, and slaves.'

If anything could have cured me of such a fault at once, it would have been serving under Lord Bathurst. I could not have fallen in with any man in whose official style there was more of the dignity

of good-nature. He could be severe when necessary ;
but in his severity there was generally a parental
tone ; and to the severest of his rebukes he could
contrive to give a colouring of consideration for the
culprit. I recollect a Scotch Minister coming home
from British Guiana, in high indignation, and in
a letter to Lord Bathurst accusing and abusing the
Governor of the Colony in the most unmeasured
terms. Lord Bathurst answered that he would have
wished to send the letter to the Governor for his
explanation of the facts alleged, but that he felt
a difficulty in doing so, not only out of respect for
the Governor, but from an unwillingness ' *to expose a
Minister of the Gospel.*'

I admired these examples, or I should not have
remembered them after the lapse of forty [1] years ; but
the hardness and crudeness of youth were incurable
except by time ; and for *some* years at least, if not
for many, the style and temper of despatches which
I drafted were such as I believe I should be very
much ashamed of were I to read them now. And at
the same time my aptitude for business, which was
considerable, and my laboriousness, placed in my
hands a measure of authority which was probably
never before exercised by so young a man in a
position so subordinate ; indeed, a larger measure
than in most of the years of my maturer official life ;
for in after years there were abler men in office
over me.

---

[1] Written in 1865.

Some time in the first decade of my service a nobleman was Governor of an important Colony. From the commencement of his administration I had strongly disapproved his policy and course of proceeding, and at length I urged upon the Secretary of State (not Lord Bathurst, but one of his early successors) that it was necessary that he should be recalled. My urgency was in vain ; the Secretary of State was not prepared for such strong measures. Nowise discouraged by his reluctance, I proceeded to draw up an elaborate and voluminous despatch recapitulating the Governor's errors and misdoings from the commencement of his administration, and ending with his recall. The Secretary of State gave way, the despatch was signed, and the Governor came home accordingly.

I dare say there were faults enough of tone in this despatch,[1] as in my other proceedings of a like character ; but I believe that substantially I was in the right ; and there was this to be said for a strong exercise of authority in those days and on the question with which I was chiefly occupied—that it was the great question of the melioration, leading to the abolition, of slavery, and· that the Governors of the slave colonies were almost all of them identified in feeling and opinion with the slave-owners, and constituted to a great extent ' His Majesty's opposition ' in that portion of his dominions.

---

[1] I have now procured a copy of the despatch and I do not find the faults in it which I had expected to find.

My exercise of authority, singular and anomalous as it was, would perhaps have been still more uncontrolled, had it not been that at this time, and for many years afterwards, my manners were against me.

Whether from nature or from the silence in which I had lived up to this time, I was unusually taciturn. It was not easy to me to say anything ; and if à man has nothing to say naturally, and finds something to say with much effort and difficulty, he can scarcely have what is called a natural manner. Mine was, with strangers or men with whom I was not intimate, far from natural, I believe, and anything but easy. I had a quick social sensitiveness ; by which I do not mean that I was apt to be hurt or to take offence, but that I was keenly alive to the minuter phenomena and effects of social intercourse. This over-quick consciousness of what is passing in the minds and what impressions are made on the feelings of those with whom we are holding intercourse is fatal to ease and simplicity of manner. It is necessarily accompanied by a continual consciousness of one's own effect upon them ; and this, with no more than an average share of vanity, or even with less than an average share, will often be enough to produce a disturbed and affected manner. I was quite aware of the defect ; few people, I think, had a better taste in manner than myself ; no one admired simplicity of manner more than I did, or desired more to be possessed of it ; but the very importance which I attached to it made it all the more unattainable. Nothing but time and the conversancy with society which brings indifference or a sufficiently light social sensibility, could place it within my reach.

I think, too, that there was something at work worse than what I have described ; a certain amount of plebeian pride and jealousy of social distinctions. The manners of a gentleman should be liberal, not only in avoiding to assert social superiority of his own, but in recognising that of others. In measuring his distances he should give the benefit of a doubt to familiarity with those below him in rank and to form with those above him ; and if he be independent in his feelings and make no more of social superiorities than they are worth, he will naturally do so,—at least if he have a natural kindness and desire to please. I missed my way very much in these matters. In my utter ignorance of society and of relative social positions, I was afraid of seeming to defer too much to rank and station, and affected not to recognise them at all. Lord Bathurst combined all sorts of titles to be treated with deference,—office, rank, age, manners, and talents ; and I had a very genuine admiration and respect for him, and would have expressed it by a duly deferential manner if I had known how. But the only effect of my feelings upon my manner was to make it more than usually infelicitous, awkward, blunt, and shy.

CHAPTER V.

EARLY FRIENDS AND ASSOCIATES—HYDE VILLIERS AND HIS FAMILY —JOHN MILL—CHARLES AUSTIN—JOHN ROMILLY—EDWARD STRUTT.

ANNO DOM. 1824-27.   ANNO Æt. 24-27.

IT was not, however, to all persons nor in every species of intercourse that my manners were equally unprepossessing, or that I found myself unacceptable. My employment in the Colonial Office introduced me to a companion of my own age, Thomas Hyde Villiers, then a clerk in the office ; and from companions we became very shortly each the most intimate friend of the other.   We were associated in our work, I officially the subordinate, for something less than a year, when he quitted the office to enter upon political life in the House of Commons, and I took his place.

He was perhaps the ablest, and had he lived long enough would probably have been the most distinguished, of a very able and distinguished brotherhood. George Villiers, now Earl of Clarendon, and lately Secretary of State for Foreign Affairs, was the eldest of the brothers ; my friend, Hyde, the second ;

Charles, a member of the present Cabinet (1865), the third ; Edward, whose dear friendship was the treasure and the charm of my middle age, the fourth ; Montague, the late Bishop of Durham, the fifth ; Algernon, who died young, the sixth. And there was one sister, Theresa, then about two-and-twenty years of age.[1]

They lived with their father and mother in Kent House, Knightsbridge, occupying one half of it, whilst the other was occupied by their mother's brother, Lord Morley, and his wife,—a woman whose wit, vivacity and good humour, natural, easy, and unambitious, will probably be remembered in London society till the last of her contemporaries shall have dropped out of it. She was a woman of the world, and, with the exception, perhaps, of Lady Charlotte Lindsay, the wittiest woman of her time ; but with all that she was simple, kindly, brave and strong. George Villiers, then about twenty-six years of age, was gay, graceful, brilliant and pre-eminently popular ; Charles, with still more wit than George (who, how-ever, had not a little), was sarcastic and unpopular, but amongst friends very agreeable ; of Hyde and Edward, as those with whom my relations were close, I will speak more largely,—of the one here, of the other hereafter ; for it was not immediately that my intimacy with Edward began.

Hyde's face was that of a fair and distinguished looking child grown to the stature of manhood (he

____
[1] Born March 8, 1803.

was very tall), with as little alteration as might be
of its delicate features. He had a large forehead,
large eyes, and a sensitive mouth beautifully chiselled.
He was slenderly made, with a feminine roundness of
the muscular fabric. His manners could be what he
pleased. They were invariably highbred, and under
all ordinary circumstances expressively courteous.
He was calm, self-governed, ambitious, but with a
far-sighted ambition, caring little for present, unless
in so far as they might conduce to ultimate results ;
cool and not vain, patient and resolute, enduring
bodily pain with unshaken fortitude, and encountering
danger [1] and difficulty with an undisturbed mind.
In boyhood he had been educated at home, in the
midst of social pleasures and with the worst of tutors ;
and, with his personal attractiveness and talents for
society, he was in the way to an epicene course of
life ; but having gone to Cambridge, he there fell in
with some young men of striking abilities, great
attainments, and democratic opinions ; learnt to look
with little favour upon the ways of life in the classes

[1] Duelling had not yet come to an end, and I was once the bearer
of a hostile message (in the nature of demand for an apology) from
Hyde Villiers to an electioneering opponent, who, in one of his
speeches, had exceeded the bounds of electioneering privilege. The
negotiations took some time. Hyde was suffering severe pain from
an abscess in the head, behind the ear, of which he died soon after.
Throughout the affair he continued labouring almost without intermission at a report of a Committee of which he had been chairman.
His brother, George, showed as little anxiety about the result of the
proceedings. On my return from my first interview, he asked me
what sort of fellow Mr. S. was. 'A mild prig,' was my answer. 'A
very dangerous person indeed !' said George Villiers, with a smile.
The gentleman made an apology, however, and there was no duel.

of society to which he had been accustomed ; and
deploring his miseducation and the ignorance of
which he now became conscious, applied himself to
retrieve the time so far as might be still possible.
Before he and I made each other's acquaintance he
had made up his mind to renounce London society
and its pleasures ; and soon after that he took a
house in Suffolk Street which I shared with him ;
and as I had hardly any other acquaintances, and he
desired to avoid the swarm of his who were idle and
uncultivated, we lived a great deal together.

When I quoted in a previous page the greater
part of a poem in which I had taken (about the year
1829) a retrospect of the formation of my own mind
by intercourse with others, I reserved as more appo-
site in this place the two following stanzas :

> The other was in age my own compeer :
>   Of a severe philosophy was he
> A searching pupil—from his natural sphere
>   Exorbitant, for he was bred to be
>   At Fashion's shrine a favoured devotee :
> But pleasure's bonds were not of strength to hold
>   A strenuous mind that struggled to be free ;
> Love grew as tedious as a tale twice told
> And beauty's eye met his, impassive, calm, and cold.
>
> I gathered from his converse,—shall I say
>   A reverence too exclusive and supreme
> For Reason in her logical array
>   And most recluse abstraction : not a theme
>   Thenceforward could escape by enthymeme ;
> We nourished in each other day by day
>   A questioning spirit ; with our double team
> We drove the harrow o'er the trodden way,
> Scouting those easy words, the good old yea and nay.

If the description in the latter stanza was applicable to Hyde Villiers and myself, it was not less so to the small set of able and highly-instructed young men who had been, with one exception, his associates at Cambridge, and who, in London, continuing to be his, became mine also ; Charles Austin, John Mill, Edward Strutt, John Romilly, Charles Villiers. They were radical, Benthamite, *doctrinaires ;* and were regarded by prudent people as very clever young men who were thwarting the gifts of Providence and throwing away their prospects of worldly advancement by audaciously avowing extreme and extravagant opinions. As time went on, however, the world met them half way ; and whether they have retained or renounced their democratic views, every one of them has obtained what he sought and pursued.

· Charles Austin was in conversation the most brilliant of them all ; and there was a singular charm in his manner, which expressed the power to command along with the desire to please. It was socially genial as well as buoyant (though, perhaps, indicating some hardness and coldness at bottom), good-humoured, frank, and wholly unaffected ; and there was a sort of light and almost careless strength in his conversational diction, contrasting strangely and strikingly with the logical precision of thought which he, in common with the rest of them, cultivated as the one thing needful. *His* precision seemed inevitable and easy; that of the others more or less painstaking and circumspect. He betook himself to the Parliamentary Bar, then the most lucrative career for a lawyer, but one which, not being compatible with a seat in the House of Commons, excluded him from all the honours and dignities of the profession. He made an enormous fortune (nearly 40,000*l.* in one year I believe), with an amount of exertion which ruined his health for a time ; and all his labours, energies, abilities, knowledge, and fascination of manner and discourse, ended by placing him, in the latter stages of his life, in the position which a thousand ordinary persons occupy by mere inheritance in the earlier stages of theirs—that of a rich country gentleman and chairman of quarter sessions. Had his ambition been political instead of pecuniary, he might have been a second Lord Lyndhurst : but he got what he desired.

John Mill was the most severely single-minded of the set.   He was of an impassioned nature, but I should conjecture, though I do not *know*,[1] that in his earliest youth the passion of his nature had not found a free and unobstructed course through the affections, and had got a good deal pent up in his intellect ; in which, however large (and amongst the *scientific* intellects of his time I hardly know where to look for a larger), it was but as an eagle in an aviary.   The result was that his political philosophy, cold as was the creed and hard the forms and discipline, caught fire ; and whilst working, as in duty bound, through dry and rigorous processes of induction, was at heart

---

[1] Written before the publication of John Mill's Autobiography.

something in the nature of political fanaticism. He was pure hearted—I was going to say conscientious —but at that time he seemed so naturally and necessarily good, and so inflexible, that one hardly thought of him as having occasion for a conscience, or as a man with whom any question could arise for reference to that tribunal. But his absorption in abstract operations of the intellect, his latent ardours, and his absolute simplicity of heart, were hardly, perhaps, compatible with knowledge of men and women. and with wisdom in living his life. His manners were plain, neither graceful nor awkward ; his features refined and regular ; the eyes small relatively to the scale of the face, the jaw large, the nose straight and finely shaped, the lips thin and compressed, the forehead and head capacious ; and both face and body seemed to represent outwardly the inflexibility of the inner man. He shook hands with you from the shoulder. Though for the most part painfully grave, he was as sensible as anybody to Charles Austin's or Charles Villiers's sallies of wit, and his strong and well-built body would heave for a few moments with half-uttered laughter. He took his share in conversation, and talked, ably and well of course, but with such scrupulous solicitude to think exactly what he should and say exactly what he thought, that he spoke with an appearance of effort and as if with an impediment of the mind. His ambition—so far as he had any—his ardent desire rather, for I doubt if he had much feeling about himself in the matter—

was to impress his opinions on mankind and promote the cause of political science. His works on logic and political economy have now been for many years of the highest authority amongst the learned, and his writings on political philosophy are regarded, even by those who most differ from them, as the aberrations of a powerful and admirable intellect. He has just (1865) furnished the first example of a man sought out and summoned by a large constituency to represent them in the House of Commons, without any proposal or desire of his own to do so, partly on account of his political opinions no doubt, but chiefly on the ground of his eminence as a political philosopher. His seat for Westminster, though not in itself what he would have sought and pursued, is the result and indication of what he did seek and pursue,—a wide-spread influence over the minds of men in his day and generation : and he, too, therefore, has got what he desired.[1]

---

[1] In our Debating Society one evening the subject was propounded by John Mill, who undertook to show that 'the aristocracy is a pernicious class in this country.' In a speech of mine in reply to him, written and got off by heart, as were most of my speeches, I met his anticipated invectives against the stolid immobility of the aristocracy :—
'It will be allowed, I apprehend, that the most active and energetic men are generally not the most prudent—that they are fond of experiments which the chances are not in favour of, and are sanguine beyond the average of mankind, which is itself known to be sanguine beyond reason. Now the conclusion is, that whereas this enlightened, enterprising, and impetuous class of philosophers might persuade the country to run some awkward risks, this stubborn, benighted, and inveterate aristocracy throw their dead weight into the other scale, and keep all where it ought to be. In moments of popular restlessness, they prevent the commonwealth from falling into the hands of any rather wild

Edward Strutt was a man of sound knowledge and solid understanding, simple and honest-minded. He had a large fortune, obtained a good position in the House of Commons, became a member of the Government, and was eventually raised to the peerage by the title of Lord Belper; which was probably all the success in life to which he had aspired; if indeed he was troubled with any aspirations of the kind.

John Romilly was sensitive and reserved; judging by his countenance, of a very gentle and affectionate nature; but sensibility was not the fashion in this set of juvenile philosophers, and those who had it did not disclose it more than they could help. He had eminent abilities, and had been sedulously trained by Dumont in all the learning of the Benthamites. Men so trained were, perhaps, in general, better fitted for jurists than for judges, and better fitted for judges than for advocates; but John Romilly succeeded at the Bar, and rose in due time to be Master of the Rolls and a peer of the realm. He therefore, like the others, has been successful, according to his desires.

There remains Charles Villiers; and as I have already said, he is at this moment (1865), as he has been for several years, a Cabinet Minister. He was handsome but in a feminine way; and in order to indicate the small value that he set upon such beauty,

young gentleman who may be possessed with a very natural desire, together with some natural capability, of leading mankind where he pleases.'

he affected slovenliness in dress and neglect of his person. He generally appeared in a threadbare coat which had lost one or more of its buttons, and Hyde said of him that he was a very good-looking fellow 'when he was picked and washed.' He was idle; like his elder brothers he had been wofully ill-educated; and he was not, I think, in the habit of reading books. But he was shrewd and acute, and by living with instructed men he got the knowledge that can be so acquired; and, pretending to nothing, paid for what he got by the interest he took in the knowledge others possessed and by the keenness and brightness of his wit; in so much that he would have been as much missed in our circle as any other of us. 'So he is gone, with all his wit and all his malice,' said Johnson when Beauclerc died; as if he somewhat regretted the loss of the malice as well as that of the wit. And there was a malice of the imagination in Charles Villiers's wit[1] which was certainly very pleasant to us philosophers. It was a mischievous wit, and made him many enemies, and it was certainly not restrained by charity. But, on the other hand, I do not believe that it proceeded from any practical ill-nature. On the contrary, I have reason to know that there was in him no little kind-

---

[1] The humour of malice, without the reality, which belonged to Charles Villiers was well expressed in an answer he gave to me on my return from some months' travel on the Continent in 1844, when I asked him about the state of public affairs, and how Gladstone had been getting on, adding that, from what I could hear, he had become quite popular: 'Yes, everyone speaks well of him,—God damn him!'

ness of disposition—carefully concealed. In after years, understanding well his own aptitudes and defects, he fastened upon one subject—the Corn Laws—acquired all the knowledge requisite for dealing with that, and through that made good his footing in political life. He played an important and conspicuous part as one of the leading members of the Anti-Corn-Law League, and he took up a position in the House of Commons which, with his social rank and his family connections, so soon as it became necessary for the Whigs to conciliate the Radicals by admitting two or three of them to a share in the government of the country, gave him an easy entrance into the Cabinet. He has, no doubt, learnt all that life in the House of Commons and in office teaches, and in this year of 1865 he has carried through Parliament with much ability and perseverance the most important and the most pertinaciously opposed measure of the session—that for union-rating.

Such were the male associates with whom my friendship with Hyde Villiers brought me into more or less of intimacy. Frequent and long drawn out were the breakfastings of those days ; and when Wordsworth happened to be in London, I got *him* to come ; and though he was old, and the rest so young, and he was opposed to them in politics, yet the force and brightness of his conversation, his social geniality, and the philosophic as well as imaginative largeness of his intellect, delighted them all. Southey, too, came amongst us once or twice ; and I look back

on those meetings with the sort of feeling with
which Beaumont reverted to the gatherings at the
' Mermaid ' of Ben Jonson and the rest :—

> What things have we seen
> Done at the Mermaid ! heard words that have been
> So nimble and so full of subtile flame
> As if that every one from whence they came
> Had meant to put his whole wit in a jest,
> And had resolved to live a fool the rest
> Of his dull life.

The society of the family at Kent House was
interesting and captivating in another way.   Miss
Villiers was eminently pretty,—as pretty, I think,
as any one could be without being beautiful ; and
she was as quick and intelligent as any one could be
without being signally intellectual.   She had been
brought up in a class of society, the *élite* of which
(as I have observed elsewhere) will naturally, from
constant practice, be ' more adroit, vivacious and
versatile in their talk than others, more prompt and
nimble in their wit, and more graceful and perfect in
the performance of the many little feats of agility in
conversation which come easily to those who have
been used to consider language rather as a toy than as
an instrument.'   She had all these advantages, and she
aimed at nothing in conversation which she could not
accomplish with ease and grace ; so that one felt as
if she might have been more brilliant than she was
had she been disposed to try.   She had sense, and
strength and clearness of purpose upon all occasions ;

and a harmony and unity of the whole being, inward
and outward, which, being so perfect, was in itself a
charm. But what perhaps most charmed me in my
gravity was a fresh light-heartedness, new to my
experience as well as contrasted with my own conditions of existence—

For the hours
Had led her lightly down the vale of life,
Dancing and scattering roses, and her face
Seemed a perpetual daybreak, and the woods
Where'er she rambled echoed through their aisles
The music of a laugh so softly gay
That Spring with all her songsters and her songs
Knew nothing like it.[1]

It was of her that I so wrote, though not by
name. Of casual and superficial sensibilities she knew
nothing ; and when the deeps were broken up, which
could happen to her as to others, it seemed as if she
could suffer only in paroxysms, and that in these
she must either conquer or die. Her way was to
conquer ; but once she did nearly die ; her strong
nerves gave way, and for some months she was
unable to speak intelligibly or to walk. These
physical consequences being removed, however, and
her health restored, she resumed her constitutional
sprightliness ; the past was past, and not a trace of
a trouble remained.

[1] Ernesto.

CHAPTER VI.

ANNO DOM. 1824–28.   ANNO ÆT. 24–28.

IN 1825 I made my first attempt to speak in public.
It was made in a debating society to which the
Villiers brothers and the other men I have mentioned
belonged, and was reported in a letter to my stepmother of March 12, 1825 ; adverting first to a
speech delivered on the same evening by Hyde
Villiers :—

'I heard him make his first speech in the Academics
last week with great success. It was able, orderly,
and distinct ; with no grace of language other than
harmony and simplicity. There was no striking
embellishment in the speech; but his manner of
delivering it was extremely expressive and imposing.
I made my first attempt last night and failed. I
know of no other reason for my failure than the mere
disability to collect my thoughts and give them
connected utterance. My speech, if speech it could

be called, reminds me of Le Fevre's pulse.[1] When I
felt thoroughly embarrassed, I said that I felt myself
not capable of going through with it and therefore I
should give it up. And I do not know that I could
have done anything better. But I felt it hard to
hear some speakers string their nothings together with
ease and fluency, whilst I who had something to say
had no power to speak it. Also it could not but be
matter of some mortification to exhibit a failure to a
large audience, most of them men of ability. I do
not consider the experiment conclusive ; and disagreeable as it is, it must be renewed. If I find that
I am really unable to speak in public, it is always
useful that men should be aware of their incapacities ;
and it is necessary that I should ascertain mine in this
instance, since it would materially influence even my
present pursuits.—Since I came to Downing Street I
have had some talk with Villiers on the subject of
my *début* last night. He says I made him excessively
nervous, but he did not expect it would end as it did ;
there was no appearance of shyness, my voice was
firm and clear, and when I made my dead stands he
always thought that I was deliberately collecting
myself and that I should go on well after. He calls
my break-down the coolest thing he ever saw.'

My father and stepmother replied, the former
beginning and the latter finishing the letter :—

---

[1] The allusion is to a passage in the account of Le Fevre's death in
Tristram Shandy, vol. vi. chap. xi. :—' The pulse fluttered—stopped—
went on—throbbed—stopped again—moved—stopped—shall I go on?
—No.'

' Persevere by all means, and redeem the opinion of the society (if they be so inexperienced as to form one on a *début*) even at the expense of incurring more wounds to vanity for a while—but attempt no reply till, by premeditated speaking, you have got over the hurry of spirits from desuetude.' . . . ' Your father is hurried to get other things ready for the post, so gives me his paper to express my mortification on the very natural and most picturesque account of your feelings. The coolness that was taken for impudence was pride that would not show mortification. I have always observed an inequality in your speech when upon any argument ; sometimes fluent and rapid, and sometimes hesitating and vacant. I am glad I was not present, I should have been so very nervous. Your failure was partly nervous, though not in the way of shyness ; but I trust practice will at least give you the exercise of your full powers, whatever they may be ; and if you have them, I am impatient to have the present impression on your audience removed. Had I to speak I should feel as you did, and as I have done many a time when I had any very painful thing to say : I have fixed upon the sentence and made my tongue do it like a parrot without any sense in my head, or in my heart either but of its own thumping.'

In less than a fortnight I reported a second attempt :—

' I spoke last night sufficiently to my own satisfaction. I got off a little speech thoroughly by rote, so that I was sure I could not be prevented from speaking it except through an absolute deprivation of intellect and utterance ; I rose without any nervous excitation further than what would be of advantage to me, and with nothing of the nervous depression which had attended my former attempt, and I spoke it quite fluently to the end. I felt no want of self-possession, and made the emphasis and manner of delivery pretty much according to my ideal of what it ought to be. I felt in speaking as if I could have digressed and come back to my rote speech at pleasure ; but I had determined not to do it ; and perhaps would have found myself wrong if I had. However, till this is done, all I know respecting my talents in this way is that I can recite before any given audience any given speech I have gotten as much by heart as ever I got an alphabet.'

A copy of the speech was enclosed, and it shows that, with all my admiration for my Benthamite friends, I was far from adopting their opinions. It might be supposed indeed from the language that I was an ardent Conservative ; but the truth is that, though I was of this way of thinking when called upon to think upon the subject at all, I cared little for politics ; and for the greater part of my life I was not in the habit of even reading the newspapers. Of political economy, nevertheless, I was a sedulous student.

A few months later my letters make mention of another speech and of its success. 'The effect, however, was a good deal broken and spoiled towards the end by a sort of minim rest, as the musicians have it; that is, I made a total pause and stood upon the floor for some time, racking my recollection for what was to come next. . . . Certainly nothing could be less like impromptu speaking than the perfectly fluent delivery of the two portions and the dead stand-still between them.   However, I have not much desire to get credit for doing more than I can do, and have no objection to everyone's knowing that I get by heart all I can say, until I can say something without.   It is more satisfactory to feel a good foundation for any reputation, great or small, which one may come by.'

An extract from one of my speeches may be worth transcribing.   It was in refutation of my friends, the young Benthamites. 'That all our motives originate in selfishness is, in my opinion, though perfectly true, very immaterial.   For I believe it is not denied that by virtue of association we come to be actuated by such motives as in common language are called dis-interested; and how does it signify what be the original principles of our nature, so long as the derivative are the acting ones?   The immediate in-stigating causes of our acts are what concerns us in life, not the remote metaphysical origin.   You may trace back closely, you may follow far, the suc-cessions and dependencies of our acts and feelings; you may pursue them into the region of final causes, where they are lost in darkness; but this will not bring you to a system of morals: for moral principles

are to be found by investigating rather the consequences of our acts than their causes, and rather the
near causes than the more distant. Although, therefore, if you will seek out in selfishness the source of
every generous impulse I do not dispute that you may
find it, yet, in my mind, it is like finding a north-west
passage to the South Pole—the way is cold and
gloomy, and it is likewise a long way about. Sir,
having admitted the doctrines in question to be true,
I will further admit them to be as harmless as many
other metaphysical truths, so long as they are silently
revolving in the brain of a philosopher; but harmless
they are not to those by whom they are half understood, and of this number are the multitude who
maintain them. To this half-comprehension is to
be imputed the open profession and boast of selfishness which has grown to be a prevalent folly among
our youth,—a profession which is not always to be
taken as indicating the natural temper of him who
makes it, but which, however, sufficiently betokens
that a direction has been given to his vanity which
will tend to confirm in him what is wrong in him,
and to check any impulse of his better mind. A
philosophic teacher of this school would instruct him,
no doubt, if he would learn, that the true principle of
well-advised selfishness is to seek for happiness in
that range and region of pleasures which the influence of association has placed at his command;
to seek it in the pleasures of benevolence and in
the pleasures of sympathy; in such as contain some

principle of permanency and self-increase ; to seek
it in such as are spreading and growing and abiding,
not dwindling and wasting away. And the pupil of
this more benign philosophy will be taught that the
pleasures and passions of which self is the centre
may, according as he contrives it, either go out where
they are kindled, or may emanate thence and
redound to him from all the multiplying and magni-
fying objects within his sphere. This, he will be
taught, is the philosophy of selfishness. So it sounds,
I confess, and so I believe it to be ; but it is a philosophy which is caviare to the general ; I have never
heard of it or perceived any tokens of a belief in it
amongst the disciples of the selfish system of morals ;
and I am afraid it happens in this, as in other cases,
that when men are referred to philosophy for their
principles of action, each man will have a philosophy of
his own, and one perhaps less remarkable for its depth
than for its adaptation to his own likings and convenience. This unhappily has come to be very much the
actual state of the case. Every man who aspires to a
certain intellectual rank and precedency has his peculiar system of morals made for himself, like his easy
chair—in which he arranges himself to his own perfect
satisfaction, denouncing ex cathedrâ the easy chairs of
all the rest of mankind. There is nothing that is infirm
or out of joint in him but some dogma is put in like
a cushion to bolster it up, and whoso meddles with his
cushions is no philosopher. It is not long since I
heard a Populationist vehemently reproach a poor

but very respectable married gentleman for the sin of having nine children lawfully begotten. The Populationist, on the other hand, was a single man, and might very possibly be chargeable with sinning against another sort of philosophy. And thus do men in our days, like their brother Antinomians in Hudibras—

> Compound for sins they are inclined to
> By damning those they have no mind to.

Sir, much mischief is done—by the act and by the example—when men of larger capacities than their fellows arrogate to themselves, not only in discourse and in disquisition, but in deed, a right to set aside the commonly received principles of morality and to govern themselves by their own. A few instances I know may be cited, in which, under very extraordinary circumstances, very extraordinary men have served the world by so doing ; but in ten generations there does not arise one man who can do so without the most perilous presumption ; and if knowledge should continue to diffuse itself as it has done, the circumstances will not again occur under which that one man would stand justified. Sir, in these times I would have men think freely, and speak freely, and write freely ; where they dissent from the prevailing opinions I would have them send forth their reasons modestly, as becomes men who are contending against all, and therefore against some that are wise ; and having sent forth their reasons, I could wish that they would leave them to make their way in the world ; but in the meantime that they would hold themselves bound by the standing opinions of mankind, and not free to follow their own. Sir, I will not trust that man who tells me that his conduct to me is to be regulated by principles of his own discovering and systems of his own making. I would say to him that the *lex incognita* of his secret conscience, of his subtle philosophy, is far from satisfactory to me. Sir, am I to study every man's philosophy before I know what I have to expect from him ? If not, then it is not enough for his system that it is right, but it must be no other than that system which is commonly known and acknowledged to be right ; there must be a general recognition of the principles and reciprocity in the practice ; I must have a public pledge ; I must have Government security ; I must be assured that he respects the commonly received, the universally sanctioned, the every day principles of morality, and that he respects the public opinion which, under the bond of such respect, will hold him to the observance of those principles, but which would not hold him to the observance of any other principles. Sir, if a man have discharged his mind from the control of public feeling and commonplace morality, I know not that wickedness which he may not commit and bring me a reason for it. If, therefore, a man should show me by any act, be it good, bad, or indifferent in itself, that he has passed his mind through this process, I should thenceforth know him to be a dangerous man, and deal with him accordingly. Take the case of a resurrection-man. The work he engages in is, in its own nature, not only innocent but meritorious. The man is invariably a ruffian. The heart of human kind is against him—he has learnt to brave the abhorrent feelings of his fellow-creatures, and it is therefore not in this their misdirection only that he is ready to brave them. In like manner every man who by reason of his peculiar opinions should take up a hostile position amongst mankind, cutting himself off from the sympathies of the better part of society and creating to himself a common interest with its out-casts,—any man who should do this, would place himself in imminent peril of passing from a versatile philosophy to a reckless and driftless conduct in life, —from an isolated and unsupported morality to an utter destitution, as well of self-government as of social control.'

Though much occupied with business in 1824 and 1825, some *horæ subsecivæ* were given to literature.

I wrote, in 1824, an article for the ' Quarterly Review' on Walter Savage Landor's 'Imaginary Con-versations.' In writing of the article to my father, I characterised it, in words quoted from one of the ' Imaginary Conversations,' as ' that persecution by petulance which the commonalty call banter.' This was the last time that I offended in that kind ; and it appears that I had repented before the article was published ; and after endeavouring, at first without much success, to induce Gifford to expunge what was most injurious, I sent the article to Landor's publisher (Landor himself was in Italy), with an offer to suppress it altogether if he thought it would do the book more harm than good. He thought otherwise, and did not desire the suppression ; and after I had prevailed in a further effort to obtain some modification of its tone, it was published.

Immitigable as Gifford was disposed to be to the last in his character of critic, he was personally very kind and gracious to *me ;* and I transcribe (panegyric and all) the last portion of the last of his letters, written (July 28, 1824) not long before his death :—

'One word in confidence. The effects of age and sickness are hourly becoming more visible to me, and I must shortly retire from a situation to which my strength is unequal. I earnestly hope, however, that you will continue your assistance to the " Review " whoever may succeed me. It is not a time for me to flatter, and you may believe me when I say, that I think you have all the elements of an excellent critic, and that practice, under a careful eye, will speedily place you in a high rank among our best writers. I notice with pleasure a beautiful mixture of pathos and quiet humour, which put me often in mind of Southey, and a style that is truly English. Ambitious ornaments, which are the property of youth, you will by degrees discover and abandon. We have fine weather here, and I am pleasantly situated in full view of the channel and the shipping. This to me is a prime consideration, for I from youth much attached to the sea. With all this, I suspect that I do not get better ; my voice fails me greatly, and I rather hiss or whistle than breathe : but I retain my spirits, and with this I am more than satisfied.'

This was, I think, the last that I heard of Gifford, except the announcement of his death in the newspapers. He must have had many literary and political acquaintances and friends ; but in this year, 1824, when I knew him, sick and moribund, he appeared to be a solitary old man. He had never been married ; the 'Quarterly Review' was his only issue ; and his talents, in raising him out of the class in which he was born, had probably tended to domestic isolation. He had published some account of himself during his life, and no fuller or other biography appeared after his death. At least I have never heard of any.

In these years I wrote 'Isaac Comnenus.' With what hopes and with what doubts of its success I sent it into the world, is expressed in a letter to Southey of February 10, 1827 :—

'It was begun between three and four years ago. The first two acts were written when I was an idle man in the country—I think in two months ; the others after I had come here, in as many years, and a year more was taken for adding and altering. Now, if I were to write another play at this rate, I might die undramatically before the fifth act ; and with respect to posthumous reputation, I cannot but think that the power of Fame to please is amongst the things of this world which pass away along with it. Whatever pleasure is to be had from success, therefore, I would rather have soon than late; and with respect to disappointment from failure, I suppose I should feel it more or less, but my unhopeful habit of mind has always spared me any very keen feeling of that kind. I have always taken failure as a matter of course and been surprised when I succeeded in anything. I could not easily fancy myself feeling disappointment in a thing of this sort, though I suppose, as there must be some expectation to induce one to try, so some disappointment must follow failure. The insolence of criticism is not offensive to me except when the criticism is ill-executed, as many miserable attempts are at the tone of critical superiority and contempt. I have been used to regard criticism like burlesque, as an exercise for the faculties of wit and ridicule. Whether such criticism will be offensive to me when directed against myself, remains to be seen. I am willing to suppose that it will not. I am not what is commonly called "touchy." People for whom I have much regard or respect can offend me, indifferent people scarcely.'

It was published by Mr Murray, the most eminent publisher of the time; and in October, 1828, an article in commendation of it appeared in the 'Quarterly Review,' the writer of which, not then known by me to be so, was Southey. But the public would have nothing to say to it. Some of my

most familiar associates seem to have known nothing
about it ; and when I heard there was to be an
article on it, I expressed myself to my father as
having lost my interest in it, my mind being occupied
with other things. I suppose I saw that it had no
chance of celebrity ; and I had always felt that, to a
poet, less than celebrity was worse than nothing. It
was easy to keep a secret which nobody desired to
know, and I, as well as my book, remained in
obscurity for some years longer,—about seven.

It was as well for me, however, that I had tried
and failed. The result of the failure was to leave me
in no hurry to publish again ; and when, soon after,
I went to work upon 'Van Artevelde,' it was with
little reference to success in publication, with hardly
any anticipation of it, and with a disposition, therefore, to work only in favourable moods and when it
gave me present pleasure. 'Be not ambitious of an
early fame,' says Landor ; ' such is apt to shrivel and
drop under the tree.' And conversely early failure
is often a recoil *pour mieux sauter.*

In June and July of 1825, I joined Southey in an
expedition through France to Holland ; and I wrote
some letters to my father and my stepmother, from
the latter of which, written at Brussels on June 17, I
will take some notices of my travels, and of my
companion, than whom, though some thirty years
older than I, no young man could have been associated with one more young-hearted and easy to please.

'The cultivation, the peasantry, the villages, the

cottages, the eating and drinking, and everything that appears, betoken a more flourishing country than I expected to see, and a country clear of the abject and destitute class which is numerous at home. But the great relief is from the jealousy of classes, which forms so many knots in the English people and obstructs the free circulation of a good fellow-feeling. I, for one, never have the good feeling towards an English mechanic, being a stranger, which I have towards dogs and horses, being so. But the moment I came amongst the French I had it. Oil seemed to have taken the place of rust in the mechanism of society, and I was reminded of the easy action of the steam-engine when I looked down upon it from the deck of the steamboat that brought us over. The first evening after landing I walked out by myself about half a mile from Boulogne, and found a churchyard full of the black and white wooden crosses which are commonly placed over the graves, and of the exuberant vegetation which the French encourage there ; and in a corner (itself as large as a small English church-yard) was the burial place of the English and other Protestants. Being somewhat tired with my day's travelling, I fell asleep upon an English tombstone ; and when I woke, a boy was digging a grave at a little distance. Had he been English he would have dug to the Antipodes before he would have noticed me ; but being French, he jumped out of the grave and came up to me, and we knew each other presently. He was a very fine intelligent boy, and I liked him as much as you would have liked a very fine Newfoundland dog ; and his ways were such as the dog's would have been to you. " Voudriez-vous coucher ici?" he said to me, after we had talked for some time, and pointed to the grave he had been digging. " Non, c'est en Angleterre que je veux coucher." ' Ce n'est pas assez foncé encore ; ' and then he jumped into it and went to work again. I have found no difficulty in making myself understood, the people are so quick in catching my meaning ; nor am I often at a loss for words ; but I am not so quick in catching theirs. No doubt I do violence to His Most Christian Majesty's French, but not a tenth part so much as Southey. He speaks the language, as he says, without shame or remorse ; and never man dashed on in such fearless defiance of pronunciation and all the parts of speech. At Bouchain he gave us a verse written in imitation of Drunken Barnaby :—

> Here we call for bread and butter ;
> Thanks for it in French we utter ;
> Better bread was never broken,
> Worser French was never spoken.[1]

He said that if Barnaby's journal was written by the person to whom it was ascribed, he had not been his own hero, for he was a very respectable man (a Dr.

---

[1] Another quatrain on the same model occurs in his correspondence :—

> Amsterdam we reached by schooner,
> And not liking left the sooner.
> Never city such a sink was ;
> Weak the drink was, strong the stink was.

Brathwaite, I think he said); but whether drunk or sober, he had a high respect for him and wished he had him here. I give Southey credit for being civil in as few words as any man, for " il fait très chaud, Monsieur," has served him all the way from Boulogne; but once he bid me good morning with " il fait furieusement chaud, Monsieur," and I told him that he should not say that, because it was a point of civility to leave the superlative of your own sentiment to be given by the person to whom you addressed yourself, and if you took it yourself you left him nothing but a cold assent. So he agreed to give up "furieusement" in cases of speaking first; but that very morning the host accosted him with " Il fait très chaud, Monsieur," and Southey's " furieusement chaud, Monsieur," came out with singular zest. An invention of mine serves us for answers to all inquiries of waiters as to what we will have and how we will have it, &c. It lies in the words, " le mieux possible." We have a good deal of literary conversation and many good stories. The former has served to revive some of the little knowledge in Belles-Lettres which I had nearly forgotten that I had ever acquired, and may make the remains of it last a year or two longer. The old roots will strike again. Most of what is newly added will die away like flowers stuck in the ground. . . . I wish Miss Fenwick would come to town with you. I think it would be an excellent thing for her to do. She would serve you a good turn by keeping you com-

pany when I am in Downing Street and my father
is God knows where ; and she would see Southey
before age has taken more from the most spirited
countenance that ever human form was graced with.'

In 1826, if I recollect right, I made another tour
in Holland with Southey; and in 1827 I went to
Paris, and thence to the north of Italy with my
father. In 1828 Mrs. Villiers proposed to me to
accompany her and Miss Villiers and Edward on
a tour through Switzerland and Italy—a proposal
which at that time must have had a peculiar fascination for me ; but I was either enabled or compelled to resist it. Probably my official duties stood
in the way ; or possibly I may have thought that in
one way or another no good would come of it.

My father, I recollect, found me sadly insensible
to the charms of scenery and of other objects which
delighted him as they came before him and continued
to delight him in the remembrance to the end of his
days. If accompanied, my companion was more to
me than the face of Nature; if alone, it was not
scenery of the gay Italian type that I loved, but
rather sylvan recesses and some ' boundless con-
tiguity of shade : ' and I had a feeling which I have
never seen expressed except in three lines of George
Darley's :—

> There is a melancholy in sunbright fields
> Deeper to me than gloom ; I am ne'er so sad
> As when I sit amid bright scenes alone.[1]

---

[1] Darley's ' Sylvia.'

In Italy, instead of looking about me, I sat in the carriage and read 'Corinne.' And indeed, throughout life, and perhaps in youth as much as afterwards, though equal to work for as many hours of the day as other men, it was only for a few hours that I was capable of enjoyment. My health and constitution rendered that capability limited in duration, and liable to abatement from small bodily contingencies, —loss of sleep, indigestion, cold, heat, hunger or fatigue. I was patient enough of such things; but pleasure could not consist with them.

My visits to Miss Fenwick, at Bath, were frequent in these years, and our friendship grew and flourished. Towards the end of 1828 my stepmother writes in answer to an account I had given of one of my visits :—

' My dear cousin certainly unites in her character what makes a most endearing and admirable combination, always most delightful to me ; and I rejoice in seeing it is always so to you ; and that she feels as motherly towards you as I do myself, but more indulgent to your failings, which must make her more dear to you, and perhaps more useful in the end ; for rare indeed are those who can receive any hint of their errors but from those they most deeply love ; and yet I never met with anyone (the insensible excepted) who was so candid and so perfectly true in such discussions as yourself.'

My answer expresses my view of myself at twenty-seven years of age.

' I do not know whether Miss Fenwick is more

indulgent to me than you are. I daresay you are
both very foolish in that way ; but if you were less
so, I cannot think that there would be any love lost
thereby. I think that generally speaking I *can* take
the credit you give me for candour in discussions
concerning my own merits and demerits. I am not
what is called touchy on such occasions ; that is, not
generally : for instances might be found of the kind,
and some which have given me much pain in the
recollection. They are imputable to aspirations after
a certain dignity of character which there is not
strength to attain, and the sense of humiliation from
being made conscious that it has not been attained.
There must be a consciousness of weakness to give
rise to such resentments. Where the point censured
brings my understanding only in question, nothing
of the kind arises ; for I have no diffidence of the
strength of my intellect. But I have felt for several
years that there was in me a want of independent and
self-subsisting strength of character, and an occasional
susceptibility of vain and trivial impressions, the
consciousness of which gives me pain, of course,
whether brought to my mind by my own reflex
observation or by the animadversions of others.
Much of this I am willing to think is less belonging
to my mind as it now is, than owing to habits formed
in a previous state of it. But such habits remaining
from a previous state are still important parts of the
actual mind, and give a consciousness of original and
native weakness. They are never presented to me in

stronger relief than when I am with Miss Fenwick. The faults which one might suppose to be, or to have been, in *her* character would be all from too much vehemence of an independent nature and an ill-considered direction of strong and generous feelings. Whatever the errors might be, one would see power and dignity all through them.   Errors of this kind I would almost wish myself capable of committing.   I should look back upon them with sorrow, perhaps, for their consequences, but without humiliation. But *my* errors are of no such manly and vigorous character ; my only strength is in a temperance of mind, and my hope is in improvement to be worked out by habits of meditation and that sort of self-analysis which is always going on where a subtle intellect is united with a solicitous temper.'

To which she made answer :—

' I don't quite understand your view of your own character, or what you aim at.   You certainly are not independent of the opinion of others ; nor is it fitting that at your age you should ; experience only ought to bring that ; arrogance often does it, and an over-rated approbation by those who are as inexperienced, but who, feeling something of the power of intellect, are impatient to be blown up like an air-cushion ; and then people gather in crowds and say—If you will blow me up, I will blow you up.   That dignity you aim at, I suppose from what you remark justly in Miss Fenwick, will not exist in the mind that harbours a trait of vanity, nor even in a mind that *delights* in being admired or looked up to even by wise men : but different minds pursue different ways with regard to working out their own characters ; and none seem to me desirable when worked out but such as are humble with a sense of their own imperfections. *That, well established,* brings all that is right where there is real intellect ; and makes them interesting and good even where the intellect is very poor. I have been writing all day, and my little share of intellect is feeble, and going and going, and gone. . . . —Yours ever, J. T.

' What you tell us of your friend T—— shows a great interest in your favour, and is satisfactory in many points of view ; you have sad temptations to vanity.'

I replied :—

' You do not understand what I would be at about my character. To get rid of the vanity of it *is* my aim ; and that would bring with it an independence of the opinions of others so far as they regard what may be called objects of vanity. I agree with you that an entire independence of opinion, as regards questions of utility, is as undesirable as it is unattainable. Hare,[1] the Irishman at Edinburgh, seems to have made the nearest approach to it one has heard of. As to humility, I do not quite know what is meant by that, when it is spoken of as a commendable quality. I like people to have neither a low estimate nor a high estimate of themselves, but

---

[1] He was a celebrated murderer, who murdered people in order to sell their bodies to the surgeon for dissection.

simply a *true* estimate.   If by humility is meant, not the estimate itself, but the feelings to which it gives rise, then I think certainly it is desirable that a full consciousness of imperfections (which is implied in a true estimate) should be attended by feelings of mortification ; and that the full consciousness of powers (also implied) should not be attended with feelings of exultation ; because such feelings are apt to disturb the judgment, and to render the *enjoyment* of the powers more the object than what is more important in the application of them ; which feelings are, however, seldom consequent upon merely a true estimate ; at least they are so then in a very slight degree.   They are, when they exist in greater potency, the *cause* of an *untrue* estimate.   I think I have not much of this sort of exultation in such powers as I have, though I believe I have a full consciousness of them.   I think I have much more pleasure in their exercise than in the acknowledgment of them by others ; at least when that acknowledgment is unattended by anything else that is agreeable. I sometimes have a great desire to gain an influence over certain individuals.   My sense of admiration is strong, and where I admire I wish to be admired—a wish which is compounded perhaps as much of the sympathies as of the vanities of human nature : but exclude these objects, and present me with the admiration and applause of T—— (which you seem to think so dangerous), and I assure you the feeling falls as flat as a flounder.'

CHAPTER VII.

THE HISTORY OF PHILIP VAN ARTEVELDE ADOPTED AS THE SUBJECT OF A DRAMA—PROPOSAL OF A NEW EMPLOYMENT WHICH DOES NOT TAKE EFFECT—MISS VILLIERS.

ANNO DOM. 1828-29.   ANNO ÆT. 28-29.

IN the spring of 1828 I was meditating another drama ; and Southey, after dissuading me from founding one upon the story of Patkul, suggested that of Philip van Artevelde, which I at once adopted, writing on March 9 :—

'I have finished Artevelde's story in Barante. A play could not develop the character from first to last, or comprise the story, unless it were, like Wallenstein, divided into parts. The first part should conduct him from obscurity to his conquest of Bruges,—everywhere the fairest, and at the latter point the brightest of his history. And the second part might bring him from the splendour of his first achievement through the consequent moral changes to his death. I agree with you that there are fine materials for an historical drama.'

And ten days later I wrote that 'Philip Van Artevelde' was begun ; without much notion pro-

bably at that time that six years would be required
to complete it.

But my official tasks were heavy for some of those
years, if not for all; and I find from a letter to
Southey in September, 1828, that I meditated taking
upon myself new labours, which would have put
poetry out of the question :—

' The proposal which is now made is that I should
retain my present office under the Colonial Secretary
of State, and give my spare time to another member
of the Cabinet, my income being raised to 1,200*l.* a
year. Beyond this accession to my income, my new
employer says he promises nothing, and should hold
himself perfectly clear in honour and in everything
else if he did nothing for me ; but he adds that, if
circumstances favoured it, his object would be to
cultivate a close alliance and undertake " the structure
of my fortunes." Perhaps that is a structure which
(if raised at all) is more likely to be the work of my
own hands than of any other person's ; but he or any
man is welcome to carry the bricks and mortar. I
think it likely that this arrangement will be concluded, and then farewell to Philip Van Artevelde
and all other my recreations ! For heavy will be the
burthen I shall have taken up ! I shall have nothing
but the objects of political life to repay me, and I
must cultivate the sort of ambition which gives them
their value.'

There are traces here of a spirit of pride and
self-assertion, which I had not then learnt to be as

alien as I afterwards knew them to be, from a pure and genuine spirit of independence. In a letter to my father I adverted to the proposed employment as one which, 'if it led to any advancement would lead me into the line of life of a political adventurer without private fortune, which I know and see is a hard, anxious, and unquiet life, and I think a life of more excitement than any except those of an actor or of a highwayman. . . . On the other hand, advancement has of course its charms with me as with other people, though I do not occupy myself with doubtful prospects of it, or dwell upon them, or care so much about them as that their removal would give me a moment's concern.'

The negotiation came to nothing, and Van Artevelde went on his way.

But my father had misgivings as to the division of my powers between business and poetry, quoting the example of a person [name illegible] of whom it was said he might have been a good poet if he had not attempted to be a statesman, and a good statesman if he had not attempted to be a poet ; and he expressed a hope that I would only take poetry as a pleasant change in the application of my powers, and not let it engross them at the expense of my health or the real business of life. His chief solicitude was about my health, which was far from strong ; and he was by no means ambitious for me, or desirous that I should aim at a political career.

He may probably have thought that I was un-

fitted for such a career by other wants than the want
of health ; and if so he was not altogether wrong.
Mr. Gladstone, I was told the other day, says of me
that 'I had wanted nothing but ambition to have
been a great man ; ' meaning, no doubt, great in the
way that he is great himself, politically. I think
there were more things wanting. I might have done
well enough as a subordinate and co-operative politician, but I was unfitted to be a political leader in
such times as those in which my lot was cast. In
respect of organic politics I have always been of a
sceptical turn—a man of uncertain opinions, and
rather glad not to have occasion to form any. Such
a man, if he be but moderately conscientious, must
be unfitted for projecting great organic changes in
complex politics, or for taking any high command
in a battle for them. If I regarded the Reform Bill
of 1832 as justifiable, it was not with sanguine
expectations of the result, and only because there
might be more danger in doing nothing or doing less.
It is true that I was prepared to act with any amount
of vigour and intrepidity on the question of West
Indian Slavery ; but that was one of the simplest of
all questions of organic change. I was thoroughly
conversant with the dangers and horrors of the
system in existence, and though I was not wholly
free from doubts as to what might ensue upon
emancipation, I could have no doubt that whatever
else it might be, it would be better than what it
supplanted.

But if my father formed a just estimate of my disqualifications for political life, he probably saw no sufficient reason for believing (have I myself the belief even now ? I suppose I have, or I would not now be writing this autobiography) that I would be one of the few who attain to permanent celebrity as a poet.

I did not defend my course upon any such ground : if I thought it so defensible, which I can only have done in a doubtful way, for my forecasts have never been sanguine or positive, I suppressed my thoughts, and only answered that no doubt I should be a worse man of business for being a writer of poetry, and the worse poet for being a man of business ; but that as writing plays was the only pleasure in which I indulged, I was enabled to dispatch my business regularly and competently in the main ; adding, 'If I were more devoted to business I should probably grasp more of it into my own hands which is properly belonging to others ; but my own share, considered in the widest extent of what can be called mine, would not be otherwise dealt with than it is now. What I do I very seldom do incompletely ; for I have always had an aversion to incompleteness in anything. If I were to go into society, or to do anything else but dispatch business and write plays, I could not get on certainly with both. But I read almost nothing and go nowhere. Ask my cousin too [meaning Miss Fenwick], and she will say, that if I have an imagination it was meant to be exercised.'

This habit of 'going nowhere' was not altogether satisfactory to my mother, especially as there was one exception. 'I wish you could tell us,' she had said, 'of any pleasant new acquaintances. You will grow old without variety, and if the Villiers family disappoint you, or be separated from you by the events of life, then you will have no intimates at all; and it is always bad to keep to one set of acquaintances; your thoughts and your opinions become contracted, and it forms a prejudiced mind; and then to avoid that, people assume a kind of allowance for other opinions that they call candour; but it does not deserve the name; it is more frequently a piece of deceit, and instead of producing the delightful effect of truth upon an honest mind of another way of thinking, it gives a strong muscular sensation of the right arm, that might produce a box on the ear, but for the habit of control.'

No doubt what was in my stepmother's mind was that I had been passing two or three years in much intimacy with one young lady, and with one only; that this one was attractive to all the world, and as she would know from the descriptions of her in my letters, could not but be peculiarly so to me; an l that it was highly improbable that the consequences would be favourable to my happiness.

Her mother had become a great friend of mine. I frequented Kent House continually, and when the

London season was over and the family left town,
Mrs. Villiers and I kept up a weekly correspondence.
She was a woman of a strong and ardent nature,
but also a woman of the world ; and neither she nor
I could have thought of a nearer connection as possible, except in certain contingencies of worldly
advancement not likely to occur at any early period.
I had been brought up in what she would think
poverty. I had no objection to it, and I was rash
and ready for anything ; but it would have been
wholly unreasonable to expect either the mother or
the daughter to be so. Nor did I in point of fact
expect it, or make at this time more than a contingent
proposal, such as did not require or receive an explicit
or decisive answer. But after some months of absence,
between the end of one London season and the
beginning of another, I became impatient of my
position ; and on the occurrence of one of those
casual jars to which a man in such a position is
always liable, I resolved to bring the question to a
determinate issue, and I was distinctly rejected.

I have sometimes since, though rarely, met Miss
Villiers (or rather Lady Theresa, as she became on
her brother's succession to the earldom of Clarendon), in a casual way, in society ; but our intimacy
has not been renewed. She was married, in 1830,
to Mr. Lister, a refined and accomplished gentleman,
who, besides works of fiction and contributions to
the periodical literature of the day, rendered valuable
services to the public on Commissions and otherwise ;

and after his early death, in 1842, to Sir George
Cornewall Lewis, said by some competent judges to
be one of the most profound and accurate scholars of
his time, author of some solid and learned books,
and afterwards Chancellor of the Exchequer and
Secretary of State in two or three successive Governments, who also died prematurely, at a time when he
was believed by many to be on the way to the post
of First Minister.

She is now (1865) living in that same Kent
House in which her life began, and to which, by an
unusual course of things, she took home her first and
second husbands to live with her and her mother,
and which she has not ceased to inhabit from her
girl days throughout her first married life, her first
widowhood, her second married life, and her second
widowhood; and whence may she pass, in God's
peace and the peace of her own bright and happy
nature, to the mansions where age and youth and
time and eternity are reconciled, and those who have
once been friends will be friends again and for ever.[1]

[1] She died in November, 1865, a few months after this was written.

CHAPTER VIII.

MEN AND AFFAIRS IN THE COLONIAL OFFICE—LORDS GODERICH AND HOWICK—BUSINESS OR POETRY, WHICH?—QUESTION OF SLAVERY—LORDS GODERICH AND HOWICK SUCCEEDED BY MR. STANLEY AND MR. LEFEVRE.

ANNO DOM. 1828-33.   ANNO ÆT. 28-33.

1828 and 1829 had been years of torpor in the Colonial Office. Sir George Murray was at the head of it,—an old soldier and a high-bred gentleman, whose countenance and natural stateliness and simple dignity of demeanour were all that can be desired in a Secretary of State, if to look the character were the one thing needful. The Duke of Wellington had induced him to undertake the office ; but when looking back upon it some years after, he told me that he knew himself to have been unfit for it, and that he would never again accept an office of the kind. No doubt his estimate of his unfitness was just. But there was a worse element of obstruction. I find, in a letter to my mother, the political Under Secretary of the time described as ' of all the Under Secretaries who had ever laid the weight of their authority upon the transactions of the Colonial Office, " the fleshliest incubus." ' If this political Under Secretary was obstructive through timidity and indecisiveness, the permanent Under Secretary was obtuse but bold. The one was for ever occupied with details and incapable of coming to a conclusion—routing and grunting and tearing up the soil to get at a grain of the subject; the other went straight to a decision, which was right or wrong as might happen. I remember applying to him the proverb that 'mettle is dangerous in a blind horse.'

With these men over me, it may be imagined that in these years my interest and activity in colonial business was much abated, and I made comparatively rapid progress with my play. But with the beginning of 1831 there came a change. Lord Goderich came into office as Secretary of State, and I found him a man of more activity than I had expected, and easy and good-humoured in personal intercourse; which, I observed to my mother, was a matter of some importance to me. I had 'always been apt,' I said, 'to forget the modesty of my official position, and to take a tone which I knew to be equally contrary to good policy and good taste;' and I added that I had 'caught myself haranguing Lord Goderich and Lord Althorp in a style which would have been more becoming if they had been my own confidential servants instead of His Majesty's,—a distinction which I should not perhaps have recollected if I had not observed that I was exciting a little good-humoured surprise.'

But what was most important was the change in

the office of political Under Secretary, now entered
upon by Lord Howick, son of the First Minister,
Lord Grey.   I spoke of him as active, vigorous, and
decisive in business, honest-minded, and ardent, and
in his nature and manners particularly gentlemanly ;
and I liked him much.   Under his influence projects
and interests which had long lain dormant sprang
into life and activity, and I was occupied in my office
and out of my office all day long in business and in
nothing else but business.

'In the midst of this life,' I wrote to my mother
' I often have a great longing after poetry, and feel as
if all time was thrown away of which a portion is not
given to it.   Perhaps if I were to be guided strictly
and solely by a sense of duty I should devote myself
wholly to a business in which I have so much opportunity of being useful, and think no more thoughts
about poetry for the rest of my life.   That, I suppose,
would be the conscientious line to take ; but personal
considerations are all the other way,—the bent of
my mind is the other way.   I can be active and
sedulous in business, and take a certain degree of
pleasure in drafting good despatches, and setting
things to rights where they are wrong, and putting
down oppression so far as may be done by my efforts
in the slave colonies ; but I can never devote myself
to business with my whole heart as I have done and
could do to poetry.   What ambition I have, too, is
poetical and not political ; and if it is not founded
upon reasonable prospects of success, I still feel that

the employment is in itself a pleasure, and that no further repayment of the labour is wanting, and that if I were disappointed of success it would still be nearly the same resource to me that it is when I am working under an expectation (such as it is) of that kind.'

And in glancing at the objects of ambition to be accomplished by an exclusive devotion to business, and rejecting the notion of political life without private fortune, I said, in a tone of levity which indicated the small measure of regard I entertained for my permanent chief, the blindly bold,—

'Perhaps the best thing that I can reasonably look forward to is to succeed Hay (if it would please God to take him) in his permanent Under Secretary-ship,—a succession which Charles Greville suggested to me the other day as a proper thing to be brought about under the present Administration, if any means could be found of providing for Hay otherwise (supposing it should not please God to take him just immediately): but I know of no such means, nor have I any idea that they would so promote me if they could; because, though they are all in the way of bringing forward obscure men who are likely to be useful, I do not see how I could be much more useful to them in Hay's place than I am at present.'

And upon the whole I concluded that there was no reason, unless it were from a sense of duty, that I should leave off writing plays.

But for the next two or three years the sense of duty was put under high pressure. The great question of slavery was approaching its inevitable close; and the approach was made through paths of exceeding difficulty and fearful danger.

In 1824 the Government of Lord Liverpool had taken up a position of mediator between the saints and the planters; finding an escape for themselves from the dilemma of the moment by one of those compromises in which an endeavour is made to reconcile oppugnant principles and implacable opponents. The slaves were not to be enfranchised, but their condition was to be 'meliorated,' as the word went: A model code was devised according to which the lash was to be taken out of the hands of the driver, punishments were to be inflicted only under the authority of stipendiary magistrates, the hours of labour were to be limited, the allowances of food were to be regulated, husbands and wives and their children were not to be sold apart, and protectors were to be appointed who were to watch over the enforcement of the code and make half-yearly reports on all matters affecting the welfare of the slaves.

The saints accepted the measure as all they could get for the moment, profoundly convinced, however, that so long as slaves were slaves, they must continue to be the victims of cruelty and wrong; whilst the planters, on the other hand, knew well enough that, whether or not negroes would be induced to work for wages if freed (which they absolutely refused to believe), nothing short of the lash in the hand of the driver would make them work as slaves.

In the West Indian Colonies, with few exceptions, all legislative authority, and, along with the power of granting or withholding supplies, almost all executive authority, was in the hands of the planters. If the Assemblies refused to enact the 'meliorating' code, there was no power in the Crown to coerce them. We tried everything. Many a conciliatory despatch was written ; not a single Assembly was conciliated.   Many were the minatory despatches that followed ; and threats were found equally unavailing.   The controversy went on year after year ; the Assemblies raged abroad ; the saints wailed and howled at home ; the Crown maintained an outward aspect of moderation :   'Not so, my sons, not so !' But in the Colonial Office we knew what we were about.   We had established protectors of slaves in the few colonies in which we had legislative power ; they made their half-yearly reports in which every outrage and enormity perpetrated on the slaves was duly detailed, with the usual result of trials and acquittals by colonial juries, and perhaps a banquet given by the principal colonists in honour of the offenders ; we [1] wrote despatches in answer, careful and cautious in their tone, but distinctly marking each atrocity, and bringing its salient points into the

---

[1] A junior clerk under me (now Sir Clinton Murdoch) took a large share in these operations.

light ; we laid the reports and despatches before Parliament as fast as they were received and written ; Zachary Macaulay forthwith transferred them to the pages of his ' Monthly Anti-Slavery Reporter,' by which they were circulated far and wide through the country ; the howlings and wailings of the saints were seen to be supported by unquestionable facts officially authenticated ; the cry of the country for the abolition of slavery waxed louder every year ; strange rumours reached the ears of the negroes ; they became excited and disturbed, imagining that the King had given them their freedom and that the fact and the freedom were kept from them by their owners ; there was plotting and conspiracy ; and at length came the insurrection of 1831 in Jamaica ; in which, of the negroes some hundreds lost their lives, of the whites not one.

This terrible event, with all its horrors and cruelties, its military slaughters and its many murders by flogging, though failing of its object as a direct means, was indirectly a death-blow to slavery. The reform of Parliament was almost simultaneous with it, and might have been sufficient of itself. Under the operation of both, the only questions that remained were, whether it was to be effected abruptly and at once, or through some transitional process, and whether with or without compensation to the planters. James Stephen, who, under the title of Counsel to the Colonial Department, had, for some years, more than any other man, ruled the Colonial Empire, was now prepared to go all lengths with his uncle, Mr. Wilberforce, and the Anti-slavery party; and simple and immediate emancipation was what they desired.

From the first years in which I had been called upon to consider the question, I had been resolute for emancipation; but I had not been satisfied, nor at that time was Stephen or any one else, that emancipation ought to be total and immediate. In a letter to Edward Villiers, of April, 1826, I adverted to the only example in existence of sudden emancipation, that given by the French in St. Domingo, where massacres, more frightful even than those of La Vendée, were succeeded by the ferocious tyranny of Christophe, and by the ' Code Henri,' which provided that any man found during prescribed hours of the day off the land assigned to him to cultivate, should be shot by the police; and I referred to the compulsory manumission clause of the meliorating Order in Council, as contended for in Lord Bathurst's despatches, for an indication of the principle on which gradual emancipation might be combined with indemnity to the owners. In 1831, I was still unprepared for immediate emancipation; but I thought that I could see my way to the immediate commencement of a self-accelerating process of emancipation.

Lord Howick, whose strong understanding, political courage, and pure and vehement public spirit, had by this time put much power in his hands, had a scheme of his own for effecting emancipation, and at the same time saving the planters, by laws against vagrancy, and by so taxing the land available for cultivating provisions as to make it impossible for the negroes to obtain a subsistence without working on the plantations.   But it was determined on all hands that I was to 'take the initiative and draw out a scheme of proceeding which might form the basis of discussion,' first in the Colonial Office, and, if approved there, in the Cabinet.

I did not agree with Lord Howick any more than with Mr. Stephen.   As to the land-tax, I thought that in countries where unoccupied land of exuberant fertility was to be found in large tracts both near and remote, no restraints of law could so far deprive the negroes of the use of it as to bring them under a necessity of working on the plantations; and as it was in evidence that the labour of not much more than one day in the week on fertile land would supply a negro with all the food he had been accustomed to, I did not believe that, when freed, he would continue to work on the plantations for any wages which the planter could afford to pay.   As to the other course, the pure and simple and immediate emancipation, I did not feel sure that it could be effected without disorder and bloodshed.

'Buxton may ask,' I said in a letter to Lord Howick, 'what more have the negroes to contend for when they have got their freedom?   For what end or object could they be riotous or spill blood?   To which I answer, there will remain as objects of contention the land, the buildings, the produce,—in short, all the property of which emancipation would not be intended to deprive the planters. The slave has not been taught hitherto to make any distinction between the planter's right to his land and buildings and to his gang : when he sees the one right abrogated, will he still think the other sacred ? To an uninstructed mind, or to one in which respect for the rights of property has been impaired, an agrarian partition will probably seem as consonant to natural justice as an abolition of slavery.'

I might have added as not beyond the range of conjecture, such an event as a war of races,—a rising of the blacks to exterminate the whites.

The results which I regarded as not impossible did *not* follow upon emancipation as effected six years later (in 1838). Another result, which not only I, but even Stephen himself, anticipated, did follow. The negroes sank into a state of barbarous indolence, the plantations were deserted, the exports of sugar from Jamaica fell to one-fourth of their previous quantity; and I may add that when a more or less humble and grateful, though lazy, generation of negroes had passed away, the Jamaica rebellion of 1865 broke out, of which the declared object was to seize the plantations and exterminate the male whites, and which might easily have been successful so far forth, but for the energy and military abilities of a civil Governor.

Perhaps, therefore, it was not unreasonable on my

part to look upon immediate emancipation as involving possible risks as well as some almost certain disadvantages.

But I was of opinion also that it would not be just if unaccompanied by compensation to the slave-owners. I had calculated the compensation required at 20 millions (the precise sum eventually granted), and I had erroneously conceived—in common, if I recollect right, with Stephen and Lord Howick—that no Government would venture to propose such a grant to the House of Commons, or if proposing, would succeed in obtaining it.

My own project was founded on the Spanish *coartado* system, under which a slave, *if he had the means*, could buy himself out of slavery by instalments. I proposed to *give* him the means for a first instalment out of public money, leaving him to provide himself, by his own industry, with the means of further self-purchase. I would have bought, say, Monday and Tuesday for him, leaving him so to employ Monday and Tuesday as in no long time to buy Wednesday ; so to employ Monday and Tuesday and Wednesday, as in less time still to buy Thursday, and thus day by day with progressive ease and speed to buy out the working days of the week and consummate his freedom. I computed (it must have been very conjecturally) the time required for this consummation by an able-bodied male slave at three years and sixteen days.

On this plan I conceived that before his bondage

ceased, he would have acquired habits of self-command and voluntary industry to take with him into freedom, by which habits *he* would be saved from a life of savage sloth and the planter from ruin.

I propounded my plan in an elaborate paper of 85 folio printed pages [1] deducing from voluminous evidence taken by recent Parliamentary Committees and other sources as full and authentic an account as I could exhibit of the state of West Indian society, and founding upon it the views I took of other schemes and the arguments by which I contended for my own.

The paper was designed for the Cabinet ; but I counted on converting Lord Howick, through whom only it could make its way there. Lord Howick, I need scarcely say, was not a very convertible person.

We had a lively discussion, and he declared that if my plan were adopted, he would go out of office and vote against it, though with his own father at the head of the Government. He naturally desired to make use of so much of my paper as suited his own views and throw aside what suited mine ; to this I demurred, though I was hardly entitled to do so ; and I think the paper never went beyond the walls of the office either in whole or in part.

Looking at the merits of my plan by the light of experience since obtained, I think that if I could have been sure that no worse results would follow than did follow from wholesale emancipation, and if I had believed that Parliament would grant the

---

[1] Written at the end of 1832.

20 millions which was granted, I ought not to have preferred my own plan, and perhaps I would not have preferred it; though I think that it was well calculated to avert the result of a barbarous indolence which I believed would follow upon wholesale emancipation, and which did in fact follow. The strongest objection was, perhaps, the political one,—that, at that eleventh hour, it would not have silenced the saints or the people. When there is a popular cry for anything, it can only be satisfied by something broad and simple and almost as inarticulate as the cry itself. It appears that, whether from the growing importance of this objection or from succeeding events and louder alarms, I came shortly to regard my plan as no longer eligible, at all events in its integrity, and that a plan, of the particulars of which I can find no account, was devised (probably by Stephen) which met the views of Lord Howick, Stephen, and myself. This plan was rejected by the Cabinet,[1]

[1] The rejection was mainly due to Lord Brougham. After the substitution of Lord Stanley's measure, or that which went by his name, Lord Howick wrote (9th October), ‘I quite agree with you that it is enough to provoke one beyond all bearing to hear the Chancellor say that he will willingly take upon himself the whole responsibility of any mischief which may result from granting freedom to the slave. If I had been at the dinner, I should certainly have complimented him upon the fairness and candour of this avowal, saying that it is perfectly clear, that if any mischief does happen, it will be owing to the grant of freedom being *incomplete*, and that, knowing him to be really responsible for this, I was glad that he acknowledged himself to be so. —— might make good use of his old inflammatory speeches in favour of the full rights of the negroes contrasted with the measure of which he declares himself willing to take the responsibility, and which *we know* that he was mainly instrumental in causing to be substituted for a more complete one.’

and soon after, though not for this reason, Lord Goderich and Lord Howick resigned, and were succeeded by Mr. Stanley and Mr. Shaw-Lefevre.

The immediate effect of the change was to deprive Stephen and myself of our usurped functions, and remand us to our original insignificance. A rumour had gone abroad amongst the West Indian merchants and proprietors that we exercised an undue and over-ruling influence over our political chiefs. Stephen was by far the most feared of the two, and with the most reason ; but it appears that I also had begun to be suspected before 1833. Writing to my mother in February, 1831, I mentioned that Mr. Robert Grant, the Judge Advocate, had told Stephen he understood there was a man named Taylor in the office who had both Lord Goderich and Lord Howick in pupilage. Stephen answered that the same Taylor was the man who had just left the room. ' No, no,' said Mr. Grant, ' that is a young man, but the man I mean must be much older.' I expressed my regret that such rumours should get abroad, as they might do harm ; and ' moreover,' I said, ' these two Viscounts are not more in pupilage than it is necessary and natural that men should be who are new to their work, and are not foolish or jealous about taking the assistance that is properly within their reach.'

Mr. Stanley was not content to take the assistance within his reach, and to take the consequences of taking it. And indeed some of the consequences were such as a man in his position might naturally be expected to dislike. The Press had been assailing, not Stephen and me only for assuming, as we were said to do, but also our political chiefs for devolving, duties which it was maintained ought to be discharged by those who were accountable to Parliament, and not by unknown and irresponsible persons. Lord Howick cared little for what was thought or written about him. Mr. Stanley was a hardy man too, but of a very different type.

He was greatly admired by a large party in the country,—perhaps by the country generally,—throughout a long life ; and it was customary to call him 'chivalrous.' I think he was not chivalrous.[1] He was a very able and capable man ; he had force, energy, and vivacity ; and he was an effective speaker, always clear and strong, sometimes commonplace, but not seldom brilliant. He was not a man of genius ; nor could it be said that he had a great intellect. He had the gifts of a party politician, such as eminent party politicians were in the generations immediately preceding his own rather than *in* his own,—subsisting throughout his life, so far as literature is concerned, mainly upon the scholarship and academical accomplishments with which he began it and playing the game of politics with more of party than of public spirit, and with not much perhaps of personal friendliness. In his latter life, when the American Civil War brought what was called 'the

---

[1] 'Autolycus Hotspur' was the name given him by Aubrey de Vere.

cotton famine' upon the districts in or near which his
estates were situated, the misery around him brought
into energetic action what was benevolent and hu-
mane in his disposition, and he exerted himself to
the utmost, devoting his daily labour for long periods
to organising and regulating the relief given to the
sufferers. But for this I should have said that he
was a hard and cold man. But out of the Colonial
Office I have hardly any *personal* knowledge to found
a judgment upon, and I may have been prejudiced
against him by the course which he took in regard to
Stephen and myself; contrasting it with what had
been generous in Lord Howick,—his pure and single
desire to do the best he could for the cause by all
means and appliances at his command, and, though
tenacious of his opinions, wholly careless to whom
the credit of playing an important part might attach,
—not even caring much perhaps for the political and
official proprieties fairly deserving consideration in
comparison with the momentous issues at stake in
dealing with the question of slavery.

Mr. Stanley took counsel with Sir James Graham,
one of the ablest of his colleagues. I doubt if either
of them had more knowledge of the matter than
might have come to them casually in Parliament and
in the newspapers. But Mr. Stanley could make the
most of the least. His skill as a debater enabled him
to do without knowledge of his own. He took his
topics from his opponents. Of anything of which he
knew nothing, let but one view be presented to him,

and he had not the slightest difficulty in presenting another and opposite one ; and in this way, so far as information was concerned, he lived upon the enemy's country. But this could suffice only for what was incidental and preliminary. The time came for propounding a measure, and Mr. Stanley and his colleague concocted one between them. Mr. Stanley introduced it into the House of Commons, and it was forthwith blown into the air.

The explosion cleared our atmosphere in the Colonial Office. Mr. Stanley became conscious of difficulties which could not be conquered by political courage and natural ability unassisted and un-informed ; he must have felt, too, that there were more ways than one in which his political reputa-tion might suffer ; and he now, very graciously, had recourse to Mr. Stephen. With his aid the Abolition Act of 1833 was devised and constructed ; and the speech by which Mr. Stanley recommended it to the acceptance of the House of Commons was, if my view of it at the time is to be trusted, much more Stephen's than his own.

Up to this point I do not know that any fault could be found with Mr. Stanley's ways of dealing with his subordinates. I, personally, had nothing to complain of. There was no reason why Mr. Stanley, who knew nothing about me, should place any confidence in me ; and there were some reasons why he should not be reputed to do so. The same might be said of Stephen at first. But when he had felt the necessity of obtaining Stephen's advice and assistance, and had profited by them to the utmost, he was as cold, unfriendly, and repulsive as he had been before the necessity arose; and as soon as he was able to dispense with him he cast him off, and even gave orders that he should not be allowed to see any public documents but such as might be officially referred to him as Counsel for the Colonial Department.

The Abolition Act which was passed provided for what was called an apprenticeship to last for six years; and on that total emancipation was to follow; and it provided also for a grant of 20 millions to compensate the slaveowners.

In writing about the measure I said that if it should succeed, its success would be owing to the 'circumstance of Stephen's putting his own designs into enactments and Mr. Stanley's into a preamble. It is owing to this circumstance, indeed,' I added, ' as far as I can judge, that any slavery measure whatever was passed in the late session; for after the wild plunge with which Stanley entered upon the subject, I am persuaded that he would have been unable to carry through a measure if Stephen had not held himself bound in duty to the cause to disencumber him, so far as was then possible, of his own schemes, and construct a measure that with all its faults might have a chance of success. The personal history of the Slavery Bill is, in truth, a remarkable part of the whole business. There have been many misbegotten measures before it which have brought upon their putative parents reproaches no otherwise due to them than as having undertaken tasks it was impossible that they could perform with their own hands, and many measures also which have reflected honour on those to whom mighty little of the merit of them was really due ; but I doubt if a great measure was ever brought into the world by a Minister of the Crown of which one could say that the responsibility for all that was evil in it had been so undividedly as well as wantonly and perversely incurred, and the credit for what was good so surreptitiously obtained.　And Stephen, after all that he has done for Stanley,—after having his services haughtily repudiated in the first instance, solicited when the emergency came, and profited by to the utmost extent without compunction or moderation,—is now treated with supreme in-difference and neglect, as if there was nothing to be ashamed of, nothing to be grateful for, and as if nothing were to be observed in him which should entitle him to respect.　There seems to be everything that is ungenerous and grasping in Stanley's com-position, and everything that is worldly,—worldly wisdom excepted,—for there is no wisdom of any kind in thus dealing with such a man as Stephen.　He is at the Isle of Wight gradually recovering from a nervous affection of the head which was the con-sequence of over-exertion in the summer.　You, who know what his habitual exertions are ' [the letter was addressed to Lord Howick], ' and what extraordinary exertions he can make without in the least suffering by them, will judge what the labour must have been that did him this injury. With all his easiness of nature [1] he is fully sensible that he is ill-treated, and I do not think that his connection with this office will last much longer on its present footing.'

There was, no doubt, a good deal of the exaggeration of anger in this invective, due perhaps not only to my regard for Stephen (who in the last three or four years had become one of my intimate friends), and to my indignation at *his* being *ill*-used, but also to my own little personal feeling about being *not* used.

The Act brought about the emancipation in four years instead of six (for the apprenticeship pleased nobody), and in 1838 the negroes passed in all tranquillity and good order into the life of indolent freedom.

Before the Act of 1833 had come into operation (which was on August 1, 1834), we of the Colonial Office had been relieved from *our* oppressor.[2] Mr. Stanley had been succeeded by Mr. Spring Rice ; and Stephen, who for so many years might better have been called the Colonial Department itself than the ' Counsel to the Colonial Department,' was

---

[1] I should rather have said ' his sense of subordination.' I do not think that easiness of nature did really belong to him.

[2] I find that my first impressions of Mr. Stanley when I came into communication with him at an earlier period,—that is, when he was political Under Secretary of State in December, 1827,—were very different from those which I received in 1833. In a letter to my father of December 29, 1827, I mentioned that I had accidentally had two or three conversations with him and liked him exceedingly:— ' Great frankness and simplicity, with a head clear and strong, is my impression of him.'

brought from Lincoln's Inn to Downing Street, and established in a newly created office of Assistant Under Secretary of State, from which he passed on in another year to that of Under Secretary of State, vacated by Mr. Hay.

I have said that the language of my letter about Lord Stanley and Stephen was probably inspired in part by some feeling of personal resentment on my part, for which there were no just grounds. I do not think, however, that this feeling was either lively or lasting. For my other vocation was much more truly my own, and for two years it had been almost entirely surrendered to the exigencies of official work ; so that the relief from the one and the resumption of the other brought with it a substantial solace and satisfaction.

CHAPTER IX.

Anno Dom. 1833.   Anno Æt. 33.

I have forgotten, and I might very well be glad to
forget, a transaction by which I aimed at throwing
overboard a part of my official burthens before I and
they were stranded together.   Previously to the
advent of Mr. Stanley, circumstances had arisen
which, in my opinion, gave me a claim to increased
emoluments.   I preferred the claim, and in a private
interview between the Secretary of State and the
Chancellor of the Exchequer, a decision was taken in
its favour.   But in taking this decision the Secretary
of the Treasury had been passed over.   Now it is
well known that, borne upon the strength of the
Treasury, there is a necessary and indispensable
office, commonly called, or which ought to be commonly called, that of Treasury Curmudgeon.   The
Chancellor of the Exchequer was not the Treasury
Curmudgeon of the day.   The Political Secretary
was.   The good easy Chancellor of the Exchequer

was overruled by the stout and unamenable Secretary, and my claim was rejected.

Till now everything had come to me unasked, and this repulse made me angry. I conceived that Lord Howick had not supported my claim as stubbornly as he ought, and I wrote him a letter in which I insisted upon taking in time what was refused in money, and applying to my own purposes the hours at home which I had hitherto devoted to official work. Had I contented myself with contending for this right in a simple and seemly manner, I should not have much fault to find with the proceeding; but my letter was full of inflated and arrogant self-assertion :—

'I cannot tell you how odious it was to me,' I wrote, ' to prefer my claim in the first instance, nor with what reluctance I brought myself to do so. But now that it is disposed of, I feel greatly relieved and quite able to mention the subject. . . . From the first year that I was in this office I have been employed, not in the business of a clerk, but in that of a statesman. So far as the West Indian Colonies have been concerned, I have at all times since that period done more for the Secretary and Under Secretary of State for the time being, of their peculiar and appropriate business, than they have done for themselves. I have been accustomed to relieve them from the trouble of taking decisions, of giving directions, of reading despatches, and of writing them. In ninety-nine cases out of a hundred the consideration which has been given to a subject by the Secretary of State has consisted in reading the draft submitted to him, and his decision has consisted in adopting it ; and the more important the question has been, the more have I found my judgment to be leant upon.   Since the year 1823, this department has been written up from the lowest condition of disrepute to, upon the whole I believe, a respectable, though not perhaps a very high place in public estimation ; and whilst the primary contribution to this effect has been made of course by Stephen, I feel that I have contributed the secondary share.'   I then recapitulated some facts of the case and proceeded :—

'Under these circumstances it is natural for me to take a review of my position and see what means are in my power to make the best of my prospects. In considering this matter I cannot but look at Stephen's case as having a direct bearing upon the judgment which I ought to form for myself ; and without presuming for a moment to compare my power of transacting business with his, I think that I in my degree may profit by his experience.   Looking then to his case, I perceive that a man may give his days and nights to public business—that he may possess every attribute of a philosophical and practical politician—the largest views, the minutest accuracy—the most comprehensive and unerring judgment ;—that he may be a man of infinite dexterity and resource ;—that he may be from time to time producing in the ordinary dispatch of business

such State Papers as the public archives of the
kingdom for all the centuries over which they extend
will probably afford few to equal ;—that every day
that he lives he may solve difficult questions and dispose of intricate cases and complicated masses of
documents to an extent to which it might be supposed that no human industry could reach ;—that he
may take upon himself the heaviest burdens of other
men and transfer to them his own singular accomplishments ;—that he may clear away their daily
perplexities and sustain their reputation ;—and after
a long term of such service find himself, so far as his
own emoluments, interests, standing, and consideration in the country are concerned, precisely where
he was at the beginning,—each successive Secretary
of State having professed himself very much obliged
and there leaving him. Can it be consistent with good
sense in any man, having such an example before his
eyes, and believing himself, in however inferior a
degree, to belong nevertheless to the same intellectual
order of mankind, to rely exclusively for his advancement upon the system of merging himself in other
men ? That my powers of doing business are unequal to Stephen's only makes the example an *à
fortiori* illustration of the futility of any expectations
on my part of profiting more by the exercise in this
way of my less capabilities. Stephen may have
attained—I trust he has—after many years employed
upon this plan, within a certain limited circle of
official men, a certain quantum of credit as a man

of business. I had imagined that to me too the
same thing might have attached in a less degree:
but I confess that when I consider all the circumstances of Stephen's case, and that at this moment
the Board of Trade are grudging him what they
give him, I am by no means surprised to find
that my official reputation has not travelled even
so far as from Downing Street to the Treasury.
Feeling therefore that it is in vain in these times
to attempt to obtain a hold upon the Government,
I conceive it to be no more than reasonable in any
man who believes himself to be possessed of the
power, to endeavour to acquire a hold upon the
Public. If I take a wrong measure of my own
capacity, it is at my own peril. I know that a more
fatal mistake cannot be made. But fallible though a
man's judgment may be on such points, it is all that
he has for his guidance in life, and he must necessarily act upon it. My habits and tastes have been
from boyhood essentially literary, and I was entering
upon literature as a profession to live by, when a
Clerkship in this office was offered to me. In performing my official duties I believe myself to have
sacrificed a literary reputation,—which, had the
sacrifice been a condition of the office, I should not
have mentioned as any mistake; because I consider
the certainty of subsistence, however obscure, to be
the preferable object. But had I confined myself to
transacting my fair proportion of business and no
more, I might have combined both objects: and this

is what it is my purpose to do for the future. The
far greater part of my drafts have been written at
home at night; the hours of my attendance at the
office being chiefly consumed in seeing people upon
business, giving directions to my assistants and
juniors, and conferring with the Secretary or Under
Secretary of State or with Mr. Stephen. My object
now is that the portion of time should be defined
which is considered to be fairly due from me to the
public, and that while I pledge myself to a punctual
attendance at the office during these hours, my time
at home should be discharged from all official claims
upon it.

'I do not complain of the species of duty which has
hitherto been devolved upon me, nor do I wish to decline it in future. On the contrary, I will readily do
my utmost to make my services, as far as they will go
within the prescribed limits of time, available in any
way which shall be considered advantageous to the
public service.

'Pray do not misapprehend the object of this
letter. It is by no means my wish to promote a
reconsideration of the decision taken at the Treasury,
or in any way to object to it. It is as much for my
interest as it can possibly be for that of the public,
to have thrown upon my hands that portion of my
time which the Government are, under the present
circumstances of the country, unable to pay for.
My wish is, not to sell my extra time, but to possess
it. If their Lordships were willing to grant the

highest amount of remuneration which has been proposed, it would not, in truth, be an equivalent to me for the leisure which I am desirous to resume.'

In giving an account of the commencement of my official life, I have said that the faults which I should imagine to have been most conspicuous in my official style would be 'arrogance and impertinence, and this, not only in the beggar-on-horseback beginnings, but for several years afterwards.' At the date of the above letter, about nine years of my official life had elapsed ; and it is clear that these faults had not been corrected then.

I hope, however, that the state of mind was exceptional, seeing what I said of it to my mother :—
'For myself, I am plunged in quarrels and contentions, some of which touch my feelings and others my interests ; but I am well and strong and going stoutly through all things. Indeed, if my spirits had not been in a state of vivacity, I should not, perhaps, have done battle for my interests ; because they are not what I am apt to stand up for when it costs me much in the way of discomposure. But I stood forth in their defence, upon this occasion, with as fine a spirit of lively pugnacity as ever launched an Irishman into a row.'

And though it is only in the retrospect that I perceive the true character of my own proceedings, I recognised at the time the character of the man with whom I was dealing :—

' There is much less to be objected to him,' I wrote in another letter, ' than to the great majority of men of his nurture. A thoughtful zeal for the interests of others is not to be expected from such men, and this is all that has been wanting in him. There is more generosity of temper, more freedom from little- nesses of feeling in him, than I have met with before in any public man with whom I have been in the habit of transacting public business.'

Owing to this temper in the man to whom the letter was addressed, our friendly relations were unimpaired and no harm came of it. Perhaps no good either; for even if I acted upon my intention of transferring some portion of my time and atten- tion to my play (which I doubt), a few weeks or months only elapsed before Mr. Stanley took office in the manner I have described, and placed my whole time at my disposal.

CHAPTER X.

DEATH OF HYDE VILLIERS--COMMISSION OF INQUIRY INTO THE
POOR LAWS—PART TAKEN BY MY FATHER IN ITS OPERATIONS.

ANNO DOM. 1832.   ANNO ÆT. 32.

I REVERT to my life in its personal relations.

In December, 1832, in the midst of the most
pressing and anxious labour which had yet fallen to
my lot,—the preparation for the Cabinet of my paper
on Slavery,—I lost the dearest of my friends,—of
my male friends at least the dearest,—and indeed
the only *very* intimate friend of my own age that I
possessed,—Hyde Villiers.

We had passed eight or nine years, not in friendship only, but in close companionship; and it is
companionship—is it not?—which takes the measure
of friendship. Wordsworth thought so; for I remember when the affection of a certain couple of
friends for each other was spoken of, he said,—'Are
they, so far as circumstances permit, continually
together; for that is the test?' Now circumstances
had varied much from year to year in what they
would permit to Hyde Villiers and me, and latterly

we had both had much work to do and much in
which we were much interested ; but I doubt if ever
the approach of the one was felt as an interruption
by the other. Certainly there was no moment of the
day or night when his approach was inopportune to
me. As I have mentioned before, we lived together
for some time in a house in Suffolk Street. The
House of Commons had even then begun to keep
late hours, and the hours I kept were early ; but
when he came home from the House, if he had anything interesting to tell, he woke me up, with the
certainty that it would give me nothing but pleasure ;
he sate down upon my bed and we talked together as
youth only can talk between two and three in the
morning. For the last eighteen months of his life
he had been in political office, and he had been
fashioned by nature for a politician ;—personally
attractive by gracefulness and a manner not the less
expressive for being high-bred ; invariably calm and
self-possessed ; a man who harmonised patience and
gentleness with strength.

The office he filled was that of Secretary to the
Board of Control ; the duty of the time was the
momentous one of determining in what manner
Ministers should propose to Parliament that the
Indian Empire should thenceforth be governed ; and
his Chief was the high-minded, accomplished, and
occasionally eloquent, but habitually and incurably
sluggish and somnolent, Charles Grant. I came to
know him afterwards, under the title of Lord Glenelg,

by four years of personal experience in the Colonial
Office ; and, amiable and excellent as he was, a more
incompetent man could not have been found to fill
an office requiring activity and a ready judgment.
A dart flung at him by Lord Brougham in 1838,
points to his notorious defect, as a Minister called
upon to deal with a crisis.   The then crisis was that
of the Canadian Rebellion :—' It is indeed,' said Lord
Brougham, 'a most alarming and frightful state of
things, and I am sure it must have given my noble
friend many a sleepless *day*.'

It was under such a chief as this that Hyde
Villiers had to handle the arduous and complex and
vitally important Indian question of 1832 ; and the
duty of guiding the Government to a conclusion
devolved, I believe, mainly, if not entirely, upon him.
In the session of that year, at his instance, six
Committees of the House of Commons had been
appointed, or rather, I think, one Committee to be
divided into six sub-Committees, by which the
several branches of the multifarious theme were to be
examined.   He had to watch the proceedings of these
Committees, to preside over another Indian Committee, to transact the current business of his office
in the morning, and to waste weary nights in the
House of Commons ; and as soon as the session was
over, he was threatened with being deprived of a seat
in Parliament, and had the cares and quarrels of an
unsuccessful contest to accompany the anxious work
of dealing with and drafting the Committee's report

(by the Speaker's permission, though the session had closed) and preparing a scheme of measures to be submitted to the Cabinet.

In a letter written after his death, along with some account of his work and the difficulties he had to meet, I described his way of working :—

' With all this was going on the perpetual toil of dragging Charles Grant to decisions,—a waste of time and spirits which those only can estimate who have known what it is to act under the inactive and decide for the indecisive. These burthens he bore with a steady and invariably tranquil outward demeanour, never complaining of them as oppressive,—partly perhaps from a feeling that it was injurious to a man's reputation to have it supposed that he felt his business to be too much for him. But in point of fact, whilst there was an excess of energy in his mind, there was too little elasticity. He became more and more deeply involved in intellectual labours, from which he could not or did not withdraw himself for intervals of relaxation. There was great vigour of intellect, but it was not a free and elastic vigour. His mind got enthralled by the subject of his meditations ' . . . .

He was suffering from an abscess in his head when he had to canvass another borough, travelled 280 miles in the mail without stopping, commenced his canvass on his arrival (three weeks before his death), went from house to house for twelve hours daily, his strength breaking down from day to day, and through intense suffering and with desperate energy prosecuted his canvass, not even then desisting from his official work, up to the verge of the delirium which ended in his death.

My father and stepmother, brooding over my loss in the solitude of Witton, felt it sorely and were full of fears for the effect of it upon my mind. Partly for their sakes perhaps, and partly in sincerity of belief and in a just estimate of the terminable, though not transitory, hold of sorrow and dejection upon a multifarious mind, I wrote to reassure them :—
'I do not fear any lasting depression of spirits from this event ; for I do not think the nature of my mind is liable to that from any event. I have mobility of mind, though not elasticity of spirits ; and as long as bodily health and strength remain to me I shall get over every misfortune.'

It was, I think, not long afterwards that I wrote in the person of Van Artevelde, what he had to say when looking back upon the death of Adriana :—

> 'Well, well,—she's gone,
> And I have tamed my sorrow.   Pain and grief
> Are transitory things no less than joy,
> And though they leave us not the men we were
> Yet they do leave us.   You behold me here
> A man bereaved, with something of a blight
> Upon the early blossoms of his life
> And its first verdure, having not the less
> A living root, and drawing from the earth
> Its vital juices, from the air its powers :

And surely as man's health and strength are whole
His appetites regerminate, his heart
Reopens, and his objects and desires
Shoot up renewed.'

The society of Hyde Villiers, and the interest I took in his topics, had made me pay more attention before his death than I did after it to political matters with which I had no official connection. In 1828 he travelled in Ireland, with a view to inform himself on the Irish questions then in agitation, and he wrote me long letters embodying ' the sundry contemplation of his travels.' I wish I could produce them, but I think they were borrowed for the information of some of his colleagues, and I fear they are lost. A long letter of mine in reply is extant ; and if a selection from my correspondence should be published, it will probably be found there.

On the English poor laws also we had much consultation and discussion ; and it was at the suggestion of Hyde Villiers, in a letter addressed by him to another member of the Government of 1831, that the Commission was appointed whose widespread inquiries and elaborate reports laid the foundation for the new Poor Law of the succeeding year. The Bishop of London, Sturges Bourne (*ci-devant* Secretary of State for the Home Department), Nassau Senior, and, at my suggestion, the Rev. Mr. Davison, who had written on the subject in 1817, were to be the Commissioners [1] ; and by Hyde Villiers' and Lord

[1] I rather think Mr. Davison declined.

Howick's advice, application was made to my father to act as its Secretary.

My father, for once, had no doubt or misgiving as to his qualifications for the task proposed to him. But domestic circumstances were sadly adverse. He had recently gone with his wife to stay for an indefinite time with her mother, a charming old lady between 80 and 90 years of age, and who now seemed to be approaching her end. It was a very anxious case of nursing ; my stepmother's health and spirits were weak and worn ; and, except her husband, she had no one to give her solace or support.

It was the first occasion in my father's life which had afforded a prospect of putting his abilities and attainments to use for the benefit of mankind, and the benefit of mankind was certainly what he had always had much at heart. He is the only man I have known in whom philanthropy could be the source of emotions such as arise in other men from personal distress. A gentleman in Scotland had achieved some celebrity by what was believed to be an enthusiastic devotion of his life to the founding and supervising schools for the poor. My father shared the general admiration, and had been conducted over the schools by the gentleman himself. But some years afterwards this person was detected in some scandalous immoralities which led to his being excluded from society. I mentioned the fact to my father. He was astonished and incredulous at first ;

and when I convinced him of the truth, he received it with tears.

But whatever power philanthropic feelings had to move him, domestic affections reigned supreme ; and the question whether he should leave home at this conjuncture he left entirely to his wife. It was impossible that she should leave her mother in the state she then was ; the separation from my father was an almost intolerable grief to her ; but she kept her sorrows as silent as she could, and the decision was to accept.

My father, emerging from a life of seclusion and inaction at sixty years of age, was found a most energetic and effective Secretary. But it became necessary that the sittings should be prolonged beyond the three or four months originally contemplated, and the strain upon my mother's fortitude was more than she could bear. Though silent as to her sufferings in her letters to my father, in one or two of those to me she had been more confiding : and before five months were out she was laid up with nervous fever, and my father at once resolved to resign his appointment and go home.

At the next meeting of the Commissioners, Mr. Senior observed that he supposed my father's reports must be the groundwork of the report finally to be made by the Commission ; to which Sturges Bourne replied that he did not see that they had anything else to go to. But this must have been a generous exaggeration.

What was the precise measure of my father's contribution to the final result of the Commission I do not venture to say. That result was one of the most important laws of our time ; and the credit of it was generally, and, I believe, quite justly, given to Mr. Senior, as its principal and essential author.

I have a few more words to say on the subject before I quit it. I have always looked upon the case as affording an instructive example of one of the ways in which the public mind in this country,.or the mind of some preponderating portion of the public, can be brought to bear upon a great public question with such weight as to enable the Government to pass an unpopular law. The series of searching interrogatories to which I have adverted were circulated to all authorities and agencies connected with the administration of relief to the poor, from the overseers upwards, in every parish in the country. Those who drew up and issued those interrogatories could themselves have answered most of them perfectly well. Their object was not so much to learn as to teach. Many of those to whom they applied for the information could not give it without inquiring from others ; whilst these, again, may have had to gather information not already possessed or recall what they had forgotten : and thus it was that thousands of people throughout the land were brought to ask or to answer questions, and to give and take instruction and think for themselves on the subject of those interrogatories ;

and on the foundation of all this questioning and answering a body of public opinion was built up. 'An index,' says Lord Bacon, 'is chiefly useful to the maker thereof.' And the person who answers a question is not seldom the person who is chiefly the wiser for the answer.

·If the public proceedings may be thought to have afforded an example for a politician to take note of, my father's conduct in the matter, in the view which I took of it, furnished a case for a casuist.

When he had been some three months at this task, I wrote to my stepmother, in answer to some of the letters I have spoken of, thus : 'I do believe that there never was a more perfect adaptation of a man to a task and a task to a man, and this must be your consolation, and you must think of the many millions of people who will benefit by that which brings suffering to you. You have not been in the way or in the habit of appreciating *public* duties, or I scarcely think that you could have reconciled it to a sense of what a man owes to his fellow-creatures that my father should have declined to undertake this business, any more than, having undertaken it, to persevere. It seems to me that scarcely any sacrifice of private feelings and interests, however much in a private view to be lamented, could be a consideration powerful enough to deter a very conscientious man from giving his assistance in a matter of such momentous public interest as this.'

My mother had said, in one of the confidential

letters to which I was replying, 'I am divided, like one who would serve two masters;' but at length she made up her mind to speak out, and my father did not hesitate a moment on the question whether the domestic or the public duty were the more sacred.

'I cannot easily imagine,' I wrote to my step-mother, 'by what process it is that any one person's absence makes any other person so ill; but I have not a bit the less sympathy for you on that account. Illness is illness and distress is distress, come how they may;' and then I said all I could find to say to extenuate the sacrifice she was occasioning, and console her for being the occasion of it, and added :—

'Even if all these considerations had not come in to render the resignation a matter of less moment in my eyes, I should have been fully satisfied with his taking the measure which he might think most con-ducive to your happiness and his. It has never been the way of our family to interfere with each other's independence of judgment and action, and if the father does not so by the son, why should the son by the father? . . . As to the question of conscience and duty and so forth, I should have held different doc-trines from yours, but I should not have had the least objection to you and my father satisfying your own consciences according to your own opinions : on the contrary, as my feelings would have been all in the interest of your opinions and not of my own, I should have been far better pleased that that could be done by you and him with a good conscience, which, I doubt not, I in your place would have done all the same, only with a bad one.'

I cannot find that she entered upon the case of conscience in the way of argument ; she only said,— ' The debates I have had with myself *how far* I was to allow my life to be nibbled away without injuring your father's peace more than giving up his situation would do, were debates that wore my mind and exhausted my body frightfully ; but unless you know all, which you never can do, you must still wonder and still condemn ; and that cannot be helped. I thank you most affectionately for the allowance you make.'

To Miss Fenwick I spoke my mind on the moral question with still less reserve : 'It is well that *their* tender consciences go along with them in the proceeding, which I, in the hardihood of mine, would have adopted with a full sense of its flagrant immorality. For my part, I never can twist my conscience, though I can easily defy it. " The last infirmity of evil," " to justify my deeds unto myself," is an infirmity with which I am not conscious that I was ever much afflicted ; and it is one to which I imagine stout consciences are seldom liable to the same degree as tender ones.'

Miss Fenwick took the opposite side :—'I not only suppose that he *thought* himself right in returning to her, but I think he *was* right ; for he contracted the obligation of cherishing her in sickness and in

health, before he contracted any obligation to the
Poor Law Commission ; and when that interfered
with what was his first duty, the other surely ceased
to be one, and his charity then had to return home
and act in that narrow sphere in which all charities
begin.'

There is the case of conscience ; and not being
myself much of a casuist, there I leave it.

CHAPTER XI.

THE ELLIOTS—FRIENDSHIP IN THE BUD AND IN THE YELLOW LEAF
—VERSES—VISIT TO WALTER SCOTT—WORDSWORTH—SYDNEY
SMITH.

ANNO DOM. 1830-34.   ANNO ÆT. 30-34.

BEFORE I pass to the period of sudden celebrity which broke upon me in June 1834—sudden and somewhat startling at first, but in the course of subsequent years not a little overclouded, or perhaps I should say outshone—before I pass to this period I will say something of a few friendships which had accrued to me in the latter years of my obscurity.

The little group of doctrinaires had broken up, as such groups of the young are wont to do when the maturer men go forth upon their several paths and become occupied and absorbed in professions or in political life, or when they marry themselves away. The death of Hyde Villiers would probably have dissolved the group, had it not been, as I rather think it was, dispersed at an earlier date. No more of breakfasts prolonged from ten o'clock to three by the charm of Charles Austin's bold and buoyant vivacities, set off by the gentle and thoughtful precision of John

Romilly, the searching insights of John Mill, the steady and sterling sense of Edward Strutt, the gibes and mockeries of Charles Villiers, and the almost feminine grace combined with the masculine intellect of Hyde. These were at an end. And in Kent House, with all its attractions, its gaiety and wit, my place knew me no more. It was after going past it one evening that I wrote the lines in ' Van Artevelde' beginning—

> There is a gate in Ghent—I passed beside it—
> A threshold there, worn of my frequent feet, .
> Which I shall cross no more.

And no doubt much of what had brightened my life had been taken out of it.

Edward Villiers remained to me for ten years longer. What he was in himself and what he was to me I have endeavoured to express in poetry, and it would be vain for me to attempt it in prose. He could not be said to restore what I had lost in Hyde ; there was but little resemblance between the two brothers ; but his friendship, though in another kind, was a not less precious possession. My father regarded it as a rare instance of a vacancy so fortunately filled—filled as it only could be at so early a moment through a loving remembrance, common to both, of a loss which both had suffered : and he remarked how much more frequently we may say with Shenstone, ' Heu ! quanto minùs est cùm reliquis versari quàm tui meminisse ! ' We were both at that time mournful men ; both at all times constitutionally subject to dejection ;

and each was to the other rather consolatory than cheering.

If Edward was unlike Hyde, who resolutely went his way in life with a calm and equable energy, he was still more unlike those of his family whose gaiety and wit were everywhere seen in society and everywhere admired. With all the ease and grace of his manner there was an habitual reserve—not forbidding and perfectly well-bred—but belonging to the tone of his spirits, which indisposed him to mix much in general society ; and one result was, that the few with whom he preferred to live were the more devoted to him. In his intercourse with them the genial liveliness of his mind came to the surface ; and if his constitutional melancholy could not be quite dissipated, it gave an additional charm to the brightness that broke through it ; and never in any man that I have known, and rarely in any woman, has nature accomplished a harmony so perfect between the countenance and the mind :—

> There was a brightening paleness in his face
> Such as Diana, rising o'er the rocks,
> Showered on the lonely Latmian : on his brow
> Sorrow there was, but sorrow not severe.[1]

There were times, however, when neither of us could enliven the other. I remember the tone of humorous reproach with which he said to me one day when we had been taking one of our long walks together in sombre silence, that ' he had not animal

____

[1] 'Gebir.'

spirits for two ; ' and it is a satisfaction to think that he found not long after, in a nearer relation of life than that of friendship, the strength and elasticity of temperament of which he had felt the want in me as well as in himself.

I was longer than he in finding the all-sufficient support ; but in the meantime sundry gains accrued to set off against my losses. About half a year after Hyde Villiers left the Colonial Office, Frederick Elliot entered it—in July 1825. He cannot have been then much more than 16 years of age ; but he was a lively and engaging boy, with a head in which youth and age had met and come to terms and made an alliance not yet, I think, altogether dissolved, though he must now (in 1872) have reached his ' grand climacteric.' His life exemplified the value of money in giving the right direction to the abilities of men whose natural aptitude is for a political career, by showing the way in which they are turned aside for want of it. His faculties in dealing with administrative affairs were known to the official class ; his social and conversational gifts, his range of knowledge, and the ease, lightness, and versatility with which he could bring it to bear, were known in London society ; but his political judgment and penetration were known to few, and might have been wholly unknown, had he not been sent to Canada in 1835, at the age of 26, as Secretary to Lord Gosford's Commission of Inquiry into Canadian affairs, then in a very critical condition. In that and the following year I received from him long letters giving an account of what he saw and heard, with the conclusions at which he arrived. I showed them to Lord Grey (then in the Cabinet, though not in the Colonial Office), and of one of them he wrote to me thus :—

'I return Elliot's letters, which I think decidedly the best papers on Canadian affairs I have ever read. Indeed, I do not know that I ever saw an account of the state of parties and politics in any country drawn up with equal judgment and discrimination. . . . I trust that you will show this letter to Lord Glenelg, and I even wish you could feel yourself at liberty to allow him to show to Lord Melbourne and the King a copy of all the more important parts of it.' In Charles Greville's 'Diary' (20th December, 1835) vol. iii., of the 'Greville Memoirs,' he writes :—

'I have just seen an excellent letter from F. Elliot to Taylor, with a description of the state of parties and politics in Lower Canada, which has been shown to the Ministers, who think it the ablest *exposé* on those heads that has been transmitted from thence. I have very little doubt that he will *go far* ; he has an admirable talent for business, a clear head, liberal and unprejudiced opinions, and he writes remarkably well.' And far he might have gone, but that he had not money to pay his way. In the course of a few years a friendship grew up between us ; and through him I became acquainted with the attractive, strong-hearted, genial, mettlesome race to which he belonged—frank, friendly, luminous, spirited 'sons of the morning;' sons—and daughters none the less.

Hugh Elliot, the stock from which they came, sometime Minister at the Court of Frederick the Great, has been presented to this generation, I may say, 'in his habit as he lived,' by his grand-daughter, Lady Minto, in one of the pleasantest biographies in which one century could be invited to take a look at another. Of his sailor son, Charles, I gave some account to Miss Fenwick, writing from the 'Star and Garter' at Richmond in March 1834 :—

'Charles, whom I should have been delighted to bring you acquainted with, is on his way to China. He is of all the men whom I have met with in life the one whose feelings are the fullest and freshest, and, with a great strength and buoyancy of temperament, the most tender : and he has a manliness of character which places him in a condition to let them take their free course without fear or shame. I have seen nothing like him in this landward society, where people think what will be thought of them, and fear their neighbours more than they love them, till their hearts become reserved and debilitated. In the present state of society a sailor may be that which scarcely any other man can. But Charles Elliot is ploughing the seas, which, as he now is, may be said to have produced him ; and so you will not see him ; and it may be many a long year before I shall, more's the pity !'

And I gave a much more particular account of him in ' Edwin the Fair ; ' for in that play he performs the part of Earl Athulf. I was already engaged in this portraiture when Sir James Stephen, in ignorance that he was giving the sanction of his sentiments to a foregone conclusion, wrote to me (18th November, 1841) :—' I return your letter with great admiration of Charles Elliot, who certainly seems as fine a fellow as ever sat for his portrait to painter or poet.'

I have often compounded one of my ' dramatis personæ ' from materials known to me in life, taking this from one person and that from another, and trusting to my imagination to harmonise what was diverse ; but except in this instance I do not remember that I have ever put a real man into a play in his totality. The part was conceived in the heart of my imagination, and there is nothing said or done by Athulf which is other than what would have been done or said by Charles Elliot in the like circumstances. Wulfstan the Wise (of whom Coleridge was the prototype) takes a psychological view of him :—

Much mirth he hath and yet less mirth than fancy :
His is that nature of humanity
Which both ways doth redound, rejoicing now
With soarings of the soul, anon brought low ;
For such the law that rules the larger spirits.
This soul of man, this elemental crasis,
Completed, should present the universe
Abounding in all kinds ; and unto all
One law is common,—that their act and reach

> Stretched to the farthest is resilient ever,
> And in resilience hath its plenary force.
> Against the gust remitting fiercelier burns
> The fire, than with the gust it burnt before.
> The richest mirth, the richest sadness too,
> Stands from a groundwork of its opposite;
> For these extremes upon the way to meet
> Take a wide sweep of nature, gathering in
> Harvests of sundry seasons.

In 1834, however, Charles Elliot's capabilities of sadness had not been developed, as they were unhappily at a later period, by domestic afflictions; nor had he at that time met with any reverses in his public career; and Ethilda's description of him, in Act i. scene 5, as 'wild with pleasantness and mirth' may be taken as not needing to be much qualified in the earliest years of our friendship: and even when his gallant, and I will say heroic, services as plenipotentiary in China, being rendered at a crisis of inevitable disaster, had been received by the British populace in the spirit in which unsuccessful heroism always has been and always will be received by every populace,—not many besides the Duke of Wellington and Lord Melbourne being clear-sighted and intrepid enough to applaud him publicly according to his deserts,—even then his hardy hilarity was but little the worse for mere popular ingratitude: Elgiva depicts him—

> Not so thoughtless now,
> And more in broken lights; but Nature's flag
> Is flying still, whose revels in his heart
> Hardly can care suspend.

And so throughout the play, whensoever there is nothing worse than warfare carried on with indifferent instrumentalities, or cares and oppositions in public life to be encountered, the heart of the fictitious commander and politician is, like that of the real one, rather vexed than oppressed ; and in scenes such as the following between Athulf and the Clown Grimbald, it is not so much an imitation of Charles Elliot that is given, as a mere plagiarism or transcription :—

> ATHULF. There—take my truncheon ; thou couldst rule
>   my force
> With more acceptance in the general mind
> Than I. By Heaven I am ashamed to see
> Such bickerings in a camp. Give me a cowl
> And let me rule a monastery rather.
>
> GRIMBALD. There—take my cap and bells ; I'll rule
>   your force,
> And wisely too ; but when I look for love
> In change for wisdom from the multitude,
> Give me again my good old cap and bells.
>
> ATHULF. Ah, fool, you're right, and that man is not
>   wise
> That cannot bear to be accounted foolish.
> I must be patient ; yet it frets my heart,
> Amongst my many cares, to be reviled
> By shallow coxcombs whom I daily save,
> Rescue, redeem, snatch from a rubbishy tomb
> Amongst the ruins of their wits, pulled down
> By their own hands upon their heads, God help them !
> Well, I'll be patient.

And if there was something peculiar to himself in the mixture or alternation of the splenetic and the gay and good-humoured with which Charles Elliot met and defeated hostility and unjust reproach, hardly less singular was the compound of natural impetuosity with self-enforced caution which marked his conduct of affairs in China, both when he rescued the British residents of Canton from their perilous imprisonment, and when, in the hour of victory, justly distinguishing between the guilty authorities and the innocent people, he saved that multitudinous and not unfriendly city from the consequences of being taken by storm.[1]

And again let Wulfstan the Wise (preparing himself with a speech to be delivered in the Synod) supply the delineation :—

> Earl Athulf's disposition shall I then
> Duly develop; him shall I disclose
> As one whose courage high and humour gay
> Cover a vein of caution, his true heart,
> Intrepid though it be, not blind to danger,
> But through imagination's optic glass
> Discerning, yea, and magnifying it may be,
> What still he dares : him in these colours dressed
> I shall set forth as prompt for enterprise,
> By reason of his boldness, and yet apt

---

[1] I may mention a trait of Charles Elliot's humour by which those who have read the memoir of Hugh Elliot may recognise the father in the son. When, under circumstances of the gravest responsibility, he had to make his way up the river to Canton, it became necessary to pass under the fire of a Chinese battery ; and by way of indicating the importance he attached to it, he had an arm-chair placed on the deck of his cutter, and sat in it, holding an umbrella over his head to protect him from the *sun*. His contempt was not altogether justified, for the Chinese gunners did manage to hit the cutter.

> For composition, owing to that vein
> Of fancy that enhances, prudence which wards
> Contingencies of peril.

Whilst, of the descendants of Hugh Elliot, Charles probably resembled him the most, to others of them the same brightness of spirit belonged in different degrees and in different ways,—coruscating in some, lambent in others. There was a sort of careless thoughtfulness that went along with it in some of them ; and for me, in my dull and melancholy moods, it had a charm which, perhaps, none *but* a melancholy man can fully appreciate. Hamlet felt it when he took to his heart a friend

> That no revenue had but his good spirits
> To feed and clothe him.

And when he tells how it was that he chose Horatio, he might be supposed to be describing Charles Elliot :—

> Since my dear soul was mistress of her choice
> And could of men distinguish her election,
> She hath sealed thee for herself ; for thou hast been
> As one in suffering all that suffers nothing,
> A man that Fortune's buffets and rewards
> Hast ta'en with equal thanks : and blessed are those
> Whose blood and judgment are so well co-mingled
> That they are not a pipe for Fortune's finger
> To sound what stop she please : give me that man
> That is not passion's slave, and I will wear him
> In my heart's core, ay, in my heart of heart,
> As I do thee.

Perhaps I should proceed with the quotation and add,—' something too much of this : ' especially as there was another of the family with whom I was in equally intimate relations, and of whom also I have something to say. For the genial vivacity, the liveliness of the heart and mind and whole nature which drew me to him, in like manner and in like measure charmed me in his eldest sister, Lady Hislop.

She was in young middle life, and was the wife of a distinguished General Officer, much older than herself, who had commanded the British army in the Deccan in 1817, and fought and won the battle of Maihidpore. When I knew him he was a simple-hearted, kindly, courteous gentleman, not easily brought into conversation, but happy and contented, sitting under his fig-tree and enjoying the honours and repose which a life of eminent military services had earned. Count Ugo, 'the gallant and magnanimous old man,' in the 'Sicilian Summer,' was mainly, though not, perhaps, so literally as in the case of Charles Elliot, drawn from Sir Thomas Hislop; and Rosalba does him no more than justice when she says that he was 'ever a just, courteous, and bountiful man, of good life and conversation, with a gentle and generous heart, and peradventure as much under- standing as innocence has occasion for.'

Lady Hislop had been, I believe, much *répandue* in society before her marriage; and she was singularly fitted to play a part in it; but the General's health was not strong, and at this time they were living in retirement at Charlton, about eight miles from Lon- don, where I became, about the year 1833, a frequent visitor. In June of that year I wrote to my father :—

'Pray take your excursion up the Tyne. It is always desirable to have a change of scene now and then, and shake oneself out of the dream that one gets into by living in a circle. *I* have been changing my scene to Charlton on Blackheath for two or three days in each of these two weeks last past, and getting more and more delighted with my friend there, Lady Hislop, whom I had scarcely seen for the last twelve months. She is ingenuous, impetuous, and vivacious in her talk and manner, and essentially discreet in her conduct ; behaving like an angel to her mild, simple, and kind-hearted old husband.'

For that old husband I had a great regard, and, in the course of time, I think even an affection. And there was an only child, a girl of about eight years of age, to whom I was very much devoted even in those days. How much and how long I continued to be devoted to her, may be inferred from these two stanzas, addressed to her, I do not remember exactly when, but after she had passed into middle age :—

> Dear Nina, how betides it that with you
> Sickness and sorrow, which since Time was born
> Were Youth's destroyers, seem but to renew
> The twilight softness of your dewy morn ?
> Ye days of Charlton, how you laugh'd to scorn
> The imminent Future ! Portion it its due ;
> I look in those large eyes whose tender blue
> The darken'd hair now deepens, and maintain
> That Time with all his following forlorn,
> Sickness and sorrow, injury and pain,
> If a Destroyer, is an Angel too.

Dante, the glorious dreamer, was he wrong
  The ' Mount of Preparation ' to invest
With sapphire hues and people with a throng
  Of happy spirits ? one, at his behest
  Sang the remembered strain he loved the best,
Whereby he knew that early loves are strong
Met in the ' Second Region ; ' I so long
    There wandering, bear a voice when daylight fades
  And shines the Love-Star singly in the West
    Sweeter than what was sweetest in the shades
Of Purgatory, Casella's broken song.

During the years 1834 and 1835, Charlton Villa was a great resource and comfort to me. Along with the charm of a bright intelligence, not uninformed by books as well as by commerce with society, and especially, I think, foreign and diplomatic society, Lady Hislop had a faculty, rarely to be met with in lively women, of giving rest to the weary.

And rest was what I stood greatly in need of; for though in the ten years which had elapsed since I left Witton, I had ceased to be subject to nervous depression, lassitude had remained to me, alternating with excitement. In the middle of my work at the Colonial Office it was not unusual with me to lie down for an hour or more and ' go into abeyance,' as Hyde Villiers called it, neither speaking nor listening nor thinking; and in the evening my exhaustion was so incapacitating that I often went to bed at eight or nine o'clock. A letter to Lady Hislop of January, 1834, betokens what my condition was in those years :—

' I suppose you will hear of Charles to-morrow.

I should miss him a good deal if I had sense and spirit enough to miss anything in the sort of life which I lead, dividing the day between hours of languor when nothing is felt, and hours of occupation when things present are all in all. It has not happened to me to meet with anyone whose society was so attractive to me, nor to part from anyone with so much regret ; unless it be those whom I met with in a fresher season of life, and whom I have been parted from for ever. We shall see him again in a few years, I hope ; and probably less changed by the lapse of a few years than most people. Thanks for your inquiry about my teeth. As to dismissing the dentist, if there were to be any dismissal it should be that of the teeth ; the fault is in them, not in him.' And after adverting to the advantages which artificial have over natural teeth :—' I believe there are very many occasions on which we patch when we ought to substitute ; and for my part I wish it were possible to substitute another body altogether for the very inconvenient one which I carry about. Pope went by water one day from London to Twickenham, and getting into dispute with the waterman about the fare, happened to make use of his favourite ejaculation of " God mend me ! " " Mend you, indeed ! " said the waterman, " much easier to make another." I am afraid I am in Pope's predicament, both in my teeth and in more important parts of this fabric,—in body and soul. You are very kind, and so is Sir Thomas (my best regards to him), in backing Nina's invitation. When will you have me ?—

> Shall't be to-morrow night; or Tuesday morn;
> Or Tuesday noon or night; or Wednesday morn?
> I pray thee name the time; but let it not
> Exceed three days.

Some gossip followed, and I told her of a new acquaintance I had made : ' The night before last I plunged deep into the acquaintance of Mrs. Norton. I came to the top again dripping with beauty ; but I shook my ears and found myself no worse.'

My visits to Charlton continued till the autumn of 1835, when the Hislops went abroad. After their departure I wrote some letters to Lady Hislop, but not many. She had, or supposed she had, a difficulty in writing letters, and I think the correspondence drooped and dropped ; and when in a year or two they returned to this country, Sir Thomas's health was much broken, and she was so wholly engrossed by it that I believe my visits to Charlton were less frequent than before. About this time too I induced Miss Fenwick to take a house in London during the winter months of each year ; in these months we lived together, and this domestication withdrew me more or less from visits out of town ; and when, after the death of Sir Thomas, Lady Hislop came to live in London, another and still closer domestication had taken place, and in no long time I had ceased to live there myself.

My friend's life in London was occupied with

many and multiplying concernments.   Her daughter
was married at an early age to Lord Melgund (now
Earl of Minto), and lived near her ; and four grand-
children were born to her ; and a daughter of her
brother Charles, who was serving abroad, was consigned to her care and was to be brought up and
brought out and married in due season.[1]   And with
her, every member of her family who had occasion
for help or kindness or care, sought and found what
they wanted.   These were the true and constant and
abiding interests of her life from first to last, and in
London as well as elsewhere ; and at the same time she
played with the world and society, and took as much
interest in doing so as the nature of the game would
permit. Under all these conditions her life was filled up.

Lady Hislop and I never had a quarrel ; never, as
far as I know, even a misunderstanding ; but with
each successive change of outward circumstance, other
changes crept along, and all else was not as it had been.

Very various are the ways in which friendships
grow old. An old friendship may or may not be a better
thing than a new one, but it is not the same thing.   It
may have struck a deeper root, but the flower and the
freshness have faded. The anxieties and sorrows which
will naturally attend a friendship of many years, and
the serious joys which take their turn, will exercise the
affections in their entire scope and capacity, and what
is strong will be established in its strength.   Arthur

---

[1] To Mr. Russell, afterwards Lord de Clifford.

Hallam has written,—' Pain is the deepest thing that we have in our nature, and union through pain has always seemed more real and more holy than any other ; '—and on the other hand joy, though not the deepest, may be a deep thing nevertheless, and some sorts of gladness there may be, and some victories and some consolations, which do their part in ministering to the strength and stability of the affections, and contribute to make the old friendship the graver stake and the more precious possession. But for all this, there are imaginative pleasures dancing round the beginnings of loves and friendships which will not dance on for ever, and the perishable garland they weave has some odours and colours that are wanting even to the best and fairest fruitions of the riper season,—even, I will venture to say, to the triumphs of the harvest-home when those who have sown and reaped come again with joy and bring their sheaves with them.

In the days of those Charlton visits I had lent Lady Hislop the copy of Barante's ' Histoire des Ducs de Bourgogne de la Maison de Valois,' in which I had been studying the story of Philip van Artevelde and his times. After the lapse of many a long year, I was sitting up in my bed (obliged to do so every night from severe spasmodic asthma), and studying Barante once more for the story which is dramatised in ' St. Clement's Eve ; ' and in turning over the pages I came upon some flowers and leaves which Lady Hislop had put between them thirty years before ; and this gave occasion to a few verses which may find a better place here than elsewhere :—

Oh tender leaves and flowers,
  Tho' withered tender yet,
What privilege of joy was ours
  In youth when first we met !

Bright eyes beheld your bloom,
  Fair hands your charms caressed,
And not irreverent was the doom
  Which laid you here to rest.

Sweet phantoms, from your bed
  Thus re-arisen, you paint
The likeness of a love long dead
  In faded colours faint.

Oh tender flowers and leaves,
  By all our vanish'd joys—
By glittering spring-tide that deceives,
  By winter that destroys,—

Though nought can now restore
  The perished to its place,
Eyes dimmed by time and tears once more
  Shall look you in the face.

My stepmother seems to have felt something of what I feel about what belongs to the beginnings of friendships. It was hardly in her nature to have a quarrel; but one of her friends did quarrel with her once; and it was in allusion to what passed upon the occasion that she wrote thus :—' She certainly has not risen in my estimation by this discourse ; but dear she must ever be to me with all her faults, and I trust that I must still be so to her with all mine. Such only can be the friendship of many years of frequent intercourse, when the fabric built by imagination has crumbled away and the realities of human nature are no longer clothed with the charms of early attachments.'

The case of Lady Hislop and myself was, as I have said, a case of crumbling, not of quarrelling. The friendship underwent a change, but it never ceased. I have survived her, but I have not survived the affection.

In the autumn of 1831 I paid a visit to the Lakes, and after passing some time in the society of Southey and Wordsworth, it occurred to me that I ought to make an effort to see Walter Scott, whose health had been broken by more than one shock of paralysis, and who might not be much longer to be seen in this world. With this view I procured myself an invitation to spend two or three days at Chief's Wood, near Abbotsford, the abode of Mr. Lockhart. Scott dined at Chief's Wood on one of these days, and I dined at Abbotsford on another. I was much and mournfully impressed with his manner and appearance. There was a homely dignity and a sad composure in them, which perhaps belonged to his state of health and to a consciousness that his end was not far off ; and along with these there was the simplicity and single-ness he must have had from nature. The animation and fertility of discourse with which also nature had gifted him were brought low. I witnessed only one

little quickening of the spirit. There was to be a
pic-nic party, and a question arose whether two
elderly ladies in the neighbourhood should be
invited. One of the family intimated an opinion
that the two elderly ladies would not add to the
liveliness of the party,—in fact, that they would be ' a
bore ; '—on which a light came into the sick man's
eyes and a flush into his cheeks, and he exclaimed,—
' I cannot call that good breeding.' He could not
bear that the good old ladies, his neighbours, should
be considered unacceptable.

I had brought him word that Wordsworth
intended to pay him a visit later in the autumn.
He answered, ' Wordsworth must come soon or he
will not find me here.' I understood this as said in
contemplation of his approaching death ; but perhaps
it had reference only to his intended departure for
Naples, whither he went not long after to escape the
English winter. Wordsworth paid him the proposed
visit, and of that came the sonnet written on the
occasion of his departure. It is a sonnet which I
often repeat to myself, and I will take this opportunity of repeating it to others :—

A trouble, not of clouds or weeping rain,
   Nor of the setting sun's pathetic light
   Engendered, hangs o'er Eildon's triple height :
Spirits of Power, assembled there, complain
   For kindred power departing from their sight ;
While Tweed, best pleased in chanting a blithe strain,
Saddens his voice again, and yet again.

> Lift up your hearts, ye mourners, for the might
> Of the whole world's good wishes with him goes;
>   Blessings and prayers in nobler retinue
> Than sceptred king or laurelled conqueror knows
>   Follow this wondrous Potentate. Be true,
> Ye winds of ocean and the midland sea
> Wafting your charge to soft Parthenope.

Wordsworth and Scott dwelt in regions as far apart as it was possible for men to occupy who each covered so large a space. Neither, I should think, could appreciate the other in full measure ; but Scott would perhaps go nearer to a full appreciation of Wordsworth than Wordsworth of Scott ; and I value the more on this account the feeling expressed in this grand valedictory sonnet.

They were as little alike in their aspect as in their genius. The only thing common to both countenances was that neither expressed a limitation. You might not have divined from either frontispiece the treasures of the volume,—it was not likely that you should ;—but when you knew that there they were, there was nothing but what harmonised with your knowledge. Both were the faces of considerable men. Scott's had a character of rusticity. Wordsworth's was a face which did not assign itself to any class. It was a hardy weather-beaten old face which might have belonged to a nobleman, a yeoman, a mariner, or a philosopher ; for there was so much of a man that you lost sight of superadded distinctions. For my own part I should not, judging by his face, have guessed him to be a poet. To my eyes there was more of strength than refinement in the face. But I think he took a different view of it himself. Whatever view he took, if occasion arose, he would be sure to disclose it; for his thoughts went naked. I was once discussing with him the merits of a picture of himself, hanging on the wall in Lockhart's house in London.   Some one had said it was like :—

'Yes,' he replied, 'I cannot deny that there is a likeness; such a likeness as the artist could produce; it is like me so far as *he* could go in me; it is like if you suppose all the finer faculties of the mind to be withdrawn : that, I should say, is Wordsworth the Chancellor of the Exchequer,—Wordsworth the Speaker of the House of Commons.'

In this there was not more vanity than belongs to other men; the difference being that what there was, like everything else in him, was wholly undisguised. He naturally took an interest in his own looks, and wished to take the most favourable view of them; as most men do, though most men do not make mention of it.   And there is something to be said for his view. Perhaps what was wanting was only *physical* refinement.   It was a rough grey face, full of rifts and clefts and fissures, out of which, some one said, you might expect lichens to grow.   But Miss Fenwick, who was familiar with the face in all its moods, could see *through* all this; and so could I too at times. The failure of the face to express all that it might have expressed was indicated by Coleridge with characteristic subtlety and significance.   He said that

Chantrey's bust of Wordsworth was more like Words-worth than Wordsworth was like himself.

In Scotland great men were not the only objects of interest to me. There was a girl in a remote district who had a singular charm of freshness, pleasantness, and Scotch friendliness, with simplicity and originality. I knew her in London afterwards—but London is not a place in which simplicity and originality can live and flourish as in their native soil. Even the admiration they may meet with—for it is quite possible that they may be admired—may not be good for them. A young lady finds that her simplicity is charming, and she thinks she will be more simple than ever. She is fearlessly natural, original, and unconventional in her ways, and becom-ing conscious that her ways are winning, she pushes naturalness a step or two beyond Nature's need. The charm is not lost, but it is just a little impaired.

Miss Fenwick did not sympathise with the light and casual admirations which came across me ; she thought them likely to interfere with sentiments which might be more to the purpose ; for her purpose was that I should be married. But there was one nugatory admiration to which she could not refuse her sympathy, the object being a sister of her own, much younger than she was, married to a Somerset-shire country gentleman. From Miss Fenwick's house in Bath I wrote to my mother :—

' Mrs. —— is here, whom I had not seen for three

years, and it is seldom I see anything which interests me more. I scarcely think that any artist could paint, or any visionary imagine, a creature more beautiful in her kind ; and though one is conscious that a great deal of brilliancy has passed away, yet the tender tone of the complexion has not ; and the contour of the features, which is so perfect, and the purity of expression, make the remains of her beauty more attractive than the unimpaired beauty of most other angels.'

I have seen many specimens of young beauty since that was written, and some of beauty outlasting youth ; but with the unfading recollection I still have of Mrs. ——, I could almost write it again, and say with Donne,—

> No Spring nor Summer's beauty hath such grace
> As I have seen in one Autumnal face.

My mother replied :—

' Mrs. —— is indeed a very interesting person, and her beauty of that kind which time has less power over than most kinds. Brilliancy or animation never was hers. One used to feel, in a manner, quite obliged to her if she smiled when the rest of the party were all mirth and folly. Yet she never was what might be termed melancholy, never dull. She retains that enchanting grace which always distinguished her, and an elegance of figure, though I don't think any one part of her or her proportions was really good. Altogether I have seldom seen anyone I more admired.'

In order to be near her sister, whose abode was Bagborough House, not far from Taunton, Miss Fenwick occupied for a few years the house of an absentee vicar of Halse, a few miles distant. Thither went I on a visit in the summer of one of those years; and thither went with me Edward Villiers and his wife; for he had then lately married Miss Elizabeth Liddell, a daughter of the first Lord Ravensworth, and they had both entered into a sort of partnership in the friendship between Miss Fenwick and me. They loved and admired her with all their hearts; and Miss Fenwick felt about them as I did.

Sydney Smith's parsonage of Combe Fleury was within a few miles of Halse, and we paid him a visit. He was in high spirits, and took us round his grounds, showing us the beautiful prospects to be seen from each point of view, for Combe Fleury is situated in one of the richest tracts of Somerset-shire :—

' An extensive prospect there to the East ; Galatia —Mesopotamia—lie in that direction.'

And when our visit was over and we rose to take leave, he asked Mrs. Villiers whither she was bound when she left Halse.—' To Bath,' was the answer.

' To Bath ! ' he said ; ' what can take you to Bath ? '

' Well, I have an aunt there, whom I really ought to go and see.'

' Ah ! an aunt—you have an aunt at Bath ; yes, everybody has an aunt at Bath—a perfect ant-hill.

I have an aunt at Bath : " Go to the ant, thou sluggard," has been ringing in my ears for a century ; but I've never gone.'

And then followed the loud but soft volley of cordial laughter with which he usually speeded his own jests on their way.

Miss Fenwick could well appreciate his wit and humour, but she could not always approve his sentiments and opinions ; and she was capable of observing upon them with some severity. When he said he could not see what there was in Wordsworth's poetry, she replied,—' There are some things which must be spiritually discerned.' She was told afterwards that he had called her ' a sensible woman ; ' and then she considered that he had taken his revenge.

Another visit which we paid in the neighbourhood of Halse brought me acquainted with a daughter of Sir Thomas Lethbridge, in whose family beauty seemed to be inherited as a sort of heirloom, like poetry in the Tennysons and intellect in the Coleridges. Miss Anna Maria Lethbridge, now Lady Clarges, was of that beautiful family the most beautiful member. If there were any of my admirations at this time which could be called frivolous or foolish this was not one, for there was a dignity of beauty in her which lent something of its own nature and character to the feeling it inspired.

CHAPTER XII.

ANNO DOM. 1834-36.   ANNO ÆT. 34-36.

'PHILIP VAN ARTEVELDE' had been in progress for
about five years before the summer of 1833, and the
revision of it extended over nearly another year.

For about ten years before its publication the
popular appetite for poetry had not been of a craving
character. The enthusiasm for Lord Byron's impassioned but often rather empty moroseness and
despair, though it may not have suffered a general
collapse, had passed away from some of the more
cultivated classes, and found perhaps its surest
retreat in the schoolboy's study and in the back
shop. And thither also had retired the sympathy
which, when it is accompanied by anything dazzling
in personal attributes or circumstances, intensity
of self-love can sometimes excite in the popular
mind.

The more just admiration felt for his brilliancy

and wit and his general poetic power remained in
large measure ; but even this, perhaps, drooped more
or less from being entangled with the dead body of
the other enthusiasm. For myself, I have never
been able to rekindle my youthful infatuation (as it
seems to me now) for Lord Byron's poetry, and I
rather think I am not a competent judge of it. It
is not easy for a passion to pass into a reasonably
warm regard.

Moore had not excited amongst his admirers the
peculiar personal interest which attached to Lord
Byron ; but having by some years the start of him,
with much more of poetic sensibility and metrical
art than the country had been accustomed to in the
eighteenth century, he shone as a morning star in
the awakening eye of the nineteenth ; and though
he was apt to disfigure his songs by what he meant
for a crowning ornament—a metaphor artificially
set forth and too much like 'the posy of a ring,'—
yet in his more genuine poetic moods, whether
plaintive or festive, or, as he could sometimes contrive it, a graceful combination of the two, he could
not but charm an audience who had forgotten the
songsters of Elizabeth and James, and so far as the
poetry of song was concerned, had had nothing
better to listen to in their own times than what was
called 'the Della Cruscan School,' or 'the School of
Laura Matilda.'

But Moore's genius, though of course with much
diversity, was yet too much akin to Byron's for the

one not to have lost by the apposition of the other. At the dawn of Byron's day

> It 'gan to pale its uneffectual fire,

and when that day declined, its own lustre was so far bedimmed as to make extinction seem to some cold calculators little more than a question of time.

In this state of things the two great poetic *intellects* of the age, which had been passing through a tunnel, as it were, since the end of the preceding century, issued forth of it and were seen and known. The depths to which the genius of the one or of the other had penetrated might be measured with the same rod, but the range was very different ; so far, at least, as was to be seen in the space covered by their published poetry. Wordsworth had produced four or five times as much as Coleridge, whose product was scanty. Coleridge, as Wordsworth once expressed it to me, had been 'in blossom' only for four years—from 1796 to 1800. The plant was perennial, but the flowers were few. That the greatest imaginative intellect of the age should, so far as poetry is concerned, have done little more in a long life than show what it *could* have done, may tend to reconcile one to the fate by which some who appeared destined to be great poets have died in early youth. 'Christabel,' the 'Ancient Mariner,' and some others of his early poems were enough, no doubt, to make an era in poetry, and they did make an era ; for though they did not themselves at once and in direct action reach the popular mind, they took immediate effect upon those whose fortune it was to be the popular poets of the time ; and poetry could never again be content to dance in a court dress with Pope, or to go through a course of gymnastics with Dryden, or to sit by the fireside with Cowper, or to mount the pulpit with Young.

If Coleridge produced little in his after life that equalled the richness of those blossoming years from 1796 to 1800, it was not that intellectual or imaginative activity fell short ; the activities were all there, but they revolved into themselves ; and the moral will, enervated by opium, was wanting in power to determine and give effect to them. I have always thought that Coleridge was describing his own states of mind when he speaks of—

> joy above the name of pleasure,
> Deep self-possession, an intense repose. . . . .
> No other than as Eastern sages paint
> The God who floats upon a lotos leaf,
> Dreams for a thousand ages, then awaking,
> Creates a world, and smiling at the bubble
> Relapses into bliss.

Wordsworth, on the contrary, wrote, in my opinion, too much poetry ; as most men will who live long and write little else, and have no employment save that of meditation and composition. But his poetry takes concentrated forms as well as those which permit him to be diffuse ; and when at last it

found its field of operation free from the rank
growths of the first quarter of this century, it
exercised a great fertilising and cultivating power ;
insomuch that, within the limits of the thoughtful
classes, the mind of at least one generation may be
said to have been moulded by it. The first opening
of their minds to Wordsworth was effected by Pro-
fessor Wilson and his associates in 'Blackwood's
Magazine ;' and this opening was widened, I think,
by two articles of mine in the 'Quarterly Review,'
one of which, I was told by the publisher at the
time, had doubled the sale of his works. His popularity with these classes, and through them with
others, lasted for some twenty years. He never lost
his hold of the generation by which he had first
been appreciated ; but another generation arose which
preferred to have a poet of its own,—a great poet in
his kind,—and Wordsworth went into occultation
during the transit of Tennyson.[1]

The case of Coleridge was somewhat different.
He too, though he did not write largely like Wordsworth, wrote a good many poems which were hardly
worthy to stand by the side of those on which his
fame was founded. But his best poems had received
from the first the profound admiration, not only of
the writers of poetry who caught some breath of his
inspiration, but also of a small circle of its readers

---

[1] *July* 1879. The occultation did not last many years, and I think
that now Wordsworth's poetry shines through the higher order of
minds everywhere with a radiance again unrivalled.

sitting at his feet; and if for many a long year he was not read by the reading multitude, yet even with them a vague notion had grown up that there was something in him 'rich and strange,' though they may have imagined that, as far as they were concerned, it might as well be at the bottom of the sea.

This partial insensibility lasted as long as Coleridge lived, but not a day longer :—

> The gates of fame and of the grave
> Stand under the same architrave.[1]

So it was at least in the case of Coleridge : for in the history of the rise and fall of poetic reputations, inexplicable as it so often is, there is nothing more curious than the way in which the long silence of the outer world was broken in 1834 when Coleridge died. For some twelve months or more he was the favourite theme of every magazine and journal. Lights will sometimes flicker over a newly filled grave, but this was more like the noisy inebriety of an Irish funeral. Like other paroxysms it passed over ; and it is hard to guess now, as one popular poet rises after another,—hard to guess and impossible to distinguish, amid the trampling of the triumphal processions,—what voices may still be repeating to themselves the poetry of the past, and how many may still be treasuring in their hearts the love of a greatness which has grown old.

---

[1] Walter Savage Landor.

In June, 1834, when 'Philip van Artevelde' appeared, Coleridge was still living, though his end was near,[1] and Wordsworth was not yet far famed. It was a flat time. Publishers would have nothing to say to poets, regarding them as an unprofitable people. My MS. seems to have been in search of a publisher some months before. On the 4th February, I told my father that I had been reported to be the author of 'The Doctor,' and also of 'Contarini Fleming;' and having expressed my amusement at finding myself the Father General of foundling publications and my satisfaction at it as showing that my name might go for something on the title-page of 'Philip van Artevelde,' I proceeded :—'That personage is now in the hands of John Murray, to enable him to judge whether he is, like most other demagogues, a marketable commodity. . . . Whatever be the fate of that work, it is off my hands. I do not say so in any way as being glad to get rid of it—quite the contrary—but only to express that the interest that has been with me for some six years past must now give place to something new.'

Murray, though strongly advised by Lockhart to accept the publication, remembered what he had lost seven years before by 'Isaac Comnenus,' and was not prepared for such another venture. He referred me to Moxon, then commencing business. Moxon told me that when authors applied to Murray to publish

---

[1] I heard with much interest from John Sterling that he read it before he died.

works likely to involve a loss, Murray was very much
in the habit of referring them to him. But as I was
ready to take the risk, he of course was glad enough
to publish.

I had shown the manuscript to four friends :
James Stephen, Charles Greville, Spencer Walpole,
and Frederick Elliot. I think Frederick Elliot was
the only one who had confidence in its success. On
the question whether I should publish 'Van Artevelde' at my own expense, my father wrote to me in
March 1834 : ' I do not expect " Artevelde " to be
popular. It is so opposite a style of composition to
that on which the tastes of this generation have been
formed. Those are few who form their taste for
themselves, and those are many who suffer their
taste to be formed by popularity ; and it is the many
who make a work pay or lose. The influence of the
few, with the aid of "Artevelde" himself, may slowly
and at last, in another generation perhaps, change the
taste of the many ; but this will go to the account of
your fame, not of your exchequer ; for fame, you
know, " is an exchequer of words and I think no other
treasure." Still I say that in your situation, as you
can afford the risk, I would incur it.'

To which I answered :—' I agree with you as to
" Van Artevelde " being at issue with popular taste,
and I infer that it can only succeed by creating the
taste by which it is to be appreciated,—an inference
which seems almost to amount to a conclusion
against its success. Nevertheless I am determined

to take no discouragement from anything but the actual result, knowing by experience that it is a sort of disappointment which needs no preparation, inasmuch as it does not bring with it one day's depression or one hour's annoyance. If I want the energies of ambition, I enjoy at least the indemnities of indifference ; and that, not only as regards acceptation by this present public. My interest in the pursuit will survive another failure—another and another—being the interest of excitabilities connected with the exercise of the art, and in a great degree independent of anything ulterior. Yet what ambition I have is directed in this line ; and standing now within the precincts of middle age, with deliberation and with food for deliberation in the experience of several years devoted mainly to other endeavours, and without any reason to be dissatisfied, on the whole, with the result of those endeavours, I do unquestionably conceive that my vocation is to write plays, and that my life will give out the larger sum total of results in proportion as it shall be more devoted to this employment.'

The principal question which arose amongst my friends was as to the prudence of the preface.

' Charles Greville says that it is all wrong from beginning to end, and that it will not do to invite people to read my book by telling them that it is what won't suit their taste. He says it will be called dogmatical, and that people will not bear to be called upon to conform to my taste, instead of to read something which is conformable to theirs. Edward Villiers is partly of the same mind; but Frederick Elliot only requires some additional humilities and then would let it go.'

I referred the question to Southey.

'Let your preface stand,' he said. 'A preface that provokes contradiction does no harm. One that attempts to defend or apologise for the book it introduces serves only to show the enemy what the garrison look upon as the weakest part of their works. Any such introduction is sure to bring on the attack that it deprecates.'

'I keep my preface,' was my reply, 'only withdrawing my humilities. They were introduced by advice, to avoid the effect of arrogance, and they produced the effect of egoism. Moreover they were too solemn—too much in the manner of "your humble man's man, Emperor Peter." The preface is now tolerably impersonal, and I must risk the charge of arrogance.'

So these preliminaries were settled, and, as my mother expressed it, quoting the words of a certain Lady Chaytor living near her, over which we had made ourselves merry some time before—'Now for a leap into the lap of the public.'

The leap was made with the advantage of a lift and a toss. The publication had been kept back so as to appear along with an article by Lockhart in the 'Quarterly Review.' There were one or two other plauditory articles written from personal motives;

then notices, more or less slight or elaborate, swarmed in every direction ; and one of my reviewers applied to me what had been said formerly of some one else (I forget of whom) that I had 'awakened one morning and found myself famous.' The sale was rapid, and as the edition had numbered only 500 copies, another had to be put in preparation without delay. Lansdowne House and Holland House, then the great receiving houses of London society, opened their gates wide. In that society I found that I was going by the name of my hero ; and one lady, more fashionable than well informed, sent me an invitation addressed to ' Philip van Artevelde, Esq.'

I enjoyed my success very much for its own sake, and I valued it greatly for the pleasure and interest it excited in my father and mother. They were not for the present at Witton Hall ; as I have said, they had temporarily left that dreary abode ; and it was for one almost as solitary—the house of my mother's mother, Mrs. Mills. She was in her eighty-seventh year, and greatly needed her daughter's care and attendance, which were given till her death in 1836 ;—it was not till then that they returned to Witton. Even the aged mother's mother, an accomplished and cultivated person, had taken an ardent interest in the work, had read it again and again, and had expressed an expectation that it ' would give a new turn to the taste of the day, and revive a purer and higher love of poetry than had been abroad for some years.'

My mother wrote in July :—

' I suppose you are sick of the sound of praise by this time. The praise of friends is sweet ; the praise of strangers more flattering ; and the praise of enemies the most delightful of all. Yet none of these will make you think better or worse of your poem than you did before it burst forth to the world.'

' I am not in the least sick of the sound of praise,' I answered ; ' but, on the contrary, begin to think that I can digest any quantity of it. . . . If it were not that the sale is less than it was, I should imagine, from what I hear and what I see in print, that the book was getting a great reputation. . . . If I were to tell the truth, I believe I should say that just at this moment I am thinking little about praise or dis- praise, and less about what is accruing to me than what is going away from me ; and what is going away from me is C—— F——. She starts for Scotland to- morrow. . . . When you say that there is in the character of Van Artevelde, what none of the critics have perceived, a kind of hardness mixed with his softness, you have got (to use a flower of speech) the right sow by the ear.'

She had spoken also of an occasional want of refinement in Clara ; to which I answered, that the want of refinement might be a fact and might be a fault ; but that, judging from my own observation, I doubted whether the vivacity of Clara would be natural without a capability of coarseness, any more than the strength of Artevelde without the capability of harshness.

In so saying, I think I was hard upon Clara. The better answer would have been that Clara's manners were not modern but mediæval. If modern manners were to be the standard, where would Rosalind be, and where even Desdemona? Much of our modern refinement is conventional, and as such has its own value as an outwork. Much of what may seem to us coarse in mediæval manners was in those days consistent with innate and essential delicacy.

Divers other views were interchanged. My father, who had read the work piecemeal in MS., rejoiced in it more and more when he came to read it in print and in sequence. His wonder was that a man who had read so little should have so much to say. But he was anxious, and so was I, that I should read more before I wrote again.

This, however, it was not easy to accomplish. The celebrity of my work had brought about a change in my daily life which was by no means favourable to reading or to any other profitable employment of my time. Of course I, like every other successful author at his first coming forth from the jungle, was put under pressure of London society. I had some advantages for a *first* appearance in it. But taking me all in all I was unapt. My strength was not equal to the effect of late hours and social excitements, and as my weakness of health did not appear in my looks, it was not accepted as an excuse for refusing repeated invitations, and the refusals gave offence, while the invitations I accepted were numerous enough to incapacitate me for anything more than the work of my office.

There was another unfitness ; it did not occur to me that social popularity was an object to be aimed at, nor consequently that it was worth while to give some thought to the ways of gaining or keeping it. This was a moral as well as a social mistake. Miss Fenwick says in one of her letters :—' Any kind of liking is a precious thing, to be cherished, whether it comes suddenly or slowly.' Perhaps popularity in London society would not have entered into her contemplation as included in the maxim ; but from some points of view it is worthy to be included. An honest and disinterested conciliation, a desire to please simply for the love of giving pleasure, are commendable ; and the genial sympathies of our nature cannot be cherished without a desire that those we like should like us ; and they may be fitly carried forward a little farther, in a desire to be liked by whosoever is not likely to be the worse for liking us. If a man can rely upon himself for making truth and sincerity paramount, and for not being weakened and wasted and spoilt, there is no reason why he should not study the arts of pleasing, and seek to make himself acceptable in society.

Nothing of this entered into my ways of thinking in 1834. I had real good nature, and as good nature

is at the root of good breeding, I ought to have been
well-bred.   But I was not myself easily displeased or
offended ; and giving others credit for a hardihood
similar to my own, I went on my tactless way,
hurting people without knowing it ; and it was only
in retrospect that I seem to have seen how much
social popularity had accrued to me and how wantonly
I had thrown it away.   Had I perceived it at the
time I should probably have thought that it signified
very little ; but it does not follow that this would
have been a just estimate.

All this may have been, in some respects, a dis-
advantage ; but, on the other hand, if I had continued
long to be as much liked and sought in society as I
was in 1834-5, my time and strength would have
been wasted and I might have become good for little
else.   This was the view I took of the access and
recess of my popularity, when, in 1844, I wrote a
short poem (not published nor intended for publication) in which I reviewed the successive stages of my
career from the seclusion of Witton Hall to the date,
then recent, of my marriage :—

> A change again ;—my name had travell'd far,
>   And in the World's applausive countenance kind
> I sunned myself ; not fearing so to mar
>   That strength of heart and liberty of mind
>   Which comes but by hard nurture : Me tho' blind
> God's mercy spared—from social snares with ease ·
> Saved by that gracious gift, inaptitude to please.

I had scruples, too, which came in aid of this

gracious gift. I had greatly enjoyed the society of Holland House ; that of Lansdowne House not so much. The former was made up of the men of wit and the eminent political men of the day, with an occasional man of letters. The dinners at Lansdowne House were now and then of the like composition and still more agreeable because there were more women ; but for the most part they, or those of them to which I was invited, consisted of men of letters almost exclusively ; and as I had no love of knowledge or of instructive conversation and none of my own to produce, they did not charm me much. But greatly as I preferred the society of Holland House, a scruple came across me which led me to withdraw from it. I did not like Lady Holland, and I found myself speaking of her accordingly. I was not sufficiently a man of the world to think this compatible with accepting her hospitalities, and I refused one invitation after another till she became aware that more would be sent in vain.[1] This, I have no doubt, had its effect in reducing the social demands upon me ; for it may well have caused me to be looked upon as a person who thought himself of infinite importance and whom it was not easy to deal with. Nothing

[1] In the diaries of Miss Caroline Fox, published in 1882, an account is given of my secession, taken by her to be my exclusion, from Holland House, which is founded on a fact, but unfounded in the inference. It is true that in conversation with Lady Holland, she sneered at Wordsworth's poetry, and I answered by saying, ' Let me beg you to believe, Lady Holland, that that has not been the sort of thing to say about Wordsworth for the last ten years.' But she sent me more than one invitation to dinner after this misdemeanour.

could be better calculated to relieve me from the pressure of many who might have been candidates for the honour of my 'good company and gracious speech.'

If this was the view taken, I was misunderstood. Self-sufficiency and self-importance were not, I think, in the number of my weaknesses.   But the misunderstanding was a natural one, and it may have been useful in preserving me from some of the 'social snares' spoken of in the poem.

I offended in another way.   In May, 1836, I published a little volume which I misnamed 'The Statesman.'   It had no right to so large a title. 'Pragmatic precepts' would have been a better, if the·word 'pragmatic' had not in these latter times got away from its origin, so as to be used in a dyslogistic sense.   But I have found more than once that there is no page of a book so difficult to write as the title-page ; and at the same time there is probably no one page taken singly which is of equal importance to its fortunes.   This book had the advantage, and it was a very great advantage, of revision in the proof-sheets by three capable critics, Spedding, Gladstone, and E. Villiers ; but on referring to their comments I do not find that any question was raised upon that important page.

The work contains commentaries upon official life and the ways in which men may best be managed and administrative business conducted ; and in so far as official and unofficial life occupy a common field, it looks indirectly into the ways of the world. The preface is more modest than the title-page. Adverting to Lord Bacon's Book 'De Negotiis' (the 8th of the 'De Augmentis'), and to the large note of deficiency there set down, the preface proceeds :—

'I should be much indeed misunderstood if, in pointing to this want in our literature, I were supposed to advance, on the part of the volume thus introduced, the slightest pretension to supply it. Amongst the dreams of juvenile presumption it had, I acknowledge, at one time entered into my fancy that if life should be long continued to me and leisure should by any happy accident accrue upon it, I might, in the course of years, undertake such an enterprise. When this vision lost some of its original brightness I still conceived that I might be able to blot from Lord Bacon's note of "deficients" so much of the doctrine "De Negotiis" as belongs to the division which he has entitled "De Occasionibus sparsis." But the colours of this exhalation also faded in due season, and when the scheme came to be chilled and condensed, the contents of the following volume were the only result that, for the present at least, I could hope to realise.'

The offence given was not, however, in the overweening title, any more than in the blushing preface ; but I believe chiefly in a chapter (the 7th) on 'popularity,' and in another (the 14th) on the 'arts of rising.' One sentence in the former chapter would have been enough. I affirmed that 'popularity is most commonly obtained by an abuse of humility and a large indulgence for all qualities and proceedings which are not denounced as flagitious by the society to which a man belongs ;' and 'one of the doctrines of this popular humility,' I proceeded, 'is much the same with that which Machiavelli ascribes to the Romish Church in his time—the doctrine "come è male del male dir male ?" There is a better doctrine which teaches that men are not only the subjects, but the instruments of God's moral government. The judgments of the street and of the market-place, the sentences which men pronounce upon each other in the ordinary intercourse of life, constitute the most essential of all social jurisdictions, and he who would serve the great Lawgiver with fidelity must carry the sword of justice in his mouth.'

There are certainly a good many worthy persons in society who would rather not meet a man with the sword of justice in his mouth.

But there was something worse still :—

'In the earlier stages of a man's career he will find it his interest, if it be consonant with his character (for nothing, be it observed, can be for a man's interest in the long run which is not founded upon his character), I say, if it fall in with his nature and dispositions it will answer to his interests to have a speaking acquaintance with large numbers of people of all classes and parties. A general acquaintance of this kind can be kept lightly in hand at no great cost

of time or trouble. By taking care that it shall
cover a due proportion of men of obscure and middle
station, the discredit of courting the great may be
partly escaped ; and he who has a speaking acquaintance with a thousand individuals will hardly find
himself in any circumstances in which he cannot
make some use of somebody. Out of the multitude ,
of the obscure some will emerge to distinction ; the
relations with this man or that may be drawn closer
as circumstances suggest ; and acquaintances which
could not be *made* at particular conjunctures without
imputations of interested motives, may be *improved*
at such moments with much less inconvenience. It
is always to be borne in mind that, as in commerce
large fortunes are most commonly made by dealing
in articles for which the poor (that is, the multitude) are customers, so in this traffic with society a
man should take into account, not the rich and the
great only, but the many. When a man shall have
mounted to a higher level of fortune, he will, doubtless, find the numerousness of his acquaintance in
obscure life to be more troublesome than useful.
But if he have taken proper care not to lavish himself in wanton intimacies, and whilst multiplying his
potential friendships as much as possible, not to cultivate them into actual friendships oftener than his
occasions required, he will find the burden of his
superfluous acquaintance lie hardly so heavy upon
him in any circumstances as to make it worth his
while to throw it off. In his more exalted station

bows and smiles will be abundantly sufficient for those with whom bows and smiles had, at all times, constituted the warp and woof of his connection. From those with whom his intercourse has gone further, he may probably be enabled to earn a dispensation for the future by doing them some substantial service which costs him nothing ; and with regard to some still closer alliances in which he may be entangled with obscure and unserviceable men, he will do well to single out some individual from time to time, in whose behalf he should make some great and well-known exertion as a tribute to friendship. This will enable him to spare trouble in other instances, and yet avoid being charged generally with the pride of a *parvenu*.'

It might be supposed that the spirit in which these passages were written could not well be misconstrued, and that in amusing myself with this kind of inquisition and exposition, I ran no risk of being understood to recommend seriously the arts I expounded. But it was not so. Men who were themselves more or less artists in this kind, thought they could best acquit themselves by exclamations of disgust and contempt, and that they could best suppress the book in which the arts were exposed by misrepresenting it as a book in which they were taught and recommended. At least I had some reason to think so.

In this way I believe the *book* suffered at its first appearance as well as the author; but had it possessed the requisites for popularity, it would soon have forced its way. It did not force its way either soon or late. So long as it was in print it never actually ceased to sell. About once a month for 36 years, it occurred to some person that he would like to read it, and in some such numbers as 12 in a year, a single edition of 750 or 1,000 copies—I forget which—dribbled away, and in this year of 1873, for the first time the book is out of print.

Fra Paolo di Sarpi said of a book of his (it could scarcely be his great work) that it would have a dozen readers in every age, and that that was enough. I think Fra Paolo was a man of very moderate desires.

CHAPTER XIII.

MR. SPRING RICE SUCCEEDS MR. STANLEY AS SECRETARY OF STATE
—MR. SPRING RICE AND HIS FAMILY—'THE FOUR AGES' OF
TITIAN—A PROPOSAL OF MARRIAGE, AND WHAT FOLLOWED.

ANNO DOM. 1834-38.   ANNO ÆT. 34-38.

IN August, 1834, Mr. Stanley and Mr. Lefevre left
the Government and were succeeded in the Colonial
Office by Mr. Spring Rice and Sir George Grey; an
event which brought with it a great change in my
official life, and led in the course of a few years to
the greatest change that can happen to a man in his
personal life, my marriage.

I wrote to Miss Fenwick on the 8th September,—
'We have had a general pacification at this office,
which, after having been torn with civil convulsions
for a year and a half, is now to enjoy all the blessings
of peace. Spring Rice has offered Stephen something
in the shape of promotion, and perhaps all that it was
in his power to offer him at present; he is to be
made an Assistant Under-Secretary of State; that
is, that office is to be created for him, and he is to
hold it along with his present office, and with the
same salary. This is not much of a step, but

Stephen is content to take it and to come into renewed activity ; and I, being of his faction, am to do likewise ! '

My father thought that I might be brought into more activity than was good for me ; but I told him that he ' need not be afraid that I should work as I had done, either for love or money.'

Mr. Spring Rice had not been above a week or two in office, before he asked me to spend a couple of days with him at a house he had taken at Petersham. In a fortnight this visit was followed by another ; and I wish it were allowable, connected as I now am with them, to repeat what I said of the family, collectively and individually, in my letters.   A little of it I may :—

' If conciliation was his object he succeeded,— would have succeeded by himself, and succeeded all the more with the help of his wife and daughters and his little boys. . . . The boys are nice boys, and the ways of the family altogether very pleasing and very expressive of happiness and affection.   I liked them much and got on very well with them, as I generally do with women and children.'

In a letter to Southey (9th September, 1834) I spoke of the father :—' Spring Rice is the only popular man whom I have found it possible to like ; but there is a genuine though an indiscriminating cordiality of temper about him, and a prodigality of kindness to every one which is certainly agreeable to see if it has no higher value ; and after seeing him in his family at Petersham (a very pleasing family) for a couple of days I found it impossible, notwithstanding my habitual distrust of men who conciliate all the world, not to believe that there was something substantial in his nature. We went down in an open carriage at sunset, and he took care not to let the sun disappear without the proper quotation from " Madoc ; " and the next day he took a fitting opportunity to pay a similar compliment to " Thalaba." He seems to have filled his daughters as full of Wordsworth as they could hold, and after coming from church turned to " The Happy Warrior," and said it was worth a thousand sermons.'

In another letter I described the manners of the young ones in the family as ' lively and gentle, fond and free.' . . . 'I have never seen a household which it was more satisfactory and pleasant to look upon.' Speaking of the eldest daughter, I said,— ' She has Wordsworth at her fingers' ends, and is full of poetry from her fingers' ends to her toes. This, however, seems to be the way of the family : Spring Rice himself seems to have a real love of it, and to have taught his children to admire Wordsworth as that which was most admirable. . . . Spring Rice is a man of a light heart and happy nature and particularly cordial manners, and when our parting breakfast came to a close (he being bound for Windsor on a visit to the King) he rubbed his hands and ejaculated a wish that now we were all together, we could all stay where we were for the rest of the day ; and I really have an idea that we all *had* amused each other very well,—tossing poetry and quotations from hand to hand ; for the house is as full of poetry as any circulating library can be full of novels. So I like my Secretary of State of this day, —him and his ; and he takes my views to a great degree of what ought to be done in the office.'

In the office, so long as he remained in it, all went well ; at least in Stephen's estimation and in mine. He was a man who had opinions of his own, but he was entirely free from arrogance or presumption ; and ready therefore, on fit occasions, to listen to the opinions of others and give them whatever preference might be due to opinions founded upon a knowledge of many years, over the opinions of one who was, for the time being, new to his work. I have known few men, however, whose knowledge of all sorts of subjects, literary and political, was more extensive, and none who could acquire knowledge, and make it ready for use, more swiftly as well as effectively. Stephen said of him, I remember,—' If you multiply his matter into his velocity you get a very considerable momentum.' He was then, or had been down to a recent date, perhaps the most popular man of his party. ' Spring Rice,' I wrote to Southey, 16th November, 1834, ' is the first person since Lord Bathurst whose departure from these doors I have seen with regret ; a light-hearted, warm-hearted man, with a mind, not powerful certainly, but acute and active, accomplished, and versed in literature and poetry as well as equal to business. He took his family down to Hastings the other day to remain there for the winter, that Lady Theodosia (who is consumptive, I fear) might have the benefit of that warmer climate. I asked him when he came back if he had planted them to his satisfaction, and he answered me by an allusion to the passage in " The Excursion," in which the Solitary describes his having taken his wife—

> To a low cottage in a sunny bay
> Where the salt sea innocuously breaks,
> And the sea-breeze as innocently breathes
> On Devon's leafy shore—

saying that he had thought of it on the way back till his eyes had filled. And in truth I never met with a man, much less a public man, whose heart was more devoted to his fireside. I see him go with concern, therefore, and without any expectation that His Majesty will transfer the seals of the Colonial Department to any person who will be half as much to my mind.'

In no long time he lost his popularity. He had done nothing to forfeit it; but how it came and how it went is not difficult to understand. Having from nature a genial Irish temperament, he had a cordial greeting for every man he met. The cordiality, however general and indiscriminating, was perfectly sincere. But it did not mean what an equal cordiality on the part of a dry Englishman would have meant. Englishmen, however, construed it by an English standard, and an untold multitude of casual acquaintances took him for a fast friend. This redounded to his popularity till the period when he attained to high office with patronage at his command. Then came the time of trial ; the untold multitude expected each man a loaf or a fish : no miracle was wrought ; and the Minister, not being more than human, was accounted less than friendly. In public life cordial manners have their value and their charm ; but in order that the popular favour they bring may be liable to no reaction, there should be a lightness and carelessness in the cordiality, showing that it is referable to the source rather than to the object,— scattered, not elicited. So qualified it gives birth to no unreasonable expectations, no embittered disappointments.

The Government fell in a few months, and Mr. Spring Rice was succeeded by Lord Aberdeen. After this I saw less of him and his family than before ; no more, indeed, than I saw casually in society or in occasional visits at their house in London during the season. But the youngest daughter, Theodosia Alice by name,[1] whom I had taken to be a child when I first saw her in 1834, had grown to be more of an object of attention to me than, with all my love for children, it was possible that a child could be.

It is not for me, situated as I now am, to describe her ; but it is open to me or any one to quote what is printed in a book ; and in the life of Archbishop Whately, vol. i., p. 487, I find a letter from the

---

[1] Hereafter called 'Alice.'

Archbishop to Mr. Senior, dated 21st July, 1841, in which it is mentioned that she was beautiful. If so she was in 1841, it may be presumed that she was not less so in 1836, when she was in her eighteenth year ; and at that time I conceived that I had met with a picture of her by Titian. The work of Titian's in which I found it I described in a letter to Miss Fenwick, of the 3rd July, 1836.

'It belongs to the collection of Bridgwater House, and commonly goes by the name of "The Four Ages," inasmuch as the several groups in the picture represent the several stages of human life. The group on the left hand consists of three children. Two of them are in a deep sleep, and the third is setting its foot upon one of the others as a stepping stone to a tree which it is about to climb. Infancy is thus represented by the careless animation of its waking moments and by the deadness of its sleep ; for the waking child puts his foot upon the one that lies asleep, and, nevertheless, the one that lies asleep is not wakened. The next group consists of a man half reclining and a girl sitting beside him with a musical instrument in her hand. In the background is old age represented by an old man meditating upon a skull. There is a controversy concerning the intent and meaning of this picture ; some saying that it represents three ages, some four. If it re-presents four, the man and girl in the second group, who seem to be lovers, must stand for two of them. The girl bears a strong resemblance to Alice Spring Rice.'

The letter proceeds to give some account of a declaration and proposal.

The family, or at least the father, was startled. Mr. Spring Rice, in his first reception of the proposal, though not refusing to consider it, was cautious and cold. He complained justly of being taken by surprise, and alleged that neither of the parties could know much of the other.

This was true. It was very little indeed that we knew of each other. And how little is it that is ordinarily known in such cases! Mr. Rogers observed to me once that it matters very little whom one marries, for one finds next day that one has married somebody else. Milton complains that 'there is no such freedom of access granted or presumed as may suffice for a perfect discerning till too late.' The habits and circumstances of society are no doubt much changed since Milton's time ; perhaps they are a little changed even since the time of Rogers ; but the changes operate in more ways than one. In Northumberland, I remember, when I was a boy, it was said by some old gentleman that the marriages of last century were commonly between relations or near neighbours ; on which a shrewd uncle of mine observed that 'that was before the roads were mended.' Amongst cousins and near neighbours a husband or a wife can be chosen with a real knowledge of what may be expected of them in domestic life. But not only have the roads been mended ; the rail has been laid down ; and girls and men from the remotest counties go to London and meet in a concourse and a crowd ; and though it is true that there is more frequency and more freedom than there used to be in such intercourse as a concourse concedes, yet all the conclusions that can commonly be drawn from intercourse of this kind are such as have reference to looks, manners, intelligence and tone. 'Didst thou see him whisper her in the *compassed window?*' says an observant person in one of Shakespeare's plays ; and a 'compassed window' is, in London, about as much of an opportunity for intercourse apart as a couple who may be gravitating towards each other can well hope to enjoy.

Had I waited for a knowledge which was not to be had, my proceedings might have been as much too slow as they were held to be too precipitate. In some of the great occasions of life, if we did not act upon an impulse we should probably let slip the time of action. But Nature has made provision for such cases. The greater the stake the greater the pains of anxiety and the troubles of a mind tossed to and fro ; they become intolerable and we rush to a decision. A man pre-occupied with his own deliberations walks up to a stone wall and runs his head against it ; the man who has not only a lure beyond, but a goad from behind, takes a run and a leap and clears it. I have never ceased to rejoice that on this greatest occasion of my life I was a little rash.

From a sonnet in my common-place book it appears that I had either met with or imagined some

monitor who strongly disapproved of my proceeding.
My father thought me rash, but it is certainly not
his disapproval to which the sonnet replies, or, if his,
I must have been making the most of a little for the
purposes of my argument.   It is entitled,—

A Charge Repelled.

From slight communion slender knowledge snatched,
  On slender knowledge serious purpose built,
Of purpose so upstarting issue hatched
  Showing a rashness near akin to guilt,
And folly with misfortune mostly matched!
  Grave tho' the charge, the Panel can allege
A solid plea for that precipitate pledge :
  There is a wisdom, scorn it as thou wilt,
Much reasoning Sophist, which the mind receives
  By impulse; there is knowledge that is met
Than what is sought more certain; Reason weaves
  Simply a snare for him who, thought-beset,
Prudentially refuses trust to place
  In the clear honesty of that fair face.

When the proposal was made in July the family
were on the point of departure for Ireland.   In
November Mr. Spring Rice returned to London,
leaving his family in Ireland ; and within a week
after his return, he asked me to a very domestic
dinner—himself, his eldest son, and one very intimate
friend—cooked by a housemaid, and served in a back-
room of his empty house.   This, which was repeated
in another week, was plainly a measure; and we
remained in the relations it indicated till his family
were about to join him in April, 1837.

I thought it time then that I should ascertain

more distinctly where I stood, and I reopened communications. Mr. Spring Rice, in his answer to my
letter, held still to the objection of inadequate knowledge, declining to sanction an engagement, whilst
he consented to our seeing more of each other on
an unengaged footing. But early in June religious
questions were raised at the instance of a member of
the family ; and after an explanatory correspondence
with Mr. Spring Rice, the engagement was broken
off by his daughter, on religious grounds.

With some natures, revelations of love are made
chiefly through pain, and perhaps it was through the
shock of the disruption that I first knew of the depths
to which mine had reached. But in no long time
there were some glimmerings of renewed hope. Hope
is said by Crashaw (or is it by Cowley ?) to be the
brother of Faith :—

> Hope, of all ills that men endure
> The only cheap and universal cure !
> Thou captive's freedom and thou sick man's health,
> Thou loser's victory and thou beggar's wealth,
>
> .   .   .   .   .   .
>
> Brother of Faith, 'twixt whom and thee
> The joys of Heaven and Earth divided be,
> Though Faith be heir and have the fixed estate,
> Thy portion yet in moveables is great !

In my case the moveables and the fixed estate were
to be one inheritance or one forfeiture.

Opinions had never been strong in me—at least
on matters not susceptible of proof ; and I think I
can acquit myself altogether of intellectual pride.

The nature of my intellect in its philosophic field was large, loose, and reconciling. I conceived the hope of such an approximation in the course of time as would make the difficulty on the score of religion not unsurmountable. During these months I sought for assistance, at Miss Fenwick's suggestion, from two friends of hers and mine, widely differing on points of ecclesiastical doctrines and discipline, but in spirit equally devout—Sir James Stephen and Mr. Gladstone. In point of intellectual range I regarded them as belonging to the same order of minds as my own, my inferiority lying mainly in the region of intellectual operations in which the intellect is dependent for its power and scope upon spiritual discernment. I need not say that their assistance was most gladly given.

Southey took perhaps a still more ardent interest in my endeavours; but his mind did not bear upon mine. It was too habitually and constitutionally confident on many sorts of questions, temporal and spiritual, on which my own was habitually diffident. In his view of the state of my mind, with which he had long been well acquainted, there had been nothing in it from the first which should have prevented the marriage on religious grounds, though he was fully aware that my convictions fell far short of my aspirations. Had the case been his own, he said, he should have greatly preferred me to a Roman Catholic. I could not understand the preference, but it was emphatically expressed.

So supported, my endeavours were not unsuccessful. There was a lifting of the mists and by degrees

> The burthen of the mystery
> Of all this unintelligible world
> Was lightened.

In January, 1838, I reopened communications with Mr. Spring Rice, and submitted to him my confession of faith. I think it may be regarded as having a rather close affinity to that section of Abraham Tucker's 'Lights of Nature' which he entitles 'Lights of Nature and Gospel Lights Blended.' After some delay it was accepted as sufficient, and intercourse was to be resumed on the footing of ' a valued friend ; ' but on no other footing till the month of June following, when the young lady would be of age.

On this my mother wrote :—' How the unnatural restraint is to be kept up for four months when each party knows the feelings of the other and each is resolved that such restraint shall end on the 2nd of June, I can't imagine. I am not sure whether I would not rather be without the intercourse till that day, lest the feelings grow dull and the temper of the parties wearied. . . .'

I resolved to submit to the condition : for, under all circumstances of life, errors of acquiescence have been more according to my nature than errors of opposition. But my mother's doubts were fully justified in the result. After some months the young lady's courage failed and she broke off the engagement.

On the 21st of April, just a month after the catastrophe, I told my mother that my health, which had been somewhat shaken, was re-established ; that I had found a refuge in my imagination ; and that, relinquishing a long meditated design of dramatising 'Thomas A'Becket,' for which the preparations seemed interminable, I had resumed a former project of dramatising 'Edwin the Fair,' where I was 'free to do what I liked, and needed not to ask, "Wit, whither wilt ?"'

Into this project I plunged, seasonably for a diversion, but far too hastily for the purposes of art. A dramatist, before he begins to execute, should see his way in his plot from beginning to end. It may be that accidents will happen on the road, and some deviations become permissible or desirable ; but the more the preconceived main drift is kept in view the better. I did not give myself time for this fore and aft completion of design before I began to write.

Still the state of mind and the course of events which had hurried me brought some compensations in dramatic and poetic detail for grave structural defects. Trouble and sorrow are not destitute of results to the mind and imagination ;—

The tree
Sucks kindlier nurture from a soil enriched
By its own fallen leaves ; and man is made
In heart and spirit from deciduous hopes
And things that seem to perish.

Those lines were written after my earlier disappointment.   It was after my later that Leolf found himself
on the shore at Hastings (the scene was *written* there,
as well as laid there),—

> Discoursing to the sea
> Of ebbs and flows ; explaining to the rocks
> How from the excavating tide they win
> A voice poetic, solacing though sad,
> Which when the passionate winds revisit them
> Gives utterance to the injuries of time.

And he tells them that ' poets are thus made.'
    The Leolf of the play is no more an impersonation
of myself than the Elgiva is an impersonation of
Alice ; but the one being

> A man upon whose head
> Already peepeth out the willowy grey,

and the other a young girl who had been incon-
stant to him, there was of course an opportunity of
bringing into the story some outgrowths of the life
I had been living ; and in the last scene between
Leolf and Elgiva there is enough of this mixed with
what belongs to the tale to make some portion of it
not come amiss in quotation here,—not amiss at least
to those, and some there may be, who may like to
see in what manner life and poetry and truth and
fiction will sometimes take occasion to embrace and
inosculate :—

> Leolf.   This is the last time we shall speak together ;
> Forgive me therefore if my speech be bold
> And need not an expositor to come.
> I loved you once ; and in such sort I loved

That anguish hath but burnt the image in,
And I must bear it with me to my grave.
I loved you once; dearest Elgiva, yes,
My heart, even now, is feeding on that love
As in its flower and freshness, ere the grace
And beauty of the fashion of it perished.
It was too anxious to be fortunate,
And it must now be buried, self-embalmed
Within my breast, or living there recluse
Talk to itself and traffic with itself;
And like a miser that puts nothing out
And asks for no return, must I tell o'er
The treasures of the past.
    Elgiva.   Can no return
Be rendered?　And is gratitude then nothing?
    Leolf. To me 'tis nothing, being less than love;
But cherish it as to your own soul precious;
The heavenliest lot that earthly natures know
Is to be affluent in gratitude.
Be grateful and be happy.　For myself
If sorrow be my portion, yet shall hope
That springs from sorrow and aspires to Heaven
Be with me still.　　　.　　　.　　　.

  .　　.　　.　　.　　.　　.　　.　　.

    Elgiva.   Oh Leolf, Leolf,
So tender, so severe!　　.　　.　　.
    Leolf.   Mistake me not;
I would not be unjust.　Our lives were linked
By one misfortune and a double fault;
It was my folly to have fixed my hopes
Upon the fruitage of a budding heart;
It was your fault,—the lighter fault by far,—
Being the bud to seem to be the berry.
The first inconstancy of unripe years
Is nature's error on the way to truth.

Happily, in my case, it was the berry which had
seemed to be the bud.

CHAPTER XIV.

LORD ABERDEEN AND MR. GLADSTONE—SCHEME FOR A LITERARY
INSTITUTE—LITERARY PENSIONS—LORD ABERDEEN IS SUCCEEDED
BY LORD GLENELG AND MR. HAY BY MR. STEPHEN—JAMES
SPEDDING IN THE COLONIAL OFFICE—HIS WAYS AND WORKS—
HIS BACON AND HIS SONNET—MR. MANNING (NOW ARCHBISHOP
OF WESTMINSTER) RESIGNS HIS JUNIOR CLERKSHIP.

ANNO DOM. 1834-38.   ANNO ÆT. 34-38.

A MONTH after I had set to work upon ' Edwin the
Fair,' an official task was provided for me which my
father thought ' would afford me as much interest
with less fatigue.'   But before I proceed, I must
bring up to date the history of my office, as Sterne
does that of the kitchen and Rapin that of the
church.

I have said that in 1834 Mr. Spring Rice was
succeeded in the post of Secretary of State for the
Colonies by the Earl of Aberdeen.   From no one of
the twenty-six Secretaries of State under whom I
have served have I met with more kindness and consideration than from Lord Aberdeen, and to none
have I been able to give in return for kindness,—or
rather not in return for it, since what I have given
must have been given whether for value received or

not,—a larger measure of admiration,—due for his absolute simplicity and singleness of character, kept pure by reason of its inherent strength through a long political life, and combined with no ordinary measure of political sagacity and prudence, and with high literary cultivation. It was the last probably which brought us into more intimate relations than public business alone could have generated.

Lord Brougham, when Chancellor, had written to Southey to ask his opinion as to what could be done by the Government to promote the interests of literature. Southey's reply indicated a distrust of Brougham's sincerity, and merely glanced at the possibility of some Government not preoccupied like the then existing one with the more urgent task of saving the country from dangers they themselves had created, undertaking to devise some scheme by which young men, with literary ability, might be enabled to subsist, and spared the temptation of pandering to the appetite of the populace for seditious and inflammatory writings. Southey had sent me a copy of the correspondence, which I had kept ; and I showed it to Lord Aberdeen, and he to Sir R. Peel. They took up the subject, and I was asked to con-sider whether something could not be done in the direction to which Southey had pointed.

I accordingly produced a scheme, founded partly upon one of which Southey's letter had given a sketch, partly upon the model of the French Institute, and partly upon notions of my own. The British

Institute was to be divided into four Academies ; 1st.
Physics and Mathematics ; 2nd. Moral and Political
Science ; 3rd. General Literature ; 4th. Classics
and Antiquarian Learning :—which were to consist
each of eight salaried and four honorary members,
those under thirty years of age receiving 200l. a-year,
those above thirty receiving 500l., and one, as president, receiving 800l.   The members were to be, at
the inchoation of the bodies, named by the Crown,
and vacancies thereafter to be filled alternately by
the Crown's selection from three candidates chosen
by the Academy, and by the Academy's selection
from three candidates chosen by the Crown.   The
paper I wrote enters at some length into the
grounds and pleas for establishing such an institute,
and the difficulties and objections which would
have to be encountered.   It was regarded with some
favour.

'Lord A.,' I wrote to my mother, 'thought it
would be as likely to succeed as any other measure
they might bring forward ; but (speaking the day
after the division on the Speakership), he added that
he did not know what the measure was in which they
were not likely to be defeated.   However, he said,
Peel would keep it by him in case of the times
affording an opportunity.'

The Government lasted, I think, only till the
April following ; and all that Sir Robert could do
was to appropriate to literature the annual 1,200l.
already on the Civil List for pensions to be granted

by the Crown. I was asked to suggest the names of literary men to whom pensions should be offered.

Southey was, of course, the one who stood first ; but, oddly enough, a personal friend of his own in the Cabinet raised the question whether the grant of a pension to him would not expose the Government to violent attacks in the House of Commons. On learning this I had recourse to Mr. Spring Rice, who assured me that not only he would not oppose such a grant, but he ' would fight for it if it were against all the devils in the Domdaniel caverns ; ' [1] and he added that he could answer for his party in the House being with him. Sir Robert Peel, being in constant expectation of the fall of his Government, reserved any announcement of the pension till its last days, and in the meantime wrote to Mr. Southey, to offer him a baronetcy, and to ask in what way he could assist him, and was answered in the admirable and touching letter now published in ' Southey's Life and Correspondence,' wherein he explains his pecuniary circumstances, and how utterly unbecoming it would be in him to accept the baronetcy, and adverting to the shock he had sustained by the insanity of his wife, forbodes the loss of his own faculties, hitherto almost the sole support of his family, and intimates that a pension would be the only way of helping him ; and that though, as he conceived, this way could not be thought of, under

[1] See Southey's ' Thalaba.'

present circumstances, as a boon to himself individually, yet it might perhaps be practicable as part of a general plan for the encouragement of literature.

The pension, however, had already been resolved upon and the warrant signed. The amount was 300*l.* per annum. In the course of a year or two Southey's forebodings came true; a softening of the brain crept upon him; and in 1839 his decaying powers sank into total imbecility. From that time to his death in 1843 the pension afforded the family a chief means of support. After his death they were provided for by the produce of life assurances.

I felt grateful to Lord Aberdeen for the part he had taken in this matter, and for much besides; and I was very sorry that my official connection with him came so soon to an end. Our friendly intercourse continued as long as he lived.

During the few months—from January to April, 1835—for which Lord Aberdeen continued Secretary for the Colonies, Mr. Gladstone, then first entering upon official life, was Under Secretary.

'I rather like Gladstone,' I wrote, on making his acquaintance; 'but he is said to have more of the devil in him than appears—in a virtuous way, that is —only self-willed. He may be all the more useful here for that.'

His amiable manner and looks deluded Sir James Stephen, who said that, for success in political life, he wanted pugnacity!

By the time that he quitted office (in April), I had of course come to know more about him, and what I said then was:—

'Gladstone left with us a paper on Negro Education, which confirmed me in the impression that he is a very considerable man,—by far the most so of any man I have seen amongst our rising statesmen. He has, together with his abilities, great strength of character and excellent dispositions.'

Soon after Lord Aberdeen had entered the office he had said to Charles Greville that he was ashamed to see me there. I suppose because it was in the position of a clerk. I have never myself felt that I was misplaced in that position; and when that of Under Secretary of State was offered me in 1847, it was without any feeling of regret that I refused it. Acting under men of the order of those under whom it was my fortune to act after the first few years of my service, subordination presented no difficulties (according to my observation of life, subordination comes more easily to men—at least to gentlemen— than the exercise of authority does); and even in a political career, unless as First Minister, subordination would still have been part and lot of the life; whilst that life would have been less suited to me, and would probably have afforded me, on the whole and in and out of office, no larger opportunities for doing the State some service than I enjoyed during the unbroken forty-eight years for which I served as a clerk.

Acting according to this view, when Greville told me in January, 1835, that 'if the present Government were to subsist for a while, they would wish to place me in some more prominent position,' a letter to my mother says :—

' I gave him to understand that I did not wish to be placed in any situation which would imply more activity than I am called upon to exercise where I am ; and, indeed, it would be difficult for the Government, in these days of no sinecures, to better my condition in my own estimation.'

And looking back upon my life over an interval of forty years, if political office was in contemplation, I cannot think that I was wrong. Strong health and an independent fortune would have made more of a doubt ; but even with those elements to vary the question, I think the answer should have been the same. I had no strong political opinions, nor had I any special aptitude for political life ; and I have no reason to suppose that any place I might have occupied in it has not been better filled by others. Even had it been otherwise, every year of many years has detracted from the value of individual mind and character in a political career, whilst adding to the demand for co-operation, compromise, and sub-serviency to popular impulse or opinion ; and the mere capable and flexible tactician—the Lord Palmer-ston of the day—could hold his ground as well as the man of large intellect and devoted patriotism—the man who, in this month of April, 1873, has just remounted to his uncertain seat, after having been upset into the ditch upon a question of third-rate importance.

With every year, moreover, the labours and troubles and trials of political life have increased and multiplied ; and what Sir Philip Sidney says to Lord Brooke in Landor's 'Imaginary Conversation,' if true of other times, is more eminently true of these :—

'How many who have abandoned for public life the studies of philosophy and poetry, may be compared to brooks and rivers which, in the beginning of their course, have assuaged our thirst and have invited us to tranquillity by their bright resemblance of it, and which afterwards partake the nature of that vast body whereinto they run,—its dreariness, its bitterness, its foam, its storms, its everlasting noise and commotion.'

In April, 1835, Lord Aberdeen was succeeded by Lord Glenelg. This change brought about the downfall of our then permanent Under Secretary, Mr. Robert William Hay. He was almost the only man I have served under who was disagreeable to me. In the early days of my acquaintance with Sydney Smith, I think it was the first time I saw him, he called upon me at the Colonial Office, and, probably by way of finding something to say, observed that Mr. Hay was a very agreeable man. I replied,— 'Perhaps so, but I have a personal dislike to him.' The old man of the world laughed at my frankness, and, exchanging the word 'dislike' for 'hatred,' made the most of it in society.

The object of my dislike was now on the point of being removed out of my way. His politics were Conservative; he lived much with Conservative politicians, and Lord Melbourne's Government did not like him any better than I did. Whilst his friends were in office he had obtained a grant of a dormant retiring pension, to be enjoyed, he conceived, whenever it should please him to retire. Lord Melbourne's Government said it should be whenever it pleased *them*; and that was at once. He was certainly not equal to the office he held; and, in point of fact, the duties of it had always been performed by others, and the far greater portion of them by Sir James Stephen.

Lord Glenelg was a friend of Stephen's; but he was far from sharing the desire of his colleagues to force Hay into retirement and put Stephen in his place. He was an amiable man and exceedingly averse from strong measures; and, moreover, a brother-in-law of his was Under Secretary for the Home Department, and he was averse from a precedent for dealing with such offices as if held by a terminable tenure. Stephen insisted that, as he had done Hay's work for many years, if he was not to have the office, he ought to have the retiring pension; and he refused to do Hay's work any longer if this was denied. Mr. Hay, who was probably unaware to what extent the Government was a party to what was going on, waited upon Lord Melbourne to complain of the course Stephen was taking, and having described what he suspected it to be, asked if it was not plain that Stephen's design was to supplant him in his office. All the answer he got from Lord Melbourne was, 'It looks devilish like it.' Lord Glenelg, however, still hung back, and for some days found a refuge from the painful dilemma in which he was placed by shutting himself up in his house. But this, alas! could be but a temporary resource; his colleagues were inexorable; and in the end Mr. Hay took his departure and Stephen reigned in his stead.

For the four or five years for which Lord Glenelg held the seals,—indeed for many other years before and after,—Stephen virtually ruled the Colonial Empire. The result to me was a considerable acquisition of leisure time. He had an enormous appetite for work, and I almost think he preferred to engross it into his own hands and not to be much helped; and I, for my part, could make him perfectly welcome to any amount of it that passed away from me.

One of the first measures which he recommended to Lord Glenelg was to offer me the Government of Upper Canada. I wavered for a moment, thinking I might have a quieter life there than I had lately had in London. My father, with the generosity which was natural to him, was ready to make small account of his own feelings in such a separation; but the knowledge of what his feelings would be was scarcely required to turn the balance, and I decided against it.

At this time I obtained another relief, and in obtaining it obtained a friend for life. James Spedding was the younger son of a Cumberland squire who had been a friend of my father's in former, though I think they had not met in latter days. In the notes to 'Van Artevelde' I had quoted a passage from an admirable speech of his spoken in a debating club at Cambridge when he was an undergraduate. This led to my making his acquaintance ; and when some very laborious business of detail had to be executed, I obtained authority to offer him the employment with a remuneration of 150*l.* a year. He was in a difficulty at the time about the choice of a profession, and feeling that a life without business and occupation of some kind was dangerous, was glad to accept this employment as one which might answer the purpose well enough, if he proved suited to it, and if not might be relinquished without difficulty and exchanged for some other. I wrote to Mr. Southey, 24th January, 1836 :—

' Spedding has been and will be invaluable, and they owe me much for him. He is regarded on all hands, not only as a man of first rate capacity, but as having quite a genius for business. I, for my part, have never seen anything like him in business on this side Stephen. . . . When I contemplate the easy labours of Stephen and one or two others. I am disposed to think that there are giants in *these* days.'

For six years Spedding worked away with universal approbation, and all this time he would have been willing to accept a post of précis-writer with 300*l.* a year, or any other such recognised position, and attach himself permanently to the office. But none such was placed at his disposal. Stephen had once said to me, when advising me to depend upon the public and upon literature for advancement, and not upon the Government,—' You may write off the first joint of your fingers for them, and then you may write off the second joint, and all that they will say of you is, " What a remarkably short-fingered man ! " '

They did not say this of Spedding, but they did nothing for him, and he took the opportunity of the Whig Government going out in 1841 to give up his employment. He then applied himself to edit the works and vindicate the fame of Lord Bacon. In 1847, on Sir James Stephen's retirement, the office of Under Secretary of State, with 2,000*l.* a year, was offered to him by Lord Grey, before it was offered to me, and he could not be induced to accept it. He could not be brought to believe, what no one else doubted, that he was equal to the duties.

Be this as it may, the fact that the man, being well known and close at hand for six years, who could have been had for 300*l.* a year in 1841, should have been let slip, though he was thought worth 2,000*l.* a year in 1847, if not a rare, is a clear example

of the little heed given by the Government of this
country to the choice and use of instruments.

It was at my suggestion that the offer was made ;
but I am not sorry that it was declined. He has
devoted his singular abilities and his infinite industry
in research, during a long life, to a great cause, and
Lord Bacon will become known to posterity, gradually
perhaps but surely, as the man that he truly was,—
illustrious beyond all others except Shakespeare in
his intellect, and with whatever infirmities, still not
less than noble in his moral mind.

In Spedding, who seemed to us in the Colonial
Office the most mild and imperturbable of men, the
detractors of Lord Bacon had awakened a passion of
indignation the capability for which even those who
knew him more than superficially could scarcely have
believed to be lying hidden in his heart. In the
course of a search amongst old papers, I have come
upon a sonnet and a letter, in which the passion finds
a language to express itself both in prose and verse.
The letter speaks of the sonnet :—‘ It sprang out of
a very strong emotion that used to visit me from
time to time, and from the occasional agitation of
which I am not yet secure. And the emotion is
roused as often as I consider what kind of creatures
they are who so complacently take it for granted that
they are nobler beings than Bacon—being as I believe
the beggarliest souls that have been gifted with the
faculty of expressing themselves—insomuch that if
the administration of the divine judgments were

deputed to me for half an hour, I think I would employ it in making the scales fall from their eyes, and letting them see and understand Bacon as he was, and themselves as they are. The contemplation of the two for half an hour would at least leave them speechless. My only doubt is whether any power whatever could enable them to understand either his greatness or their own littleness without making them over again quite new, which would be more trouble than they are worth. Well then, if this is what ought to be done, why is it not done? Why are these people permitted to go on strutting and moralising and making the angels weep, when a sudden gift of insight into themselves would make them go and hide out of the way? I can think of no likelier reason than that Bacon himself would be sorry that any of those who were once his fellow-creatures should suffer such a punishment on his account. And it was to relieve myself from the pressure of this thought (which, as you may see, is apt to put me out of my proprieties) by shutting it up in a sonnet that I began. . . .'

And then he proceeds to say how he conceives that he had ended in a failure. But the truth is that from beginning to end the sonnet is one of Miltonic force and fervour, and here it is :

When I have heard sleek worldlings quote thy name
And sigh o'er great parts gone in evil ways,
And thank the God they serve on Sabbath days
That they are not as thou, meek Verulam,

> Then have I marvelled that the searching flame
> Lingered in God's uplifted hand which lays
> The filmed bosom bare to its own gaze
> And makes men die with horror of their shame :
> But when I thought how humbly thou didst walk
> On earth,—how kiss that merciless rod,—I said
> Surely 'twas thy prevailing voice that prayed
> For patience with those men and their rash talk,
> Because they knew thy deeds but not thy heart,
> And who knows partly can but judge in part.

It was not on one subject only that Spedding could be impassioned. There is rather a wide range between Lord Bacon and Jenny Lind, but I find a letter (2nd September, 1847) in which he reproves me for not going to hear that celebrated songstress sing :—'I cannot approve of your conduct with regard to Jenny Lind. . . . The experiment might have failed, but it was worth trying. Failing, it would only have spoiled an evening ; succeeding, it would have enriched a life. Heaven has never been so opened in my time. I was reading the " Winter's Tale " the other day, and was surprised to observe how like Perdita had grown to Jenny Lind since I last saw her.' This was not the enthusiasm of a person devoted to music. I had never known, nor I think had anyone else, that he cared for music at all.

James Spedding was well quit of the Colonial Office. His friends, it is true, were highly dissatisfied with his decision to refuse the office of Under Secretary of State ; but he maintained that he knew himself and his deficiencies better than they ; and no doubt he did know what were the tasks that suited him best.   He observed, with the quiet humour which was characteristic of him, that ' it was fortunate *he* was by when the decision was taken.'   The work to which he gave his life is a work of great labour, a work of great love, and a work which will be a lantern unto the feet and a light unto the paths of many generations of mankind,—of as many as shall care to look back to the greatest secondary cause of their being what, in the progress of science and discovery, they shall have become.

This loss of Spedding was not the end of our losses.   I wrote to my father in August, 1839, from the Colonial Office :—' Another of our very best men [1] will leave us in a few weeks for Canada, in the capacity of Secretary to Poulett Thomson, who (strange to say !) is going there as Governor-General, with all sorts of powers, and probably with a peerage, " Levia sursum ! " ' [2]

Some years before, another great fish had been caught and let go.   The present Archbishop of Westminster, Cardinal Manning, was for a short time a junior clerk in the Colonial Office.   But him it might not have been easy to retain upon any terms. He is a man of dignified and graceful manners, with what I should call, though I hardly know on what

---

[1] He who is now Sir Thomas Clinton Murdoch.

[2] This disparagement does no credit to my judgment of men.   I believe Lord Sydenham did his work exceedingly well.

grounds, a mediæval countenance, austere but gentle,
and some qualities which have deservedly given him
a personal influence, as well as an ecclesiastical pre-
eminence, in the Church to which he was converted,
though there is one party in it to which he is anything but acceptable. Indeed, it has been said by a
cynical member of that Church that the greatest
misfortune it has suffered in this century was the
death of *Mrs.* Manning. After many a long year he
and I met once more I passed a few months in
London in the winter of 1872, and in a letter to
Lord Blachford of November in that year I wrote :—
' He sent me a message of remembrance when he heard
we were in London and I went to see him. He was
a sight to see—much changed from his former face
—most meagre and strangely mediæval, and the
austerity had lost the sweetness which went with it
formerly, though still there was nothing ungentle.
He considers that Aubrey de Vere has at last produced
a great work. He had not thought so highly as I
did of Aubrey's poetry before " The Legends of St.
Patrick." '

From Lord Glenelg's accession to office in 1835
to the summer of 1838, what with the aid given by
Spedding and the voracious ways of Stephen, I doubt
whether my official employments were much of a
burthen to me. But, in 1838, a critical period had
arrived for the negro populations of the West Indies ;
and as the sugar colonies were my special charge, my
duties in 1838-9 came to be of a more engrossing
character.

Since the questions with which I had to deal are of some historical interest and importance, and what took place is, in my opinion, instructive, as showing in what manner and with what consequences our Colonial policy becomes entangled with our system of government by political parties at home, I shall venture, in this instance, to do more than glance at my operations in the Colonial Office ; and I propose to treat of the subject at some length.   Indeed, what I did is entitled to a prominent place in my life on its official side, being the only instance in which, if I did not singly and absolutely originate (which I rather think I did), I was, at all events, chiefly instrumental in originating, a measure of importance in Home as well as in Colonial politics ; inasmuch as the way in which it was dealt with in the Cabinet and in Parliament proved vital to the existence of the Government.   When I say vital I mean mortal.

CHAPTER XV.

TRANSITION OF THE NEGROES FROM APPRENTICESHIP INTO FREEDOM —MEASURE FOR THEIR WELFARE PROPOUNDED AND MUTILATED IN THE CABINET AND DEFEATED BY SIR R. PEEL IN THE HOUSE OF COMMONS—LORD MELBOURNE'S GOVERNMENT RESIGNS : IT IS RECONSTITUTED, BUT THE MEASURE IS GONE—THE NEGROES SUFFER THE CONSEQUENCES FOR TWENTY-SIX YEARS.

ANNO DOM. 1838-39.   ANNO ÆT. 38-39.

IN MAY, 1838, I wrote to my father that I was in doubt whether I could take any holidays in that year, and enclosed an official minute addressed to me and my answer to it by way of explanation, adding, —' The task proposed to me was one which I could not, with a good conscience, consider myself at liberty to decline or devolve. It is, in fact, that of preparing the West Indies for the transition from apprenticeship to freedom.'

The six years' apprenticeship, commenced under the Imperial Abolition of Slavery Act on the 1st August, 1834, had no sooner been established than its inherent and incurable evils began to be developed. The stipendiary justices sent out from England, if they could not prevent, could materially mitigate and control, the oppression of the negroes by their masters, so far as that oppression was exercised in the exaction of labour ; but the master so controlled regarded the amount of labour exacted as ruinously insufficient.   On the other hand, the planters, in their capacity of local justices, could perpetrate all manner of cruelty and wrong under the shelter of local laws, —sending men and women to their horribly over-crowded prisons, to be put on the treadmill and flogged without mercy upon the flimsiest pretexts. The superior courts were partisans of slavery ; the legislatures were worse than the judicatures ; all were embittered and enraged against the negroes and their friends, and the police were fit agents for giving effect to the passions of their employers.

The Anti-Slavery party in this country renewed their agitation, and on the 11th April, 1838, an Act was passed by Parliament (1 Vic., c. 19) to amend the Act for the Abolition of Slavery, the object of which was to remove various evils and abuses in the apprenticeship system for which no remedies could be obtained from the local legislatures ; and another Act was passed to enable the Crown to shut up such of the West Indian prisons as might be found unfit for use, and thereby compel the legislatures to provide others.

The result was more anger than ever on the part of the Jamaica Assembly, manifested by a protest in which they grossly insulted both Houses of Parliament, and indeed the English nation. The Governor, an excellent old soldier, Sir Lionel Smith (described

by the Duke of Wellington in a private letter to the
Secretary of State as fit for any situation in which he
could be placed), wrote confidentially to Lord Glenelg,
17th May, 1838 :—‘It is impossible for any one to
answer for the conduct of the House of Assembly.
Many are there in the island who would be delighted
to get up an insurrection for the pleasure of destroying
the negroes and missionaries. They are, in fact, mad.
I have received a letter from a magistrate, telling me
that some militia officers threaten, if I do not call
out the militia, that they will assemble of their own
accord ; but for what I know not. . . . Also that I
am to be shot. I mention these silly things to your
Lordship to show some of the consequences of a
seditious press upon the minds of the people.’

By this time the apprenticeship had become intolerable to all parties ; the dangers resulting from it
were manifest ; one local legislature—that of Antigua
—had renounced it from the beginning; several others
had done so after experience of it ; and the Jamaica
Assembly itself, in June, 1838, came to the same
conclusion, and passed an Act under which final
emancipation was to take effect on the 1st August
following, instead of the 1st August, 1840.

It was now more urgently necessary than ever
that laws should be enacted to provide for the exigencies of the new state of society, and that laws
should be repealed which were utterly at variance
with the liberty of the subject.

How little the liberty of the subject was provided

for by the mere abolition of prædial servitude, is
shown by an article written by James Spedding in
the 'Edinourgh Review' for July, 1839. 'A single
illustration will be sufficient. The following case
may occur at any time, may be occurring whilst we
write. . . . The great mass of the labourers are
tenants at will of their former masters and have no
homes but such as belong to them. The manager
calls on them to enter into a contract involving heavy
duties and small pay and lasting for a long time. If
they consent they bind themselves to a bad bargain,
and in case of any kind of failure to fulfil the entire
conditions of it, *which need not be expressed in writing*,
they may be deprived of all their wages, or imprisoned
for three months in a Jamaica prison, at the discretion of any justice of the peace. If they refuse, they
are liable, at the discretion of any two justices, to be
summarily ejected from the estate. Being ejected,
they may be brought before the nearest justice as
vagrants wandering abroad . . . and sentenced to
hard labour in the house of correction for six months
. . . they may besides, be they males or females,
receive thirty-nine lashes.'

I had written in the summer of 1838, four long
papers on the preparatory measures proper to be
taken by the Government. My views had met with
the concurrence of every one in the Colonial Office
and had been brought before the Government. I
have no copies of them and no recollection of their
substance ; but in October, it appears I was not

content with the course of action which the Government was contemplating, and on the 24th of that month I wrote on the subject to Mr. Stephen:—

'. . . I cannot help expressing to you privately my persuasion that the Government is in danger of falling into a system of erroneous policy on this question and creating great and continual discontent to no purpose. What they are doing and about to do is, in fact, a repetition of the policy pursued from 1823 to 1834, on Slave melioration, and I think the experience of the effects of that policy, contrasted with the experience of the effects of reversing it which we have had subsequently, should teach us a different lesson. I observe, indeed, that Lord Howick[1] considers the question at issue to be now of a different character, and the position of the Government with the Assemblies to be totally altered, insomuch as the interests of the planters are now identified with the general interest, and they must be equally desirous with the Government that order, industry and contentment should prevail. So far forth, it is true there is a common object; and it may be likewise true that the liberal and protective laws which the Government would desire to establish would be the best means of attaining it. But the planters would not see this. I believe that to have been true which was so often urged, that many of the meliorating laws proposed from 1823 to 1834 would have

---

[1] Lord Howick was in the Cabinet, but not at this time in the Colonial Office.

been equally for the interest of the planter and of the slave. But these laws were as much resisted by the Assemblies as those which were for the interest of the slaves solely. Liberality, charity, forbearance, equal dealing, &c., would be, no doubt, like honesty, the best policy in the present circumstances of the planters ; but it is nevertheless certain that this is not the policy by which their legislation will be guided, and we have already had specimens, in the St. Vincent's Vagrancy and Contract for Service Acts, that every effort will be made to enact laws at direct variance with this policy ; and it may be reasonably feared that all persuasion to the contrary will be of no more avail than the annual meliorating circulars and the daily animadversions on acts of assembly in the previous controversy of ten years long. Now I cannot but think, that if we are to learn anything from experience, it should be this :— That assuming the objects of the Government to be necessary to the establishment of the liberty and promotion of the industry of the negroes, and that the habits and prejudices, if not the interests of the planters, are strongly opposed to them, then the only method of accomplishing them effectually and completely, and the best method as regards irritation and discontent, will be by exerting at once and conclusively, a power which shall overrule all opposition and set the question at rest. The persuasory and recommendatory process may appear to be the more conciliatory at first ; but I am convinced that the appearance is fallacious. The West Indian legislatures have neither the will nor the skill to make such laws as you want made ; and they cannot be converted on the point of willingness, and they will not be instructed. You have Acts sent you which *mean* a great deal of mischief, and which, for want of legal knowledge and technical ingenuity, may do a great deal that was not meant. You object and advise and suspend the Queen's decision, —and is there one case in ten, in which an Assembly has been either conciliated or brought to reason by such a process? Is not neglect at the best, or in the case of the most important Colonies, anger and contumely, the ordinary result ? . . . This process, then, leads to irritation in detail, a slow, never-ending, rankling quarrel. . . . It may be remarked that the Assemblies have taken very quietly every actual exercise of supreme authority by Parliamentary legislation, inasmuch as it was done and there was no help for it; but have resented most bitterly every recommendation of the Government by the adoption of which they might have averted Parliamentary interference : and nothing has kept them in a more implacable state of hostility than that constant setting up and knocking down of their authority which has been misdeemed a system of conciliation. There was, in truth, nothing . of the substance of conciliation about it ; and the mere phrases and outward show were regarded as nothing better than a cool attempt to play upon their credulity.

They were told that the utmost respect was entertained for their constitutional privileges of legislation, and they were respectfully advised to legislate in this way or that, with a sufficient intimation at the same time, that if they were to legislate much otherwise they might just as well not legislate at all, for their Acts would be disallowed. The result almost always was that they did nothing, that their functions were paralysed and their passions kept in a state of great activity. . . .'

What I proposed at this time was that Parliament should be asked to enact the laws which the Assemblies refused to enact.

But before the year was out, the Jamaica Assembly had taken a further step; and in resentment of the interference already exercised by Parliament, and in anticipation of further interference, had absolutely refused to do business; whilst the Governor reported that the small owners and overseers 'might irritate and persecute the peaceable negroes into resistance,' endeavouring 'to make out a case for calling out the militia,' which militia he describes as 'lawless,' and 'officered by men who have been generally slaveholders and are now burning with hatred and vengeance against the negroes for being free.' Under these circumstances measures of a more comprehensive character than had been hitherto contemplated seemed to be required : and on the 14th January, 1839, a decision had been arrived at in the department, and I drew up a Minute (with a

voluminous appendix) for submission to the Cabinet
by Lord Glenelg, 'on the course to be taken with
the West Indian Assemblies.' The main drift of it
may be gathered from the following extracts :—

' The exigency now created unavoidably brings
under the view of the Government the question
whether the West Indian Assemblies be or be not,
by their constitution and the nature of the societies
for which they legislate, absolutely incompetent and
unfit to deal with the new state of things and to provide for the peace and well-being of Her Majesty's
subjects in those parts. And as the immediate crisis
arises in Jamaica, and that island from its magnitude
must carry the whole question along with it, it will
be convenient to consider the subject with reference
to Jamaica individually so far as regards any specific
circumstances of the case. But the general features
of society are the same throughout the West Indies,
and they present views which cover the whole of the
question.

' The first inquiry which presents itself is, what
field or basis for a really representative system is
to be found in the West Indian communities ; and
whether it is in the nature of things that the elements
of which they are constituted can furnish one ? Let
the society of Jamaica be taken for an example—
320,000 black people just emancipated, still in the
depths of ignorance and by their African temperament highly excitable; about 28,000 people partly
coloured, partly black, whose freedom is of earlier

date than that of the emancipated class, of whom
many may have property, but so few are decently
educated that it was thought by the Governor that
their own friends would not wish to see the Assembly
chiefly composed of them; and lastly, 9,000 Whites
possessed by all the passions and the inveterate
prejudices growing out of the slave system. Throw
these elements into what forms or combinations we
will, is it possible to bring out of them anything like
a representative system properly so called? The
Blacks have neither property nor knowledge, and
cannot therefore have political power, or communicate it through any exercise of the rights of a constituency. Yet they are the mass of the people, and
if there is to be any representation it ought to be
their interests mainly that are represented. The
coloured class have some property and such a portion
of knowledge as may just enable them to possess
political influence, but hardly to make a good use of
it ; and though they have no good will to the Whites,
yet are they still worse affected towards the Blacks;
and standing between two classes to which they are
equally akin, they have naturally shown themselves
disposed to make an alliance with the dominant and
aristocratic class, and to join them in trampling upon
the Blacks to whom they feel it to be their shame
and misfortune to be allied in blood. There are, it
is believed, twelve coloured members of Assembly,
and the Governor reports that out of these there
are only three who did not go over to the Whites

and desert the Government in the recent divisions.
The obvious truth is that every attempt at a
representative system in such a community must
result in an oligarchy. Such the Assembly of
Jamaica always has been, now is, and will inevitably
continue to be, until the mass of the population
shall have been educated and raised in the scale of
society.'

  .   .   .   .   .   .

'Such being the organisation of this body, it is
important to observe that the structure of the society
affording no support to the Crown either from an
extended public opinion (which has no existence) or
from proprietary connection with the Government,
the royal authority in Jamaica resolves itself into the
power of imposing inaction by the veto. The Crown
in former times had no adequate object to gain by
engaging in struggles in which the Assembly was
always prepared to·go to the extreme of stopping
the supplies, and the result was the usurpation by
the Assembly of the chief administrative as well as
legislative powers of the State. Thus (under the
authority either of its own resolutions or of acts of
the legislature assented to by the Crown in former
times and to which, when renewed, the Crown con-
tinues to assent as a matter of immemorial usage
and necessity) it is accustomed to delegate to committees or commissioners consisting of members of
its own body, some of the most important administrative offices, and especially that of expending the

money voted by itself. Some of these boards and committees sit and exercise their delegated powers in permanent session, notwithstanding prorogation or even dissolution of the body from which their powers are derived. Moreover it is not necessary in the Assembly of Jamaica, as in the House of Commons, that a proposal for a grant of money should come from the Government ; any member of Assembly may propose any grant of money for any purpose. Under this system the levy and expenditure of public money is conducted with a responsibility which travels in a circle amongst a body of forty-four men. The tax levied on the property of the colony, which is chiefly the property of absentees, is paid into the Treasury ; the forty-four vote it away as an Assembly; the same forty-four or any five of them give effect to the expenditure by making contracts and issuing orders, warrants or resolutions ; and the same forty-four, or a quorum of them, act as auditors.

' Looking at the Assembly therefore on the side of financial affairs, it presents the aspect which might be expected in a body representing no considerable class, responsible to none, and mixing executive with legislative functions. We see the virtue of its members corrupted, the revenues of the island diverted from their proper application, and the Government left without the necessary resources for administering justice, spreading instruction, preventing crime, and administering to the public welfare in the most important and vital points ; these objects having been hitherto either scandalously neglected, abusively pursued, or effected, so far as they have been effected at all, at the expense of this country. Although there is hardly an instance of money being granted for any useful object recommended by Her Majesty's Government, the colony is now declared by the Governor to owe about a million of money and to be fast advancing towards bankruptcy.

'But still more important than the point of financial integrity is that of political feeling ; and in this respect the Assembly of Jamaica may be said to be the very result and representative of slavery—proud and stubborn, and at all times inaccessible to any motives connected even with justice or humanity to the negroes, let alone their advancement in civilisation and qualification for civil rights.   Their refusal to do business is, no doubt, founded in reality less on the Parliamentary interference with the prisons, than upon their desire to evade giving an answer to the specific applications about to be made to them for laws of protection for the negroes.

'Now there can hardly be a doubt that these laws themselves are indispensable in the present state of affairs, and that such changes must be made as will admit of their enactment and execution.   But further, there can be as little doubt that the establishment of a governing power consentaneous with the spirit of those laws, and fitted to mould the whole state of things into conformity with that spirit, is the only remedy for the existing discordancy between the old institutions of these colonies and the new rights given to the negroes.

‘ Looking to what the state of society has been in the West Indies, and then looking to what it is to be, it would seem to be an almost necessary *à priori* conclusion that the laws and polity which were adapted to the one state of things cannot be fit for the other. To effect by a force from without the greatest of all social changes,—a change of the most practical and pervasive character, penetrating everywhere and affecting every man's relations with every other man and every hour's transactions,—to force this social change, and yet to leave the political framework of this totally different society the same as it was, would seem, even in a mere theoretical view, to be in the nature of a political solecism. And when we look to the character of the Assembly of Jamaica, and to the fact of their refusing to enact the indispensable measures required at the very outset of the career of improvement, no further confirmation of such a view can be needed ; and it must surely be acknowledged in every quarter, except amongst the resident West India planters, that such a body as this, unfit to exist in any state of society, is eminently disqualified for the great task of educating and improving a people newly born into freedom as it were.

‘ If the abolition of the Assembly is loudly called for by the immediate exigency and urgently demanded also by considerations of general and prospective policy, the present conjuncture offers certainly peculiar facilities for carrying that measure into effect.

'Those who wish to get rid of the Assembly of Jamaica could not desire to see it put itself more imprudently and extravagantly in the wrong than it has done in the last twelve months ; and in the wrong, not only as regards Her Majesty's Government, but also with Parliament, and more especially with the House of Lords, in which House, if in any quarter, it might have hoped to find a few advocates.'

The memorandum quotes resolutions of the Jamaica Assembly, in which the House of Lords is accused of either 'cowardice and imbecility,' or 'fraud and malice,' and the House of Commons of 'perjury' and 'corruption,' and proceeds :—

'It is thus, after treating with insult the first of the two acts of Parliamentary interposition, that they met the second—that about the prisons—with the resolution of obstinate inaction which calls upon the already insulted Parliament to take the matter up : and Her Majesty's Government will now go to a Parliament where (to judge by the divisions of last session even) the Assembly has not a single friend, with an acknowledgment on all sides that a crisis has arrived in which they have no choice but to propose a large and decisive measure.

'But there is another and, in truth, a very serious point of view in which the present moment offers opportunities which might very shortly be irretrievably lost.   It is not impossible, indeed the Governor looks upon it as extremely probable, that in no long time under the operation of the existing ten-pound franchise, and with the facilities which exist for creating fictitious freeholds, every white member may be turned out of the Assembly and the revolution of affairs may bring up suddenly a coloured and black ascendency.

'This would change the complexion of the evil to be dealt with, but not reduce its magnitude.   The mass of the population is, and must long be, ignorant and bedarkened ; and whether the men who sit in the Assembly be white, black, or coloured, they will inevitably be irresponsible and unrepresentative of the interests of the people.   A black oligarchy will certainly oppress a white minority of the people, but it will not protect the population at large ; for no irresponsible oligarchy of any colour will ever do that.

'And in what position would the Government be placed if it had to deal with a black ascendency in the Assembly ?   The people of colour would join either the whites through inclination or the blacks through fear ; and whichever way the coalition might take place, there would be ample ground to apprehend that the inveterate feelings by which the colonists are divided would lead to measures of legislative oppression and, in the end, break out into acts of violence.

'Here, then, would be a new call upon the

Government to arbitrate and protect. And it may be said, perhaps, that the Crown has its veto ; that the legislation of the Assembly is altogether by permission ; that acts of violence and oppression of one class towards another may thus be prevented ; and that the only evil to be feared is that which has been hitherto experienced, namely, a Legislature inoperative to any good purpose.

' On this, however, serious doubts may be suggested, if we are to contemplate a change in the allotment of political power. So long as the Assembly was white and the populace black and coloured, the Crown could quarrel with the Assembly and take the part of the black and coloured classes, without fear of any other consequence than that which actually followed, namely, that the Crown partially neutralised the proceedings of the Assembly, whilst the Assembly paralysed the Government. But if, in the course of time, the black and coloured classes should predominate in the Assembly, and should take measures, as might naturally be expected of them, to oppress the whites ; or if the blacks alone should be paramount and oppress the white and coloured ; that is, if by any change the Crown should be called upon to take part with a numerical minority of the population, against political power *combined* with physical force (instead of, as heretofore, *opposed* to it)—against a black or coloured interest in the Assembly, backed by the black or coloured population of the island— then the quarrel between the Government and the

Jamaica Assembly would be totally different in its features from those we have been accustomed to, and of a far more dangerous character.

'But if we are looking to the establishment of a polity in Jamaica which shall be adapted to the circumstances of the to come, years we must contemplate the possibility of having to thwart the coloured and black interest as well as the white ; we must expect the oppresseb to decome the oppressor in his turn ; we must anticipate that new powers will be used with little moderation, and that the gratitude of a people to a Government for rights conceded and benefits conferred will not last longer than other popular sentiments, or constitute a tie of such strength as to control accruing influences and the passions of the day. There is perhaps no contingency which the Government of this country should more earnestly deprecate than one which might bring them, from being the allies and advocates of the black and coloured classes, into a relation of opposition and resistance to them ; and yet if that ignorant, prejudiced, excitable, and relatively numerous people should jump into exercise of political functions for which they are unfit, in a state of society which requires much legislative management, contingencies of this kind are by no means to be regarded as of improbable occurrence.

'And if by a very probable progress of events, a black or coloured ascendency were once established, would the Government be enabled, as now, to command an undivided support in this country for measures of control? Would auditories in Exeter Hall sympathise with oppressed *Whites?* or would it be believed that black or coloured representatives would be guilty of abuse, malversation, or contumacious refusals of supplies? And if the Government would be likely to obtain but a doubtful adherency to measures for the control of such an Assembly, still less could it rely upon finding any support in going to Parliament for its abolition.

'It is at the present moment therefore, if ever, that the Assembly can be got rid of. It is perhaps itself aware that a black ascendency may possibly impend; and this may account in part for the apparent rashness with which it seems almost to court a death-blow at the hands of the Government.'

The memorandum concludes by proposing that the Government should apply to Parliament for the abolition of the Assemblies and the substitution of Legislatures in the chartered colonies based on the model of the Legislatures already existing in the Crown Colonies, in which the power of the Crown was paramount.

The memorandum was 'circulated' as it is called, *i.e.* sent round to each Minister; and Lord Melbourne expressed his concurrence in it. After the circulation I met Lord Howick in society. To his question whether it was not I who had written the paper, I answered I did not know why he should think so;

and he rejoined, 'I am only sure of one thing, that it is *not* Glenelg's.'

Lord Howick was entirely with me in the matter; but unfortunately it devolved upon Lord Glenelg to bring it before the Cabinet. He read my paper to his colleagues, and three Cabinets were held upon it. The measure it proposed was warmly advocated by some of the Ministers, but I have reason to know that Lord Glenelg's support of his adopted child was but faint-hearted, and in the end its adversaries prevailed to the extent of reducing it to a measure for suspending the Jamaica Assembly during five years (or even a less term, for the Government seems to have intimated that the term might be curtailed in Committee) instead of abolishing all the West Indian Assemblies and substituting Crown Colony Councils.

This was fatal. The justification of the measure lay in the total unfitness of such bodies as the Assemblies, whether in Jamaica or elsewhere, and whether during or after five years or any other number of years, to legislate for communities of freed negroes. In cutting away half the measure, —indeed far more than half—the Cabinet had cut away the whole of the principle on which it was founded. Sir Robert Peel led the opposition in the House of Commons; the majority for the Bill was no more than five; and on the day following (7th May, 1839) the Government quitted office.

It is, no doubt, an evil incident to our form of government that half measures are often the only measures that can be carried through Parliament; but the habit of halving measures is not a wholesome habit for Cabinets to acquire; and in this instance it was the opinion of one of the most distinguished members of the Cabinet that if the measure had not been halved it would have been carried.

The fate of the measure is instructive, as showing the occasional effect of our system of party government upon the welfare of our Colonial dependencies. Sir Robert Peel and his party threw out the Government (to very little purpose, as it proved, for Sir Robert met with what he considered an insuperable difficulty in forming another); and the well-being of about a million negroes was sacrificed for a term of about six-and-twenty years. Corruption, malversation, waste, and ruin went on in Jamaica and elsewhere. No provision was made for the due administration of justice or an efficient police; none for securing to the negro the fruits of his industry, if industrious; none for his education; none for saving him from the consequences of vagrancy and squatting on unoccupied lands, in barbarous solitudes, when driven from the plantations by the conduct of the planters: the docile and grateful generation of negroes that had worshipped God and the missionaries passed away; new and inferior missionaries had to beg their bread from flocks which gave them a beggarly return, and indeed regarded them as little better than beggars; wild black missionaries broke into the fold, and, under the name of revivalists, led roving multitudes of negroes into an extravagance of debauchery compared with which their ordinary condition of concubinage was decent and respectable ; roving gàngs of another kind lived by plundering the provision grounds of their fellows, who had no resource but to rove and plunder in their turn ; political agitators of the mixed blood arose and pointed to Hayti ; plots were formed for slaughtering the planters and taking possession of the plantations ; companies of negroes were secretly embodied and drilled under black leaders in the remote and mountainous districts ; and at length, in October 1865, the blow was struck in St. Thomas'-in-the-East which was designed to raise the whole black population of Jamaica in revolt and exterminate the whites. Twenty-six magistrates and others, assembled with other persons in sessions, saw large bodies of the negroes march down upon them in military array, and having no means of defence, eighteen were killed in cold blood, and thirty-one wounded, of whom I think some died of their wounds. It so happened that Mr. Eyre, the Governor of the colony, though a civilian, was a man with a military faculty ; and by the exercise of his gifts of this kind with military promptitude and decision, he contrived to cut off the communication of the rebels with their friends in the northern and western districts, and very speedily to crush them within their own.

The negro population throughout the colony was

intimidated, and peace was restored. But the Assembly which had been preserved in 1839 for twenty-six years more of misrule, was frightened *into* its senses at the state of things it had brought to pass, and voluntarily put an end to its existence.[1]

Thus, in about the term of one generation, Sir Robert Peel's error, following on the half-and-half policy of Lord Melbourne's Cabinet, was corrected by its own consequences, and the government by the Crown, which the Colonial Department had vainly advocated in 1839, was established in 1866. The reign of peace and prosperity then began, and every year since then has shown a considerable advance in the colony's commercial and financial condition (I am writing in 1873) ; and though moral and social progress is not so palpably ascertainable and must be less swift, yet there can be no doubt that it has

---

[1] On this subject I had a correspondence with Lord Grey in 1876. He was at first disposed to acquit Sir R. Peel, but on reference to the debates owned that I was substantially right. No doubt, as Lord Grey contended, the measure was miserably defective, and did not deserve to succeed ; but so far as Jamaica was concerned it would have enabled the Crown to enact during the five years of suspension of the Assembly, a system of laws consonant with freedom, so far as the then state of society would permit. What would have happened after the Assembly should have resumed its functions can only be conjectured. But Sir R. Peel rested his opposition on the principle of preserving West Indian Representative Legislatures as embodying principles of *liberty*, quoting as analogous the case of the North American Colonies in 1774, calling them *popular* Assemblies, and citing Burke's declamation on the ' high and haughty spirit of *liberty* ' which animated the planters of Virginia and Carolina, where slavery existed, as well as the Northern States. And in short throughout his speech he is the advocate of the system by which the planters were to legislate for the negroes. *See his speech of 3rd May*, 1839. *Hansard*, p. 766.

begun, and I trust that the measures adopted to ensure it will bear their full fruits in due season.

One drawback there will be. As in 1839, so in 1869, the home politics of England operated to the prejudice of her West Indian colonies. The question between disendowment of the Anglican Church and equal concurrent endowment of that, along with other Christian communions, in the West Indies, was unhappily decided in favour of the disendowment, as most consistent with English opinion and the principles of the party by whom Mr. Gladstone's Government was supported and by whose aid the Anglican Church in Ireland had been disendowed. But to apply what is called ' the voluntary principle ' to negro populations, is about as reasonable as it would be to call upon a flock of sheep to find themselves a shepherd.

Such is the story of my official operations in 1838–9. Though Lord Melbourne's Government was reconstituted, the division in the Cabinet connected with the Jamaica question led to a change in the office of Secretary of State for the Colonies. Lord Normanby succeeded to Lord Glenelg (February, 1839), and in a few months after Lord John Russell succeeded to Lord Normanby.

In October, 1839, I find myself writing to Edward Villiers,—

' You once asked me how Stephen and I liked Lord John's way of doing business. Very much— very different from anything before him.'

When Lord Glenelg left us there was a desire on the part of some members of the Government that Stephen should be transferred to some other office.

'Some of the Ministers,' I wrote to my father, 'are furious with Stephen for having advised poor. Lord Glenelg not to accept the Privy Seal' (this had been offered to him as a sop); 'and most of them, I believe, are annoyed by the imputations cast upon them in the world, of being tools in Stephen's hands in all affairs connected with the colonies. It is said that they want to get Stephen out (on honourable terms for him); and I rather think they are justly chargeable with the gross folly of this wish . . . Some persons suppose that if Stephen goes I shall be asked to take his place. If I should be asked I shall give a reasonable answer; but I shall not stir a step to get myself the offer.'

My father was anxious that I should take into account the preference to be given to 2,000*l.* a year over 1,000*l.*, in addition to the superior official rank, as enabling me to marry; or rather enabling me to have a wider field of choice in marriage. I agreed that the appointment would be a facility in that way. 'The official rank would go for a good deal with the middle classes, the country gentlemen, and the humdrum aristocracy.[1] Amongst the fashionable aristocracy it would not go for much; because my position in that society would hardly be more

[1] Called by Sydney Smith 'The table-land of Society,—high and flat.'

improved by being Under Secretary of State than Sir Walter Scott's was—elsewhere than at Selkirk—by being " the Shirra."   But no doubt the difference between 1,000*l.* and 2,000*l.* a year is recognised in all classes. .. . . As to applications and claims, I am satisfied that my best course is to have nothing to do with them.   I know by experience that the parts of candidate and claimant are parts which I cannot perform, and it is in vain for me to undertake them. I know also what Her Majesty's Ministers are made of.   I am personally acquainted with almost all the members of the present Cabinet, and am on terms of rather friendly acquaintanceship with some of them. Lord —— had a partiality for me two or three years ago—" absolutely loved me," as Lady —— expressed it.   That was for the first two seasons after I was known in the world.   But Lord ——'s heart is like Iago's purse :—

" 'Twas mine, 'tis his, and has been slave to thousands."

. . . Moreover my claims are not so strong as they were seven years ago.   I was much more zealous and laborious the first eight years of my service than I have been the last seven.   And, all these things considered, I hope you will approve of my leaving the Government to make me the offer of the place at the suggestion of their own convenience if they make it at all—which I think unlikely.   The only men in public life on whose friendships I would place any reliance are Gladstone and Lord Aberdeen.'

The language of this letter sounds as though I thought Cabinet Ministers who did not care to be of use to me, were to blame. Such language is often thoughtlessly employed when not much is meant. But if I did mean it I was unreasonable. There was no reason why these gentlemen should take trouble about me simply because they were acquainted with me. And as to the one of them who liked me less when he knew me more, that may very well have come to pass without any fault of his.

Stephen remained where he was ; no offer was made to me ; and for some years my official life was uneventful.

CHAPTER XVI.

DILIGENT ENDEAVOURS OF FRIENDS TO FIND ME A WIFE.

Anno Dom. 1838-39.   Anno Æt. 38-39.

I HAVE spoken of the distress which was suffered by my father and mother and Miss Fenwick through the overthrow of my hopes in April, 1838. And mixed with the sorrow was the fear either that I might not marry at all, or that I might be a long time in finding my way to a wife.

They and other of my friends had for some years been anxious to see me safely married, believing that I would not be happy in single life; and also, perhaps, believing that, through some sudden captivation or some inadvertency of commitment, I might very possibly one day or another make a marriage in which I would be less happy still.

So far as the blankness of celibacy was concerned, I had seen no reason to differ from them, even in earlier years ; and I had now arrived at an age at which the forecasts of life, never with me very bright, begin to darken, and men are not so self-sufficing as in their youth, whilst they feel, as well as know, that they will be less and less so in the years to come.

When half our threescore years and ten have been left behind, we get a glimpse of a still somewhat distant, but what we perceive must be a rather dreary tract to be traversed, if the wayfarer is to perform the journey alone.   For, as I expressed it at the time—

> Think what it must be
> To watch in solitude our own decay,
> Jealously asking of our observation
> If ears or eyes or brains or body fail,
> And not to see the while new bodies, brains,
> New eyes, new ears, about us springing fresh
> And to ourselves more precious than are ours.[1]

So much for the alternative of not marrying at all. As to marrying amiss, that was less to be apprehended.   I was no longer in the condition of St. Augustine in his youth, when he was 'in love with being loved, and hated safety and a way without snares.'   Under this change of conditions I took counsel with Wulfstan the Wise, as to the sort of marriage which would be suitable for my time of life ; and Wulfstan in his wisdom made answer thus :—

> . . . Love changes with the changing life of man :
> In its first youth sufficient to itself,
> Heedless of all beside, it reigns alone,
> Revels or storms and spends itself in passion :
> In middle age,—a garden through whose soil
> The roots of neighbouring forest trees have crept,—
> It strikes on stringy customs bedded deep,
> Perhaps on alien passions ; still it grows

---

[1] 'Edwin the Fair,' Act ii. sc. 2.

And lacks not force nor freshness; but this age
Shall aptly choose as answering best its own
A love that clings not nor is exigent,
Encumbers not the active purposes
Nor drains their source; but proffers with free grace
Pleasure at pleasure touched, at pleasure waived,
A washing of the weary traveller's feet,
A quenching of his thirst, a sweet repose,
Alternate and preparative, in groves
Where loving much the flower that loves the shade
And loving much the shade that that flower loves,
He yet is unbewildered, unenslaved,
Thence starting light and pleasantly let go
When serious service calls.[1]

In no long time my friends began to look about and see what resources remained for me. I looked on ; and with a view to lighten the gloom of Witton Hall and quicken it with new images and interests I gave minute accounts to my mother (accounts which would by no means conduce to the romance of this history) of the various potential wives that were sought out for me and duly considered. My mother was not well disposed towards London society :—

' I think nothing more surely injures a man's happiness than having acquired a taste for the stimulating qualities so much cultivated by women whose sole pursuit is to please in society ; that society being also of the light, gay, fashionable sort. . . . The qualities which promote cheerfulness in domestic life *may* appear dull in society ; whilst the woman who gives her soul to attract admiration, or who is after

---

[1] 'Edwin the Fair,' Act ii. sc. 2.

her own nature the delight and delighted one in company, is I believe very rarely cheerful and contented in the sameness of domestic life. And if it is bad for the woman to acquire such tastes, it is no less detrimental that the man should have cultivated his taste to admire these butterflies to the exclusion of more rational companionship.'

This was said with reference to one lady in particular ; and I said in reply :—

' Thanks for your solicitude, but she will do me no harm. Two or three years ago perhaps she might ; but not now.'

And indeed I was myself rather tired of London society, as it was of me ; and I was not of opinion that it was the place in which a man in my position could expect to find the best of wives.

But London society was the only society to which I had easy or habitual access ; and though once in a way I could (and did) make an expedition to a remote hill-side and give a passing admiration to ' the flower that loves the shade,' and though this might have been enough in the days when I was liable to sudden fancies, yet in these very different days, when it only remained for me, as Southey expresses it, ' to walk into love,' the devotion of a few holidays to that ambulatory process was not enough.

And another difficulty presented itself. I had always had a strong leaning towards youthfulness (probably from not having seen enough of it in my

own youth) ; and now when it had become unseasonable, the perverse partiality remained almost as strong
as ever.   I could reason as Donne did,—

> Since such Love's natural station is, may still
> My love descend and journey down the hill ;
> · Not panting after growing beauties ; so
> I shall ebb on with them that homeward go. [1]

But I am not sure that Donne did actually feel as he
saw reason to feel ; and neither did I.

And what I further fancied was gaiety of heart
and high spirits.   I thought that, though I might
not be able to *make* a woman happy, yet if nature
had made her to be so, I could let her.   On both
points Miss Fenwick gave me a word of warning.

'I hold strongly to the opinion, that any dis-
parity in age without some peculiar fitness in the
individual, could not but tell injuriously on your
future welfare ; and that fitness must proceed from
her having got beyond *her* years, not in what you
have not lost by yours.   You are not an old
boy, and never were a young one.   Even when you
were one-and-twenty, I question that it would have
answered to you to marry a *girl*, though then you
might better have relied on "the genial sense of
youth" for guiding you to one who would ripen
into the character that would suit you.   *Now*
you must have it ready found for you.   Youthful
spirits are tender as well as gay, and are easily

---

[1] 'Elegies,' 2.

damped.   They require companionship : and youthful
feelings and affections demand both a sympathy and
a return that only youth can bestow.   Should you
get them in a wife it would be in all likelihood but
to see them die away before their time, or turn to
other objects for their gratification.   Now, in a country life there are many objects to which she might
turn with safety and advantage ;—to nature in
general,—a garden, animals (tame and wild), a
school, and household cares : but in a town there is
but the miserable world and its vanities to turn to ;
and how full of danger it is you know better than I
can tell.   Look around you ; the world is full of
women taking this course, and men who are suffering
from it.   But who would suffer more than you? not
from what you lose ; for you have not much happiness
to lose ; but from what you will have failed to gain.
No, my dear cousin ; the wife to suit you is one whose
spring is past, whose youthful spirits have stood the
trials that all women must meet before thirty, and have
settled into a steady cheerfulness ; and whose youthful feelings, still retaining their warmth, have been
disciplined by some suffering and are regulated by
principle.   Such a woman loves both well and wisely;
and you would be happy in her love and she in yours.
Indeed in marriage there can be no advantage which
is not mutual.   It is losing sight of this truth and
seeking a separate advantage that leads men to those
ill-assorted marriages which cause so much misery.
It becomes you to think more wisely and worthily ;

or rather it becomes you to act as wisely as you think, and to endeavour to bring your taste up to your judgment. For I doubt not your agreeing in every word I say ;—and why should I say all this when you can say it so much better to yourself? I know not ; only that I am ever turning in my mind all that affects your happiness, and desiring it and praying for it with an earnest, anxious, full and loving heart.'

I knew it all, and I knew more. I knew, as I have observed before, that I had become, or was fast becoming, too old to be successful with young girls. My mother once said of girls that they were as easily won at eighteen as at eight-and-twenty ; and that may be correct in the application of it which she intended —*i.e.* when a man is young too ;—but it is not girls of eighteen, but girls of eight-and-twenty, that are easily won by men of eight-and-thirty. Till the last year or two I had looked about six years younger than my age. But now I looked the age I was, and I was the age I looked. Some very visionary person has spoken of 'poets ever young :' eternal youth might better be predicated of farmers or fox-hunters. Without any confusion of reckonings, however, it might fairly be supposed that in some cases my poetry might be a sort of compensation for ten years of youth past and gone, and give me a chance the more. But with some it went for nothing, and I had to say with Touchstone,—' When a man's verses cannot be read, nor a man's good wit seconded

with the forward child Understanding, it strikes a
man more dead than a great reckoning in a small
room. Truly, I would the gods had made thee
poetical.'

CHAPTER XVII.

RETREAT FROM TROUBLES INTO IMAGINATIVE WRITING—'EDWIN THE FAIR'—SOUTHEY'S BRAIN SOFTENS AND HE IS LOST TO ME.

ANNO DOM. 1838-39.   ANNO ÆT. 38-39.

ACROSS these outlooks into the future and these friendly quests and speculations, there had fallen, more than once or twice, some flickering and uncertain lights out of the past. *Ignes fatui*, they might be, or they might be signals of distress.

I had heard of some such, but I attached little importance to what I had heard; I told my mother that I regarded the question as at an end; and in no long time my mind was sufficiently dispossessed to take refuge in my imagination. 'Guide my way,' said Akenside,—

> Thro' fair Lyceum's walk, the green retreats
> Of Academus, and the thymy vale
> Where oft enchanted with Socratic sounds
> Ilissus pure devolved his tuneful stream
> In gentle murmurs.

The guidance I invoked, led by a rougher road to groves and streams of an enchantment less classic, but to my fancy not less seductive; and by the close

of the autumn I had withdrawn myself into my
dramatic romance.

The way in which my days were passed at this
time is described in a letter to Miss Fenwick :—

'These ten days that I have been in town I have
been living quite alone, and have found myself very
pleasant. It is only when I am thus delivered over
to myself in absolute possession that I have the full
use and enjoyment of my poetical faculties ; and it is
certainly a pleasure not to be despised, though it only
lasts for three or four hours of the day, and leaves
me in a state of lassitude. With my hours so much at
my own disposal as they are in this manner of living,
I can arrange them so that the worst of the languor
shall come when I have nothing to do but to bear it
and get over it. I get up at seven in the morning,
and run riot till half-past eleven. By that time the
excitement which has been pleasurable turns to a nervous fulness and irritability about the forehead ; and
my fancy is like a cat which purrs and is pleased to be
stroked for a certain time, and then scratches. I am
in the sort of state described by Byron, when he says,—

> I feel my brain turn round,
> And all my fancies whirling like a mill ;
> Which is a signal to the nerves and brain
> To take a quiet ride in some green lane.

With me it is a walk through the Park to my office ;
and there I cool down to business ; get through a
moderate amount of it ; and go home to dinner at

five o'clock ; from which time I sink more and more into exhaustion, and just contrive to linger through the evening with reading, lying on the sofa, and a walk round Grosvenor Square, till half-past nine or ten, when I go to bed ; as pleased as much lassitude and a little lowness will allow me to be, that I have made something out of six or seven hours of the twenty-four.'

The time was now approaching when I was to have another need for a retreat, whether into poetry or into business, from sad thoughts and contemplations. Mrs. Southey's mental malady, which terminated only with her death, had preyed upon her husband's mind for three or four years before that termination came. On the 12th January, 1834, he writes :— 'From a house that was once full of children, I shall soon have only two left at home, both of whom have arrived at a grave, or at least a serious age, and each of whom ought to depart when a proper opportunity offers. What remains for me in life is to take my degree as Grandfather and be left alone with my wife —whose spirits are irrecoverably broken—and with my books. But these are sufficient society for me, and by God's blessing I have never yet felt the want of sunshine in myself.' And the sunshine breaks out in the very same letter. 'The Doctor' had been recently published anonymously ; and who was the author was a subject of much controversy in literary circles. This was an amusement to him, and in order to divert suspicion from himself, in a letter to me, meant to be shown, for I was almost the only one of his friends by whom he was known to be the author, he writes thus :—'I have read "The Doctor," one of the strangest books that has ever fallen in my way, but in spite of its affected strangeness, a very clever one. It has come to me with the author's compliments in a disguised hand, and with my name printed in red letters on the back of the title-page. From the studied eccentricity I should suspect it to be young Disraeli's, if it were more objectionable and offensive on the score of personalities ; and I should suspect his father from the sort of reading which it displays, but the style is too good to be his. Can it be old Mathias? who has been concocting it for years in Italy, and farcing it *more suo* with quotations ; the number of Italian ones from authors one has never heard of seems to indicate him, and this conjecture is strengthened by the fact that the book is printed by Nicol, whose father published the "Pursuits of Literature." Besides, the opinions in the book agree with Mathias's, while they do not with Disraeli's. I can think of no other known author so likely, and the book is evidently not the work of a novice.'

He continued to apply himself to his literary tasks with his usual diligence and not without effect, but he sunk into an unaccustomed silence in his family, and was living in what seemed in him an almost unnatural abstraction from those of them who were about him. No physical cause for such a change was then suspected ; and Miss Fenwick, in relating what she had heard of it, adds :—

'This, no doubt, arose from the wretched state of his family during his wife's illness, when it seemed well that he should be able to forget it in his books. Yet, in the long run I question that it has answered to him. I believe that it would have been better for him in all respects to have been more present to the circumstances of his family, however painful ; and better also for them all. Kate, who is wise, as good loving beings always are, observed most feelingly on the effect on his mind of the silence into which he had fallen. Yet she was of too timid a spirit to venture to break through it ; and she and Bertha confined themselves to the silent ministering of love. They provided for all his little wants,— laid the books he wanted in his way, mended his pens, replenished his ink-bottle, stirred the fire, and said nothing. And for whole days nothing was said. The storms that sometimes visit the Mount[1] are more healthful and invigorating than such calms.'

In thus speaking 'of the effect on his mind of the silence into which he had fallen,' there was a reversal of the real relation of cause and effect. The brain had been shaken by all he had gone through ; and the silence and inattention to his family were probably the first symptoms of the softening of the brain of which further symptoms became apparent in 1838. The death of his wife,—

---

[1] Rydal Mount is meant.

'the passage from life into death, or rather, in this case, from death into life,' as he expressed it in a letter to me, took place in November, 1837. It might naturally have been expected that this would have been a relief; but it was otherwise felt by him. On the 29th November he wrote that he was meditating a tour with his daughters :—

'It is for them that change of place and circumstance is necessary, not for me. No change of place can make me cease to feel the great change in my own relations to this world. The bitterness of the loss was past, and this termination was to be desired from the time that mental recovery became hopeless. But to the last there was a recognition of who and what I was, a reliance, a dependence upon me ; and it was not till all was over that I felt how much of my own life had been taken from me.'

He was still equal to literary labour, and his letters and manner of writing seemed very much what they had ever been. In a postscript to a letter of 1st May, 1838, he writes:—'To-day I have a companion in my walk. In dull weather I walk alone, but when the sun shines as, I thank him, he does now, I and my shadow are as good company as I could desire—so good that I sometimes put my book in my pocket for the shadow's sake.' Nor did his bodily strength fail, nor was he sensible of any other failure except in his spirits :—

'I am as well as need be,' he says, on the 19th May, 1838, 'in all respects but one—the main one of spirits.   My way of life is not likely to produce any amendment in them, nor can I look forward to any change in my way of life.   But I have had a full and overflowing share of happiness.'

Within ten days from this time, however, he wrote that he had been engaged in a correspondence, the subject of which he mentioned as yet to none but me ; and before the end of July he intimated that there was every prospect of the purpose of this correspondence being accomplished.   This was his marriage to Miss Bowles.   He went soon after to stay with her at Lymington, where, I think, he remained some months.

The accounts of him I received in February, 1839, from his brother Dr. Southey, who had paid him a visit at Lymington, was that he worked slowly and with an abstraction which was not usual to him, and found it an effort sometimes even to write a letter. The strange thing was that what he did write was as well written as ever,—even a letter to me of which, owing to confusion of mind, the latter part was addressed to his daughter Kate ; and I indulged a belief that the infirmity, whatever it was, from which he suffered, did not 'extend in any case to the operations of the intellect or reason—only to the mechanical or methodical faculty and the memory.' An abundance of muscular strength still remained to him.   He lost his way in the New ·Forest, and walked fourteen miles before he found it again, and this was without apparent fatigue.

He returned to Keswick for his daughter Bertha's marriage; and Miss Fenwick saw him there and wrote to me in March, 1839, of his state of health and of his pre-occupation of mind, which was such as to make him give little apparent attention to an illness of his daughter Kate. I replied that I wished his marriage was over, attributing his ways, in some measure, to the fact that it was impending :—

'In all cases I imagine that the interval between an engagement and a marriage—" between the acting of a dreadful thing and the first motion"—is one of much distraction and disturbance. In youth a man may be driven through it by passion, or borne over it by elasticity or vigour of temperament; and in Southey's case the soundness of his nervous constitution might have stood in the place of youth if it had not been so severely worked upon by the trials of these latter years.'

But I added, in allusion to his apparent indifference to his daughter's illness, 'Grosvenor Bedford' [this was his old schoolfellow and most intimate friend] 'says that Southey used formerly to be anything but unobservant in his family;—that he was, on the contrary, painfully and immoderately susceptible of alarm if anything was the matter with any of them.'

He went back to Lymington very shortly, and the marriage took place there in the summer; and in August I saw him and his wife as they passed through London on their way to Keswick.

He spoke to me, in London, of being unable to

find his way about the streets, and of finding himself looking at his watch for some time before he collected from it what was the time of day ; and I described him to Miss Fenwick, 26th August, 1839, as in a state of great exhaustion :—

'The meaning and spirit of what he says are quite according to his former mind, and the tone is cheerful and happy.   But there is a placid languor in the manner which is very different from the strength and animation of his healthier state ; and once or twice in the course of four visits which I have paid him since he arrived, I could see that he had lost himself in the conversation for a moment, and had got confused. He was conscious of it, and patient under the consciousness, and just let it pass without troubling himself to get right again. . . I have no doubt that his present infirmity is to be ascribed to the three or four years of strain upon a heart and nervous system which had appeared to him to be of unconquerable strength, and which he consequently took no pains to spare.'

He was now conscious of inefficiency and nervous about the journey home ; and when I told him I had arranged that Mr. and Mrs. F. Elliot, who were going the same road, should travel with him, he answered, with a smile,—'If they will take care of me, I will be as helpless as they please.'

The purport of the account I received of him from Miss Fenwick after his arrival at Keswick may be gathered from my answer :—

'Thank you, my dearest cousin, for your half letter from Keswick, with its other half from Ambleside. Melancholy enough the former half is, and a letter which I had a day or two before from Mrs. Southey was not less so. The only consolation I can think of is that his great mind will still exist upon earth in the least perishable form which is permitted to earthly existences, and that his spirit will pass into a world which is more akin to it than this. His state is most painfully interesting at present; and yet painful as the interest was, I never felt the charm of his mind and manner more than when I saw him last. His mind was all his own in its nature, frame, tone, and complexion, and was beautiful in its debility. And in parts also it seemed so perfect!'

I continued to write to him longer, I think, than he could read or understand my letters; but I never heard from him again.

Thus clouded to its close was that unhappy year 1838; and thus did the clouds pass on and spread themselves over the summer of 1839. But before that summer was quite past, there was an outbreak of light and a blue sky. Intercourse was renewed with the Spring Rices. On the 17th October, 1839, I was married, and the epilogue to this chapter may be borrowed from the sonnets of Spenser:—

> Lyke as a huntsman after weary chace
> Seeing the game from him escapt away
> Sits down to rest him in some shady place
> With panting hounds beguiled of their prey,

So after long pursuit and vaine assay
When I all weary had the chace forsooke,
  The gentle deer returned the selfsame way,
Thinking to quench her thirst at the next brooke :
There she beholding me with milder looke
  Sought not to fly, but fearlesse still did bide,
  And with her owne goodwill her fyrmely tyde.
  Strange thing, meseemed, to see a beast so wyld
  So goodly wonne, with her owne will beguyled !

CHAPTER XVIII.

WITTON HALL 'SURPRISED WITH JOY'—STANZAS—DEATH OF LADY
THEODOSIA SPRING RICE—AN ILLNESS—A PAMPHLET—CHARLES
ELLIOT IN CHINA—AN ODE.

ANNO DOM. 1838-39.   ANNO ÆT. 38-39.

AND when a man is married, what more is there to
be said about him. 'Living happily ever after' is
proverbially what should be let alone by reason of
dullness; and there are other reasons for other
reticences.   When Donne was about to take his
departure for the Continent, he addressed some
stanzas to his wife; and one of them was this :—

> Then let us part and make no noise,
> No tear-floods or sigh-tempests prove ;
> 'Twere profanation of our joys
> To tell the Laity our love.

I will try, however, to find something in my life
after marriage which, being worth telling, may not
unfitly be told.

Within the first week of it, we presented ourselves
at Witton ; and it is no profanation to tell of the joy
which then lit up the gloomy old border tower,—lit
it up then and never left it so long as life lasted in
the two affectionate old hearts there abiding.   My
father was in his sixty-eighth year, my mother in her

seventieth. My father lived for eleven years more, my mother for thirteen. My old maiden aunt in the village was ten years older than my father, and she was equally devoted to him and me. She lived for some six or seven years. My marriage made, I think, almost as great a change in their lives as in mine ; for there was a peace as well as a brightness they had not known for many years in the new loves and hopes and interests which sprang up ; and from that time the letters which 'old Jacky' brought up to the Hall were as many and as long and as loving from their daughter-in-law as from their son.

Some ten years before, on revisiting Witton Hall after an unusual length of absence, I had begun a poem addressed to the Lynn (the little brook or burn which had been my haunt when the Hall was my abode), of which I have had occasion to quote one stanza in a former chapter, and two or three years after my marriage I resumed and finished it ; and as it is autobiographical and reaches to the time at which my narrative has now arrived, it shall take its place here :—

THE LYNNBURN.

I.

Again, oh stream, beloved in earlier years
  And not unsung, within thy wooded glen
I stand, and inwardly my hushed heart hears
    The same remembrancer that murmured then ;
    For thou wert with me ere the haunts of men
Were trodden of my feet, and thou couldst gloze
Even in the days long passed of younger days than those.

II.

And I would ask, melodious recluse
  Whose sameness measures change, if I be still
Like him who whilom turned his fancy loose
  To chase the shadows thro' thy woods at will;
  I would be told of change for good and ill,
And know if I be capable as once
To thy low call to make a musical response.

III.

The old plank bridge is gone—the stone-built arch
  Is but a sorry substitute to me;
But mining still beneath that leaning larch
  The same slow current spreads itself: I see
  Reflected there a face how changed since we
Were neighbours and so oft at eventide
(Then was thy sweet voice sweetest) wandered side by side.

IV.

Some twenty years have held since then their course
  In lights and shade, in smiles and bitterness,
And so long I have been to thee perforce
  Occasional, not constant; not the less
  In gladness have I sought thee and in distress,
And counsel sweet we still together took
At every change of life in this sequestered nook.

V.

What didst thou witness first? the life of dreams,
  Of genial nights and mornings run to waste,
Ambitious hopes, a fancy fired by themes
  Of thoughtless passion, labour much misplaced
  In aping wild effusions where false taste
Bedecks false feeling, visionary love
For what not earth below affords nor Heav'n above.

VI.

This ere I left thee : Then the sturdier state
   Of youthful manhood, prompt for action, proud
Of self-reliance, strenuous in debate,
   Presumptuous in decision, by a crowd
   Of busy cares encompassed which allowed
For dreaming sensibilities scant scope ;—
Yet room for one fair face vouchsafed, one fearful hope.

VII.

A will disordered, hurried mind, and heart
   Though wearied yet intolerant of rest,
Thou cunning'st adept in the healing art
   I brought to thee ; well knowing thou wert blest
   With wondrous power to still the troubled breast ;—
Than thou none more, save Siloa's brook which feeds
The flowers that breathe their balm from sempiternal meads.

VIII.

Another change ;—the face was no more seen,
   The hope expired : the appetite for rule,
Advancement, civil station, that had been
   Therewith allied, began thenceforth to cool :
   To be the powerful, serviceable tool
Of statecraft seemed inglorious, and with feet
Less shackled did I then revisit this retreat.

IX.

'Twas summer and I heard the cushat coo,
   And saw the dog-rose blooming in the groves ;
All was as fresh as when the world was new ;
   I plucked the roses, listened to the doves,
   Forgetful for a season of fixed loves
And fugitive caresses—I was free :
Then came the Muse and laid her thrilling hand on me.

u 2

X.

Not wholly slighted had she been before,
   But now my heart was hers by night and day ;
I loved her not for honours that she wore
    In the World's eye, rich robe and wreath of bay,
    But for herself—and therefore did I pay
My service due with labour slow and sure
In secret many a year, content to be obscure.

XI.

A change again ;—my name had travelled far
   And in the World's applausive countenance kind
I sunned myself—not fearing so to mar
    That strength of heart and liberty of mind
    Which comes but by hard nurture : Me tho' blind
God's mercy spared—from social snares with ease
Saved by that gracious gift, inaptitude to please.

XII.

To thee I fled ; and it was then thy mood
   To teach Autumnal lessons ; for a blast
Blown by the north had weeded from thy wood
    The yellow leaf, but o'er the russet past,
    That graver beauty leaving to the last
By strength of stem preserved : Thou saidst 'Behold
Such colours life should keep when skies are dark and cold .'

XIII.

My 'yea' fell flat : The interests that are youth's
   And youth's alone, could now no more be mine ;
The soul's deep, sacred and sufficing truths
    Seemed to dim eyes too distantly divine ;
    A world that will not flatter, to resign
Costs little : but life's wherewithal ran low
When bounty at my need new sources bade to flow.

xiv.

For of the many one who smiled at first
  On better knowledge wore a smile as bright;
And still when dreariness had done its worst
  And dryness weaned the multitude, despite
  Of doubts and sore disturbance that pure light
Burnt up reanimate; wherein to live
Was the one genuine joy that Earth had now to give.

xv.

Last change of all, I hither brought my bride,
  At whom each sweetest, freshest woodland flower
Laughed as to see a sister by its side;
  And old eyes glistened in that gladdening hour;
  For who are they in yon square border tower
Half up the hill? and in the cottage near
Whose is the old grey face so tender and so dear?

xvi.

My weal had been their last and only stake
  In life's decline; and doubt and fear and pain
Long, largely had they suffered for my sake.
  To them whose hearts did never touch profane
  Of worldly cares corrode or pleasure stain,
How peaceful but for me! at length I brought
The charm that soothed to rest full many an anxious thought.

xvii.

Thou garrulous stream, my youth's companion sweet,
  In earlier years if I have loved thee well,
In after years if oft my faithful feet
  Assiduously have sought thy sylvan dell,
  If to my heart thy voluble voice can tell
So much so softly, am I wrong to raise
My voice above thine own in publishing thy praise?

Our married life was not, however, all sunshine even from the first. Two clouds hung over it, one of which broke and fell within two months; the other spread a veil, thin and transparent, but not impalpable, over several years. The one arose from the state of health of Lady Theodosia, now to be called Lady Monteagle (Mr. Spring Rice had been raised to the peerage in 1839), the other from the state of my own health.

Lady Monteagle's condition had been one of increasing illness ever since I had known the family; and she died at Hastings in December 1839. She was a high-minded, devout, gentle, thoughtful person, whose patience and resignation had made her long illness less of a preparation for the loss of her than otherwise it might have been. And shortly before this time Lord Monteagle's house had been emptied in other ways. His second daughter had been married some time before our marriage, and his eldest and only remaining daughter had been attached to the court as Maid of Honour to the Queen.

Under these circumstances, when he and his family removed from Hastings to London, I was led to acquiesce in his wish that my wife and I should pass the winter with him in his house, whilst looking about for a house of our own.

It was Christmas; the house had been long unoccupied, and the walls were dripping. What modicum of health and strength I had possessed before 1837, having had a good deal to contend with in the years that followed, had been not a little worn and weakened ; and shortly after the removal I had a gastric fever, from which I escaped with life but not without injury.

It was very unseasonable ; for just at this time the proceedings of Charles Elliot, then Minister Plenipotentiary in China, were about to be attacked in the House of Commons, and I was anxious to contribute to his defence. With this view, as soon as my fever left me, I prepared a digest of his despatches, with connecting comments and an argumentative summary, which was hurried through the press and published a few days before the debate.

It was a successful effort. Lord Palmerston saw it in the proof sheets, and said it would be of the greatest use in setting public opinion right ; and after the debate I wrote to my mother, 18th May, 1840 :— ' Charles Elliot has got nothing but credit on all hands, as far as I can hear ; and my digest, that is, in point of fact, his own despatches, have had all the effect I could have wished.'

The Duke of Wellington told Rogers that he had been converted by it. He spoke in the House of Lords, and his speech was ' delivered without any of the hesitation and repetition which have been usual with him, and was ardent, masterly, and impressive. He said that Charles Elliot " had had no authority for doing what he had done, but had done it at his own risk, and that the Government and the country owed him a debt of gratitude for having performed that service on his personal responsibility, and with a courage and self-devotion which few men have had an opportunity of showing, and still fewer would have shown if they had had the opportunity." '

Charles Greville saw the Duke soon after, and, expressing the pleasure he had felt in reading his speech, added that, however, many of the party were very angry with it; to which the Duke replied,—' I know they are, and I don't care a damn. I have no time not to do what is right.'

A ' twopenny ' damn was, I believe, the form usually employed by the Duke, as an expression of value ; but on the present occasion he seems to have been less precise.

Lord Melbourne had spoken before the Duke, and said that Charles Elliot ' had acted with the greatest coolness, the greatest ability, and the greatest judgment.'

These encomiums were no more than were to be expected from the two statesmen of the time who, when they spoke at all, spoke their minds ; and indeed they expressed what could scarcely fail to be the sentiments of any just and competent person who had read the despatches.

But the digest had had a further effect which was less to be looked for. To the letter from which I have quoted there is a postscript, saying :—' Lord Clarendon has just written me word that my pamphlet has been translated into German, and has effected a sudden and complete revolution in Austrian public opinion on the subject. How strange it seems that Austria should trouble its head about such things to such an extent! Germany seems to be the nation which is to stand by and read and contemplate, whilst other nations act.'

Of the digest, probably there are not more than two or three copies, if so many, in existence ; and if it were to be had, nobody would read it now, for it was a voluminous and elaborate affair. But Charles Elliot's operations and adventures in China, both those recorded in the pamphlet and those of subsequent date, make up a scrap of history which I can write probably better than anyone else, and which ought to be written with care, for it is instructive as well as personally interesting ; and as the subject matter gave occasion, not only to the pamphlet, but to one of the only two odes I have written, the story is not unconnected with my autobiography, and it will be found in an Appendix,—not relegated thither as of secondary interest ; quite the contrary ; but in the hope that it will be read in that compact and separated shape, with a more undivided interest than if it were to occur where it might seem to be a digression.

It will there be seen, that after the operations recorded in the digest, a squadron and a small body of troops having been sent from India, Elliot was enabled by alternately fighting and negotiating, first to take possession of Hong-Kong, and next, by a series of rapid and masterly movements on the part of the naval and military forces, in the course of which a formidable flotilla of about one hundred fireships and other war-craft were destroyed, a long line of fortified works obstinately defended and batteries mounting sixty guns were carried, an entrenched camp taken and a numerous force routed,—to stand before the gates of Canton, and holding the City at his mercy, possess himself of a sum of six million dollars there collected by the Emperor's Commissioners for the purpose of carrying on the war, and to exact divers other important concessions, as the terms of a local truce ; which concluded, he could leave our interests in the South secure from molestation, and so soon as reinforcements should arrive, and with them the favourable monsoon, be enabled to move the forces to the North and threaten Pekin from the mouth of the Grand Canal.

Thither he was about to proceed, when the Government, goaded by popular clamour at his supposed failures, and not knowing that the news of his successes was already on its way home, was so much misled, or rather misdriven, as to supersede him in his office, and was moreover so unlucky as to allege for the ground of his recall, ' disobedience of instructions *not justified by success.*'

They had heard of the ineffectual attempt to negotiate off the mouth of the Peiho, of the transference of the seat of negotiation to Canton, of the evacuation of Chusan, and of the unpromising transactions with Keshen ; but the tidings of what followed had not yet arrived, and they were under an entire misapprehension as to the further operations about to be undertaken.

That they were ill informed as to the last point was no doubt by Elliot's own default; for in the rapid succession of emergencies in which he had been called to act, he had not found time to write.

What was known up to the time when Canton was invested, if it wore an aspect of failure to the Government, was still more confidently assumed to be failure by the people and the press ; and of course their confidence was all the more boisterous when the Government lent it their countenance by Charles Elliot's recall. John Bull raged and bellowed and would have liked to toss Charles Elliot on his horns ; and even when the tidings arrived of the investment of Canton, on which such rich results had followed, John was by no means pacified ; for unhappily that event was first announced in a despatch from the General in command of the forces, which was un-accompanied for the moment by any despatch from Elliot (always least occupied with what most concerned himself) ; and the General wrote in a spirit of grievous mortification and disappointment, as if, when Elliot had prevented Canton from being taken by storm, he had substituted some tame treaty for a magnificent feat of arms. Though at the date of the General's despatch, he and Charles Elliot were living together in the same house and on cordial and friendly terms, the despatch was not shown to him, and he only knew of its tenor when the return mail brought him the results of it in a clamorous echo by the press and the people of the General's cry of distress. [1]

Sir Henry Pottinger was sent out and Elliot came home ; and then another tale was told. He repaired the omission to explain what he had been about. His motives, proceedings, and plans were fully set forth in a letter to Lord Aberdeen, who had succeeded Lord Palmerston at the Foreign Office ; and both with the men in office and the men who had quitted office, he stood, perhaps, on higher ground than ever. I wrote to my father, 13th November, 1841 :—

' Poor fellow ! he is bethumped with words as you will have seen ; but I trust he cares as little for the press as for a Chinese battery. I believe there is no doubt now that he was right. I know that to be the opinion of Lord Palmerston [it was he who had recalled him], Lord Lansdowne, Lord John Russell,[2] Lord Clarendon, and Lord Auckland.'

I might have added, but that it had not then come to my knowledge, of Lord Melbourne, Lord Aberdeen, and Sir Robert Peel.

Sir Henry Pottinger performed his part with unquestionable judgment and ability ; and his judg-

---

[1] The six million dollars which Charles Elliot secured towards an indemnity for the destruction of the cargoes would have accrued to the General and his troops as prize of war if the city had been taken by storm.

[2] Lord John Russell once told me that, according to his experience, we had no better diplomatists than our sea-captains.

ment was in nothing more clearly shown than in the adoption and prosecution of the plans of his predecessor.

When the news of his triumph arrived, Lord Aberdeen wrote to Charles Elliot, then Minister at Texas, to congratulate him on the termination of the war by his successor, as being distinctly the result of operations designed by himself.

But all he had done and all he had enabled and guided others to do, was known only to a few official men ; it was decided that, for public reasons, public opinion could not be corrected by laying the requisite papers before Parliament ; he remained unhonoured by the multitude ; and I, being minded that at all events he should not remain unsung, delivered myself of the ode which follows, entitled :—

HEROISM IN THE SHADE.

Written after the return of Sir H. Pottinger from China.

I.

The Million smiles ; the taverns ring with toasts ;
    A thousand journals teem with good report
And plauditory paragraph ; with hosts
    Of thankful deputations swarm the streets;
His native city of her hero boasts ;
      The minister who chose him, in the choice
    Exults ; and prompted to its part, the court
      The echo of the country's praise repeats,
        And by the popular pitchpipe tunes its voice.

II.

But where is he whose genius led the way
    To all this triumph ?　Elliot, where is he ?

—When first that Monster of the Eastern sea,
That hugest empire that for ages lay
    Becalm'd beneath the sun, with strange see-saws
    Convulsively unsheath'd its quivering claws,
'Twas he that watch'd its motions many a day,
    Foreseeing and foretelling that the sleep
    For those unnumber'd centuries so deep
Would pass ; and when its rage and fear at length
Shook off the numbness from its labouring strength,
'Twas he whose skill and courage gagg'd its gaping jaws.

III.

Justice, Truth, Mercy,—these his weapons were ;
    And if the sword, 'twas wielded but to spare
    Through timely terror worse event.   With rare
    And excellent contemperature he knew
How best on martial ardour to confer
    The honours that are then alone its due
    When patience, prudence, ruth are honour'd too.
When to relent he saw, and when to dare,
Sudden to strike, magnanimous to forbear !
Prone lay the second city of that land,
    Third of the world, a suppliant at the feet
    Of him whom erst she gloried to maltreat !
    But then a great heart to itself was true—
On the rash soldier's bridle was the hand
Of Elliot laid, with calm but firm command.

IV.

Thou mighty city with thy million souls !
    To England, through that rescue, art thou made
    A treasure-house of tribute and of trade !
To England, whose street-statesmen, blind as moles,
    Scribe-taught, and ravening like wolves for blood,
    Spared not his wisdom's temperance to upbraid
    Who thus thy ruin righteously withstood !
Thou mighty city, for thy ruler's faults,
    Not thine, how many an innocent had bled,
    How many a wife and mother hung her head
In agony above thy funeral vaults,

What horrors had been thine, what shame were ours,
  If he, by popular impulses betray'd,
   Or of rash judgments selfishly afraid,
     Had render'd up thy wealth and blood to feast
     That hunger of the many-headed beast
Which its own seed-corn tramples and devours.

V.

But service such as his, to virtue vow'd,
Ne'er tax'd for noise the weasand of the crowd,
  Most thankless in their ignorance and spleen.
  His glory blossoms in the shade, unseen
    Save by the few and wise; to them alone
    His daring, prudence, fortitude are known.
—In the beginning had his portion been,
Even as a pilot's in a sea unplough'd
By cursive keel before, when winds pipe loud
    And all is undiscover'd and untried,
  To take the difficult soundings in the dark ;
  And then with tentative and wary course,
    And changing oft with change of wind and tide,
  The shoals to pass, evade the current's force,
  And keep unhurt his unappointed bark ;—
A tentative and wary course to steer,
But ever with a gay and gallant cheer.
This task perform'd, when now the way was clear,
  The armament provided, and the mark,
    Though hard to be attain'd, was full in sight,
    Upon his prosperous path there fell a blight,
Distrust arrested him in mid-career.

VI.

Another reap'd where he had sown : success,
  Doubtless well-won, attended him to whom
  The harvesting was given : his honours bloom
Brightly, and many a rapturous caress
The populace bestows—what could they less ?

Far be from me malignly to assume
  That popular praise, how oft soe'er it swerved
  From a just mark, must needs be undeserved:
But knowing by whom the burthen and the heat
  Was borne,—with what intrepid zeal, what skill,
    Care, enterprise, and scope of politic thought,—
  Through labours, dangers, obloquy, ill-will,
  Battles, captivities, and shipwreck, still,
With means or wanting means, alert to meet
    In all conjunctures all events,—if aught
Could make a wise man wonder at the ways
Of fortune, and the world's awards of praise,
    'Twould be, whilst taverns ring and tankards foam
    Healths to this hero of the harvest-home,
      To think what welcome had been his whose toil
      Had fell'd the forest and prepared the soil.

VII.

What makes a hero ?—Not success, not fame,
Inebriate merchants and the loud acclaim
  Of glutted avarice,—caps toss'd up in the air,
  Or pen of journalist with flourish fair,
Bells peal'd, stars, ribands, and a titular name,—
  These, though his rightful tribute, he can spare ;
His rightful tribute, not his end or aim,
Or true reward ; for never yet did these
Refresh the soul or set the heart at ease.
—What makes a hero ?   An heroic mind
  Express'd in action, in endurance proved :
    And if there be pre-eminence of right,
    Derived through pain well suffer'd, to the height
  Of rank heroic, 'tis to bear unmoved,
Not toil, not risk, not rage of sea or wind,
Not the brute fury of barbarians blind,
  But worse,—ingratitude and poisonous darts
    Launch'd by the country he had served and loved :
This with a free unclouded spirit pure,
This in the strength of silence to endure,

> A dignity to noble deeds imparts
> 　Beyond the gauds and trappings of renown
> 　This is the hero's complement and crown ;
> This miss'd, one struggle had been wanting still,
> One glorious triumph of the heroic will,
> 　One self-approval in his heart of hearts.

Lord Aberdeen wrote to me on the subject of these stanzas, and said he believed them to be 'not more friendly than just.'

CHAPTER XIX.

OUR FRIENDS RESPECTIVELY BECOME FRIENDS IN COMMON—AUBREY
DE VERE. LADY HARRIET BARING. SIR EDMUND HEAD. GEORGE
CORNEWALL LEWIS. CHARLES GREVILLE—MEETING BETWEEN
LORD MONTEAGLE AND MY FATHER.

Anno Dom. 1840–44.   Æt. 40–44.

One incident of the change from single to married
life is, that two circles of friends and associates meet
and cut each other—or, if that phrase be equivocal,
let it be said that the two circles meet and kiss each
other. In our case the impact was enriching to both
husband and wife. The best friends of each became
equally, or almost equally, the friends of the other ;
and in our respective contingents we were more upon
a par than might be inferred from the difference of
age. I had had the time and opportunities of nearly
seventeen years more to provide myself with chosen
friends ; but, on the other hand, I had no brothers
or sisters, whereas my wife had seven ; and, beyond
that immediate bound, but only just beyond it,
she had a first cousin who was a brother in everything except the one remove in blood—Aubrey, a
younger son of Sir Aubrey de Vere, whose wife was

Lord Monteagle's sister.   My wife had no other very intimate friend; but that one was worth a thousand.

Bearing in mind what I have said of certain others, I am afraid to speak of him as he deserves, lest I should be supposed by some unbeliever to have a way of considering all my own friends as food for the Gods and my wife's as the salt wherewith it is salted. There is a natural disposition in many people to revolt against anything which looks like exaggeration in a man's estimate of his friends, as being not radically very distinguishable from an exaggerated estimate of himself.   And some, though I hope not quite so many, find the language of panegyric distasteful, even when free from the taint of friendship; being of opinion with Sir Philip Francis, that praise is never tolerable but when it is *in odium tertii*.   It may be well, therefore, to be a little careful, and rather to let my friends' letters describe them than say all I think about some of them.

But as to Aubrey de Vere, his rank in poetry is now quite as much recognised as some of our now famous poets were in their own lifetime, and every year of these latter years has been extending the recognition in wider circles.   In 1848, when his poems were but little read, Walter Savage Landor, then I think 74 years of age, gave him as cordial a salutation as ever old poet bestowed upon a young one—

> Welcome who last hast climbed the cloven hill
> Forsaken by its Muses and their God!

Show us the way; we miss it, young and old.
Roses that cannot clasp their languid leaves,
Puffy and colourless and overblown,
Encumber all our walks of poetry.
The satin slipper and the mirror boot
 Delight in pressing them ; but who hath trackt
A Grace's naked foot amid them all ?
Or who hath seen (Ah ! how few care to see !)
The close-bound tresses and the robe succinct ?
Thou hast ; and she hath placed her palm in thine ;
Walk ye together in our fields and groves.
We have gay birds and graver ; we have none
Of varied note, none to whose harmony
Late hours will listen, none who sings alone.
Make thy proud name yet prouder for thy sons,
Aubrey de Vere !   Fling far aside all heed [1]
Of that hyæna race whose growl and smiles
Alternate, and which neither blows nor food
Nor stern nor gentle brow domesticate.
Await some Cromwell who alone hath strength
Of heart to dash down its wild wantonness
And fasten its fierce grin with steady gaze.
Come reascend with me the steeps of Greece
With firmer foot than mine ; none stop the road,
And few will follow ; we shall breathe apart
That pure fresh air, and drink the untroubled spring.
Lead thou the way ; I knew it once ; my sight
May miss old marks ; lend me thy hand ; press on ;
Elastic is thy step, thy guidance sure.

If Landor had known Aubrey de Vere personally,
he might have testified to other and higher attributes
than those of the intellect and imagination.   And
indeed as to mere matter of intellect, it ought not to

____

[1] Aubrey de Vere had published a pamphlet entitled 'English
Misrule and Irish Misdeeds,' which probably Mr. Landor thought a
little too indulgent to the latter.

be otherwise than easy of belief that the friends of an
intellectual man are intellectual. For such persons
fall naturally enough into groups, whether through
kindred of blood and brain or through mutual attraction and a common field. It was in both ways
that the Spring Rices and the De Veres had been
brought together in the preceding generation ; it was
thus, too, that a daughter of the one and a son of
the other, having each, however diverse in kind and
degree, an inheritance of intellectual gifts, were
brought into relations of more than ordinary intimacy ; and after my marriage I was not long in
finding how rich a dowry of friendship my wife had
brought me in Aubrey de Vere.

Of those that *I* brought to *her* it is but two or
three that have not been made known already.

One of them, Lady Harriet Baring, afterwards
Lady Ashburton, became very shortly, I think, even
more attached to my wife than to myself. She was
for some years before her premature death the most
brilliant phenomenon of London society, drawing
round her all of it that was much distinguished in
social, political, and literary life. She is one of the
persons of whom Lord Houghton has given an
account in a book called ' Monographs,' published in
1873 ; but he has described her, I think, with less
felicity than some others. Nor do I know that I
could describe her better. For there was much of
her that is indescribable, especially her wit. Lord
Houghton has endeavoured to reproduce it ; but it

was a wit which could not be written down—too subtle, too swift, too essentially born of the moment and of evanescent circumstance, to be capable of lending itself to a record. It was inseparable from herself, her manners, and her ways, and one hardly knew whether it was the woman or the wit that was so charming.

Our relations for three or four years before my marriage had been what I should call rather familiar than intimate, though I know not that there was, just at that time, any one with whom she was *more* intimate. Notwithstanding the warmth of personal regard, which I fully recognised and returned, and the almost reckless sallies of intellectual gaiety of which I felt the attraction, I was conscious that there stood beyond these a barrier of reserve, rarely, and then but for a moment, surmounted ; and that with what lay on the other side she had no desire, or only now and then a momentary desire, that I should intermeddle. Nor had I, on my part, any disposition to do so ; for it was my way, with her and others, to take what measure of confidence came and be thankful ; and not to press, and hardly, I think, even to wish for more. The outpourings of some persons are interesting ; in others, silence may be more interesting still—

> Sacred Silence, thou that art
> Floodgate of the deepest heart—— [1]

---

[1] The lines are from Flecknoe ; and they may be set against much derision inflicted upon him by Dryden. .

and of all the heart's litanies, silence is that to which it was most within my competence to respond.

It was otherwise with my wife. Lady Harriet and she became ardently attached to each other, and the floodgate was washed away.

Miss Fenwick was a little afraid of her influence, regarding it as allied to the influences of fashionable society ; and I find myself, in reply, vindicating her claim to be considered as more and other than a woman of the world :—' Lady Ashburton is, in my view of her, a person of a continually deepening nature, and of great truth, strength and constancy in friendship.'

Another friend, hitherto not named, whom I rejoiced in presenting to my wife, was Sir Edmund Head ; a man whose endowments and attainments taken together might have achieved a high literary reputation, had he not, almost of necessity, for he was not rich, betaken himself to public employments instead of literary labours. It seems to be often assumed, as a matter of course, that the latter labours give birth to more lasting results than the former. All that ought to be assumed is, that the labourer will probably be longer known by name, and that the results of his labours will be more distinctly traceable to himself. The good done by Sir Edmund Head in his public employments will bear fruit in successive generations of consequences, long after any portions of it have ceased to be referred to their original. It is personal reputation only which is more lasting in the case of literary achievements.

Some men—a very few—in our time may have rivalled Sir Edmund Head in knowledge of books and some in knowledge of art ; but probably no one was equal to him in knowledge of both together ; and when I first knew him there was, along with this, a gaiety of heart which, in so laborious a student, made perhaps the rarest combination of all.   It was subdued afterwards, though not extinguished, by some years of ill-health : through which, with manly energy,

he kept
The citadel unconquered,

doing the State excellent service, first as Poor Law Commissioner, then as Lieutenant-Governor of New Brunswick, and, finally, as Governor-General of Canada.   He died suddenly in 1868.   A memoir of him was written by Herman Merivale, and I edited a collection of his poems.

At the time of my marriage he was the mirthful member of the small and, but for him, somewhat grave circle of friends of which Edward Villiers was the centre.   It was as a friend of Edward's that he became a friend of mine ;   and there was another, George Cornewall Lewis, whom I think I accounted, at that time, equally a friend.   I have mentioned him already in connection with his marriage some years after to Lady Theresa Lister (born Villiers). But the tie between us must have depended very much on Edward Villiers, and if friendship at all, can only have been friendship at second-hand ; for it slackened after our loss of Edward ; and after my change of abode to the suburbs it was very rarely that we met.   He was a singular man ; his manners were dry and phlegmatic, though too simple to be supercilious ; he was thoroughly honest-minded ; he was of an imperturbable temper, though cynical ; and, externally frigid as he was, he had two or three attachments of which the secret strength was to be inferred from an unvarying constancy.   His success in political life never received a check ; and it showed how unessential popular manners are to such success in this country, so long as integrity and sincerity are unquestioned ; proving also that coldness and comparative indifference, with the requisite conscientiousness and intellectual power, may inspire more general and durable confidence than political ardours howsoever patriotic.   His well-known saying that ' life would be tolerable enough but for its amusements ' was genuinely characteristic ; and I doubt whether politics were much more congenial to him than amusements, or work in his office, whether as Chancellor of the Exchequer or Secretary of State, equally acceptable with work in his study.   Even when in office he seemed to prefer laborious literary research and the composition of able, but dry, literary works, to administrative industries ; though for these also he was well fitted by the largeness of his understanding ; for with all his devotion to learning and scholastic literature, his mind was in no sense pedantic. He had a highly cultivated logical faculty; but he knew that faculty to be instrumental only,—designed to serve the higher reason, not to master it. What limitation there was of his intellect was on the imaginative side. His mind was essentially prosaic. One of the few meetings which took place between us after he had entered upon political life, was an accidental one at Grove Mill House, then the abode of Mrs. Edward Villiers. It was just after Wordsworth's death, and during the vacancy of the laureateship. He told me he had suggested to his colleague, the First Minister, that the laureateship should be offered to me, and had been surprised to hear that Tennyson was in question, conceiving that Tennyson was little known, and that his claims would not be generally recognised. I, on the other hand, was abundantly surprised that he should think so, and I assured him that there could be no greater mistake. Living amongst the men in London who were the most eminent in literature, he had yet lived so far apart from poetry, that the poet who for some years past had eclipsed every other in popularity was supposed by him to be obscure.

In a letter to my father, 17th September, 1844, after mentioning the marriage then about to take place, I wrote :—'He is a calm, immoveable man, very learned and very active in mind, and perhaps the most potent of the Poor Law Triumvirate at Somerset House. Carlyle says he is a " melancholy, mournful man, like an old ruined barn filled with owlets ; " but I think the mournfulness is Carlyle's own, who takes a mournful view of everything.'

Sir Edmund Head, in editing after his death a collection of his essays, gives an ardent, and, I think, a just account of his public and private virtues ; and if there are one or two minor particulars in the portraiture which do not quite accord with what were my own previous impressions, I do not the less adopt his ; for these two were true and unalterable friends from first to last ; whereas the relations between George Lewis and myself, always less close, underwent, as I have said, at an early period, a change amounting almost to extinction.

Then there was Charles Greville, a friend of mine, a friend of many, and always most a friend when friendship was most wanted ; high born, high bred, avowedly Epicurean, with a somewhat square and sturdy figure, adorned by a face both solid and refined, noble in its outline, the mouth terse and ex-quisitely chiselled, and without perhaps much other expression, expressing his aristocratic extraction as only such mouths can ; for, rarely as they are seen at all, I have never observed, amongst males, the sort of mouth I mean except in connection with high birth ; as if Nature must have been at work through successive generations polishing the *material* ; for it is material refinement that is distinctively expressed, with or without other refinement as the case may be.

Friendly though Charles Greville was, and active

and zealous in his friendship, he did not profess, nor did it perhaps at any time happen to him, to be possessed by any ardent affections ; nor is celibate life in London favourable to such ardours. But the warmth which belonged to him was genuine and consistent, and being largely diffused and not ungenerous, made up in multiplied values for the absence of intensity and concentration. He had more than ordinary abilities, a clear judgment, and no little cultivation, and lived in constant intercourse with the most eminent political men of all parties, except, perhaps, the Radicals, and with men of letters, and with every other class to be met with in what is called ' Society ' in London. His grandfather, the Duke of Portland, had conferred on him (with other sinecures) the valuable office of Clerk of the Council ; the effect of which unhappy boon was to substitute the turf for the House of Commons as his field of action, and to divert from a political career a man who was, perhaps on the whole and certainly in some important qualifications, more fitted, if not more likely, to have been First Minister, than at least three of the First Ministers of his generation. But, though disabled for entering Parliament or holding political office, he was by no means excluded from exercising political influence. Being in relations of social intimacy with Whigs and Tories alike, and trusted by both, he was constantly resorted to as an adviser, and upon occasions as an intermediary ; and no one knew better how, with an acute, adroit, impartial, and temperate handling, to adjust what may be called the personalities of political life. He kept diaries, some volumes of which he showed me from time to time, and all of which will probably be published sooner or later ; those preceding the Queen's accession sooner, the others later. Like most records of the kind, there will be insurmountable objections to the publication of them *in their totality*, till some distant day when their colours will have faded.[1]

All our common friends in London life came across each other easily enough ; but it was rather oddly that my father and my father-in-law first met. In September, 1841, Lord Monteagle went to Durham on some business connected with the University, contemplating a visit to Witton before he returned, but saying nothing of his whereabouts till he could see his way. My father and mother happened to be on a visit to a connection of my mother's at Durham, and my mother wrote to me on the 27th September :— ' I must now tell you of yesterday's adventure, which will surprise you a little. Your father attended Lady Milbanke to the Galilee Chapel, where he was delighted with the service. Mr. Townshend preached. The crowd was great. I did not go. After the service had just commenced, Dr. Gilly brought a gentle-

---

[1] As all the world knows, the diaries preceding the Queen's accession were published soon after Mr. Greville's death by his friend, Mr. Henry Reeve, to whom he had committed the task, and they have attained an unexampled celebrity as a living likeness of the time which gave them birth in its historical, political, social, and personal aspects.

man to a vacant place by your father's side, saying, "An acquaintance of yours, Mr. Taylor," and passed on. The gentleman took the vacant seat, your father slightly bowing to him and not at all recognizing him. He looked at him from time to time, but found it impossible to recollect him. When the service was concluded Dr. Gilly came back and introduced— LORD MONTEAGLE,—and the most animated and cordial greetings ensued. . . . Since I wrote the above, I have been out and met Lord M. and your father in the street, as merry and cordial as if they were discoursing of the affairs of their youth and of the same age.' . . . A letter from Lord Monteagle to his daughter gave an account of the meeting and of the man he met. 'We became much more than acquainted ; we became intimate and friendly in the portion of two days we passed together. He is a man after my own heart.'

Under ordinary circumstances it was not easy to become intimate with my father ; I find myself saying to him in one of my letters,—' Like all retired persons you are difficult to please ; ' and certainly the way into his acquaintance seemed often in the nature of a voyage of discovery, and the voyage in the nature of a North-West passage ; but anything which touched his domestic heart thawed him at once. The man of action and the man of lettered seclusion did not meet often in the few years that remained of my father's life ; but first and last it was with the same friendly feeling.

CHAPTER XX.

FRIENDLY ACQUAINTANCES—SAMUEL ROGERS—ARCHBISHOP WHATELY
THOMAS CARLYLE.

LEAVING the muster of my friends, I may pass on to three or four of my friendly acquaintances,—those of them who may be said to belong, in some sort, to the history of their time.

Samuel Rogers I only knew when he was, I should think, more than seventy years of age ; and if I were to call him a friend, it is only as a hundred others could ; for his friends were so many that I doubt if he had any in the first degree, at least when I knew him ; but by that time he might have outlived those of his own generation. He was a sleeping partner in a bank and a wealthy man. His house in St. James's Place, not a very large one, for he was a bachelor, was filled with works of art, and in its interior might be called a work of art in itself ; and at his table had dined almost every eminent man of his time—men of letters and artists, statesmen, men of wit, naval and military heroes. I remember his telling me of a dinner at which Lord Nelson was one of his guests ; and on the only two occasions on which I ever met the Duke of Wellington as one of a few, Rogers was the host. It was at a *partie carrée* at his house that I met Turner for the first and last time ; and there I made the acquaintance of Tennyson. There, too, I had the honour,—I cannot say that either there or elsewhere it was a pleasure, —to meet Sir Robert Peel ; and of course Sydney Smith was a frequent guest ; as were the three heiresses in the second generation of the genius and wit of Sheridan—Mrs. Norton, Lady Dufferin, and the Duchess of Somerset.

The poems of which Rogers was the author would scarcely have attained to the celebrity they once enjoyed, had they been published at any other time than in the 18th century or the very beginning of the 19th. But at that time they may have done something towards giving him the high position in society which he occupied for half a century. His social talents and his wit did more. Through them he was admired ; and what, perhaps, availed him equally, he was feared.

In giving up his life to society, he probably made the most of it. Miss Fenwick met him in the autumn of 1840, paying visits to Southey and Wordsworth at the Lakes, where he was somewhat dwarfed by what surrounded him. In answering her letter I wrote :—'No doubt Rogers would be as much lost amongst the mountains as Southey used to be at a great dinner-party in London. But I am disposed to think that Rogers chose the line of life in which he was best bestowed, as well as that which suited

him best.   If he had attempted to adapt his mind to
mountain solitudes, he would have committed as
great an error of judgment as the citizen who
castellates a villa at Richmond.'

His wit was perhaps in higher repute than any in
his time, except that of Sydney Smith; but whilst
Sydney's wit was genial and good-humoured, and
even his mockeries gave no offence, that of Rogers
was sarcastic and bitter; and the plea which I have
heard him advance for its bitterness was, in itself, a
satire :—' They tell me I say ill-natured things,' he
observed in his slow, quiet, deliberate way; 'I have
a very weak voice; if I did not say ill-natured things,
no one would hear what I said.'

It was owing to this weakness of voice that no
candles were put on his dinner-table; for glare and
noise go together, and dimness subdues the voices in
conversation as a handkerchief thrown over the cage
of a canary subdues its song.   The light we dined
by was thrown upon the walls and the pictures, and
shaded from the room.   This did not suit Sydney
Smith, who said that a dinner in St. James's Place
was 'a flood of light on all above, and below nothing
but darkness and gnashing of teeth.'

However one might be tormented, it was not
safe to complain.   I remember one victim,—it was
the widow of Sir Humphry Davy,—venturing to
do so. 'Now, Mr. Rogers,' she said in a tone of
aggrieved expostulation, 'you are always attacking

mc.' 'Attacking you, Lady Davy! I waste my life in defending you.'

But with all the acrimony of his wit, he was by no means wanting in practical benevolence, in tender sympathies, or in kindnesses, bounties, and charities.

Whilst the wit of Rogers was the wit of satire, and that of Sydney Smith the wit of comedy, the wit of Whately, Archbishop of Dublin, might be designated as the wit of logic.

Soon after my marriage we met him at Ems, whither we had gone for the benefit of my wife's health. He was of a gigantic size and a gaunt aspect, with a strange unconsciousness of the body ; and, what is perhaps the next best thing to a perfect manner, he had *no* manner. What his legs and arms were about was best known to themselves. His rank placed him by the side of the Lord-Lieutenant's wife when dining at the Castle, and the wife of one of the Lord-Lieutenants has told me that she had occasionally to remove the Archbishop's foot out of her lap. His life has been written in two volumes, but without any attempt to represent his powers as appearing in conversation, always vigorous and significant, often delightfully epigrammatic. He never wasted a thought upon his dignity. If he had, the dignity would have been an unwelcome weight ; but, without any intentional arrogance, he was accustomed to assume the intellectual dictatorship of every company in which he found himself. There could be no greater mistake than to infer from this that there

was any tincture in him of ecclesiastical intolerance.
He was in reality intolerant of intolerance, and of not
many things beside.   He lived upon easy terms with
the young men about the Viceregal Court, and one of
them, a young nobleman who was Aide-de-camp to the
Lord-Lieutenant, made a little mistake in assuming
that a scoff at the Roman Catholic Bishops would be
acceptable :—‘My Lord Archbishop,’ said the Aide-
de-camp, ‘do you know what is the difference between
a Roman Catholic Bishop and a donkey?’   ‘No,’
said the Archbishop.   ‘The one has a cross on his
breast and the other on his back,’ said the Aide-de-
camp.   ‘Ha!’ said the Archbishop ; ‘do you know the
difference between an Aide-de-camp and a donkey?’
‘No,’ said the Aide-de-camp.   ‘Neither do I,’ said
the Archbishop.

His Grace had approved highly of ‘The Statesman,’ and had published anonymously a book
modelled upon it and quoting from it largely, which
was entitled ‘The Bishop’; and in regard to literature
generally, with which he was perhaps not much more
conversant than myself, we were, so far as we went,
very much in accord.   But in the matter of poetry
I found him of a different way of thinking from
mine.   His mind, versatile and open as it was, was
not imaginative ; and I was somewhat vexed to find
that Wordsworth’s mind, with all its doctrinal
thoughtfulness and philosophic generalisations, could
find no entrance into his ; and, perceiving that I
could not force the entrance in conversation, I made

a more elaborate endeavour to work Wordsworth
into minds of his order and quality by writing an
article on his sonnets for the 'Quarterly Review.'[1]
I treated the sonnets in some such way as Dante
treats his own verses in the 'Vita Nuova,' developing
the more or less latent meanings, and occasionally
perhaps, in the manner of a preacher upon a text,
adding a little doctrine which may have been rather
suggested by the sonnet than derived from it. The
inexorable Archbishop seized upon these instances of
extra-development, and (in a letter to a friend which
reached my hands) observed with characteristic
sharpness that they reminded him of 'pebble soup,
which is said to be very savoury and nutritive if you
season it with pepper and salt, a few sweet herbs,
and a neck of mutton.'

I have yet, however, to exemplify what I mean
when I say that his wit was of the logical type. In
a debate upon the introduction into the House of
Lords of the Poor Law for Ireland, some peer (I
think Lord Clanricarde) supported it by saying that
if the landowners lived upon their estates, and *if* the
boards of guardians were attentive to their duties,
and *if* the overseers examined strictly into the
circumstances of the applicants for relief, the law
would have a most beneficial operation. The Arch-

---

[1] It appeared in No. 137, December, 1841, and this and another
article on Wordsworth (No. 104, December, 1834) were published with
one or two other reprints from reviews in a volume entitled 'Notes
from Books.'—*Note*, 1878. They are now to be found in the fifth
volume of my collective works.—H. T.

bishop strode across the floor to my brother-in-law, Stephen Spring Rice, who was sitting on the steps of the throne, and said to him aside, ' *If* my aunt had been a man, she would have been my uncle ; that's his argument.'

We parted great friends at Ems : the Archbishop said if he were to see no more of us he should be sorry to have seen so much ; and glad indeed should we have been to have renewed and prolonged the intercourse. But opportunities were few, and after that parting it was but seldom that we met.

I have reserved to the last place—why I know not, unless it be on the principle that the last should be first and the first last—one with whom England, Scotland, and Germany have almost as intimate and as friendly an acquaintance as I can claim for myself —Thomas Carlyle : and yet the acquaintance I can claim is very intimate and most friendly.

His relations with the people are without a pre-cedent, as far as I am aware, in these times or in any ; the human paradox of the period. He is their ' chartered libertine,' assailing them and their rights, insisting that they should be everywhere ruled with a rod of iron, and yet more honoured and admired by them than any demagogue who pays them knee-wor-ship. In courting the people it is easy, no doubt, to err on the side of obsequiousness, and to lose their respect. But it is far from easy to defy them and yet to conquer. How the conquest has been achieved by Carlyle is a perplexing problem. Is it that the man being beyond all question a genuine man, there is nevertheless something unreal about his opinions ; so that the splendid apparitions of them are admired and applauded by the people, as they would admire a great actor in the character of Coriolanus and another in the character of Menenius Agrippa, and still more one who could play both parts in turn ?

But then it may be asked, how are we to reconcile the undoubted sincerity of the man with the questionable reality of the opinions ?   And it is the solution of this problem which, to my apprehension, discloses the peculiar constitution of Carlyle's mind.

He is impatient of the slow process by which most thoughtful men arrive at a conclusion.   His own mind is not logical ; and, whilst other eminent writers of his generation have had perhaps too much reverence for logic, he has had too little.   With infinite industry in searching out historical facts, his way of coming by political doctrines is sudden and precipitate.   What can be known by insight without conscious reasoning, or at least without self-questioning operations of the reason, he knows well, and can flash upon us with words which are almost like the ' word which Isaiah the son of Amos *saw*.'   But when he deals with what is not so to be known, being intolerant of lawful courses, and yet not content with a negative, or passive, or neutral position, he snatches his opinions, and holds them, as men commonly do hold what they have snatched, tenaciously for the moment, but not securely.   And thence comes the

sort of unreality of opinion which I have ventured
to impute to the most faithful and true-hearted of
mankind.

An unlimited freedom of speech is permitted to
his friends, and I remember when some wild sentiments escaped him long ago, telling him that he was
an excellent man in all the relations of life, but that
he did not know the difference between right and
wrong. And if such casualties of conversation were
to be accepted as an exposition of his moral mind,
anyone might suppose that these luminous shafts of
his came out of the blackness of darkness.

Perhaps, too, he is a little dazzled by the reflex
of his wild-fire, and feels for a moment that what is
so bright must needs show forth what is true ; not
recognising the fact that most truths are as dull as
they are precious ; simply because in the course of
ages they have worked their way to the exalted, but
not interesting, position of truisms.

He was one of the most valued and cherished
friends of Lady Ashburton ; and as he and I were
both in the habit of paying her long visits in the
country (at Bay House, Alverstoke, when she was
Lady Harriet Baring, at the Grange when her husband had succeeded his father), I had opportunities
of knowing him such as London cannot provide.
And from Bay House I find myself writing of him to
Miss Fenwick thus, 22nd January, 1848 :—

'We have had Carlyle here all the time,—a
longer time than I have hitherto seen him for. His

conversation is as bright as ever, and as striking in its imaginative effects. But his mind seems utterly incapable of coming to any conclusion about anything ; and if he says something that seems for the moment direct, as well as forcible, in the way of an opinion, it is hardly out of his mouth before he says something else that breaks it in pieces. He can see nothing but the chaos of his own mind reflected in the universe. Guidance, therefore, there is none to be got from him ; nor any illumination, save that of storm-lights. But I suppose one cannot see anything so rich and strange as his mind is without gaining by it in some unconscious way, as well as finding pleasure and pain in it. It is fruitful of both.'

And I wrote in the same sense to my mother and to Aubrey de Vere. To her :—' The society of the house is gay and pleasant, divers visitors coming and going and some abiding. The only one you have any knowledge of is Carlyle, than whom none is more interesting—a striking element of the wild and grotesque to mix up with the more gay and graceful material of a fashionable set.'

To Aubrey :—' As to the rest of the people we have had at Alverstoke, some of them were agreeable, but none interesting except Carlyle, who from time to time threw his blue lights across the conversation. Strange and brilliant he was as ever, but more than ever adrift in his opinions, if opinions he could be said to have ; for they darted about like the monsters of the solar microscope, perpetually devouring each other.'

I did not mean to imply, of course, that he had not, what he has made known to all the world that he had in a superlative degree, divers rooted predilections and unchangeable aversions. Both are strong in him ; whether equally strong, it is not easy to say. There have been eminent men in all ages who have combined in different measures and proportions the attributes of idolater and iconoclast. They are undoubtedly combined in Carlyle ; the former perhaps predominating in his writings, the latter in his conversation. What was unaccountable was that such a man should have chosen as the object of his idolatry, 'iste stultorum magister'—Success. Long before his life of Cromwell came out, I heard him insisting in conversation upon the fact that Cromwell had been throughout his career invariably successful ; and having with much satisfaction traced the long line of his successes from the beginning to the end, he added, 'it is true they got him out of his grave at the Restoration and they stuck his head up over the gate at Tyburn, but not till he had quite done with it.'

He would scarcely have sympathised with the sentiment to which the last breath of Brutus gave utterance,—

> I shall have glory by this losing day
> More than Octavius and Marc Antony
> By their vile conquest shall attain unto——

and the vile conqueror Frederick could engage more

of his admiration than most honest men will be disposed to share.   Perhaps, however, it was a waning
admiration,—less as he proceeded with his history
than when he began it ; and it should not be forgotten
that he ended by entitling it a life of Frederick
' called ' the Great.

His powers of invective and disparagement, on the
other hand, are exercised in conversation sometimes
in a manifest spirit of contradiction and generally
with an infusion of humour, giving them at one time
the character of a passage of arms in a tournament or
sham fight, at another that of a grotesque dance of
mummers ; so that forcible as they often are, they are
not serious enough to give offence.

He delights in knocking over any pageantry
of another man's setting up.   One evening at the
Grange a party of gentlemen, returning from a walk
in the dusk, had seen a magnificent meteor, one which
filled a place in the newspapers for some days afterwards.   They described what they had beheld in
glowing colours and with much enthusiasm.   Carlyle
having heard them in silence to the end, gave his
view of the phenomenon :—

' Aye, some sulphuretted hydrogen, I suppose, or
some rubbish of that kind.'

In the autumn of 1845, Monckton Milnes [1] was

---

[1] Now Lord Houghton.   Called by Sydney Smith ' the Cool of the
Evening.'   Some little eccentricities of manner there may have been
to suggest the epithet ; but those who have known him in his acts and
deeds are conversant with what is anything but cool in his nature ;
and there is a large measure of ardour as well as grace in his poetry.

one of a party at the Grange at the same time with Carlyle and myself. He was famous for the interest he took in notorieties, and especially in notorious sinners, always finding some good reason for taking an indulgent view of their misdeeds. I have heard that on the occasion of some murderer being hanged, his sister, Lady Galway, expressed her satisfaction, saying that if he had been acquitted she would have been sure to have met him next week at one of her brother's Thursday morning breakfasts. At the time of this visit, Sir Robert Peel had just formed his Government, and had not found a place in it for Monckton Milnes, who appeared to be somewhat dissatisfied with Sir Robert on the occasion. Carlyle took a different view : he highly commended Sir Robert's judgment and penetration, insisting that no man knew better who would suit his purposes and who not, and ended by pronouncing his own opinion, that the only office Monckton Milnes was fit for was that of 'Perpetual President of the Heaven and Hell Amalgamation Society.'

In Carlyle's invectives as well as in effusions where it would be less unexpected, there would generally be something which met the eye. When he spoke of a thing, under whatever feeling or impulse, he seemed to see it. He paid a visit to Lord Ashburton at a shooting-box in Scotland, at a time when the cholera was supposed to be approaching, and there was a retired physician staying in the house to be ready for any emergency. Carlyle was not well and was very gloomy, and shut himself up in his room for some days, admitting no one.   At last Lady Ashburton was a little disturbed at his ways, and begged Dr. Wilson just to go in to him and see whether there was anything seriously amiss.   The Doctor went into his room and presently came flying out again ; and his account was that Carlyle had received him with a volley of invectives against himself and his profession, saying that ' of all the sons of Adam they were the most eminently unprofitable, and that a man might as well pour his sorrows into the long hairy ear of a jackass.'   As in most of his sallies of this kind, the extravagance and the grotesqueness of the attack sheathed the sharpness of it, and the little touch of the picturesque,—the 'long hairy ear,'— seemed to give it the character of a vision rather than a vituperation.

CHAPTER XXI.

MISS FENWICK WITH MR. AND MRS. WORDSWORTH.

ANNO DOM. 1840-41.   ANNO ÆT. 40-41.

I HAVE said that the change made by my marriage in
the lives of my father and mother was a change full
of happiness and peace.

To Miss Fenwick, also, it brought joy and great
gladness of heart, and if not perfect peace, yet all the
peace which her nature and the nature of her affections permitted. For in all her affections there was
an element of diffidence and disturbance working up
and betraying itself from time to time, as well as a
profounder element of peace,—profounder far,—the
peace of the deep sea,—the

> central peace subsisting at the heart
> Of endless agitation.

Perhaps there are no natures, having a rare and
extraordinary largeness of love, which can hold themselves in a constant and invariable contentment with
the objects of their love. It cannot be expected that,
in this commonplace world, what is rare and extraordinary will fall in with what is equally rare and
extraordinary; and yet absolute and uninterrupted

contentment is not to be expected in the relations engendered by unequal attributes and capacities.

Vainly heart with heart would mingle,
For the deepest still is single—

says some one,—I think Aubrey de Vere,—and there is truth in the aphorism, though, like most aphoristic truths, it is to be taken as approximate only, and with sundry notes of reservation.

Miss Fenwick was like myself, constitutionally liable to fits of oppression and dejection, though not to the flatness which accompanied mine ; and in the ebbing years which preceded my marriage, there had been, now and then, some grating on the shallows. But with my marriage came the flood-tide ; love flowed in upon her from all sides ; from my wife as well as from myself ; and not from us only.

For happily at this time she was brought into relations of the closest intimacy with Wordsworth. Her admiration for him as a poet, always supreme, allied itself with affection for him as a man ; and her admiration and affection for him was equalled, if not exceeded, by his for her. She took a house within an easy walk of Rydal Mount, and when that house ceased to be at her disposal, she took up her abode for some time at Rydal Mount itself. Mrs. Wordsworth, who has been justly as well as *exquisitely* described in her husband's verse (and I may use that word, not only as it is commonly used, but also in its derivative sense, as it is used by Milton, for the verses

are a real *searching out* of what was in her), attached
herself to Miss Fenwick with a warmth and energy
of nature which took no account of years ; and it
can seldom have happened that a friendship of three
persons first formed in advanced life has been so
fervent and so inward.

In the spring of 1840 she writes, dating from
Rydal Mount,—' Before I arrived here I thought I
would write you a very cross letter' [I had been
dilatory in writing to her], ' but I must have been
the very devil to retain my ill humour in the
midst of all this beauty and the love that so harmo-
nises all the feelings as to make them sensible to it,
and almost to it alone. The poor body also seems
at ease here ; the atmosphere is perfect, and I can
almost walk about like other people, just with so much
remembrance of my late oppression as gives a feeling
of relief as well as of enjoyment, in a degree such as
those blessed spirits must feel in Heaven who have
" come out of great troubles." You are very happy,
I trust, my dear cousins ; but still in this atmosphere
—moral, intellectual, and spiritual—I think you
would be more blessedly happy ; and so I wish you
were here. No season can be so delightful as this.
It is a beauty giving the impression of *progress* which
makes the spring the most precious of all seasons. I
grieve that you are where you know nothing of it
but chickens and asparagus and dust and dissipation.
Though of the last you may not much partake, still
you see " the madness of the people." '

And shortly after she writes :—

' I have got this house to the end of October, but that is all.   It is likely that I shall then go to Rydal Mount.   It is just ten years since I first went there.   I think I said to you then, I would be content to be a servant in the house to hear his wisdom.   Losing sight of all the intermediate steps which have led me hither, how wonderful does it seem to me that I should take up my abode there almost as a matter of necessity ; for could I get another house I would not be there, though I value his wisdom quite as much as I could have done then, and I love him ten thousand times more than I ever expected I should.'

What Miss Fenwick greatly prized in the family was the openness and sincerity with which all thoughts and feelings were expressed ;   and this she regarded as of infinite value in the regulation of Wordsworth's life and mind.   ' There is no domestic altar in that house,' she once said to me ; and if she found none there, neither did she set up one.   As the intimacy became closer, her admiration for the personal qualities of the wife became, I think, more unmixed than her admiration for the personal qualities of the husband ; but even when she had arrived at the knowledge of all his faults—and no man's were less hidden—she retained a profound sense of what *was* great in his personal character, as well as an undiminished appreciation of his genius and powers.

At this time her influence over him was invaluable

to the family. His love for his only daughter was passionately jealous, and the marriage which was indispensable to her peace and happiness was intolerable to his feelings. The emotions,—I may say the throes and agonies of emotion,—he underwent, were such as an old man could not have endured without suffering in health, had he not been a very strong old man. But he was like nobody else,—old or young. He would pass the night, or most part of it, in struggles and storms, to the moment of coming down to breakfast; and then, if strangers were present, be as easy and delightful in conversation as if nothing was the matter. But if his own health did not suffer, his daughter's did; and this consequence of his resistance, mainly aided, I believe, by the temperate but persistent pressure exercised by Miss Fenwick, brought him at length, though far too tardily, to consent to the marriage. On the 6th May, 1841, Miss Fenwick writes from Bath :—' Our marriage still stands for the 11th, and I do sincerely trust nothing will interfere with its taking place on that day, for all parties seem prepared for it. Mr. Wordsworth behaves beautifully.'

It did take place accordingly, and Mrs. Quillinan was granted about six years of happiness in married life, before her death in July 1847.

On leaving Bath, Wordsworth, Mrs. Wordsworth, and Miss Fenwick paid a visit to Miss Fenwick's brother-in-law and sister, in Somersetshire, and on

their way made excursions to the places in which
Wordsworth and Coleridge had set up their rest when
they lived so much together, in those years of their
youth (1796 to 1800) when Coleridge was ' in
blossom.'

' We had two perfect days,' Miss Fenwick writes
on the 20th May, 1841, ' for our visit to Wells,
Alfoxden, &c. They were worthy of a page or two
in the poet's life. Forty-two years, perhaps, never
passed over any human head with more gain and less
loss than over his. There he was again, after that
long period, in the full vigour of his intellect, and
with all the fervent feelings which have accompanied
him through life ; his bodily strength little impaired,
but grey-headed, with an old wife and not a young
daughter. The thought of what his sister, who had
been his companion here, was then and now is,
seemed the only painful feeling that moved in his
mind. He was delighted to see again those scenes
(and they were beautiful in their kind) where he had
been so happy—where he had felt and thought so
much. He pointed out the spots where he had
written many of his early poems, and told us how
they had been suggested. . . . Dear Dora and Mr.
Quillinan parted with us at Bridgewater ; they proceeded to Rydal Mount and we to Bagborough,
where we have been spending some very pleasant
days. Mr. Wordsworth and the Squire do very well
together. The latter thinks the former a very

sensible man, and the former thinks the latter a very pleasant one. The people in Somersetshire know nothing of the poet. They call him Wentworth and Wedgewood and all sorts of names. But they are kind and hospitable, and he likes to be met on the ground of his common humanity.'

CHAPTER XXII.

PUBLICATION OF ‘EDWIN THE FAIR’—MACAULAY’S OPINION OF IT—
HEALTH BROKEN—LEAVING ENGLAND FOR ITALY.

ANNO DOM. 1842-43.   ANNO ÆT. 42-43.

I HAVE mentioned in a previous chapter the precipitate way in which, under the exigencies of 1838, being in want of an immediate diversion from unhappy thoughts and recollections, I threw myself into the composition of ‘Edwin the Fair.’

Two years before I had been in search of a subject. Lord Aberdeen had suggested the conquest of Naples by Charles of Anjou. I rejected it as too romantic, thinking that I should stand more firmly upon plainer ground. I had thought of Sixtus the Fifth and of Thomas A’Becket as well as of Edwin the Fair. The characters and certain scenes in the lives of each of them are eminently dramatic ; but their histories do not admit of a consecutive action terminating in a catastrophe in which they should be the principal actors and objects of interest throughout ; whilst the presentation of them as occasional objects would strike the light out of any hero or heroine who might be brought within range of them.

At a later date Macaulay made a suggestion. He

wrote :—' I am more and more struck by what I think I once mentioned to you, the resemblance between your poetry and Schiller's. I wish to God that you would take that great subject of which he touches only a portion, the greatest subject of modern times, Mary Queen of Scots, and give her life and death in three parts. The first part should end with the death of Darnley, and the second with the flight into England.'

This was written after the publication of 'Edwin the Fair;' but I think I had had the subject under consideration before. It involves the difficulty of a catastrophe separated by seventeen years from the main action ; and there is the further objection of the principal characters being too familiar to the readers of history to afford so fair a chance as a dramatist would desire of the ideal taking possession of their imaginations undisturbed by the real. But these objections notwithstanding, I am disposed to agree with Macaulay that the subject is the best that modern history supplies ; or at least that it will become so in the course of two or three centuries, when it shall be seen in a dimmer distance.

My choice of Edwin the Fair was determined, I think, by the desire for a subject which did not present any formidable array of structural and *preliminary* difficulties. But it was not a good choice ; and if I had foreseen, what my experience should have enabled me to foresee, that the play would occupy me for four years, perhaps I might have bestowed more labour than I was willing to bestow on the selection and construction of a story. Once embarked in it, however, I put on board all merchandise which those four years had in them to supply.

The play on its publication in June, 1842, was received well enough, but not with the warmth of welcome which had so much surprised its predecessor eight years before. Macaulay, in the letter which I have quoted, gave me his impressions on a first reading ; and perhaps they may be taken as foreshowing what was to be the general feeling about it :—

' I think that, considered as an intellectual effort, the tragedy is fully equal to " Van Artevelde " Indeed I think that it contains finer specimens of diction. It moves the feelings less, at least my feelings. But this I attribute to a cause which was, perhaps, beyond your control. Van Artevelde and his Italian mistress are persons of far higher powers and stronger characters than Edwy and his queen. And the cracking of tough natures is the most affecting thing that a dramatist can exhibit. Othello is the great example. Poor Edwy and his bride go down like the willows before the hurricane. I should say that you have succeeded, on the whole, better in exhibiting the character of the age and of the two parties than the character of individuals. In this respect the play reminds me of Shakspeare's " Henry the Sixth," which, though not eminent, at least among his works, for delineation of particular men and women, exhibits a peculiar state of society with a vivacity and truth such as no historian has approached. Your monastic and secular factions are admirable. Dunstan I cannot make up my mind about. I must wait for another reading.'

In writing to my wife, who was at Tunbridge Wells, to tell her that the last scene had been accomplished, I mentioned that if I had not been alone when I finished it, I might have been said to have made a scene in more senses than one. The sort of weakness I alluded to may be taken as an indication of what was more distinctly shown in no long time after, that my health was breaking down. In the following year, on my way home from my office after some work there which, perhaps, I had performed with more excitement than was necessary, I fell down in the street with a momentary unconsciousness ; and, as will often happen, this overt and palpable sign of broken health was of more use as a warning than many months of creeping and crawling indisposition. I knew then that something must be done ; and, in October, 1843, I obtained six months' leave of absence from my office,[1] to be prolonged if necessary, and I passed the winter of 1843–44 in Italy.

---

[1] I proposed to place myself on half salary, but Lord Stanley was good enough to say that I should have whole salary for six months and half only for any additional term. I mention this because it may be regarded by some readers as a circumstance which should have deterred me from writing of Lord Stanley as I have written of him in a preceding chapter.

APPENDIX.

CHARLES ELLIOT'S [1] OPERATIONS IN CHINA.

CHARLES ELLIOT was British Plenipotentiary in China in 1839, when a great revolution took place in the counsels of the Emperor in regard to that large portion of the British trade at Canton which consisted in the importation of opium produced in India and consumed in China. It was chiefly paid for in Sycee silver, the exportation of which the Chinese Government imagined, in its ignorance, to be a cause of national impoverishment; and for years there had been much vacillation in their policy on the subject, decrees being issued again and again to prohibit the trade at the instance of one party, whilst the opposite party took care that they should be inoperative, and the local authorities at Canton merely used them as a facility for obtaining bribes from the merchants.

Charles Elliot had always considered that the trade was conducted on a most precarious footing, and in 1839 all vacillation at Pekin came to an end. Lin, a man of great energy and determination, was sent to Canton with supreme authority, and took the trade by surprise. Cargoes of opium to the value of two millions sterling were in the Canton waters. They were confiscated; and, in order to compel their surrender, the British merchants to whom they were consigned, in number about two

---

[1] Afterwards Admiral Sir Charles Elliot, K.C.B.

hundred, were imprisoned in their own factories, and their supplies of food and water being cut off, all were in danger of starvation, whilst some were threatened with a more violent and immediate death.

The tidings reached Charles Elliot when he was at Macao, and he forthwith took his departure for Canton, sailed up the river in defiance of the Chinese batteries, reached the factories, and threw himself amongst his imprisoned countrymen.

He found all negotiation to be ineffectual for saving at once the lives of the merchants and the cargoes in the ships; and he then took over the cargoes from the merchants in the name of the Queen, paying for them in bills drawn on the British Treasury, and delivered them up to Lin; whereupon the merchants were liberated and the ships allowed to depart.

A war with China was to be the consequence, and a great commotion arose in Parliament and in the Press and in the public mind of England.

Some preliminary discussion had already taken place in the House of Commons before my pamphlet was ready, but it was published some days before the great debate.

The principal charges against Charles Elliot with which it dealt were :—

1st. That he had countenanced or permitted the trade in opium, contrary to the laws of China, which forbade its importation, and contrary to moral obligations, inasmuch as opium was the moral poison of the Chinese nation.

2nd. That when the British merchants were shut up in the factories and threatened with death, he placed himself in the power of the Chinese by joining the imprisoned merchants, so as to be unable to act as an independent negotiator.

As to the first charge, the pamphlet quotes numerous passages from Elliot's despatches, in which year after year he had lamented and denounced the trade, and, in reply to an allegation of Sir G. Staunton, in the previous discussion, that he might have prevented it, the pamphlet proceeds as follows :—

'It is further. affirmed by Sir G. Staunton, that the Government is responsible for the opium trade down to the period when Lin's measures were taken, because Captain Elliot only ordered the receiving ships to quit the coast on the 11th September, 1839, whereas if he had given this order three years, or even seven months, before, all would have been safe. Lord Palmerston answered, that Captain Elliot had no power to do so; to which Sir G. Staunton rejoined, that he did it at last, and therefore he might have done it at first.

' Now let Captain Elliot's position be regarded, and then let us see what is the worth of such an argument as this. When the trade was a monopoly in the hands of the East India Company, the ships could not trade without licences, and the licences contained an obligation to obey the orders of the supercargo at Canton. When the trade was freed, the superintendents succeeded to the duties of the supercargoes, but not to their powers; because, as no licences were required, no obligations could be enforced. When Captain Elliot had appeared to contemplate the exercise of the supercargoes' power, by preventing a steamship from going up the river, Lord Palmerston had explained the state of the law to him, and cautioned him against the assumption of an authority which he did not possess.

' How comes it then, says Sir George Staunton, that he had the authority, and could give effect to it, on the 11th September, 1839 ? The answer is that he had no more *legal* or *official* authority then than before; but that from first to last his authority was an authority of moral influence; an authority of circumstance; an authority of guidance, persuasion, and management. In 1836 there was a trade worth millions, sanctioned by a Committee of the House of Commons, contributing largely to the revenues of British India, connived at by Chinese Viceroys, and dear as their very life's blood to this Keun-Min-Foo, and that Kwangheep. There were a set of British merchants, eager and independent, some of them certainly (Mr. Innes, for example) perverse and turbulent, and all of them, according to Sir George Robinson, divided into factions and animated by a violent party spirit; and these persons were to be governed by management without power. At that period Captain Elliot, standing alone in his opinions, may well be conceived to have taken the measure of his authority and found it wanting; and it then behoved him, in obedience to his instructions, not to issue orders which, being set at nought, would only have brought his office into contempt. These were the circumstances of 1836.

'But in September, 1839, there were a different set of circumstances; every sort of violence on the part of the Chinese, jeopardy and extremity on the part of the merchants, the trade embarrassed, two millions of property confiscated, a fleet in danger, and peace or war upon the issue. If it be asked whence came Captain Elliot's authority over the merchants in such circumstances as these, the answer is, that it was the authority of a man who had placed himself at their head when a leader was wanted; who had forced his way to them in the moment of danger; who had been ready in every emergency; had shrunk from no responsibility; whose judgment had been tried and whose foresight had been proved; who had shared their prison and accomplished their deliverance; and finally it was the authority of a commanding mind on a critical occasion. If Sir George Staunton had been upon the spot at that particular period and had himself fallen under the operation of one of Lin's edicts, bidding him to "tremble intensely," he would possibly have felt more disposed than he would have been under other circumstances to obey an order for leaving China. however little warranted by law. In the private accounts of these transactions some descriptions have been given of the breathless anxiety with which the merchants confined in the factory watched the approach of Captain Elliot, as, sailing and pulling in his four-oared gig, he eluded the chase of the Chinese guard-boats ; and a picture has been drawn, too, of the enthusiasm with which he was received when he landed on the quay. If Sir George Staunton had been one of those merchants, perhaps he would be better able to understand the nature of the authority which Captain Elliot exercised over them from that time forward, and how it came to be greater in extent than that which he had been enabled to exercise in 1836.

'But the despatches which were received in this country a few days ago (27th March, 1840) are now to be added to all the previous evidence of Captain Elliot's opinions and conduct on this head ; and that evidence may be well wound up with the following passage from his despatch of the 16th November, 1839 :—

' " If my private feelings were of the least consequence upon questions of a public and important nature, surely, I might justly say, that no man entertains a deeper detestation of the disgrace and sin of this forced traffic on the coast of China than the humble individual who signs this despatch. I see little to choose between it and piracy ; and in my place as a public officer, I have steadily discountenanced it by all the lawful means in my power, and at the total sacrifice of my private comfort in the society in which I have lived for some years past."

' We have now passed in review the main accusations which have been preferred, and have stated the conclusions to which we come in discharge of the several British parties who have been alleged to be responsible for the opium trade. But the great and governing principle to be looked to in this matter is, that moral evils are to be met by moral cures ;[1] that vice is to be encountered, not by excluding the material product which subserves to it, but by imparting to the heart of the sinner an impulse which shall give him the victory over his sin. If this remedy be within reach, trade may take its course, and will carry nothing to the shores of China but what is useful and salutary in articles of commerce, together with civilising knowledge, and in God's good time (let us hope), the doctrines of the Christian faith. Without this remedy, all legislative prohibitions and penalties will be ineffectual ; the opium of Malwa will press in when the opium of Bengal is kept out ; what cannot enter by the river will find a way by the inlet or the creek ; and even if all the Indian opium were excluded, there would remain the supply to be derived from growing the poppy in China, which was one of the schemes recommended to the Emperor by those very Ministers who advocated the prohibition of foreign opium.'

To the second charge the pamphlet replies by quoting Captain Elliot's own statement,—that he had been led to take the course of joining the merchants on consideration of the ' natural unfitness of a commercial community to take any conscntaneous course respecting the delicate and momentous question in hand in this hour of extreme peril to all interests, and indeed generally to human life.' This had carried him to the conviction that ' he must either

---

[1] This dogma was justly and provably applicable in the case in question ; but I fell into a mischievous though hackneyed error, when I stated it as a proposition universally or generally applicable. Much may be done by penal and other legislation to give moral cures a better chance.

reach these factories or some desperate calamity would ensue.'

And as to his remaining aloof in order that he might negotiate without restraint, I replied,—'The truth seems to have been that he had no power, and nothing to negotiate with except his own skill and courage; and with no other stake remaining he had to make the most of these.'

The pamphlet proceeds :—

'Seeing that the property must be surrendered, and also that his Government must be involved in measures (hostilities if necessary) for obtaining redress, he put the matter into the best shape he could, not only for saving the parties immediately in danger, but for giving his Government the clearest and most authentic ground for a demand of redress or a declaration of war.' To use his own words, the requisition which he made on British subjects for the surrender to him of British owned opium was 'founded on the principle that these violent compulsory measures being utterly unjust *per se*, and of general application for the forced surrender of any other property or of human life, or for the constraint of any unsuitable terms or concessions, it became highly necessary to vest and leave the right of exacting effectual security, and full indemnity for every loss, directly in the Queen.'

As I have mentioned in the pages to which this narrative is an Appendix, Charles Elliot's despatches, as published in my ' Digest,' sufficed for his vindication, and for much more than his vindication, so far as his proceedings in 1839 were concerned. In the debates of May 1840, the Duke of Wellington and Lord Melbourne pronounced the most ardent and emphatic encomiums upon his courage, coolness, judgment, ability, and self-devotion; and whilst public opinion in England changed colour and was a little ashamed of itself, a translation of the digest

into German effected, as I was informed by Lord Clarendon, a revolution in the public opinion of Austria.

But if the British public can be brought to blush for
one offence committed through ignorance and presumption,
it is not, therefore, the less ready to run into another;
and its second error, which had regard to Charles Elliot's
operations in China after 1839, was as precipitate as the
first; and not the less worthy of notice, because the
Government was betrayed into sharing it, wholly or in
part, or, at all events, into acting upon it as if shared.

The Government of this country must be expected to
adopt an exasperated and clamorous public opinion unless
they are provided with a plain and producible plea for re-
sisting it. In regard to the public opinion of such of
Charles Elliot's operations as followed those recorded in
the digest, unfortunately they were not provided with the
plea till too late.

After the outrage perpetrated on the British merchants,
of course there was to be a demand for reparation and indemnity, with war as the alternative. An expedition was
dispatched of such naval and military forces as could be
gathered, without delay, from India and elsewhere, and in
January, 1840, operations commenced.

From their commencement there was, no doubt, an
essential difference of view and feeling between the
English people and Charles Elliot. The English people
were naturally full of anger against the Chinese; and
when the English people are full of anger, they are very
like other people, and do not quite know what they are
about.

The questions pending were multiform and complex;
and amongst the essential distinctions to be taken, one
was that between the Chinese Government and the
Chinese people, and another, that between the Chinese

people in the North and the Chinese people in the South and especially in Canton and the adjacent districts.

The English people raged against all alike. Charles Elliot knew that the trading interests of the Southerns were identical with our own ; that this identity of interest had generated a friendly feeling ; and that the outrageous proceedings of the Emperor and his Government, if they had been intolerable to us, had been likewise deeply injurious and offensive to the people of Canton.

There was another element in the case, never forgotten by Charles Elliot, which had passed out of the popular mind of England as soon as angry passions had possessed it. He never forgot that all these troubles had grown out of an unlawful and hateful trade by which the Chinese people everywhere were drugged with opium. He knew, no doubt, that this trade had been connived at by the local, and heretofore by the Imperial authorities, and that nothing could justify the fierce and violent proceedings by which the latter authorities had now sought to abolish it. But he still felt that on our side the quarrel was tainted in its origin.

On these views and feelings the instructions he received from his Government were founded ; for the instructions he received from his Government were, in their general tenor, those which he had himself advised his Government to give him.

It was desired, if possible, to obtain indemnity and reparation by a show of force without actual conflict ; and with this view to send a force to the north, where it would be most alarming to the Emperor as well as least obnoxious to the people of Canton, and to negotiate in those parts. And in order at once to make the menace more effective, to secure a base of operations in case of prolonged hostilities, and to possess ourselves of a permanent stronghold in those parts for the protection of our trade, the instructions to the Plenipotentiary and the Admiral were to take possession of some island on the eastern coast of China.

In obedience to these instructions, Chusan had been occupied by a military force three days before the arrival there of the Admiral and the Plenipotentiary in the 'Melville' on the 6th July, 1840.

It had not been occupied without a serious conflict; the native troops and people evinced a deadly hostility, and still maintained, at no great distance, a threatening attitude. As the 'Melville' entered the harbour (of which no surveys were in existence) she struck heavily upon a rock, and was so far disabled that it became necessary to heave her down for repairs; and this involved the necessity of leaving another line-of-battle ship to heave her down to. The accident would not have been regarded by Charles Elliot as by any means unfortunate, had the Admiral concurred with him in considering it a sufficient plea for departing from their instructions in one particular in which the Secretary of State had erred through want of local knowledge. They were instructed to proceed with the squadron *to the mouth of the Peiho*, and thence to send a letter to Pekin. But they could not approach nearer to the Peiho than four leagues, and it was idle to expect that with the ships now left at their disposal and unable to come within sight of the coast, they could from that position produce any effect upon the Court of Pekin.

What Charles Elliot wished was to proceed at once with his own plan of operations, which was to send all the light-draught vessels at once up the Yang-tse-Kiang, so that the channels up the river might be ascertained and the transports with the troops moved up with safety to the mouth of the Grand Canal. He felt sure that the letter from the Secretary of State would go with much more weight from that base of operations where they would be in strength, than from an invisible and helpless squadron off the mouth of the Peiho. He wrote to the

Admiral (his cousin George Elliot, brother of Lord Minto, then First Lord of the Admiralty) pressing these views upon him as strongly as he could; but the Admiral thought himself bound to proceed to the Peiho in obedience to his instructions; and thither they went.

The result was what Charles Elliot had anticipated. No negotiations could then be brought about. The Court at Pekin took no alarm, and when Keshen, the High Minister, who was sent to communicate with them, simply proposed to meet them at Canton in the beginning of the next year, they were ready enough to accept his proposal, and to get away from a situation in which they were fully aware of their impotence.

On their way back they came upon a disastrous state of things at Chusan. The troops, closed in by a hostile and menacing population, had to meet a still more deadly enemy in the climate.

Disease had attacked them in so virulent a form that the force was sensibly diminishing day by day; and, in point of fact, during the eight months which elapsed before the evacuation of the island, out of a force of 2,300, nearly 600 were buried, and about 1,000 were invalided and sent away.

They were anxiously occupied at Chusan from the end of September till the beginning of November, in effecting such improvements as they could; and in December, Charles Elliot met Keshen at the mouth of the Canton River and entered upon a then somewhat hopeless negotiation. Keshen himself was friendly and honest, and knew what the circumstances demanded in the interest of his country. But he was the servant of a blind and obstinate Court, and was negotiating at his personal peril.

Well disposed as he was in his heart, it was shortly apparent that no effective results could be obtained without placing him under pressure.

Hostilities were indispensable, and on the 7th January, 1841, the Chinese positions at Chuenpee, commanding the mouth of the Canton River, were attacked and taken by assault. In the action more than 700 Chinese fell, without the loss of a single man on our side.

After what Charles Elliot calls in his despatches 'the melancholy slaughter of that day,' negotiations were resumed, and at the end of January a preliminary Convention was concluded with Keshen. By this Convention the Island of Hong Kong was to be ceded to the British Crown instead of Chusan; an indemnity of six million dollars was to be paid; direct intercourse on an equal footing was to be established; and the port of Canton was to be opened to the trade.

Hong Kong was taken possession of at once, and the troops which were perishing by hundreds at Chusan were ordered to the mouth of the Canton River, where the whole force, naval and military, was consolidated.

On the 17th February, 1841, Elliot having received intelligence which, though private, left no room for doubt, that Keshen had been disgraced and would be disavowed, hostilities were at once renewed, and no time was lost in carrying up the force to the waters in the more immediate neighbourhood of Canton.

From that threatening position, Elliot was enabled in March to negotiate a local truce with the Governor of the Province, whereby, with little or no loss of time as regarded operations in the North, since reinforcements were to come from India, and the favourable monsoon was not to be expected till April, the channels of commerce were reopened and the trade of the season made its escape.

But before the time arrived for going North, it came to Elliot's knowledge that works which we had disarmed in March, had been rearmed in violation of the conditions of the truce; whilst the further knowledge reached him that a large mass of treasure had been collected at Canton for the purposes of the war. The truce thus broken, hostilities were renewed, and the brilliant campaign of a few days which followed placed the city at the mercy of the British force.

Elliot described the operations, some of which were of a critical and dangerous character, in a despatch to Lord Palmerston of the 8th June:—

'I arrived in Canton on the 18th ultimo, and at once issued the inclosed Circular.'—It was a secret Circular to the merchants, advising them to withdraw from the factories gradually, in order not to attract notice, but with as much dispatch as possible.—'In order to prevent any general panic, however, it was communicated confidentially to the three senior merchants upon the spot, with a request that they would press upon all Her Majesty's subjects my advice to act upon it with promptitude. But, at the same time, having reason to believe there would be no danger in a few days' delay, and knowing that that interval would serve to complete the loading of every British ship actually taking in cargo at Whampoa, I felt anxious to afford the few remaining merchants my own countenance on shore, as long as I possibly could, with due attention to the information I was receiving respecting the secret purposes of the Government.

'On the morning of the 21st, I became aware that further delay would be unsafe, and I therefore issued a second Circular (desiring all British subjects to withdraw before sunset), and retired from the factories at about 5 o'clock P.M.

'It is satisfactory to add, that the loading of the ships receiving cargo at Whampoa had now been completed, and with the exception of a Mr. John Millar, a clerk in an American house, whose melancholy fate will be hereafter noticed, not a single British subject remained in the factories, when the perfidy of the Government manifested itself; that is, at about 11 o'clock P.M.

'Her Majesty's Government will recognise the appropriateness of this expression when I add, that on the very evening of the day that the attempt to destroy us was made, the three Commissioners placarded a proclamation assuring both the native and foreign merchants that they might remain in Canton in perfect safety.

'In order to support Her Majesty's Brig "Algerine," lying about a mile from the factories, and my own cutter before them, the senior officer on the spot (Captain Herbert of the "Calliope") had moved up Her Majesty's ships "Modeste" and "Pylades" in the evening, and the steamer "Nemesis," on board of which I had just embarked, was also lying in company with them.

'There was no interruption of the state of tranquillity until about 11 o'clock P.M., when four or five sail of fire-vessels, charged with every description of combustible, were towed down from the upper part of the river, the ebb tide being then at its close. The vessels were brought down with resolution, for they were not fired until within easy musket shot of Her Majesty's ships; and if the attempt had not been delayed till the ebb tide had so nearly exhausted itself that the direction of drift had become devious and the rate slow, there can be little doubt that some of the vessels would have fallen athwart-hawse of one or more of the ships.

'The firing of the rafts was the signal for a brisk and creditably directed cannonade from the work lately rearmed in the Shameen suburb, and also from several other masked works along shore.

'By the light of the burning vessels, too, we descried a numerous flotilla under sail, tideward of them, and obviously menacing the increased pressure of the ships by closer cannonade, or perhaps by boarding, if they should take fire.

' The rafts were towed clear of the ships by the boats, and the fire from the batteries answered with characteristic steadiness and courage. A renewed attempt by fire-vessels from the eastward upon the flood tide, was also baffled with the same coolness and success as the first.

' The enemy continued their fire throughout the night; but the measured fire of the ships upon the points of their cannonade shortly abated its vigour.

'On the next morning at daylight (22nd) the ships were moved up before the battery at Shameen, which was silenced, notwithstanding an obstinate defence and a palpable improvement in the Chinese practice; and when the people went on shore to destroy the guns it was found that a flanking work had been thrown up mounting several new guns of large calibre, one indeed of $9\frac{1}{2}$-inch diameter, which they appear to have recently discovered the art of casting.

'Above Shameen the river branches off to the northward and westward, leading to a point called Tsengpoo, distant about three and a half miles from the north wall of the city, where I had reason to believe, from private correspondence with the Major-General, he proposed to effect the disembarkation of his force. Your Lordship will, therefore, at once understand the eagerness with which Captain Herbert, embarked in the steamship " Nemesis," pursued the numerous flotilla that had taken part in the attempt of the preceding night, now rapidly retiring in the direction of Tsengpoo. As soon as the ships had silenced the Shameen battery, their boats were sent to reinforce the " Nemesis," and in the brief space of three or four hours about seventy sail of armed and fire vessels were run on shore, or destroyed by fire. On the next morning, the 23rd, another division of boats completed the destruction of this formidable flotilla; so that on the morning of the 24th the whole passage to Tsengpoo was left perfectly open.

'On that afternoon (24th) orders reached the ships in advance to move before the factories, and silence any opposition which might be offered to the landing at that point of a small division of troops, then rapidly approaching in the steamer "Atalanta." Her Majesty's ships had scarcely taken up their positions when two sail of fire-vessels lying a-head of them, with a strong tide running, were cast adrift; but fortunately there was a steady breeze across the river, which, acting powerfully upon the volume of flame and smoke, drove them on shore at the east end of the Hongs, about two cables' length from the advanced ship.

'The boats, sent away to tow off the fire-vessels and ascertain the condition of the "Dutch Folly," soon found themselves opposed by a line of works commencing nearly opposite to that point, and extending with little interval to the "French Folly." The most contiguous were immediately attacked and carried, the Chinese standing to their guns till the seamen were actually in the works, and in several instances falling in personal conflict.

'Whilst these operations proceeded before the factories, the steamship "Nemesis," towing and having on board the whole remainder of the force, was moving steadily upon Tsengpoo; and shortly after sunset the Major-General had effected his disembarkation, and ascertained, by personal reconnaissance in force, that his immediate front was clear.

'At daylight the next morning (the 25th), the whole force moved forward. The first effort of the enemy was to draw the Major-General into pursuit on the right of his present lines; that is, amongst a vast extent of paddy and difficult country leading to the north-western walls of the city; but these purposes were at once detected by the Major-General, and answered with immediate arrangements to move forward by his left.

'By a combination of masterly dispositions, ardour, and constancy, which has certainly never been surpassed, a handful of British troops (moved through a country of excessive difficulty wholly unknown to the Major-General and in the face of a numerous army with whose mode of warfare he was unacquainted) was placed in the short space of six hours in the firm possession of a line of fortified heights, not inobstinately defended, flanked on the left by large intrenched encampments, and supported by an active and respectably served artillery from the walls of the city. Several attacks of the enemy in much force, both from the town and the camp, were repelled; and finally, the intrenched camp itself was carried and destroyed, and the numerous force in its occupation entirely routed with the same coolness and distinguished success which attended the whole course of operations.

'On that day and the next (the 26th), the ships and flotilla in the front of the factories had completed the conquest of the whole line of formidable works extending from the "Dutch Folly" downwards; and late in the evening I was approached by the officers of the Government with overtures for the prevention of further hostilities.

'High-hearted conduct of this stamp is always most suitably reported in brief terms and simple language; at all events I feel myself unable to convey to your Lordship any adequate sense of the ability which has marked the conception and guidance of these admirable operations, and of the gallantry and prodigious exertion with which they have been executed by all arms of the Queen's forces. But I am performing no more than my duty in drawing the merit and claims of the whole force under your Lordship's particular attention, for submission to the gracious notice of the Queen.

'The loss which has been sustained will be a source of much concern to Her Majesty's Government; but it has been a matter of surprise to me that it has not been more considerable; for the Chinese manifested an honourable spirit of resolution at several points of operation.'

It was in the situation to which these operations led, when more than 100 armed and fire-ships had been destroyed, a line of works mounting 60 pieces of artillery had been carried, a large body of troops routed, and the gates and city of Canton were commanded by the British forces, that Elliot arrested the operations and consented to negotiate with the Chinese Commissioners. And this arrest of the operations and refusal to allow the city to be taken by assault, when it came to be known at home, called up a storm of wrath and indignation in the British breast. What the British public would have desired it may not be easy to particularise. What Charles Elliot did *not* desire is capable of explanation.

He did not desire that the 'melancholy slaughter' of Chuenpee should be repeated on a gigantic scale; he did not desire that the million of unoffending, if not secretly friendly inhabitants, should run the risk of seeing the municipal authorities and the police take to flight, leaving the city to be sacked by the rabble; he did not desire that there should be the further risk of the destruction of the town by fire. Such were the consequences which he conceived to be, if not highly probable, at all events quite within the chances of the hour, should the city be taken by storm ; and these consequences he had to apprehend, 'even on the assumption' (to use his own words in a letter[1] to the Secretary of State), 'of the utmost amount

---

[1] Not written unfortunately till after his return to England.

of military success, unqualified by a single misadventure, and accompanied and followed by perfect discipline, order, and sobriety amongst the troops, maintained in the midst of confusion and the heat of assault, with an immense city prostrate before them, and in course of being plundered by everybody but themselves.'

These were the hazards to be taken into account; and, after all, the occupation of the city by assault would not have promoted, but would have absolutely impeded and defeated, the ends, whether present or prospective, which Elliot had to accomplish.

What were they ?

1st. He had to get what he could towards indemnifying the British Treasury for the two millions sterling which had been paid for the confiscated opium. By admitting the city to ransom, he obtained at once towards this indemnity six millions of dollars collected at Canton by the Imperial Commissioners for the purpose of carrying on the war. Had he allowed the city to be taken by assault the six millions of dollars would have been prize of war,— greatly no doubt to the contentment of the naval and military officers and men, but equally to the detriment of the erring and bewildered British public.

2nd. So soon as certain reinforcements of the steam-arm should arrive, which were designed to facilitate operations up the rivers, he had to get away to the North, ascend the Yang-tse-Kiang, and make his demonstration at the mouth of the Grand Canal, with every available ship and man. Had he possessed himself of Canton, no inconsiderable portion of his force must have been left behind to hold it.

The reinforcements did not arrive as soon as they were expected ; but the interval was by no means unemployed. He made good use of it in arrangements for the security of our new possession, the Island of Hong Kong, and for the protection of our other interests in the South, that thereby he might disembarrass his rear and leave no subject of anxiety behind; and in two or three weeks after the Convention concluded at the gates of Canton, he was on the point of commencing the movement to the North.

But the stars in their courses fought against him. The movement was arrested by the occurrence of a tremendous typhoon. Most of the transports in the harbour of Hong Kong got adrift, and were more or less disabled; and along with this weakening of a force which had no strength to spare, came the last of Elliot's strange and various personal adventures in China.

I described it in a letter to Miss Fenwick, as I heard it from himself after his return to England.

He, with the Commodore, Sir Gordon Bremer, who had succeeded Admiral George Elliot in the command, were overtaken by the tempest on the way from Macao to Canton in Elliot's cutter. The only chance of escape was by getting out to sea, and the only way out was through a number of scattered islands. One of these, and a very rocky one, was but a mile and a half distant, and immediately to leeward with a terrific sea breaking upon it. The cutter's anchor was light and the chain old and worn, but by keeping the mast standing, and preparing for slipping at a moment's notice, it appeared possible that on drifting close to the island they might slip from their anchor, and wear round so as to clear the shore ; and this being done, if there was light enough in the gloom of the storm to see their way, they might clear the other scattered islands ; and as the wind, which had been north-west at the outset, veered to the east (according to the invariable custom of typhoons), there was a chance of running under the shelter of some headland, and into the creeks of the coast to the south and west of Macao. They ran from 7 A.M. till sunset, through the waves rather than over them, the cutter, however, behaving admirably. There were some young hands on board, and Elliot told the master—a fine old seaman—he must do what he could to keep them steady. The answer was,—' As long as we are here, sir, we are to do our duty, and you may be sure that I'll see to it : ' but it was not long that *he* was there. He was shortly washed overboard, with no possibility of rescue.

They went on their way, and presently 'land ahead' was shouted from the bow, and they were close on a perpendicular cliff. A sail was hoisted to bring her head round, but it was torn to ribbons; another, and all depended on keeping it full and unshaken that it might not share the same fate, whilst they ran for some time under the cliff. It stood fast, and saved them; but no sooner had they got rid of this island, than they found themselves close upon another. This the cutter could not clear; but there was a bay partially sheltered. All that could be done was to let go their remaining anchor, without a chance of its holding, merely to check her ashore; and on she went upon a rock. Elliot was, in due accordance with naval etiquette, the last to leave the cutter, and though clutched by a weaker swimmer than himself, he reached the rock—only, however, to be washed off it; then he reached it again, and at last he and all of them got safe on shore, and took refuge in a cave.

They had not been there long when a native came in upon them, shouting and flourishing a sword, with a troop of others at his back. A seaman put his hand on a cutlass; but Elliot told him to be quiet, and singling out one of the natives who looked more mild and sensible than the rest, took him apart, and wrote in Chinese on the sand that he would give him 1,000 dollars if he would

take him and the Commodore to Macao. The Chinaman
signified his assent, and persuaded his comrades to give
them over to his charge, whilst they went to see after the
wreck; first, however, stripping the whole party of everything but one garment apiece, Elliot only excepted; for
he spoke roughly to the native coming to strip him, who
thereupon went to the next man, from whom he snatched
his last and only rag.

In this state they got to their protector's hut, where
they were lodged for the night. But then a new danger
arose. The natives had found certain portions of the
armament of the wreck, and insisted that the foreigners
were the very barbarians who were fighting with China.
And hardly had they been pacified upon this point, when
another party discovered ten dead bodies of Chinese on
the shore near to the spot where the cutter had been
wrecked, and between twenty and thirty dead bodies a
little further along, which bodies were wounded and
lacerated. They were furious at this, and there was
great difficulty in convincing them of what was the fact—
that these were the bodies of the crew of a Chinese vessel,
wrecked at the same time with the cutter, and that the
wounds were only from their having been dashed upon
the rocks.

Charles Elliot took his friend apart again and told
him to promise the other natives 1,000 dollars amongst
them, and that he should himself have 2,000 dollars, provided they were off to Macao by six the next morning.

This was successful: but one more incident came in
their way. A Chinese (probably one who had escaped
from the Chinese wreck) had taken a dying boy—possibly
his son—into a hut, and the boy had died there, whereby
the hut had become, according to the native superstition,
unclean. The natives were enraged at this, and had
seized the offender and brought him out of the hut, with

the body. As the man was speaking a Fokeen dialect, Elliot could not well understand what was passing; but it appeared that, in order to save himself, he was attributing the offence in some way to the foreigners; and the grotesque and dismal spectacle of the poor man, with the boy's corpse at his feet, swaying his body in an incessant succession of Chinese obeisances and begging for mercy, was succeeded by a new quarrel between Elliot and the natives.

Through all this, however, they came clear; and at six in the morning Elliot and the Commodore started in a canoe for Macao.

Their next danger was from a boat of ladrones or pirates which made its appearance, in verification of a plea of danger from such a boat which their protector had made when he was wanting to raise the price of the ransom. But, with good rowing, they left the pirates behind; and then, as they turned a point, Elliot (who has the hawk's eye of his race) cried out to the Commodore, 'For God's sake, lie flat; I see a Mandarin flag!' They lay down in the bottom of the canoe, and the Mandarin boat came near enough to hail and ask the news from the westward, but luckily not so near as to see that there were two persons lying in the bottom. Thus they were saved once more, and reached Macao.

Before he landed, an officer came alongside and told him the news from England. The news was that he was superseded, and his successor might be expected immediately. To this Elliot made answer, that to be cast ashore at Sanchuen, and find himself adrift at Macao, was more than a man had a right to expect in one week, be he Plenipotentiary or be he not.

Providence had been kinder to him than some other authorities; and, thankful to Providence for his life, he went with the Commodore to the house which was to be no longer his at Macao. There, when they were taking some rest and refreshment, a line in a well-known poem of Dryden's came into his head, and he repeated it to the Commodore. Tom Killigrew is conceived by the poet to be returning home, after one of the fierce fights with the Dutch in the channel, only to find his gifted sister dead ; and then comes the line he quoted—

> Slack all thy sails, for thou art wrecked ashore.

Thus ends this ' strange eventful history,' so far as the scene is laid in China.

On Elliot's arrival in England, he found Lord Aberdeen in the Foreign Office instead of Lord Palmerston, for a change of Government had taken place, and it was to Lord Aberdeen that he had to address his answer to Lord Palmerston's recalling despatch.

The ground on which Lord Palmerston had rested his recall was disobedience of instructions ' not justified by success.'

At the date of this despatch it was not known in England that he had successfully invested Canton, that he had successfully expelled the Imperial Commissioners, that he had successfully destroyed the military preparations, and that he had successfully extorted six millions of dollars towards the liquidation of the British claims.

In the conclusion of the letter in his own vindication, addressed to Lord Aberdeen, he shortly reverts to the facts and pleas adduced at large in its previous pages :—

' With regard to disobedience I have endeavoured to place before your Lordship, as precisely as I can, within what limits this charge against me ought to be confined.

' With regard to success, it is not for me to judge what should be considered success in the difficulties that surrounded me. Disastrous sickness, inconvenient accident inseparable from navigation on coasts imperfectly surveyed and in latitudes liable to devastating tempests, immense masses of property lying on hand to be turned to account, extensive public and private embarrassment to prevent. In China, whilst I was concerned there, the difficulties were great, and the chances and accidents to which human affairs must always be subject were steadily adverse; but I am not ashamed of the measure of public advantage which was wrung out of such circumstances, nor of my own share in those transactions. I have devoted my days and nights to my duty, and I have been exposed to as much trial and difficulty of all kinds as any officer in the service of the British Crown; neither have I the least doubt that the course of management I have pursued through cross and hard circumstances has upheld the highest honour of our country and her interests considered in their largest and lasting aspects. Between the 24th of March, 1839, when I was made a prisoner at Canton by the Chinese Government, and the 18th of August, 1841, when I was removed by my own, we have turned a trade amounting to upwards of ten millions sterling, despatched more than fifty thousand tons of British shipping, sent to England as much produce as would pour into Her Majesty's Treasury upwards of eight millions sterling, recovered from the Chinese Treasury about 150 tons of hard silver, warded off from Her Majesty's Government pressing appeals from foreign Governments at peculiarly uneasy moments and on very delicate subjects, triumphantly manifested the prowess of the Queen's arms, and still more signally and with more enduring advantage established the character and extent of British magnanimity.

'If this has not been deemed to be success, I am, nevertheless, not without my own sense of reward; for I have prevented great public mischief and private distress, and the services of the gallant officers whose honourable exertions have done so much to accomplish my political conceptions such as they were, have already been most graciously acknowledged by Her Majesty.

'As to errors, it is not to be supposed, and I am far from having the arrogance to imagine, that in the course of the complicated and difficult transactions in which I have been engaged, so often requiring sudden decisions, I have not committed errors of judgment; but I beg your Lordship to believe, that if I were aware of any serious and important errors of that nature I would acknowledge them; and there is one fault which it is right I should acknowledge. I have to reproach myself with having insufficiently explained my proceedings to Her Majesty's Government in my despatches from China.

'The excuse which I have to offer for my deficiencies in this respect is, that I was acting in more capacities at once than it was possible for any officer, even with the strongest health and the most unremitting activity, to fulfil with entire efficiency in all. When warfare and negotiation were carried on together, I was not only charged with the negotiation, but I was perpetually in conference on the naval and military movements, and I was piloting the ships, and owing to peculiar local circumstances I was compelled to undertake various kinds of duty not usually devolving upon a person in my station. And in time of truce the heavy business of my own office was added to the urgent affairs growing out of the military and diplomatic circumstances of the period. Between the hostilities (7th January) which terminated with my Treaty with Keshen, forwarded to England on the 14th February, there was an interval of eight weeks. During these eight weeks it is my misfortune, and in part my fault, that I did not find time to write so fully to the Secretary of State as would have enabled him to judge me on just and sufficient grounds. I was burthened with the details of the negotiations (which lasted till the middle of February), and a multiplicity of arrangements for securing the benefits of the Treaty, if it should be confirmed, or providing against the contingency of a renewed rupture. I was in perpetual movement from place to place, and I allowed the urgency of the affairs immediately pressing upon me to divert me from the duty of conveying to my Government a distinct and sufficient explanation of the grounds of my measures, until a total change of circumstances took place, hostilities were renewed, and I was almost necessarily cut off from the opportunity of repairing this omission.

' But for this omission thus arising I cannot but believe that the distinguished person lately at the head of Foreign Affairs, whose kindness to me on many occasions I warmly appreciate, would have left me to reap the fruits of my hard career, which, at all events, my country may regard without shame for the things achieved, and with satisfaction for the things prevented.

'I earnestly hope, however, and I fully believe, that under the able management of the person who was appointed to succeed me, the war with China will be brought to an early and successful close.'

His vindication was complete, whether by the successes which became known after his recall had been dispatched, or by the explanations afforded in his letter of the grounds on which he had thought it right to deviate from his instructions.

Those instructions, as I have said, had been mainly, if not entirely, devised by himself, and they directed the occupation of an island on the eastern coast of China. Chusan was the island occupied in pursuance of this instruction, and Elliot had seen fit to evacuate Chusan, and to occupy instead of it the Island of Hong Kong in the south.

In the despatch of 8th June, 1841, from which I have

drawn Elliot's report of the investment of Canton, he adverts to the measures he had taken for diverting the course of trade from that city to Hong Kong, and then proceeds :—

'Her Majesty's Government and the nation may be assured that the steady encouragement of that possession upon the most liberal principles would, of itself, soon repay every expense and every sacrifice of this expedition.'

In the letter addressed to Lord Aberdeen after his return to England, he observed :—

'If Lord Palmerston had written of Hong Kong instead of an island on the eastern coast, his letters would have been going far indeed to sanction the main ground of the arrangement I was ready to have made; and I cannot help thinking it is merely my misfortune he did not write it of Hong Kong. . . . When I say my misfortune, I do not mean to imply that his Lordship was in a state of information to give me directions in that sense when this despatch was written. But it is clear that we have all been instructing ourselves— Lord Palmerston, the Governor-General of India, and myself, in this expedition of experiences, so heavily visited by sickness and accident and storm, and were all modifying our views of the best means to the same end according to our increased knowledge and reflection.'

He proceeds to show that the best island to possess was one like Hong Kong, having 'a large and safe harbour, abundance of fresh water, ease of protection by maritime ascendency, and no more extent of territory or population than may be necessary for our own convenience as occupants of a great commercial emporium, to the end that the island may be permanently held by a small land force, and governed by very moderate civil establishments. I believe that such a position in the neighbourhood of

Canton, firmly held, leaves the country independent of a
Treaty of Peace with the Emperor whilst he is unwilling
to treat, that it is the surest and least painful mode of
inducing a willingness to treat, and the single guarantee
for the faithful fulfilment of a treaty when he has been
compelled to treat.'

I turn to the ' Colonial Office List' for 1872, to see
how far Hong Kong has justified the judgment by which
Charles Elliot was guided in exchanging it for Chusan :—

'As it is a free port,' say the official editors, ' it is
impossible to give a correct return of imports and exports ;
but the enormous extent of the trade with which it is
connected may be approximately guessed at by the fact
that the British and foreign tonnage entering and leaving
the port annually averages two millions of tons. To this
must be added the immense fleets of native craft of all
sizes and forms by which much of the coasting trade of
the Chinese Empire is carried on, and also that of Siam,
Cochin China, and the Straits. The number of native
boats which visit Hong Kong annually is about 52,000,
with a tonnage of nearly 1,300,000, raising the total
tonnage to upwards of two millions and a half. From
these figures some idea of the movement and commercial
activity which pervades this great centre of eastern commerce may be formed.'

If it is needless now to say more of the eligibility of
Hong Kong, it is equally so to say *anything* of the
*in*eligibility of Chusan; for, though it was re-occupied
by Lord Palmerston's orders, issued before he had been
better informed, the policy of letting it alone was presently recognised, and it was restored under the Treaty of
Peace.

Yet Lord Palmerston told Charles Elliot that, but for
his surrender of Chusan, he would not have been recalled.

Indeed, amongst public men, whether of one party or

the other (I have named elsewhere Lord Lansdowne, Lord John Russell, Lord Clarendon, and Lord Auckland), there seems to have been but one opinion.

Sir Robert Peel told him that, whilst he did not pretend to understand Chinese affairs intimately, he certainly had a conviction that he, Elliot, understood the public interests in that quarter better than most of the authorities by whom he had been judged; and, for his own part, he fully concurred in Lord Aberdeen's opinion, that he was not blamable in the course he had taken concerning Chusan and other questioned points. Lord Melbourne told him he had been 'hastily judged.' And when tidings came of the triumph of his successor, Lord Aberdeen wrote to congratulate him, and did so the more cordially 'because the operation which had brought the war to a close was distinctly pointed out and recommended by him so early as the 21st February, 1840, in his letters to Lord Auckland and Sir Frederick Maitland.'

So ends the story of my friend's services in China. Though the Minister who recalled him had done so in ignorance of what he had achieved and in error as to what he had renounced, and in a total, though perhaps not unnatural, misconception of his motives, plans, and purposes, yet, even under these misleading conditions, he would probably have put trust in Charles Elliot and waited, had not the matter been urgent from another point of view. It was in the weak latter days of Lord Melbourne's Government that these things befell. If the Government was in some ignorance on the subject, the people were not only ignorant, but envenomed and inflamed; and the Government were goaded to what Lord Melbourne so generously admitted to have been a 'hasty judgment,' by a virulence of popular clamour and reproach which they could not afford to disregard. And it is in this aspect of the affair chiefly that I look upon it as instructive.

If I were generalising from facts in history after the manner of the 'Discorsi,' the warning which I should deduce from the narrative would be that a Government which is amenable to a representative assembly should be slow to engage in any military operations which in their progress may be liable to hindrance or vicissitude. There can be little doubt that if the House of Commons had been reformed and converted into a body truly representing popular impulses in the year 1810, the Duke of Wellington would have been recalled on his retreat to Torres Vedras.

END OF THE FIRST VOLUME.

9 783337 031237